INTO TEMPTATION

KATHRYN SMITH

INTO TEMPTATION

AVON BOOKS

An Imprint of HarperCollins*Publishers*

AVON BOOKS
An Imprint of HarperCollins*Publishers*
10 East 53rd Street
New York, New York 10022-5299

For Nathalie,

*for being the one who actually wanted to listen
to my Shaun Cassidy albums,
for providing the voice of reason
when I couldn't do it myself,
for having the best comebacks ever.
And for the most hilarious Columbo
impersonation I've ever seen.
When I grow up I want to be just like you.*

Chapter 1

*He was the kind of man who believed himself
to be always in the right—
and everyone else in the wrong.*

An Unfortunate Attachment by A Repentant Lady

Essex
April 1819

"What the devil do you mean, she is not here?"
Sir William Lewis blinked at the annoyance
in his companion's tone. "I thought you knew."

Julian Rexley, Earl Wolfram, rose from a patterned
armchair that had long ago molded itself to a much larger
backside and frowned at his host.

The trip to Essex had taken longer than usual due to the
poor quality of the roads, and Julian had been stuck inside
his carriage with nothing to look at but rain and mud. Being forced to wait upon the weak-minded baronet in this
small, hot parlor did not help. To find out it was all for
naught only added to his black mood.

"My dear sir, I would not be here had I known there
was no reason to come." But he hadn't known. Letitia
hadn't informed him of her change of plans. Why?

1

Sir William Lewis's already florid cheeks flushed darker. "This is a very embarrassing situation, Wolfram. Very embarrassing, indeed."

"Sir William," Julian said, his jaw tensing. He was so warm that the skin beneath his collar itched with sweat, and there was a sharp pounding in his head. "Where is my sister?"

The baronet sat slouched in his chair, his waistcoat straining at its buttons, and gazed at Julian with an expression of good-natured bewilderment.

"I do not know."

A faint thrumming began somewhere behind Julian's eyes. He scowled. It made the thrumming worse.

He sought to regain his composure, even as thoughts of the dangers his sister might encounter bombarded his mind and quickened his heart. Letitia was the kind of person who didn't have to look for trouble. It usually found her with little difficulty.

"You do not know? I might ask, my dear sir, why you would let a woman leave your protection unescorted without first ascertaining her destination." His tone was deceptively light. Inside he was very near panic. No one had known where Miranda had gone either, and by the time Julian had found her, she was dead. To assume the same would happen with Letitia was madness, but he couldn't stop the horrible thought from flashing through his mind.

Sir William reddened even more. "Forgive me, Lord Wolfram, but it did not seem so wholly strange as you suggest. Lady Letitia is hardly a chit fresh from the schoolroom, and she made it very clear from the time of her arrival that she would be leaving us on the fourth because of a prior obligation. She spoke of it so casually that

I detected no artifice in her tone, nor did it occur to me that she might not have your approval."

He was right of course. Why would he suspect Letitia of deceit? Sir William did not know his sister as Julian did. Kind and good-hearted, Letitia was also willful and spoilt—a fact for which Julian was to blame.

But that wasn't important now. What was important was determining just where his sly sibling had gone, and why she had considered it enough of a secret not to tell him. No doubt part of her reason had been the wish to avoid going to town for the season. Letitia was well aware that it was his wish that she would find a husband this year, just as Julian was very much aware that his younger sister did not want his assistance in that matter.

"Sir William."

The baronet eyed him warily, as one might watch a growling dog. "My lord?"

Julian forced a slight smile. "I wonder if perhaps your daughter might know my sister's whereabouts."

"By George, I wager she does," Sir William replied, brightening. "Thick as the corns on a whore's heel those two are."

With that charming analogy in his head, Julian waited for the other man to fetch his child. Sir William simply sat there flushed and dazed. Wryly, Julian wondered if the baronet's stupidity had landed him many beatings in school.

"Might I speak to her?" he asked when it became apparent that the thought wasn't going to cross the vast desert of Sir William's mind.

"Of course!" The baronet cried, leaping to his feet with as much grace as his size and gout would allow. "I shall fetch her myself."

Either a smile or a grimace curved Julian's lips—he wasn't certain which. "I am most obliged, thank you."

Sir William waved his words aside with a broad grin and shuffled from the room in search of the fruit of his loins.

Where the devil had Letitia run off to? And how could she put him through this worry? Sir William was right, Letitia was no green girl. She was a woman of four and twenty and she was old enough to know that such behavior was childish and inconsiderate. She must have known the news would alarm him. Perhaps that had been her intention. She was angry with him for trying to find her a husband and this was her way of showing her displeasure.

The brat didn't know displeasure, but she would when Julian found her. Running away was no way to deal with problems, neither was hiding. Now he had to take time out of his busy schedule to go and find his churlish sibling. He was not impressed.

Christ, he hoped nothing had happened to her.

He couldn't bear it if anything happened to Letitia. She was all he had left. He'd lost his parents at eighteen, his other sister, Miranda, less than a decade later. Only his friend Brave, who had loved Miranda, knew how he had suffered at her death. They would have to lock him up if he lost Letitia too. At times she seemed to be as much his child as his sister, and he knew that sometimes she thought him a bit of a tyrant, but he had done everything he could to give her the life she deserved. He had even agreed to allow her to choose her own husband, but that had been five years ago, and she had yet to choose.

She needed support and if he ever wanted a life of his own, he was going to have to help his sister out of his house and into someone else's. Someone who deserved her and would love her.

And most important, someone who could handle her without crushing her spirit. Letitia might be willful, but she had a sweet disposition and a romantic nature that was as inclined to melancholy as it was to joy. It would take a special kind of man to give her what she needed. That was why Julian had taken it upon himself to select possible candidates. He would do anything to ensure his sister did not allow her heart to make a disastrous attachment, as Miranda had done.

The room's stifling heat was making the pounding in his head even worse. Moving as far away from the fire as possible, Julian went to stand by the window at the far end of the parlor. It wasn't quite as uncomfortable there, and if he pressed his forehead against the cool, rain-pelted glass, he felt a little relief.

He would not be sorry to leave the shelter of Sir William's house. He would be very happy to be outside where it was cooler. He would be happier still to know where Letitia was.

"Here she is, Wolfram." Sir William's cheerful voice rang through the room, jangling what little was left of Julian's nerves.

For a split second, Julian thought Sir William spoke of Letitia, but then he remembered.

Miss Lewis looked nothing like her father, which could only serve in the girl's favor. She was petite, with fine reddish brown hair, a pert nose and large green eyes that were startlingly feline in shape. One look at her and Julian knew that this girl and his sister would be pure trouble together.

And one look at her was enough to ascertain that she

knew exactly where Letitia was. If the alarm on her face at seeing him wasn't enough, the fact that she couldn't meet his gaze was.

Choking back the urge to start demanding answers to his questions, Julian bowed. "Miss Lewis."

The girl curtsied and mumbled something in reply. Still, she did not look at him.

Julian did his best imitation of a charming smile as he walked toward Sir William and his daughter. He despised secrets and deception of any kind. Two people had tried to willfully deceive him in his lifetime: Miranda and one other. Miranda had succeeded and the other had come all too close. Even the mere suspicion of being lied to or plotted against was enough to stoke the embers of his temper.

"My dear Miss Lewis," he said softly, "I am very sorry to involve you in this . . . situation."

The girl lifted her head, but kept her gaze averted. "I am not aware of any 'situation,' my lord."

Julian's jaw tightened. He should have known better than to expect immediate cooperation.

"I refer to my sister's involving you in this scheme of hers to avoid going to London."

She looked at him—and lied outright. "I know of no scheme, Lord Wolfram."

Lips thinning, Julian met the guileless gaze with a hard one of his own. The girl's composure cracked a bit.

"I think you do."

She paled but said nothing. Perhaps he wasn't pursuing this in quite the right manner. The girl's loyalty to Letitia was admirable—if not foolish. She would not betray her friend to a blustering brother, not just because he demanded it. No, she would need stronger incentive.

Julian put on an apologetic face. "I would hate for any

scandal my sister might invite upon herself to taint you as well, especially given your circumstances."

That got her attention—her father's as well. It was no secret that Sir William wished for his only daughter to make a good match. The estate and title were to go to the baronet's son upon his death, but the inheritance wasn't a rich one. Both of Sir William's children would have to marry well to achieve the lifestyle they desired, and scandal would certainly impinge upon them doing so.

Sir William shot Julian an anxious glance before turning his attention to his daughter. "Well, miss? What do you know of Lady Letitia's whereabouts?"

"Hertford," she murmured. "She's in Hertford."

Relief flooded Julian's limbs. Lady Wickford, a very good family friend, lived in Hertford. Letitia visited her often. Her secrecy this time surely had been to delay Julian in finding her.

Miss Lewis stepped closer to her father. "She is with Lady Aberley."

All the relief Julian had felt moments before vanished, replaced by a swimming in his brain not unlike the time Fitz Parkington had pounded his head into the ground at school.

The Marchioness of Aberley was Sophia Morelle. She had been Sophia Everston when he knew her. At one time he had referred to her as his "Darling Fe." She was also the other person who had tried to deceive him. How had she managed to get her claws into Letitia?

"Are you certain that is where she has gone?" he asked when he found his voice.

Miss Lewis nodded stiffly. Both she and her father were watching him closely. No doubt both were very much aware of the scandal between himself and Lady

Aberley. Sir William was old enough to remember it first-hand, and there could be little question as to how Miss Lewis knew. Letitia had undoubtedly told her.

He would laugh if he weren't so furious. Letitia was anything but stupid, even though he sometimes had to wonder just how her thought process worked. She knew how he felt about Soph—*Lady Aberley*. She undoubtedly believed she was safe there, that Julian wouldn't come after her because he always went out of his way to avoid meeting the marchioness.

His sister couldn't be more mistaken.

He muttered his thanks and took his leave of Sir William and his daughter without any idea of whether or not they even responded. He did not care if they spoke of his behavior after he left. He didn't care what they said about him, it was Letitia he was worried about. Fortunately, Miss Lewis was a good friend to his sister and could no doubt be trusted to keep Letitia's confidence even without the hint of the scandal that might follow if word got out.

At least Letitia had *some* sense in choosing friends, he thought as he jogged down Sir William's steps. Julian's coachmen came scurrying from the shelter of the stables as one of Sir William's footmen opened the carriage door for him.

"To Hertford," he instructed his poor driver who, despite the protection of a slicker, had not escaped the cold and damp. "Get us there quickly and I shall buy you a hot meal and a bath to warm you up."

"Aye m'lord," the coachman replied as he climbed up into his seat.

Drawing the shades so that the interior of the vehicle was shrouded in murky darkness, Julian leaned back against the squabs as the carriage rolled into motion. It was cooler here than it had been in the parlor, and it eased the pounding in his head somewhat. There was little to be done about the knots in his shoulders or the sick feeling in his stomach, however, for this time they had little to do with travel and everything to do with the destination.

Sophia.

When was the last time he had seen her? A few years ago, he had caught a glimpse of her in Bath when she and the marquess had been there taking the waters for his failing health. Obviously the waters hadn't worked, because Sophia had been made a widow two and a half years ago. As was proper—strange behavior for her indeed—she had kept herself in relative seclusion for her mourning period. Julian had half expected her to show up at his friend Gabriel's wedding, but she hadn't—even though he knew she had been invited by Lilith, Gabriel's wife.

Julian had flattered himself that Sophia hadn't come to the wedding to avoid seeing him, but he knew nothing could be further from the truth. The Sophia he knew feared nothing.

On the other hand, the Sophia he knew wouldn't have hidden herself away for eighteen months of mourning—not for a husband.

When he thought of how close he had come to becoming her husband he almost shuddered. She had tried her best to trap him. Tried and failed, thank God. She had offered herself to Julian in a way that made him believe . . . Well, it didn't matter what he had believed. He had walked willingly into her web, only to find out that the whole thing had been an elaborate ruse to get her greedy little hands on his fortune.

Oh, there had been scandal. Everyone in England knew

he had been caught literally with his pants down—or rather unfastened. He could still remember the triumphant gleam in Sophia's eyes when she believed him to be well and truly caught. He could remember the hatred he saw there later as well.

The worst part about it was that he had naively allowed himself to believe she actually cared for him. That notion was quickly dispelled by her hasty engagement to the marquess and his massive fortune. Thank Christ Julian had found out the truth about Sophia and her greed before he had a chance to change his mind and offer for her. She had made a big enough fool of him as it was without that happening.

She still was making a fool of him, truth be told. The poem that had launched his career as a writer had been written about her. While later works established him as one of England's most respected poets, it was that one work that haunted him. It was the one people still talked about and referred to as the "best thing" he had ever written.

He had more such poems inspired by Sophia, a very few of which had been published. He did not want *her* to be his muse.

And now the witch had his sister—the only family he had left. It was not to be borne.

That Letitia thought to manipulate and control him in such a way proved what a danger Sophia could be. Willful and spoilt his sister might be, but she wasn't wholly deceitful. If she were, she wouldn't have told her friend where she was going. She would have wanted to make Julian suffer her absence. No, this was a power struggle. By running to Sophia, Letitia dared her brother to come and get her. She didn't think he would.

She thought wrong.

He would go to Hertford and he would remove her from Sophia's house—forcefully if he had to. And then he would take his petulant sibling back to London. If necessary, he would shackle her to his arm for the entirety of the season—or at least until he found a suitable husband for her. Hopefully, by then she would be too enamored of her betrothed to spend her time flitting all over England making trouble for her weary older brother.

Drawing a fur lap robe up over his chest to ward off the damp, Julian once again laid his head on the plush velvet padding behind him. He was getting too old for this sort of thing. He would much rather be at home with a good book and a glass of wine than out in this awful weather.

"Ah, Lettie," he sighed, closing his eyes. It would be much easier to stay furious at the girl if he didn't love her so deeply. But this latest trick was too damn much. She had defied him for the last time.

The ache in his head lessened as sleep, brought on by the sound of the rain on the roof and the darkness inside the carriage, came to collect him. Julian put all thoughts of his sister aside and tried not to think at all as he drifted off. He was almost successful, except for the thoughts that plagued him as he fell into slumber—thoughts of laughing dark eyes and the woman who possessed them.

"What, might I ask, is so interesting about the rain that keeps you watching out that window?"

Sophia Morelle, dowager Marchioness of Aberley, turned her attention from her front gate on the other side of the glass, to the young woman in marigold satin sprawled on a chaise across the room. She smiled, even though she did not feel like it.

"I am watching for your brother," she replied with a shiver that had more to do with the man in question than the draft creeping through the soft cashmere of her shawl.

Letitia rolled her doelike eyes in exasperation. "I thought we already established that Julian would never come here."

Smiling humorlessly at her friend's confidence, Sophia rose from the window seat and crossed the gently creaking oak floor to the fire where Letitia sat. "No, *you* established it. I disagreed with you then and I still do. You are quite wrong if you believe your brother will allow you to remain under my roof once he learns you are here."

The younger, thinner woman eyed her curiously as Sophia sat in the chair across from her. She did not seem moved by the warning at all.

"He is afraid of you."

Sophia snorted. "He fears nothing."

Letitia pressed forward, leaning her elbow against the pillows. "Then why does he go out of his way to avoid meeting you?"

"Because he despises me." A long time ago—it seemed a lifetime—she had despised him as well, but that had eased somewhat as she grew older. Now, she could almost understand why Julian betrayed her. Unfortunately, the wound of his betrayal had not faded with her hatred. It remained ever present in the background. Sometimes she would go months without thinking of it, but when she did, the hurt was still as sharp and raw as ever.

She had been a stupid, stupid fool where he was concerned and she had never forgiven herself.

Her friend smiled. "My brother flaunts himself in the face of those he dislikes. I think it gives him some kind of perverse pleasure. He would rather leave a place than play that game with you."

"I humiliated him," Sophia retorted, shame creeping into her cheeks. "No doubt the sight of me is a reminder of that."

"And the sound of your name as well?" Letitia arched a brow. "Is that a reminder? He cannot stand that either."

Sophia stared at her friend. Letitia made it sound like Julian's hatred was something Sophia should be proud of. At that moment, with that haughty, self-satisfied expression on her face she looked very much like her elder brother. So much so that Sophia had to turn away.

"I would imagine even the slightest mention of me would cause him discomfort," she muttered. Lord knew she cringed at the slightest reference to *him*.

"I must confess I have heard little of the story from Julian. Most of what I know I heard from the gossips."

Sophia glanced up. Julian hadn't told her the whole sordid tale? No, she supposed not. He had no way of knowing that the two of them would ever become friends, and it was hardly the sort of thing one discussed with a gently bred young woman.

"I fell in love with him." At her friend's shocked gaze, she continued, "And the sentiment was not returned, no matter how much I tried to force it." And when it wasn't returned, she lashed out in the most public and grandiose way she could.

"Oh." Letitia's expression was one of genuine discomfort and Sophia regretted having said anything at all.

There was no need to tell Letitia that Sophia had believed her feelings to have been returned at the time. It was all in the past and Julian was Letitia's brother. Sophia had no desire to paint him as a villain in his sister's eyes.

"I disgraced myself over him." Saying the words cut her to the very bone, but it was almost a relief to let the truth out. "And my behavior is the reason he will come for you. He will not risk my influencing you in any way."

Letitia's expression was one of disgust. "Your influence is not the one I need protection from. You are not the one trying to force me into marriage. You are not the one trying to make me something I am not. You have always encouraged me to be what I want."

Sophia smiled. "You see, I am a bad influence. From a male perspective at any rate."

Laughing, Letitia reached out and took one of Sophia's hands in hers. The younger woman's fingers were warm and firm. "You are the best friend I have ever had. I only wish it had not been necessary to hide our relationship all these years."

"We can thank Lady Wickford for her assistance," Sophia replied, withdrawing her hand so she could lean back in her chair. "Were it not for her we would scarce see each other."

It had happened quite innocently several years ago, when Edmund was still alive. Letitia had been in the area visiting Lady Wickford, and the two had happened upon Sophia one day while shopping in the village. Lady Wickford had always been friendly to Sophia, despite the older woman's close connection to the Rexley family. She introduced Letitia and invited Sophia to dine with them that night. Sophia had taken an instant liking to Julian's sister, and whenever Letitia came to visit Lady Wickford, Sophia spent as much time with them as possible.

But this recent visit was different. Letitia hadn't come to Lady Wickford first. She had come straight to Sophia, hoping to hide from her brother and his plans to marry her off to the gentleman who made the best offer.

"What does your Mr. Wesley have to say about all of this?"

Letitia brightened at the mention of the man she loved. Sophia both envied and feared her reaction. She knew what it was like to believe the sun rose and set on one person, knew the sweetness of such unswerving devotion. She also knew the bitterness of discovering that devotion was undeserved and unreturned. She would spare her friend that pain at any cost.

That was why she had agreed to help Letitia, so she could ascertain for herself what Mr. Wesley's intentions were and either encourage or dissuade Letitia accordingly.

"He says he wants to talk to my brother," the young woman replied with more than a touch of awe in her tone. "He believes he can persuade Julian to consent to our marriage."

Sophia liked this Mr. Wesley already. Convincing a man like Julian Rexley of anything would not be an easy task, especially when the earl already had his mind made up. But the fact that Letitia's beau would rather be open and honest about his intentions than underhanded said much for his character. After all, Mr. Wesley was not titled—not yet, though he was heir to a lord. Someday he would make a splendid match for a young woman, but right now he would hardly be able to keep Letitia in gowns, let alone the style she was accustomed to living.

"Why are you opposed to such a meeting?" Sophia queried, pouring herself a cup of tea from the pot on the tray before her. It wasn't hot, but it was warm enough, hopefully, to chase away the chill in her bones.

Letitia gazed at her as though the answer should be obvious. "Because my brother would never allow me to marry Mr. Wesley. Until Marcus comes into his inheritance, he would be unable to support us. Secondly, my brother believes that *he* is better equipped than I to determine who will make me a proper husband." She made a moue of disgust. "He wants me to marry someone as stuffy and dull as he is. As if I could ever be happy with any of the gentlemen he has in mind!"

Cup pressed against her mouth, Sophia paused, allowing the heat from the china to seep into her fingers and her lips.

Julian, stuffy and dull? Never in a million years would she attach such a description to the passionate young man she had known. At first he had been a game to her, but it did not take long for him to become much more.

That had been her greatest mistake, to believe that Julian Rexley was anything more than a man with a pretty face who knew how to make a young woman feel beautiful and special. She had set out to seduce him, but it was she who ended up being taken in.

"I am certain your brother believes he is acting in your best interest."

Letitia's Cupid's-bow lips twisted into a startlingly bitter sneer. "As he acted in yours?"

The retort hit its mark—and undoubtedly more sharply than Letitia intended. The girl—and despite her age she was just that—was too caught up in her own suffering feelings to consider whether or not she stepped on anyone else's.

"That was different," Sophia replied, her trembling fingers setting her cup on its saucer with a sharp clatter. "I was not his sister, and as you said yourself earlier, you possess too little of the facts to make any such assumptions."

Something in her tone must have gotten through Letitia's self-absorption, because her expression instantly changed to one of contrition. She reached out and caught Sophia's hand again.

"Oh, my dearest friend, what you must think of me! You are right of course. I have no right at all to pretend I know what happened between yourself and my brother. Please forgive me."

Sophia squeezed the other woman's fingers with a slight smile. She wasn't so cold now. The fire and the tea were beginning to thaw her. "There is nothing to forgive. You are upset. Anyone in your situation would be."

Letitia released her hand and slumped back against the chaise. "Oh, Sophia! *Upset* does not begin to describe my suffering! I try not to let my emotions run away with me, but it is so very difficult! Do you know what it is like to be faced with the possibility of losing that one person you love with all your heart?"

Sophia's heart constricted so sharply she almost cried out in pain. Yes. She knew that feeling.

"Of course you do," Letitia continued with a sympathetic countenance. "You lost your husband. Blast my foolish tongue! Would someone cut it out so it would flap no more!"

Sophia laughed—whether it was because Letitia assumed Sophia had loved her husband, or because of her friend's outburst, she wasn't quite sure. Perhaps it was both.

"Do not make yourself uneasy," she entreated when Letitia's mood threatened to turn as gray as the weather.

"You have done me no injury, and I will not have you act as though you have. I do not allow brooding in this house."

As quickly as the thunder clouds had appeared in the younger woman's face they disappeared again, and the sun burst through in the brightness of Letitia's laughter. The sound jarred Sophia's nerves, unused as they were to such volatile temperament. Heaven save her from passionate people, for they would surely be the end of her.

And to think she had once been one of them. Lord, she wouldn't be that girl again for anything. Except . . . Except that it would be nice to laugh like that just once more. It used to feel so good.

"I shall brood no more," Letitia promised with a smile. "But you must promise something in return."

Something in the girl's tone made Sophia wary. "What might that be?"

The smile faded. "You must answer a question for me, regardless of how impertinent it may be."

"You? Impertinent?" Sophia replied despite the fluttering in her breast at her friend's sudden seriousness. "No, I cannot believe it."

"Will you promise it?"

Sophia had already promised Letitia she would help protect her from her brother. She was loathe to make another vow that might prove unkeepable.

"I will do my best, but I can promise nothing without first hearing the question." And from the expression on Letitia's face, it was not going to be a question Sophia wanted to answer.

Letitia hesitated—something Sophia had never seen her do before. That she did so now did not bode well.

"Is it true that you and my brother were found in a state of . . . undress?"

Hot shame flooded Sophia's cheeks. She shouldn't be surprised that Letitia had questions. That her friend hadn't asked them before this was more strange.

"Yes," she replied, lifting her chin. She would not hang her head in front of Letitia, no matter how much she wanted to, because Letitia might be her friend, but she was also that bastard's sister. "We were."

The image came unbidden and unwelcome—a moment frozen forever in Sophia's mind. Hot, naive desire coupled with a mixture of fear and anticipation as Julian pressed himself between her thighs, only to be cruelly— thankfully—interrupted by the crashing of the door as Sophia's father burst into the room.

Sophia's horror was reflected in the face across from hers. Surely Letitia already knew this part of the story. "My brother ruined you."

"Not quite. I ruined myself."

Letitia appeared not to have heard. Perhaps she hadn't. Perhaps the words really had been the pathetic whisper Sophia heard them to be.

"And is it true that he refused to marry you?"

Sophia swallowed hard against the tightness in her throat. She held the other woman's fearful gaze. Poor Letitia, she already knew the truth.

"Yes," she whispered.

In fact, Julian hadn't even been asked to marry her before he refused. He seemed to think that Sophia had hoped to trick him into marriage. That was only half true. Yes, Sophia had hoped they might be discovered, but not like that. And she had hoped that by the time anyone found them Julian would have already made her his—and that he would have proposed on his own. It wasn't until she saw the hatred in his topaz gaze that Sophia realized he hadn't meant to offer for her at all, even though he would have gladly taken her innocence.

Letitia's face drained of all color. She looked so totally heartbroken, that Sophia regretted telling her the truth.

"How awful."

Glancing down at the fingers knotted in her lap, Sophia managed a small shrug. "I was as much to blame as your brother. I believed his attentions to be much more than they were, just as he believed mine to be much less."

Oh how grown up she sounded! How calm and generous and good! But she hadn't always felt so generous when it came to Julian Rexley.

Letitia shook her head, her expression one of such compassion that Sophia had to look away again.

Tell her about the book, Sophia. Then we shall see if you still have her sympathy. Wait until she discovers what a mockery you made of her brother.

And she would be certain to find out now. No doubt Julian would do whatever necessary to make certain his precious sister realized just what kind of woman Sophia was. He would show her the book and Letitia would know that Sophia had taken her revenge against her brother in her own, spiteful way.

There were times Sophia regretted avenging herself in such a manner, other times she regretted only that more people didn't know the truth behind it. For while Julian's humiliation of her had been very public, Sophia's had been much, much more subtle, and she would have liked to have seen him bleed a little all those years ago.

Voices in the hall outside the parlor made both her and

Letitia turn toward the door. Mrs. Ellis, the housekeeper, burst into the room, her bosom heaving as she gasped for breath.

"My lady, I'm so very sorry—"

The woman never got a chance to finish. Sophia rose to her feet as an ominous shadow filled the door frame. She knew who it was just as surely as she had known he would come.

He ignored her as he stepped inside. His hair was dark with rain and slicked back from his face. Water dripped onto the floor from the hem of his greatcoat. Apparently he had walked some distance through the storm to collect his sister—to get her away from Sophia.

His gaze went immediately to Letitia. "You," he said, his tone sending a sliver of ice up Sophia's spine. "Go collect your belongings. *Now.*"

He didn't even bother to wait to see if his sister obeyed before turning that icy brown gaze to Sophia. She stared at the fury in his face—a face that once had been so pretty it made angels weep. He wasn't so pretty anymore, but the sight of him hurt her more than it had a right to.

Gathering all her courage, Sophia lifted her chin and fixed him with what she hoped was a cool smile. She would not give him the satisfaction of seeing her quake before him.

"Hello, Lord Wolfram. Won't you sit down?"

Chapter 2

*Fate has a way of punishing
those who dare tempt it.*

An Unfortunate Attachment by A Repentant Lady

She wanted him to sit.

He'd come there prepared to fight, and she talked as though they were at a goddamn dinner party! If it weren't for the fact that he would know her voice—deep and husky with the faintest Spanish lilt—anywhere, he might have believed himself to have taken a wrong turn as he slogged through the rain and the mud.

But no. He would know her even if he were deaf and blind. He would know by the shiver that raced down his spine as soon as he was in her presence—an awareness that shot through his chest straight to his groin in a most arousing and infuriating fashion.

Damn, but the years had been kind to her. She was rounder than he remembered, softer, and her face had a maturity to it that hadn't been there before. Her thick, black hair was pulled back from her face in a style that would have been severe on some, but only served to accentuate the delicate bones of her face and the delicate pink and ivory of her complexion.

"I'll stand," he growled, clenching his jaw to keep his teeth from chattering.

The woman had the nerve to shrug. "Suit yourself. At least allow Mrs. Ellis to take your coat. You are dripping."

There was no rancor in her tone, yet she had a way of making Julian feel guilty. And why should he? She was the one who had tried to trap him. She was the one who was telling his sister God only knew what about him. All he had to feel bad about was leaving a water mark on her floor. And there were so many scuffs and stains under the polish now that it was unlikely anyone would notice his contribution.

Yet he allowed the matronly housekeeper to take his coat. It only made sense, he couldn't travel back to London in wet clothes. He couldn't travel back to London regardless, not until the wheel that had come off his carriage a mile down the road could be repaired. Allowing Letitia to spend another night with Sophia was out of the question. He would hire a coach if he had to, or borrow one from Sophia, but he would be leaving as soon as possible.

As cautiously as if Sophia were a wild animal, he turned his gaze to his sister. Letitia was still standing by the chaise, staring at him with a mixture of shock and hatred.

"I told you to go collect your things."

Her generous mouth flattened. "I'm not going anywhere."

Blood rushed to Julian's icy cheeks. How dare she defy him! Especially in front of Sophia. It was bad enough that he stood there, wet and shivering, but to have Letitia challenge his authority this way was unpardonable.

"You are," he informed her calmly. "Even if I have to put a sack over your head and drag you out by your heels. Now, *go pack*."

His heart twisted at the tears that sprang to his sister's eyes. He despised seeing her cry—and she knew it. This was just one more attempt to thwart him. It would not work. He stared at her impassively, waiting for her to do as she was told.

"I hate you!" she cried. "And you cannot force me to leave. You cannot!" With that declaration and a heartbroken sob, Letitia ran from the room, leaving Julian alone with Sophia.

Only the crackle of the fire and the rain against the windows broke the silence as he turned to face her and her superior smirk.

But she wasn't smirking. She watched him with an expression he couldn't quite read—something like sympathy and disgust rolled into one. He would have preferred the smirk.

"That went well," she remarked with more humor than the situation warranted.

Julian's eyes narrowed. How could she possibly be so blasé? It seemed he was so angry that even his muscles trembled at being this close to her. And she stood there staring at him as though nothing had ever happened between them.

"I blame you for this."

Sophia made a sound very much like a snort. Her ebony gaze locked with his. "Of course you do. I was the one who drove her to run out of the room in tears, after all."

Jaw tightening, Julian shifted his weight to the other foot. His boot made a squishing sound as he did so. He was soaked, his head ached and he was on the verge of throwing a fit that would make Letitia look even tempered. He was *not* in the mood to argue with this woman where his sister was concerned.

"No. You were simply the one who assisted her in deceiving her brother." He spoke through clenched teeth to keep them from chattering.

Those dark eyes flashed up at him. "Perhaps her brother should give some thought as to why she should want to deceive him."

That did it. Who did she think she was to think she had any right to comment on what was his business? "What happens between Letitia and myself is none of your concern, madam."

Sighing, Sophia gave her head a little shake. "I am afraid that it is my concern, Lord Wolfram. Your sister has given me as little choice in this matter as she has given you."

A frown drew Julian's brows together as her words drained some of the anger from his body. "What do you mean?"

She glanced away. "Letitia arrived here without invitation, my lord, something that I normally would not mind in the least, but had I known at the time that I was to be set between the two of you I should never have welcomed her as I did."

She was telling the truth, of that he was certain. It was now obvious that she was no happier to see him than he was to see her. For some reason, that rankled him as much as it pleased him. It felt good to know that he wasn't the only one with a grudge, but part of him had expected to walk in and have her throw herself at him, to resort to her old trickery.

"I am sorry she chose to involve you in this." He almost

choked on the words. Apologizing to Sophia for anything went against everything he knew of her. "We will leave as soon as she has packed."

Sophia looked at him—and seemed startled by what she saw. "I think you know as well as I, my lord, that your sister is not in her room packing. Sobbing, pitching a fit, perhaps, but not packing."

Julian would have laughed at her astuteness were she not the woman she was. "If you would be so kind as to point me in the right direction I will go talk to her."

"I think perhaps you should give her a little time to calm down."

"At the risk of being rude, my lady, I do not particularly care what you think."

She stiffened, but she didn't back down. "You do not seem to care much for what your sister thinks either."

"I beg your pardon?" His voice was muffled by the solid clench of his teeth.

Mouth set mulishly, Sophia said nothing.

Julian stepped forward. "You started this, madam. Now I demand to know what you are talking about."

Her chest rose and fell rapidly with the force of her anger, lifting the creamy swells of her breasts against the restraining neckline of her violet gown.

How typically male of him to ogle her chest whilst reflecting on how much she angered him. What would he degrade himself to next?

"You may demand all you want, my lord, but I am mistress here and my demands are the only ones that matter."

Ah, this was the Sophia he knew. That woman who treated him like a polite stranger was just that, a stranger. This woman, the one with eyes that glittered like the night sky and fists clenched at her sides, was the woman he had once wanted so badly he ached for her.

This ache he felt now was just a reminder of that, nothing more.

"And what would you have me do, Lady Aberley?" he demanded, gesturing with his hands the way he always did when his temper ran away with him. "Sit by your fire and make small talk while my sister manipulates us both?"

Some of the tension seemed to leave her as she listened to his words. "I think you should indeed sit by my fire, Lord Wolfram, if for no other reason than to dry your clothes so you do not end up with an ague and under my roof for longer than either of us would care to suffer through."

What a sharp-tongued little viper she was! But he had always known that. The sting of her words was heightened by the annoying fact that she was right.

Crossing the sagging floor to the fire, Julian seated himself in an incredibly ugly chair whose black, brown and orange pattern could only be enhanced by any stain his wet clothing might leave behind.

Sophia followed, keeping as much distance between them as was possible. This arrangement suited Julian just fine, until he noticed how she hugged her shawl around her shoulders.

"Come sit where it is warm," he instructed. "I promise not to bite." *Not yet, at any rate.*

She surprised him by taking the chair across from him. "You should take your boots off so they will dry faster."

She was right, of course, and Julian complied without speaking. He set the battered Hessians on their sides, with the tops facing the fire so the insides would dry quickly.

Turning his chair to directly face the fire, he propped his feet up on the ottoman that matched his homely seat and sighed as the fire set about driving the chill from his bones.

They sat in a silence that was eerily comfortable. Occasionally rain spattered down the chimney, drawing a sharp hiss out of the fire, but other than that there was no other hint of aggression in the room. It was as though Letitia, and the fact that they were both cold, had formed some kind of truce between them.

Refusing to allow himself to be lulled by this feeling of contentment, Julian took the opportunity to study his surroundings, looking to find some indication that Sophia was the harridan he wanted her to be. He found very little. What he did find piqued his curiosity.

Sophia lived in the dowager house on her late husband's estate, as was proper, but her abode was not what he expected. Instead of the rich opulence he equated with Sophia, he found comfortable yet shabby furnishings, wallpaper several decades out of date and floors in need of refinishing. Even Sophia herself, as lovely as she was, wore a gown that could hardly be described as the height of fashion, although it would have been, last year or the year before. Why?

Her husband had been a wealthy man. Surely he had left his widow enough blunt to live properly? Her circumstances couldn't possibly be *this* reduced, could they?

It was none of his business. As soon as he and Letitia were able to leave, he would put as much distance as possible between himself and Sophia Morelle, and then he would do everything in his power to forget having seen her again.

And to forget that, as of this moment, it was almost nice to be with her.

"If there is going to be much of a delay in repairing my carriage, might it be possible for me to beg loan of one of yours?" he asked, wiggling his toes in front of the fire. His stockings were almost dry.

"You will have to inquire at the great house, I am afraid, my lord," she replied softly. "There are no stables here."

Horses weren't a problem. He had horses. "All I need is a carriage, Lady Aberley." It felt odd to call her by that name.

When Sophia didn't reply immediately, Julian turned his head toward her. She had her hands folded in her lap and her head was bowed.

"Lady Aberley? You do have a carriage, do you not?"

Her head came up and the depth of pride in those fathomless eyes of hers struck Julian hard in the chest. "I do not."

He couldn't have been more surprised if she had told him she was considering entering a convent. Julian didn't know anyone who didn't own at least one vehicle.

"And may I ask why?" He kept his tone even, afraid that if he sounded as incredulous as he felt she would not answer honestly.

"My brother-in-law thought it a frivolous expense, since he has several carriages at the great house."

He supposed that wasn't wholly strange. "Do you agree with his assessment?"

She turned toward the fire, giving Julian a cameo-perfect view of the gentle slopes and curves of her profile.

"He handles my finances, Lord Wolfram. I have no choice but to agree with his assessment."

A suspicion took root in Julian's belly, spreading rapidly through his entire being. "And does your brother-in-law also consider decent furniture and new gowns 'frivolous' expenses?" he questioned softly, watching her expression carefully.

Sophia closed her eyes. Julian watched as she drew in a deep breath and released it again. The thick fringe of her lashes fluttered open. Then, having composed herself, she turned her head to face him.

"Recently he seems to have come to that conclusion, yes."

"*Recently?* I would think that now that your mourning period is over he would want to see you out in society. Unless of course, you choose to remain in the country?"

The longing in her gaze almost made him smile. For a split second, she looked like that girl he had once known—before he learned of her true nature.

"Oh no. I should like very much to be out and about again."

"Then why do you not tell him that?"

Her gaze shuttered, but not before Julian saw what she did not want him to see. She had told her brother-in-law. And he hadn't allowed it.

Why? What had happened during her brief return to society that made the new marquess want to keep her cloistered away in the country. What had she done?

As if sensing that he knew she had a secret, Sophia rose to her feet. She kept her gaze averted, her cheeks flushed with embarrassment.

"If you will excuse me, Lord Wolfram, I believe I will have Mrs. Ellis make some tea to warm you up. I will also have her put on some soup for you and your men. They will no doubt need it."

"That is not necessary," he replied, suddenly sorry for having discomfited her, when it was what he had wanted originally. She seemed so sincere, and yet he knew without question that she was hiding something. Sophia was always hiding *something*. Was she purposely trying to make her brother-in-law seem the villain to cover her own sins?

"No." She met his gaze with a shaky smile that he had to admire. "I think it is. Please excuse me."

She left the room without a backward glance, leaving Julian peering around the back of his chair after her. As he settled back in his seat, he couldn't help but wonder what it was that Sophia was so anxious to conceal.

And why the hell he should even care.

She would have to be more careful.

Pausing outside the parlor, Sophia pressed her forehead against the cool, whitewashed door frame and struggled to pull herself together. How could she have made such a blunder as to trust the Earl Wolfram with details of her life? She shouldn't have mentioned Charles at all. Now he would know there was something going on, and if he pressed Lady Wickford for information, he just might uncover what it was.

What if he did? Lifting her head, she thought about it for a moment. What was the worst thing that could happen? He could believe she deserved her brother-in-law's harassment and have a good chuckle at her expense. How could that hurt her? She had already suffered the worst humiliation Julian Rexley could ever heap upon her. Having him laugh at her misfortune would be a minuscule embarrassment in comparison.

She had said other things to him as well, things that

made her both anxious and giddy with power. She had told him that perhaps he should ask himself why Letitia sought to escape him. Even better, she had told him she didn't want him in her house! She hadn't been able to stop herself. No doubt Edmund would be rolling over in his grave to hear her talk in such a hoydenish manner, but Edmund was dead and couldn't hear a word she said.

Still, as good as it had felt to speak to Julian in such a frank manner, there was that little niggling of guilt in the back of her mind—a little voice telling her she should behave in a more ladylike and genteel manner. It was Edmund's voice. He might not be able to hear *her*, but she was certainly able to hear *him*, even from beyond the grave.

Drawing her shawl around her shoulders, Sophia strode across the hall to a door that led to the kitchen. Faint, yet warm and appetizing, the smells from that area of the house greeted her as she closed the door behind her. Charles may deny her everything that would make it possible for her to reenter society, but he did not deny her food. He most likely thought that would make her feel some kind of gratitude toward him.

Charles wanted her. He made that perfectly clear, but not for a wife. She was, after all, his brother's widow, and even if such a thing were done, it still wouldn't be what Charles had in mind. He took everything he could from her in the hope that she would eventually capitulate and give him what he wanted—her body.

He gave her enough money to maintain her household— he had to. Charles might be in charge of her funds, but so were Edmund's former solicitors. According to one of the many stipulations in Edmund's will, Sophia was to be given enough money to live comfortably. Charles couldn't cut her off completely lest he violate the will, but he could argue that while Sophia was virtually a prisoner in her own home, she was a "comfortable" one.

There were other stipulations in the will that Charles sought to manipulate in his favor, but since they hinged on Sophia's public conduct, they were useless. She never went out in public, so there was little chance of her breaking them. Still, she was careful around her brother-in-law. He was trying to trap her into becoming his mistress or swindle her out of her allowance—possibly even both. She would not allow him to win.

Lately, Sophia had begun to wonder if Charles wasn't growing impatient. She feared that he was done waiting, that he was going to use force to get what he wanted, and as loyal as Sophia's servants were, they worked for Charles first. She could not count on them to come to her aid if he assaulted her.

What would Lord Wolfram think of that? Would he think she deserved to be used in such a way? Probably. And yet here she was, going to the kitchen to have tea made for him. She had made him sit near the fire so his clothing would dry and he wouldn't catch cold.

She wanted him out of her house. It was that simple. If he got sick he would have to stay, and she couldn't trust herself not to do everything she could to increase his suffering. That was a lie. She would probably nurse him back to health herself, she was that much of an idiot.

"It smells wonderful in here," she announced with false cheer as she stepped into the kitchen.

The cook smiled at her over her shoulder from her spot by the stove. "Thank you, m'lady. 'Tis lamb for supper. I hope you don't mind, I took the liberty of changing the menu as it looks like the earl will be staying."

"Oh?" Sophia tried to keep the panic from her voice.

She glanced at Mrs. Ellis, who sat at the rough-hewn table sipping a cup of tea. "Have you had word from his men?"

The round-faced housekeeper nodded as she set her empty cup on the saucer. "Yes, my lady. Roger took a few men from the great house and went to give them a hand."

The great house? Oh, no! That meant Charles would know that Julian was there.

"They managed to get the carriage and the horses up to the stables," Mrs. Ellis continued, "and they hope to have the wheel fixed, or a new one on by tomorrow morning at the latest."

If it weren't for the presence of the two other women, Sophia thought she might have been ill right then and there. Julian couldn't stay the night! It had taken all her strength to face him for thirty minutes! How could she possibly manage to spend the entire night under the same roof with him? She couldn't. They would just have to have his carriage fixed and ready to go. And the rain would just have to stop. That's all there was to it.

"I see," she murmured. "Make up a room for his lordship just in case." The words were bitter in her mouth, but unless she wanted the servants gossiping, she had to pretend that Julian's presence was perfectly normal and not something that made her want to run through the house screaming.

As she turned to leave the room, feeling much like a marionette with tangled strings, she remembered why she had gone to the kitchen in the first place.

"Mrs. Ellis, would you be so good as to take Lord Wolfram some tea and soup? I would hate for him to take ill." *And have to stay here for more than one night.*

The housekeeper smiled. "Of course, Lady Aberley. Would you like me to set a cup for yourself?"

Take tea with Julian? She'd rather wash her face with lye. The man was too handsome, too much of a threat to her. When he wasn't bristling like a hedgehog, he was far too easy to talk to. He always had been, but he was the last person on earth with whom she should trust her secrets—or her regrets.

"No. But perhaps you would send a tray of tea and cakes up to Lady Letitia's room. I shall take refreshment with her."

Leaving the kitchen, Sophia walked slowly back to the hall. Her meeting with Julian had taken what little energy she had, and now she had to deal with his overly dramatic sister. It was not a chore she looked forward to, but Julian wasn't leaving without his sister, and Letitia didn't want to go with him at all. If Sophia ever wanted the two siblings out of her house, she was going to have to try her best to help repair the rift between them. It was either that or go stay with Lady Wickford until the smoke cleared.

As she crossed several of the brightly hued rugs that covered the ruin that was the hall floor, Sophia finally allowed her thoughts to turn to Julian—not as a threat, or as an earl, or even as Letitia's brother, but as a man. More important, how the man he was today compared with the young man she once favored above all others.

He was the one man—the one person—who had ever dared say no to her. Certainly her husband and his brother had no trouble denying her anything, but Julian had been the first, and his refusal hadn't come on the heels of a request for a new gown or a puppy, but from the offer of everything she had to give.

The first time she laid eyes on Julian Rexley she had thought him Adonis come to earth, so struck was she by his beauty. Standing in the middle of Almack's, the light from the chandeliers warming the gold of his skin and highlighting the thick waves of his hair, he had set her heart to pounding in a most exciting manner. Her friend Caroline had judged him "too thin," but Sophia was smitten regardless.

He hadn't changed that much over the years. There were faint lines carved in the delicate flesh around his eyes and between his brows and around his mouth—a mouth that was far too sensual to be wasted on a man. He frowned just as much as he laughed, as was usual with people whose moods were as unpredictable and volatile as the weather.

Age had fleshed out the gauntness of youth from the sharply chiseled bones of his face, just as it had with the rest of him. Julian Rexley had grown into his body in a most spectacular manner. He carried himself proudly, showing off his extraordinary height, and the limbs that had at one time been gangly and a little awkward moved with the fluid grace of a man who knew his place in the world—on top of it.

If he had been striking in his youth, he was devastating now—if one liked men who were too handsome for their own good. Personally, Sophia thought looks were horribly overrated, at least where Julian was concerned. He might look tempting, but just like the serpent who tormented Eve he had a nasty bite. She knew that firsthand, a fact she would do well to remember when his beauty threatened to overwhelm her.

Lifting her skirts, she climbed the stairs to the next floor and at the top, squared her shoulders in preparation for seeing Letitia. It was not going to be pleasant. The girl believed her brother to be totally against her, and Sophia thought she just might be right, but Sophia knew Julian's intentions weren't self-serving. He only wanted to see her settled and well matched, just as Sophia's own parents had, or at least her mother had. Her father had just wanted to be rid of her.

And truthfully, had her parents chosen so very badly for her? Edmund was from a good family, had a respected title and was incredibly wealthy. He had been the perfect candidate. Unfortunately, he had been far from the perfect husband.

Oh no, that was wrong. It had been *she* who was not perfect, as Edmund had often reminded her.

For the longest time Sophia wondered what it was about her character that was so defective that it drove men away or made them want to change her. The answer came to her one day when she witnessed Edmund's anger because the weather wasn't as he would like it. Men like to control things—including people.

It had taken Edmund some time to learn what weapons to use against her to bend her to his will. He appealed to her dignity, to her pride and to her sense of guilt to mold her into his idea of the proper wife. After his death she had been struck with sheer panic at the prospect of reentering the world without his guidance. Thankfully she had the confines of mourning to hide behind. It was only now that she longed to join the world.

And now Charles sought to control her as well. He would not find it quite as easy as his brother had. She had found a quiet strength within herself, a pride that she never knew she had, and it gave her more courage than any man could ever take away.

With a start, she realized she was standing outside Letitia's door. How long she had been standing there, she had no idea. She had been too ensconced in the past.

She tapped on the door and waited for Letitia to answer. Nothing. She knocked again, louder this time.

Thank heaven Charles didn't know about the book. Then he would truly have her right where he wanted her— almost. She would be at his mercy, but not even that would persuade her into his bed.

There was still no answer from within Letitia's chamber. Sophia frowned. Had her friend not retired to her room as she thought?

"Letitia, dearest, are you in there?" She called, rapping yet again. Her knuckles were beginning to sting.

A muffled shuffling sounded from behind the door. "Is my brother with you?"

Sophia smiled at the pathetically defiant tone. "No. He is not."

Following the subtle click of a key being turned in a lock, the door to Letitia's bedchamber slowly swung open. A red-eyed Letitia peered cautiously around the edge.

"Where is he?" she asked, her voice thick from the tears she had shed.

There was, of course, no need to say who "he" was.

"In the parlor," Sophia replied, stepping into the room. "Warming himself in front of the fire with a cup of tea."

Closing the door, Letitia shot her an accusatory glance. "You gave him tea? I hope you put hemlock in it."

Sophia smiled at the petulant tone. "I must confess the idea never occurred to me."

Flouncing over to the bed, Letitia dropped onto the coverlet in a disheveled heap of brightly colored skirts. "I cannot believe you of all people offered him any hospitality."

"What would you have me do?" Sophia asked as she

crossed the floor to sit beside her. "Toss him out into the rain?"

The younger woman's lip thrust out. "'Twould be a start."

"Come now," Sophia said firmly, placing her arm around her friend's shoulders. "This is hardly the way for a young lady to behave." Lord, she sounded just like Edmund! A bitter taste filled her mouth, despite the truth of her words.

The shoulders beneath her arm rose with a gusty sigh. "You are right," Letitia replied, lifting her gaze to Sophia's. "I should face my bully of a brother with calm and resilience, rather than running off and leaving you to his mercy. Was he absolutely horrible to you?"

"No," she replied. Other than blaming her for everything he had been surprisingly civil.

"No doubt he is saving all his rancor for me," Letitia remarked with false brightness, but there was real fear in her eyes. "Oh, Sophia. What if he forces me to wed before Mr. Wesley can prove himself?"

"He cannot force you to marry anyone, dearest," Sophia replied, squeezing her friend's shoulders. "Even if he dragged you to the altar he cannot force you to say the words." No one could force Letitia to do anything. She was stronger than Sophia had been. It had been very easy for her father to shame her into marrying Edmund. After all, she had disgraced the family name.

Shaking her head, Letitia broke free of her embrace and leapt to her feet. "You do not know Julian as I do."

That was true, but Sophia knew him better than she would have liked. "I know that he loves you."

Letitia made a scoffing sound. Hugging herself, she began to pace the length of the rug. "Do you think so?"

"He would not have come here in such weather to rescue you if he did not. Do you really believe he would use force against you?"

"My brother does not have to use his physical strength to bend someone to his will."

To her humiliation, a soft heat crept up Sophia's neck and face. Yes, she was well aware of some of the more seductive weapons in Julian Rexley's arsenal, weapons whose power and destruction his sister could have no way of knowing.

"He will coerce me," Letitia continued, her steps slowing to a stop in the middle of the room. "He will keep talking, telling me that he is right and I am wrong, that he knows what is best for me. By the time he is done with me, even I will be convinced that I am doing the right thing."

The bleakness in her friend's expression frightened Sophia. She knew how it felt to have someone else's will pressed upon her. Of course Julian would know exactly how to manipulate his sister. He was manipulative by nature—like Edmund and even her father. Men like that saw every weakness a woman had and used it to their advantage without the slightest trace of guilt.

"You have a strong will as well," she reminded her friend. "Surely you can stand against your brother and his list of suitors, especially when you have the power of love on your side."

Letitia's eyes were black with despair. "Mr. Wesley and I barely see each other once a fortnight as it is. With Julian watching my every move it will be even more difficult for us to meet." She sighed in resignation, her shoulders slumping. "He will forget me and my brother will win."

"I do not believe that for one minute," Sophia replied resolutely. "I know how determined you can be, my friend. You will persevere, but not if you talk as though you have already lost."

A weak smile curved Letitia's full lips. Coming forward, she knelt at Sophia's feet, taking her hands in her own. "You are such a good, dear friend to me, Sophia. No matter how foolish or melancholy I become you always believe the best of me and set me to rights. How I wish I had one ounce of your strength."

Strength? Letitia thought *she* had strength? Sophia would have laughed were it not for the huge lump in her throat.

"I am not strong," she whispered.

"Oh, but you are!" Letitia countered. "I saw how you stood before my brother, daring him to play lord of the manor with you. I have never seen anyone stand up to him as you did. If I have any bravery at all it is because I am with you."

How could Sophia explain that it was because of who Letitia's brother was that she had forced herself to stand proud before him? Few people disarmed her as Julian did, and she had always had more bravado than sense when it came to facing her fears.

Suddenly, a strange brightness lit Letitia's eyes, a light that made a heavy coil of unease unfurl in Sophia's stomach.

"Whatever it is you are thinking you can forget it," she told her friend.

Letitia grinned. "But I have just thought of the perfect way to foil my brother's plans."

Warily, Sophia stared at her. It didn't matter that she had known Letitia as a friend for some time, these extreme fluctuations in mood always made her uneasy.

"And how do you propose to do that?" she asked.

Letitia's smile broadened. "It is easy. You are coming to London with me."

Chapter 3

*Men are not the only creatures to ever be deceived
by a pair of fine eyes and a pretty face.*

An *Unfortunate Attachment* by A Repentant Lady

*T*rapped.

That was exactly how Julian felt as he stared out the narrow window at the rain. Even if his carriage wasn't in need of a new wheel, the roads beyond the cottage were the consistency of cold gravy—soft and lumpy. His horses would be exhausted before they made it out of the village.

He was trapped here, in Sophia's house, totally at her mercy.

And so far she had yet to take advantage of the situation. In fact, his hostess had made herself surprisingly scarce. Mrs. Ellis had shown him to this closet of a bedroom where a steaming bath had sat waiting—courtesy of the marchioness. Julian's clothes had dried in front of a comfortable fire while he soaked in the heavenly hot water.

Now, dry and as warm as he could be in the drafty cottage, he paced the length of a faded carpet so worn the floor boards peeked through in several spots, and wondered yet again why Sophia's brother-in-law allowed her to live in such lowered circumstances. What had she done?

And more important, why did she look at him as though daring him to mention it?

He didn't care. He didn't care that her house was drafty. He didn't care that her clothing was out of date and still in the subdued shades of half mourning. She was but a pale shadow of the vibrant creature she had once been. Only when she looked him in the eye and told him she did not want him in her house did he see any resemblance to the girl he had once . . .

The girl he had what? Desired? Admired?

Loved?

Standing at the window, the warmth of the fire at his back as he stared into the bleakness outside, Julian thought back to the time when Sophia could have had his heart for the asking. It had been a long time since he had thought of it, and even longer since it had actually happened, but it resurfaced in his mind with startling clarity.

He had first noticed Sophia during her first season. In a bouquet of delicate English roses she had been an exotic orchid. Her half-Spanish heritage set her apart from the other debutantes. He couldn't take his eyes off of her. What little self-confidence he possessed dissolved whenever he ventured within a few feet of her and it angered him. He made a habit of staying as far away from her as possible, even though he envied every man she danced with.

His avoidance of her went on for two seasons. It had become a habit by then. Julian had already watched several of his friends make fools of themselves over Sophia and had no desire to do the same. What other outcome could there possibly be? He was quiet and moody. He wrote poetry. She was vibrant and happy and seemed far too worldly to be impressed by the verses he scratched.

So when she walked up to him at a ball and boldly asked him why he never danced with her he had stammered something inane—he couldn't remember what. She looked up at him with those enormous, fathomless eyes of hers and asked him if he would care to dance. He said yes.

They danced twice that night. He actually asked her the second time. Even if he had known where those innocent dances would lead, he knew without a doubt he would have danced with her anyway. He would have taken that risk just to hold her in his arms, because when she looked at him he had felt as though there was nothing he could not do.

She had made him feel like a man.

The creaking of the chamber door brought him back to the present. He turned, half dreading, half hoping to see Sophia standing there.

It was Letitia.

"Yes?" He had expected her to pout longer than this.

She closed the door behind her. Dressed in an evening gown of dark copper silk, his sister was a vision of elegance. She looked so much like their mother that sometimes it brought a lump to Julian's throat. She had much of their mother's goodness as well—when she wasn't being obstinate.

"I have been thinking," she told him, raising her hesitant gaze to his.

What scheme had she come up with now? "About?"

She clasped her hands in front of her skirts. "About returning to London. I will go with you on one condition."

She was going with him and that was all there was to it.

If Miranda's death had taught him anything, it was to be firm where his youngest sister was concerned.

"And that is?" he asked curiously, leaning his shoulder against the window frame.

"I want Sophia to come to London with us."

She didn't want much, did she? "No."

Letitia met his simple declaration with a defiant lift of her chin. "Then I am not going."

Damnation! What was she trying to do, drive him to violence? Dragging a hand through his hair, Julian silently counted to ten.

"You are going," he insisted from between clenched teeth. "Even if I have to carry you out of here."

His sister's color heightened but she did not back down. "Will you force me to go to balls as well? Will you lock me in my room to keep me from seeing whom I choose? You can only force me to do so much, Julian. No one can force me to say 'I do.' Not even you."

She had him there, and the smug smile on her face told him she knew it too.

"I would never force you to marry a man you could not in time learn to love, Lettie, as you are well aware."

Her smile widened at that. Locking his gaze with hers, Julian continued, "But you will leave this house with me as soon as we are able to do so, and Lady Aberley will *not* be coming with us. That is final."

Letitia's smile crumpled into an expression somewhere between tears and rage. For a moment, Julian thought Letitia was going to either burst into tears or throw something at him, but before she could do anything, there was a knock on the door.

"Enter," he called.

Mrs. Ellis appeared in the open doorway. "Begging

your pardon my lord, but the marchioness wished me to tell you and Lady Letitia that she will wait upon you in the parlor before going in to dinner."

So Sophia wished to break bread with him, did she? No doubt this show of hospitality was for Letitia's sake.

"Thank you, Mrs. Ellis," he replied with a smile. "Please tell Lady Aberley my sister and I shall be down directly."

"I am not going anywhere with you," Letitia informed him once the housekeeper was gone.

Julian turned to face her with a heavy heart. Did she think he enjoyed denying her? For more than a decade he had been both mother and father to her. He gave her whatever she wanted, no matter how big or small. Perhaps that was the problem. Letitia was used to having her own way, but this was one time he would not give in.

"Fine," he told her. "I shall have Lady Aberley send a tray up to the nursery for you. If you wish to act like a child you can be treated as one."

If it were possible to slay someone with a glance, he would have expired right then and there, so dark was the gaze his sister fixed upon him.

"Sometimes I truly despise you," she whispered.

He knew she was angry with him, and it wasn't the first time she had said such words to him, but they still hurt all the same.

"I know," he replied with the faintest trace of regret. "Shall we go downstairs?"

She refused the arm he offered her as they met in the doorway and brushed past him with all the hauteur of a queen avoiding a peasant. Stifling a sigh, Julian didn't press the issue and left the room behind her.

Why must she always make him the villain? Why

could she not see that he was only doing what was best for her? He wanted her to have a husband who would adore her, children to love and dote upon. These were things she deserved to have. Surely she desired them as well? And now was the time to do it, before she became too set in her ways.

Plus, he needed to see her settled and cared for before he could get on with his own life, and lately Julian had felt the urge to do just that. Over the past few years he had witnessed the marriages of his two closest friends. He envied the happiness Brave and Gabriel had found and wanted it for himself, but first he had to find it for Letitia. He would not always be there for her and he needed to know she would be well looked after should anything happen to him.

One would think that Sophia would encourage Letitia to marry, and marry well. After all, she had set out to get herself a rich husband and she ended up a marchioness. How fortunate she must consider herself that Julian hadn't offered for her, otherwise she would have ended up a mere countess.

Would she prefer that to being a reclusive widow in a house with creaky floors and drafty windows?

Outside the parlor door he straightened his coat— which was, thankfully, dry and comfortable once more— and ran his fingers through his hair. He winced as several tangles pulled at his scalp. Damn stuff. It was too thick and unruly for his liking.

As soon as he stepped into the parlor, Sophia met his gaze with an expression somewhat akin to panic. Julian's brain barely had time to register that and how lovely she looked in her dark plum evening gown before realizing that he was not the only man in the room.

Charles Morelle, the present Marquess of Aberley, followed his sister-in-law's gaze and flashed Julian a smile that was no more sincere than it was welcoming.

"Wolfram." The marquess greeted him coolly. "How good it is to see you again."

"Likewise," Julian replied with a slight smile. Charles stood very close to his sister-in-law, and every nuance of the man's stance and expression made it perfectly clear that he considered Sophia and all her soft curves as his property.

Was that why Sophia looked so distressed when he entered the room? She didn't want him to see that there was something going on between herself and her dead husband's brother? Were she and Morelle lovers?

The idea soured Julian's stomach.

Sophia discreetly put some space between herself and Charles. "Lord Wolfram, I am so glad you decided to join us."

Julian arched a brow, forcing himself to look at her face and not the soft flesh exposed by the low neckline of her gown. Had she thought he would stay up in his room all evening?

"Thank you for the hospitality, Lady Aberley. I apologize for any inconvenience my presence might cause you."

Was it his imagination or did she blush at that?

"Well," she said finally, after a brief but awkward silence. "Shall we go in?"

Aberley stepped forward to escort Sophia. Julian watched her stiffen as he did so. She didn't seem any happier to take the marquess's arm than Letitia was to take his. Either Sophia had learned to become an even better actress than she had been in her youth, or she truly did not want her brother-in-law touching her.

Julian wagered it was the former. Charles Morelle was

a handsome man. He certainly wasn't as tall as Julian, nor was he as long of limb, but the marquess possessed the physique of a sporting man and a blond ruggedness that most women would find attractive. Surely Sophia wasn't immune.

His dislike for the marquess rose.

In fact, he thought as they entered the dining room, Sophia and Charles made a very handsome couple, just as she and the late marquess had. They looked as though they belonged together, and there could be no doubt that Charles wanted Sophia. The hunger in his gaze when he looked at her was unmistakable.

So why did she look more like a poor relation than a rich man's mistress?

It was none of his concern. After tomorrow, when he and Letitia were on their way to London, he wouldn't give Sophia or her lover another thought. They could go at it on the dining-room table for all he cared.

But when Julian imagined Sophia naked and writhing on that polished oak surface, it wasn't Charles Morelle he saw poised to devour her like the tart she was.

Good lord. What the hell was wrong with him? How could he even imagine making love with a woman he didn't even like? But he had liked her very much at one time. He never had Sophia as he had wanted all those years ago, perhaps that was the reason he was having these thoughts now. That had to be it.

Sophia sat at one end of the table, Charles at the other. She seemed much more relaxed with several feet of china and silverware between them. Did she hope that he wouldn't notice the way Charles looked at her? A man would have to be blind to miss that.

Dinner was an informal affair, with each of them serving themselves from platters on the table and nearby side-board. The food was simple but delicious, and Julian was thankful for it as there was little conversation.

"So you're bound for London tomorrow, eh, Wol-fram?" Charles asked around a mouthful of bread.

Lowering his fork to his plate, Julian nodded. "Yes." He didn't bother to add he'd steal a carriage if he had to.

The marquess looked very pleased to hear this. "Lady Aberley will miss your lovely sister's company, I fear."

If he feared it why did he look so damn happy about it?

"I invited Lady Aberley to join us," Letitia replied, fix-ing Julian with a mutinous expression. "But she declined."

This announcement seemed to surprise Charles as much as it surprised Julian.

"If you want to go to London, Sister, all you have to do is ask." There was a hint of innuendo in Charles's tone, a trace of intimacy that made it sound as though Sophia could have whatever she wanted, provided she asked the right way.

With her body.

It was tempting to knock the marquess's teeth into his lap. How dare he be so blatant in front of Letitia!

But Letitia didn't seem to notice. She was too busy moving her vegetables around her plate with her fork.

Julian glanced at Sophia. She looked as though she might throw something at her brother-in-law. Julian rather hoped that she would. He wanted her to refute the insinu-ation that Charles knew her more intimately than a hus-band's brother should.

Instead, she tightened her grip on her knife and fork. Disappointment stabbed at Julian's breast. "I have no de-sire to go to London," she replied politely. Only that brief flash in her eyes betrayed how truly angry she was.

She turned to Julian, her face an expressionless mask. "Please do not think I was trying to win an invitation, my lord."

In other words she didn't want to be in the same city as him, let alone the same house. It shouldn't affect him, but it did. It served to drive home the fact that she had never truly cared about him, that she had only paid attention to him because of his title and his fortune. What a fool she must think him.

Julian forced a smile. "Of course not," he replied, his chest strangely tight. "I would never assume such a thing."

She needed a drink.

Setting the heavy, silver-backed brush on the vanity, Sophia rose from the thickly padded stool, reached for the silk wrapper draped over the foot of her bed and slipped it on over her matching night rail. It wasn't very warm, but it was all she had. Edmund hadn't liked her in warm, heavy fabrics such as velvet. They hid too much, and he liked to have as much of her as possible available to his sight and touch.

The idea of running into Julian while wearing it was almost enough to send her hiding beneath her blankets, but she wasn't about to let his presence in her house interfere with her usual habits. She was going to go to the little room that served as her library, and she was going to sit by the fire and enjoy a glass of wine as she read.

There was very little chance that Julian would stumble upon her sanctuary and even less chance that he would stay there if he did. No doubt he was in his room either writing one of those morose poems of his, or he was asleep—his feet dangling over the edge of the little bed.

The idea of Julian being so uncomfortable made

Sophia smile. She imagined those long feet of his, bare and blue with cold, sticking out from beneath the quilts as he shivered and sniffled his way through the night.

Unfortunately, she also imagined the bare legs attached to those feet. And with the thought of bare legs, came the thought of a bare everything else.

"Idiot," she mumbled, fastening her robe around her. The man barged into her house, practically accused her of trying to corrupt his sister, and how did she react? She pictured him naked! And she couldn't even picture him looking disfigured and misshapen. She had to imagine him as perfect and proportionate as only Julian Rexley could dare be.

It was humiliating, degrading and just plain *wrong*. Surely it was some kind of defect in her character that made her think such improper thoughts when it came to Julian. She thought that side of her nature had been duly repressed by her marriage. Edmund had been the only man to know her so . . . *intimately*, despite all her earlier efforts with Julian. She had thought that finally knowing what all the urges were about would put an end to this longing, but it only seemed to make it worse. She knew what kinds of things a man could do to a woman, the pleasure he could give, and it had only taken one look at Julian to set her wondering what delights he was capable of bestowing.

Just the thought of it made her tingle in places that hadn't tingled in quite some time.

Opening the door to her room, Sophia tiptoed into the dark corridor, avoiding by instinct every creaky floorboard and stair on her way to the library, where Mrs. Ellis would have left a fire burning in the hearth. Sometimes the dear woman even had a glass of wine waiting as well.

The library door squeaked softly as she pushed it open. Light and warmth from the fire greeted her as she stepped inside. Entering this room was more like entering another world, it felt so different from the rest of the house. The library made the drafts and uneven floors and smoking chimneys bearable. This room gave her the strength to shoulder anything Charles threw at her.

After closing the door behind her, Sophia turned toward her chair and froze.

Julian Rexley sat in her favorite chair, a book in one hand, a glass of wine in the other. *Her* glass of wine. He was dressed in nothing but a shirt that was open at the throat, exposing a shameful amount of tan chest and the curly hair that covered it, and trousers that pulled taut across the leg he draped over the arm of the chair. His feet were bare and the glimpse of hairy shin that showed above reminded Sophia of the thoughts she'd had in her bedroom. Thoughts that had her attention flitting back to the spot between his legs where the fabric of his trousers stretched in such a way that her heart tripped at the sight.

Somehow, she managed to lift her gaze to his face before she completely humiliated herself—if she hadn't already, by looking him over like a thirsty woman looking at water. He stared at her expectantly, as though he thought her there for no other reason but to see him.

That was *it*.

"Get out." As the words reverberated in her head, she couldn't believe that she had actually said them.

His expression would be forever frozen in Sophia's memory as one of the most satisfying things she had ever seen. Those low, darkly arched brows of his lifted, creasing his forehead and widening his eyes in an expression of thick-lashed amazement.

"I beg your pardon?" He looked as though he couldn't decide whether to be angry or to laugh.

She had come this far, she couldn't turn back now. Squaring her shoulders, she met his dark gaze evenly. "It was bad enough that you arrived at my home uninvited, Lord Rexley, even worse that I was forced to offer you any hospitality at all, but to find you prowling about at this hour—"

"I am not prowling," he interrupted with an amused expression as he held up the book in his hand. "I am reading."

Heat flushed Sophia's cheeks. Trying to make a fool of her, was he? Well, she didn't need *him* to do that.

"You are sitting in my chair," she continued petulantly. "And you are drinking wine that was left here for my purposes."

Setting aside his book, Julian rose to his feet. He was so tall, so lean and intense. He reminded Sophia of a wolf she'd seen once on display. Long and rangy, the beast had looked more like a lanky dog than a wild animal. It had even let her touch it, but Sophia knew that it would kill her without hesitation if it deemed it necessary.

What would Julian Rexley do to her if he thought it necessary?

"Forgive me," he said in a deceptively mild tone. "I had no idea. There is more wine and another glass if you would like some."

"What I would like," she replied, peevish at his gentlemanly behavior, "is to have some peace and quiet. Can you not take your book and your wine back to your room?"

His lips tilted upward on one side. It made him look cute and boyish. No doubt he'd rehearsed it many times in his looking glass.

"It is warmer down here."

A wave of guilt washed over Sophia. Of course it was. His room was in the far end of the house—the coldest end.

Despite her earlier thoughts, she really didn't want him to freeze. He might catch cold—and that would mean a lengthier stay.

"Then you should stay here." How quickly her backbone dissolved where he was concerned! "I will go."

"The room is not that small," his voice came brusquely as she turned to go. "Cannot we make the best of the situation and share it?"

Lord, the man didn't live up to only the "wolf" in his name but the "ram" as well. He was as stubborn and single-minded as an old goat. Why did he want her to stay?

Frowning, she faced him. He seemed hesitant as he met her gaze. Surely he didn't desire her company, did he? No, it was impossible. He despised her—even more than she despised him, blast it all.

She raised a brow. "I cannot imagine the two of us sharing anything."

What disgustingly awful choice of words, because it conjured up all kinds of naughty images and painful memories—such as all the breath, touches, and secrets they had once shared.

Tilting his head to one side, he didn't look as though he agreed with her. "I believe we share something already."

"What?" Yes, what? A past? A creeping discomfort that was somehow strangely appealing whenever the other was near?

His expression softened, revealing just a hint of vulnerability. "Affection for my sister."

Oh! That wasn't what she had expected. "You believe I

care for Letitia then? That I am not out to corrupt her with my wickedness?"

The thinning of his mouth told her that the thought had crossed his mind—and that he hadn't completely given it up, either.

"She is a difficult young woman, Lady Aberley," he replied. "You must love her, otherwise a woman of your rank would not bother with her."

Something in the region of Sophia's heart swelled and began to ache. The blackguard. He always seemed to know what to say to her to get the reaction he wanted.

"Oh." Unable to stare into those bright eyes of his any longer, Sophia dropped her gaze to his neck. His throat was smooth, his flesh shifting over cords and muscle as he moved, his Adam's apple dipping ever so slightly when he swallowed. She could remember the feel of that warm, salty skin beneath her lips, the soft abrasion of stubble against her cheek . . .

Flushed with shame, she jerked her gaze back to his face. He was watching her with an expression of guarded heat, as though he knew exactly what she was thinking and was trying to rein in his own reaction.

Good Lord, he felt it too! Perhaps if he was any other man, Sophia wouldn't recognize it so readily, but she and Julian had never bothered to hide their desire from each other in the past, and because of that, neither of them could hide it now. So if she could see it so plainly in his eyes, then he could undoubtedly see it in hers.

Oh no.

This couldn't be. It was ludicrous! There was no way they could feel the way they did about each other and still want each other in *that* way! It was perverse.

"I had forgotten how incredible you look with your hair down." His voice was little more of a whisper, but it shook Sophia right to the very soles of her feet. She hated her hair and he knew it. It was thick and poker straight and so heavy that she couldn't wear it any longer than just past her shoulders before the weight of it started to give her headaches.

"Last time you saw me with my hair down you ruined me." It was the only thing she could think of to ease this awareness between them. Despising Julian was safe. Wanting him wasn't.

"I remember removing the pins." The heat in his gaze cooled a fraction. "You ruined me as well."

Sophia supposed he meant that his reputation had not gone unscathed either, but there was a hint of something deeper in his voice, as though he meant she had ruined him for other women as well.

She met his gaze and the trembling in her stomach intensified. "I only wanted to marry you."

"I know." He said it in such an accusatory fashion that Sophia would have to be completely witless to miss his meaning. It was no secret that he thought she had sought to trap him. What hurt was that he hadn't wanted to be trapped by her.

"Yes, well thank God I did not succeed," she replied, her voice stilted with emotion. "No doubt we both would have come to regret the union."

He had the nerve to smile at that, his mouth curving upward at one corner—mocking her pain. "Perhaps." He raked her with a stare that was nothing short of carnal. "Some aspects of the union might have proved themselves quite enjoyable."

An inferno raged beneath Sophia's skin. Indignation
and sexual attraction simmered her blood. But there was
no shame. It would be easier to despise him—and herself—
were there only a little shame.

She straightened her shoulders as the weight of his
gaze settled heavily on her breasts. "It is a little late for regrets, do you not think?"

That honey-clear gaze lifted to hers. The smile and all
trace of emotion was wiped clean. "I have no regrets."

Face flaming, Sophia turned to leave him. Let him have
her library. In the morning he would be leaving and she
would wish him good riddance.

His voice stopped her before she took a step. "Are you
and Aberley lovers?"

What? Stunned, shocked and frozen to the very core,
Sophia could only gape at him. After all that had happened between them, he had the nerve, the unmitigated
gall to ask if she and Charles were lovers?

"What in the name of heaven makes you think that my
personal life is any of your concern?" She demanded, her
fists curling tightly at her sides.

Julian's eyes brightened. In the lamplight they were a
warm chocolate brown, but Sophia knew that in reality
they were almost as amber and as dangerous as that
wolf's. He took a step toward her, those sensuous lips
curving into a slight, but assured smile.

"Because," he said, his voice soft and gravelly, "you
used to be more discriminating than that."

Staring at him, Sophia wasn't certain whether she
should laugh or scream. Of all the puffed up, stupid male
arrogance!

She fixed him with what she hoped was a haughty ex-

pression. "In fact, my preferences have much improved
since I was a girl."

The blasted man had the nerve to look more amused
than affronted. He took another step toward her. "Oh?"

Nerves jangling like warning bells, Sophia took a step
back and bumped into a chair. Her action did not go unno-
ticed. Julian's smile grew even more predatory as he took
yet another step closer.

Ashamed that she'd let him see how much he affected
her, Sophia lifted her chin defiantly. "Yes. I'm not quite as
stupid as I used to be. It takes more than a pretty face to
turn my head now."

"Does it?" He was so close now she could smell him.
He smelled of that distinctly masculine smell that was Julian and . . . lavender? Of course, Mrs. Ellis had prepared
a bath for him. The only good soap in the house was
Sophia's own. It was both unsettling and arousing to smell
her own scent mingled with the warmth of his skin.

"Of course." She held his gaze, despite the fact that he
was standing close enough to touch—close enough that
she wanted him closer, even as her brain told her to run
away. "And you?"

He tilted his head again. "I believe my taste has improved somewhat as well. Although I fear that in some re-
spects I'm every bit as stupid as I ever was."

Her heart hammering against her ribs, Sophia could
only stare at him as he lowered his head to hers. Against
her own volition, her eyelids fluttered shut as the soft
warmth of his lips brushed against hers.

It felt so good it hurt. He didn't try to force his tongue
into her mouth as Charles had that time he had grabbed
her in the parlor. He seemed content just to press the

sweetness of his lips to hers, capturing first her upper lip, then the bottom one between his own, teasing her with the hot wine sweetness of his breath as he drew her deeper and deeper into the dark ache that threatened to envelop her.

He was going to envelop her. And she was going to let him.

A sudden burst of anger exploded in Sophia's chest. Raising her hands, she braced her palms against the solid warmth of his chest. His heart was pounding—hammering against his ribs just as hard and rapidly as her own. Feeling the effect she had on him was more arousing than any kiss could ever have been.

It took all of her strength to push him away. Breathing rapidly, her body hot and eager beneath her gown and wrapper, Sophia stared at him and willed herself not to topple him to the floor and show him just what she wanted to do to him.

That heavy-lidded gaze of his did little to strengthen her resolve, but somehow she managed to keep her distance. He ran his tongue along the full length of his lower lip, and without saying a word, his eyes told Sophia exactly what he was doing.

He was tasting whatever traces of herself her lips had left behind. Molten desire pooled low in her abdomen, spreading its heat to her thighs and that part of her that didn't care if her head liked Julian or not—*it* liked him just fine.

"I was a fool once, Lord Wolfram," she whispered, and for the first time the significance of his title hit her. He was a wolf, but she had no intention of setting herself up as a lamb. "But I have no intention of ever being that foolish again."

He didn't reply. He just watched her with a gaze she couldn't read. Somehow, Sophia managed to tear her own gaze away. And as she turned to leave she couldn't help but feel that while she might not be a lamb, she was still considered prey.

Chapter 4

*Often times the best choices are those made
when one has not the time to reconsider.*

An Unfortunate Attachment by A Repentant Lady

J ulian finally returned to his room after a long, uncomfortable and sleepless night in Sophia's favorite chair. Even if he hadn't spent the entire night in the library hoping Sophia would return, he wouldn't have been any more comfortable in that cramped, cold bed.

In fact, he mused as he knotted his wrinkled cravat around his neck, he probably would have been even more uncomfortable. As it was he had spent much of the night thinking about Sophia's body and how it might feel beneath his, above his, beside his.

What was it about Sophia that made her have such an effect on him? He thought all traces of foolish sentiment for her had been wiped away years ago. Obviously, they hadn't. Last night was proof of that. He had intentionally revealed his attraction—and his disapproval of it—to her. He had wanted to make her feel as low as he himself did. It had worked, but not in the way he had hoped. The realization that she wanted him as well only made his own wanting worse.

And then when she tried to walk away—when he should have let her but couldn't—he asked if she and Aberley were lovers. The shock and outrage on her face had not been faked, he was certain of that. But she hadn't answered him—not with a definite yes or no.

Then he had kissed her. If she truly were the woman he believed her to be she would have kissed him back and invited him to do more. She had returned the kiss, but she had also put a stop to it.

Her rejection had stung. It wasn't as though he was a rake of the first order, but when he decided to kiss a woman, it eventually led to sex. Only with Sophia had it ever *not* reached that conclusion.

After he finished dressing, Julian crept downstairs as quietly as the creaky boards would allow. Mrs. Ellis was already up and starting her day's work when he entered the little hall. She fetched his greatcoat and hat for him, and told him which path to take to the great house so he could check on his own carriage.

"Your sister certainly brightens this little cottage, my lord," Mrs. Ellis gushed, handing him his hat. "We're so glad Lady Wickford introduced her to Lady Aberley."

Julian forced a smile. So, Lady W was responsible for this debacle, was she?

Stomping out into the gray morning, Julian resolved to ask his old friend just how this introduction had come about.

The path to the great house was but a short walk through the woods. Clear and smooth, the little lane obviously got a lot of use. Did Aberley skulk along it late at night, bound for Sophia's bedroom? Or did Sophia brazenly walk this route in the middle of the day to meet her lover?

Before he could give that unpleasant image another thought, he was greeted by the head groom as he entered the stables.

"John's gone into the village to fetch your new wheel now, my lord," the man told him. "We should have your carriage fixed by mid-morning."

"Excellent." He was quite happy to hear it. This slight disappointment he felt was only because he couldn't get away from Sophia soon enough.

The ride to Lady Wickford's was a pleasant one. The road was soft from yesterday's rain, but not so soft that travel would be impossible. It had had all night to dry, plus, the sun was already creeping up over the horizon. A few hours of sunshine would dry things up considerably. He and Letitia would be in London in time for dinner.

By the time he was shown into Lady Wickford's breakfast room, Julian was certain this bit of trouble between himself and Letitia could be easily mended. Once they were in London his sister would be caught up in her usual social whirl, Sophia Morelle would be forgotten and Julian could set his mind to seeing Letitia happily married.

"Wolfram, my dear boy! What brings you here at this ungodly hour?"

Phillippa Markham-Pryce, Countess Wickford, sat at a small table, sipping a cup of tea. Well into her sixth decade, she was of a robust build, round and buxom. Her pale blue eyes sparkled with good humor and a joy for life that was rare in anyone over the age of thirty. She had a

knowledge of the world that was sometimes shocking—
especially when she spoke of things that no lady should
know.

"You know why I am here," he admonished her with
mock severity as he bent to kiss her soft, pale cheek.

Lady Wickford had been a dear friend of his grand-
mother on his mother's side and a regular fixture in his life
as long as Julian could remember.

Dropping into the chair closest to hers, Julian plucked a
piece of bacon off a platter and took a bite as he stretched
his legs out before him. "Yesterday I discovered that my
sister is at the home of Lady Aberley. Today I discovered
'twas you who introduced the two."

Lady Wickford's round face showed neither concern
nor contrition. "I thought they would like each other," she
replied, dabbing her lips with her napkin. "I was right."

Straightening, Julian leaned his elbow on the table and
rubbed his hand over his face. "Sophia Morelle is deceitful and untrustworthy, and she is a poor influence for a
young woman."

Lady Wickford arched a thin brow. "Letitia is hardly a
young woman anymore, Julian." She toyed with the rim of
her tea cup, the rings on her hand sparkling in the light.
"Besides, your opinion of Sophia is colored by one unfortunate incident."

Julian choked on a disbelieving bark of laughter. "I have
seen for myself just what effect her influence has had on
my sister. Letitia refuses to come to London without her!"

The old woman's face lit up as she poured him a cup of
coffee. "London! Oh how marvelous, Sophia is due for a
trip."

Julian blinked. Was Lady W losing her senses? "There

is no way I would allow that woman to be a guest in my home."

"Why ever not?" Lady Wickford inquired, lifting her cup to her lips. "What harm could possibly befall you for taking Sophia to town?"

Julian couldn't believe they were even having this conversation! "What harm? Good lord, have you forgotten the scandal?"

Lady Wickford waved a large hand in the air. "Oh, pooh. No one will remember that foolish incident. Sophia would be there as Letitia's guest and companion, not your bit of muslin. Or is there still an attraction between the two of you?"

The shrewdness of her gaze had Julian flushing to the roots of his hair. "Of course not!"

The countess leaned forward, as though she were about to impart some great secret wisdom.

"You keep your enemies close, dear boy. What better way to determine Sophia's designs on Letitia—if indeed she has any—than to keep her under close scrutiny? And just think of how agreeable your sister will be if she can take her friend along? And who knows? You might just make an ally out of Sophia. Perhaps you can use that 'influence' you claim she has over Letitia to your advantage."

Good Lord, why hadn't he thought of any of this? Because he'd been too busy thinking what the consequences of taking Sophia along would be rather than the possible benefits. If she was truly Letitia's friend, she would want what was best for her, and if she was still the mercenary girl he remembered she would urge her friend to marry well. A few well-dropped hints and she could help him nudge Letitia to the altar.

And maybe a little more time together might cure him of this damnable attraction he felt for her. Reconcile the present with the past, prove once and for all that he was lucky to have escaped her clutches.

"Perhaps you are right," he allowed. "Perhaps I have been looking at this the wrong way."

Lady Wickford smiled patiently and Julian half expected her to pat him on the head and congratulate him on finally figuring that out.

Letitia was still in bed when he returned to the cottage. So was Sophia, Mrs. Ellis informed him. Why, Julian wasn't certain.

He bounded up the stairs, oblivious to the noise his boots and the squeaking boards made. He didn't care if he woke Sophia. In fact he hoped he did, then his head wouldn't be filled with images of her lying peacefully amongst a tangle of blankets, bare limbs peeking out.

He burst into his sister's room without even knocking. Still foggy and grumpy with sleep, she pushed herself into a sitting position against a mountain of pillows.

Her room, Julian noted, was much warmer than his own.

"What do you want?" Letitia demanded.

"Get up, brat," he ordered cheerfully, tossing her wrapper at her. "We are leaving for London later this morning."

Scowling, Letitia dropped back against the cushions as her robe fell across her lap. "I am not going."

"Oh, well, that does put a knot in things," he replied with mock austerity as he opened the wardrobe door and began emptying it of its contents. "I am not certain what Lady Aberley's servants will think when she and I leave for London and you remain behind."

"What? Oh, Julian!"

Letitia sprang from the bed and ran for him, her arms outstretched, nightgown billowing around her.

He just managed to drop the mound of gowns in his arms onto a chair before she hit him. She hugged him fiercely.

"Thank you!" she cried, feathering his face with kisses. "Oh, I love you, I love you!"

Laughing, Julian returned the embrace. Any misgivings he might have had about taking Sophia to London with them evaporated in the face of his sister's happiness. Surely he could survive a few weeks under the same roof as Sophia if it meant having his sister back. He would rarely, if ever, be alone with her and they would be so busy socializing they would scarcely see each other.

What could possibly happen?

"He changed his mind!"

Startled by the door of her room flying open, Sophia almost spilled hot coffee all over the front of her nightgown. As it was, the scalding brew splashed against her fingers as she held the cup and saucer over the carpet rather than her bed.

Hissing in pain, she set the coffee on her bedside table and wiped her smarting fingers on a serviette.

"Who?" she demanded as Letitia swung the door shut behind her. Sophia wasn't much of a morning person, and this morning she felt even less sociable than usual.

Of course her sour mood had nothing to do with the fact that she'd spent most of the night lying awake thinking about Julian Rexley and feeling hot and frustrated. Oh, no.

"Julian!" Letitia cried, oblivious to Sophia's ill humor. "He said you could come to London with us!"

Sophia's heart literally stopped. "He said what?"

Letitia practically danced over to the bed. "Is it not wonderful? Of course I had to agree to be civil to the gentlemen on his husband list, but that's of no consequence. They won't steal my heart away from my Mr. Wesley. But whatever is the matter? I thought you would be happy."

Sophia stared at her. "Happy? What in the world would make you think I would ever be happy about spending weeks in the same house as your brother?" She couldn't go to London, not with Julian. It would only be a matter of time before people remembered the scandal. What if rumors started? If she brought scandal upon the family name, Charles would move in for the kill.

Letitia's face fell. "But Sophia, you have to! How else am I to fight Julian if you are not with me?"

Sophia had to laugh at that. "My dear, your brother would stand a better chance at convincing the sun not to rise. You will be fine."

The young woman's lower lip was starting to tremble. "You have to come! I shall be dreadfully lonely without you. You are the only true friend I have!"

For once Sophia knew that her friend wasn't being overly dramatic. She honestly believed what she said, and Sophia couldn't help but be touched. And what if she was right about Julian? What if he pressured Letitia into marriage just as Sophia's father had pressured her? She would never forgive herself if that happened and she hadn't done anything to try to prevent it.

Letitia was relentless. "If you come to London I will have someone on my side when Mr. Wesley decides to approach my brother, and you will be able to go to teas and parties and balls, and Lord Aberley will not be able to stop you!"

The idea of escaping Charles and his ever-increasing attentions was appealing—very appealing. When he had shown up for dinner the night before, he had made it very clear that he expected her to soon give in to him. And it had been so long since she'd attended a ball . . .

"I haven't the wardrobe for going to town," she protested, her pride winning out over her cowardice.

Letitia dismissed her protests with a wave of her hand and a roll of her dark eyes. "I will take care of that. A gift for being such a good friend."

"You most certainly will not!" Sophia snatched her hand away. "I am not a charity case!"

Instead of being contrite, Letitia laughed. "Oh, Sophia, you are so silly! Perhaps you would prefer to have my brother foot the bill? Consider it retribution for his being such a beast to you while he has been under your roof."

Now, *that* was tempting, as underhanded as it was.

She shook her head. "I—"

"Think it over," Letitia insisted, cutting her off. "Please."

Nodding, Sophia agreed, but she knew her answer would be the same in an hour as it was then. There was no way she was going to put herself under that much of Julian's control as to agree to be a guest in his home. Why had he even suggested it? He had some ulterior motive other than just his sister's happiness, of that she was certain.

Heat crept up her cheeks as an idea occurred to her. Surely he didn't think that . . . No! It was too much, even for him. As rotten as Julian could be, he would never expect her to be his mistress right under his sister's nose!

What other reason could he possibly have for inviting her? He didn't like her any more than she liked him.

Perhaps she should just ask him.

After Letitia left to go dress for breakfast, Sophia scampered out of bed and hurriedly washed and dressed. She was still sticking pins in her hair as she hurried downstairs a little while later. She wore the best day gown she owned, a square-necked, modest dress of dark purple. It was her favorite and was still fairly stylish as she had purchased it just prior to Charles cutting off her funds. She felt pretty and confident when she wore it, and she needed all the confidence she could summon when dealing with Julian.

With her hair secured in a neat chignon, she rounded the corner at the bottom of the stairs and strolled toward the back of the house. Somehow, she knew where he would be.

He was in her library, sitting in her favorite chair, sipping a cup of coffee.

He looked up at her entrance, and immediately rose to his feet. He was dressed a bit more formally than he had been last night, but his clothing was wrinkled and a day's growth of beard lined his cheeks. He looked the part of a poet now, with his hair mussed and his eyes heavy with fatigue. Obviously he hadn't slept well last night either. Good.

"I had hoped you would come back," he said, his gaze assessing her just as she had assessed him.

She frowned. "I beg your pardon?"

He shook his head. "Never mind. I imagine my sister has already talked with you?"

"Yes," she replied with a nod. "Jul—Lord Wolfram, I—"

"Sit," he interjected, offering her the chair he had just vacated. "Please. It feels awkward to stand when we have so much to discuss."

The fact that he relinquished her favorite chair to her warmed her in ways that were both charming and annoying. Still, she accepted the offer and even passed him his coffee so he didn't have to reach for it from his seat across from her.

"I want to know why you changed your mind about inviting me to London," she blurted when they were both settled.

He took a drink of his coffee and smiled. "I imagine you do, and so I shall tell you. I changed it because Letitia would have made my life miserable if I did not."

Sophia could tell from his expression and the dry tone that he used that he spoke the truth, but there was something more.

"And?" she prodded.

He sighed. "*And* because I hoped that you might be able to help me ensure that my sister makes an attachment by the end of the season."

"Even if I had such sway over your sister I would not use it."

Julian's lips twisted into a mocking smile as he arched a brow. "Especially not for me."

Heat crept up Sophia's cheeks but she did not respond.

"We don't always have to be on opposite sides, Sophia." He said her name like it was a caress and her body reacted as such, tightening and flushing in a most shameful and delicious manner.

Setting his cup aside, he leaned forward in his chair, resting his forearms on his knees as he regarded her. "Tell me the real reason for your reservations. It is because of what happened last night, is it not?"

"A little," she whispered.

His expression was suddenly serious. "My behavior

was inexcusable and I apologize. My only excuse is that I had been drinking."

Oh, so he'd kissed her because his judgment was impaired. How flattering.

"I appreciate your attempts to soothe my fragile feminine sensibilities," she heard herself reply, "but we both know that you kissed me because you wanted to, and I allowed it for the same reason." Dear Lord, what was she doing?

His sherry-colored eyes darkened. "You did."

Swallowing against the sudden dryness in her mouth, Sophia bobbed her head. "I do not claim to understand it, nor do you, I am sure. You do not like me and I most assuredly do not like you, but I cannot deny that I am drawn to you, much like a moth to flame."

She couldn't believe she was saying these things. Apparently, neither could Julian, because he just stared at her with those heavy-lidded eyes of his. He didn't try to deny that he felt the same, however.

"Why is that, do you suppose?"

Sophia smiled. It felt bitter and twisted. "I suppose because like the moth, I am well aware of what will happen if I get too close to your flame."

His lips twitched. Whether it was with humor or regret, Sophia couldn't tell. "I suppose there is something to be said for knowing the consequences. Will my *flame* keep you from coming to London?"

He mocked her and yet it did not sting as she expected. It didn't matter that she knew the consequences—she wished to avoid them.

"*If* I decide to go to London, we must both promise that there will be no repeats of last night—or any similar behavior." Just the thought of "similar behavior" was enough to make her knees quiver.

He had the nerve to look affronted. "Do you really believe I would take advantage of your being a guest in my home?"

His wounded tone triggered something deep within her, something old and musty from the past. It filled her with a cold that numbed her from head to toe. Rising to her feet, she fixed him with a hard gaze.

"You would have taken my virginity and walked away without a backward glance. I believe you capable of almost anything."

Color blossomed on his high cheekbones as he also stood. "I think I can safely give you my word that there would be *no* repeats of last night whatsoever."

She shouldn't be hurt by his coldness—after all, she had just been as rude to him—but it stung all the same because she was the one who had been hurt all those years ago. It was her life that had been forever changed, and he didn't seem the least bit sorry for having been the cause of it.

"Good," she replied, her voice clipped. "Now if you will excuse me, I am late for breakfast."

He nodded. "I believe I will check on my carriage. I have the sudden desire to be on the road as soon as possible."

And with that he brushed past her, leaving her alone in the room and denying her the satisfaction of having had the last word.

Two hours later, Sophia stood at the dining-room window and watched as Julian's carriage rolled up the driveway. The new wheel was in place and all that was left was to load Letitia's luggage on board.

She still had yet to decide whether or not to join them.

"I was hoping to find you alone," a low voice near her ear hissed.

Sophia jumped. It was Charles. She had been so wrapped up in her own thoughts she hadn't even heard him approach.

His hands slid around her waist before she could pull away. He pressed the length of himself against her back. He was solid muscle, as hard as a brick wall. His breath was hot against her neck as he nuzzled the sensitive flesh there.

"Let me go, Charles." Damn it, even her voice was shaking!

"Never," he whispered, sliding one hand up to cup her right breast.

It was odd how one reacted to something as uncomplicated as a touch. Sophia had once cared very much about Julian and had enjoyed his touches. Charles, on the other hand, she despised, and when he touched her it felt like a thousand worms crawling on her skin.

"Please," she said, catching sight of Julian through the window. Oh, God, please don't let him see! "Let me go."

Charles's response was to grind his pelvis against her buttocks. His erection poked at her through her skirts, and Sophia knew then and there that Charles was going to have her, whether she wanted it or not.

She braced one hand against the window frame to keep from toppling headfirst into the glass as he thrust against her. With her other hand she tried to pry his fingers away from her breast.

It didn't work. In fact, it only seemed to make him

more insistent. The fingers on her breast flexed upward, gripping and tugging at the neck of her gown. The sound of tearing fabric was as frightening as it was heartbreaking. He was going to ravage her and all she could think of was the ruin of her favorite gown.

"Stop it!" she cried. "Let me go!"

Charles's teeth were sharp against her neck. "Yell all you want. No one will come help you. Wolfram's leaving and I am going to toss up your skirts and take you like the bitch you are."

He pulled her away from the window, and pushed her face down over the table. The polished wood pulled at her cheek as Charles shoved at her from behind. Tears of pain and fury sprang to Sophia's eyes as she struggled to free herself of his grasp.

It was at that moment, as tears threatened to cloud her vision that Sophia looked up—and saw Julian standing in the doorway, an expression she had never seen before hardening his face.

"Let her go." His voice was so low, so chilled that Sophia shivered.

"Wolfram," Charles said jovially, lifting his weight off her back. "I thought you were leaving."

Her arms trembling, Sophia pushed against the table-top, clinging to it for support as her legs shook beneath her.

"I am," Julian replied. He didn't look at her. "I came to see if Lady Aberley had changed her mind about accompanying us."

The two men never took their eyes off each other, yet Sophia could feel Julian watching her.

Charles smiled. "She hasn't."

"Actually—" Her voice was a mere whisper and Sophia cleared her throat. "I have."

Both men turned to her. Still holding the table for support, Sophia inched away from Charles. She kept her gaze pinned on Julian, even as her heart beat against her ribs. She expected Charles to try to stop her, but he didn't. Probably because he knew she would have to return to Hertford once the season ended.

"I would very much like to accompany you and your sister to London, if the offer still stands, Lord Wolfram."

Julian's hard gaze flickered briefly to Charles before returning to her. Some of the coldness left his eyes as he held out his hand to her. Sophia took it, cautiously.

"It still stands," he said, squeezing her fingers.

It was all Sophia could do not to squeeze back.

He had been wrong to bring her to London.

One look at Sophia's happy face as the carriage entered the city and Julian knew he was going to face the challenge of his life in resisting her allure. But he couldn't have left her in Hertford, not with that bastard Aberley.

He couldn't get the image of her frightened face from his mind. He could have killed Aberley and not have thought twice about it. Killed him, not just for hurting a woman, but for hurting Sophia. The implications of that possessive, murderous rage were not things Julian wanted to think about.

"We simply must get you a plum silk ball gown," Letitia was saying, once again turning the conversation to fashion. "With a matching feather for your hair."

Sophia smiled patiently, flashing a brief glance in Julian's direction. "I do not like feathers. Do not go overboard, Letitia. I have no desire to abuse Lord Wolfram's kindness."

Perhaps agreeing to buy some gowns for Sophia had

been weak of him, but he had seen the crushed expression on Sophia's face as she fussed over the tear Aberley had put in her gown. The dress was either her favorite or her best, and while it was pretty enough it was nothing compared to the finery she would be expected, as a marchioness, to wear in London.

He wanted to make her happy, and that was, in some ways, even more disturbing than Aberley's attack. As sorry as he felt for Sophia, as much as he regretted thinking she and Aberley had been lovers, he could not forget that the minute he let down his guard there was the chance that she would be there to take advantage of it.

He listened to their conversation with half an ear as the carriage wove through London traffic. The sound of hooves and wheels against the cobblestones was a pleasant cacophony, familiar and comforting.

He loved London. It was home. Of all the houses he owned, the London house held the most pleasant memories. The only other estate he'd ever felt such attachment to was Heatherington Park in Yorkshire, and he went there but seldom. Miranda had killed herself there, and while being there made him feel close to her, it was still far too painful to endure for long, even with Brave and Rachel nearby.

Brave and Rachel! Good lord, what would they have to say when they learned he'd brought Sophia to town? For that matter, what would Gabriel and Lilith's reaction be? Lilith might not be such a willing ally, having known Sophia in the past.

Turning, he opened his mouth to suggest to Letitia that they have a small dinner party to reintroduce Sophia to society, but the words stuck in his throat as his gaze fell upon Sophia.

She had her face pressed to the window, her black eyes as round as saucers as they stared at the passing scene beyond. They were entering Mayfair, a neighborhood as opulent as the members of the *haute ton* who made it their home. That it had been a long time since Sophia had seen it was obvious. That she loved it was even more so.

"You will want to call upon your parents as soon as possible, I expect," he remarked, smiling because her joy was infectious.

She jerked away from the window, all the pleasure disappearing from her face. Julian's own smile melted away.

"No," she replied, her gaze locking with his. "Not as soon as possible. Perhaps in a few days."

How could he be so stupid? Of course she had no desire to go running to her parents and announce that she was a guest of the man who had refused to marry her.

He would have to make certain that word spread very quickly that Sophia was Letitia's companion, that they were simply assisting her in reentering society. Julian would have to make certain that while in public he didn't treat Sophia any differently than he treated any other woman.

It was how to treat her in private that had him worried.

Thankfully the direction of his thoughts was cut off before they could wander into more dangerous territory by the distinct slowing and turning of the carriage that meant they were at Wolfram House.

The carriage rolled to a halt. The door opened, the steps were put down and Julian alighted first to assist the women to the ground.

Letitia was still chattering away as she stepped out into the late afternoon sun. Her maid followed her into the house, her head bobbing in reply to every suggestion Letitia made.

Letitia's chatter faded into the background as Julian watched Sophia lift her gaze to Wolfram House. Here in the bright of day her eyes weren't quite black and they shone with a sparkle of deep, dark velvety brown as a smile curved her full pink lips.

"It is just as lovely as I remembered," she remarked as he helped her to the ground.

"Thank you," Julian replied with pride.

Made of mellow Bath stone, Wolfram House's exterior had a golden appearance. Rows of tall, wide windows graced its smooth, clean front. Low steps climbed to the front doors—heavy twin portals of golden oak graced with large brass knockers polished to a brilliant shine.

Julian followed her inside, where Sophia's eyes grew even wider. "Oh, Julian, it is beautiful!"

Following her gaze, he surveyed the great hall, seeing it through her eyes. The entire house had been redecorated in the Robert Adam style before his mother's death and Julian had no plans to ever change it. From the gold, blue and peach marble floor with its eye-catching circular center design, to the pale peach walls with their delicate scroll work, to the high ceiling with its gold, blue and white design that complemented the floor below in true Adam fashion, the hall was a stunning example of beauty and serenity.

"Yes," he replied, his gaze dropping to her glowing face. "It is very lovely indeed."

Time seemed to stumble to a halt as Julian stared into Sophia's eyes. In the past few hours he had felt a multitude of emotions where she was concerned—desire, anger, dislike, protectiveness, understanding, amusement and now this. And what was *this* anyway? It was a hopeful feeling. It was a feeling of coming home.

Yes, that was it. He was home. Here. With her.

"Sophia!"

Never had Julian been so glad to hear his sister's voice. The spell was broken, and just in bloody time too!

"Come upstairs," Letitia called from a doorway directly across the hall. "I want to show you to your room!"

Sophia muttered something to him before turning to leave. Julian assumed she had excused herself, but she could have told him to go jump in the Thames for all he had heard.

He watched her as she crossed the floor to join Letitia, enjoying the way the generous swell of her hips swayed with every step.

All the soft hills and hidden valleys of her vista formed a sweeter garden than Eden ever dreamed.

The echo of the words inside his head jerked Julian out of his daze. Instead of going to his room and ringing for a bath as he had planned, Julian made a detour to his study. The room was exactly as he left it—a mess. Papers cluttered almost every surface. Books littered the floor, the surface of his desk and were stacked on top of each other on several shelves. Once in a while he allowed the maids to clean in there, but only when he was around to supervise where everything went. He despised anyone invading his privacy when he was working, so the staff stayed away unless he rang.

Grabbing his "idea" notebook, he uncapped his inkwell and dipped his pen into it. He scribbled the line about Sophia and then put the ink away. He would work on it later.

He turned to the wall of books behind him. Without thinking he went to the far shelves, climbed the ladder and pulled a small, blue book from the others on the highest ledge. Stepping back down to the floor, he opened it.

An Unfortunate Attachment by A Repentant Lady.

A repentant lady indeed. Not half so repentant as he had been. His gaze dropped to the handwritten inscription beneath.

> *To Julian. I hope you don't find Lord Foxton to be too unflattering a character. The description is an honest one, if not very kind.*
>
> *Warmly, Sophia*

When he first opened the book almost seven years ago he had been outraged to read what she had written. Now it made him smile. Almost. He had never read the book itself. Perhaps he should.

But not right this moment. Right now all he wanted was a bath, a shave and a change of clothes. As much as he wanted to take the book with him to read in the bath, he couldn't risk one of the servants seeing it or, heaven forbid, reading any of it. He would come back and begin it later, and then, when he had read it from beginning to end, he and Sophia would sit down and have a little talk.

And he would either tell her that she was a misguided liar, or he would make things right. He had a feeling that no matter how wronged Sophia *thought* she was, it wasn't going to be the latter.

Chapter 5

*He was the kind of gentleman mothers
advised their daughters to avoid.
That in itself made him dangerously attractive.*

An Unfortunate Attachment by A Repentant Lady

They spent two days doing nothing but shopping, eating and talking, before Letitia surprised Sophia by appearing in her chamber in the late afternoon with the announcement that Julian was *finally* taking them out.

"Not to Almack's, I hope," Sophia joked, setting her book aside. "I vowed never to darken those doors again."

"Even if your gowns were ready I would not dream of subjecting you to Sally Jersey this early in your visit," Letitia replied, plopping herself into a nearby chair. "No, he's taking us for a ride in *Hyde Park!*"

While the idea of an outing in the park was lovely indeed, it certainly didn't warrant the sparkle in Letitia's eyes, not on its own. "And?"

A broad grin curved Letitia's generous mouth. "I have sent word to Mr. Wesley that we will be there. I am certain I will be able to see him this afternoon!"

It was difficult to share her friend's enthusiasm. "Do you think that is a good idea? What if your brother notices your partiality to this gentleman? I thought you wanted to keep it a secret until Mr. Wesley could talk to him."

As usual, Letitia waved her concerns away. "Julian will never know. But never mind that, will you come to Hyde Park with us?"

Sophia found herself smiling despite her misgivings. She hoped that once Julian met Mr. Wesley and saw how much Letitia loved him, his own regard for his sister would convince him to agree to the match. She wanted Julian to be different from her father, even though thinking ill of him made it easier to dislike and distrust him.

But either way, provided her friend didn't do anything rash, Sophia would keep her secret and do what she could to help her avoid a marriage like Sophia's own.

"Of course I will come."

"Excellent!" Letitia cried, clapping her hands together. "We shall leave within the half hour." Jumping out of her seat, she stopped long enough to rake Sophia with a solemn gaze.

"Is that what you are going to wear?"

Laughing at her friend's lack of tact, Sophia also rose to her feet. "I do have a riding habit, you know. While it is not the height of fashion, I am certain it will do for today's outing."

Letitia's frown gave way to the same happy grin that had lit her face almost constantly since their arrival in London.

"Where are you going?" Sophia asked when Letitia made for a door at the far corner of her chamber.

"To tell Julian," Letitia replied as though Sophia were daft. "He was going to his room to change his coat."

An invisible hand closed around Sophia's throat and squeezed. "J . . . Your brother's chamber connects to this one?"

Letitia nodded. "Through a small parlor, but do not worry. He never uses it. You did not think I would put my dearest friend in a chamber that was below her station, did you? This was my mother's room."

And with that, Letitia opened the corner door and slipped through. It clicked shut behind her, leaving Sophia in stunned silence.

The countess's bedchamber! How could Letitia have been so idiotic as to put her in the room adjoining Julian's? It mattered not that there was little chance of anyone else ever finding out, Sophia knew, and that was bad enough.

Sucking a deep breath into her lungs, she willed herself to be calm. There was no way she could ask Letitia to move her and not raise her friend's suspicion, and even if she did, she risked hurting Letitia's feelings. Giving Sophia her mother's room was a great honor, as Sophia was well aware of how much Letitia honored her mother's memory.

She would rather have Julian close than cause injury to Letitia. Besides, having Julian but a few feet away did not mean Sophia was in any more danger of acting on her foolish attraction for the man than if he were down the hall.

They were both adults, able to control themselves, and just in case one of them forgot that, the door was sure to have locks on it.

And if that didn't convince her, the thought of the scandal that would ensue from an affair with Julian certainly did. Scandal would lead to her losing what little income she had—thanks to her late husband and his cretin of a brother. Wouldn't Charles love that, to have her penniless and completely at his mercy? The idea of that alone should be enough to keep her from losing her head where Julian was concerned.

Julian, on the other hand, she couldn't speak for. And since Sophia's limited experience with men had proven that the opposite sex was not above taking whatever it wanted from hers, she would make certain that the door remained locked from her side.

Starting now.

After checking the lock, Sophia rang for the maid Letitia had insisted she have. She had best get changed for their outing.

Twenty-five minutes later, she was washed, dressed in her old but presentable dark blue riding habit and had the matching hat pinned on over a sleek but elegant hairstyle. She made her way downstairs to the great hall to join Julian and Letitia. Fortunately only Letitia was there.

"Julian has gone to see about the horses," her friend explained. Then, in a conspiratorial tone she whispered, "He is a little upset with me for surprising him from your room."

Sophia was willing to wager it wasn't Letitia coming from the room that surprised him, but rather *where* Sophia's room was in relation to his.

Julian joined them a few moments later, looking magnificent in snug buckskin trousers that hugged his long legs, a dark green coat and beaver hat. It seemed a shame to cover up all that thick hair with a hat, but it wouldn't be very seemly for him to go out in public without one.

The glance he sent Sophia was brief at best. "Shall we go?"

Outside, three horses stood patiently waiting with two grooms. Julian immediately went to a chestnut gelding and swung himself into the saddle. Letitia made for a small gray mare, leaving the black for Sophia.

It had been a long time since she had been on a horse, but she wasn't the least bit nervous as the groom gave her a hand up into the saddle. The mare stood perfectly still as Sophia positioned herself and arranged her skirts. It felt perfectly natural to be in the saddle again as the horse clip-clopped down the densely packed drive.

Wolfram House was located on Upper Brook Street, near Grosvenor Square, so the ride to Hyde Park wasn't a long one. Still, it gave Sophia a chance to glance around at the neighborhood and soak up the excitement and motion that was London. It was as though a door had been opened for her, a door into a bright, new world where she could throw off the mantle of her former life and be herself again.

And perhaps she could. As long as Charles wasn't there to watch her she could do what she wanted, go where she wanted. As long as she didn't bring scandal upon herself she was free.

Julian rode slightly behind, leaving Letitia and her mount between them. Whether it was for his own benefit or for society's Sophia wasn't certain. There was no such thing as being too careful where gossip was concerned. Still, he had managed to avoid her for most of the last two days.

Really, she shouldn't be bothered by his lack of attention. Whether it was because of the incident with Charles, or gossip, or because he genuinely wished to avoid her, Sophia didn't know and she didn't really care, but it stung her vanity and her pride to think that he could forget that kiss in the library quite so easily as to pretend that there was nothing between them.

"How are you faring, Sophia?" Letitia asked with a jaunty grin. "Is the mare to your liking?"

Returning the smile, Sophia ran a gloved hand down the mare's glossy neck. "She's beautiful. What is her name?"

"*Amanté*," Letitia replied, and Sophia's heart faltered in her chest. "Julian named her. I do not know what it means."

"It is Spanish," Sophia replied hoarsely, her throat tight. "The Spanish word for love."

"Oh!" Letitia's smile brightened as she shot a backward glance at her brother. "How lovely!"

Sophia did not dare look at Julian to see his reaction. Nor did she want him to see hers, for then he would know that she remembered and she would have to ask why he had named this beautiful little horse one of the few Spanish words she had taught him.

Five o'clock was the fashionable hour to be seen in Hyde Park, and today was no exception. The air smelled of horse and damp grass, and rang with the sound of hooves and lively chatter. Being confronted with so many people and so much noise all at once was overwhelming for Sophia and she wished she could somehow hide herself from view.

Hiding, of course, was impossible. As they picked their way along the hoof-trodden course of Rotten Row, deftly skirting around the piles of horse droppings that dotted the track, dozens of people tipped their hats, waved or called out in greeting. It seemed everyone knew Letitia—and even more knew her brother.

A group of four gentlemen and three ladies stopped to chat. Sophia recognized one of the gentlemen as a friend of her father's. Now her parents were sure to hear that she was in town.

Letitia made the introductions. Sophia almost choked when Letitia got to the fourth gentleman. His name was Mr. Wesley. Even if she hadn't heard his name, she would have known who he was by the quick but ardent glance that passed between him and Letitia.

Thankfully Julian was too busy talking to Lord Penderthal, her father's friend, to notice his sister making cow eyes at the young Mr. Wesley.

Their conversation lasted but a few moments. Sophia noticed that Letitia didn't seem too upset to bid farewell to her lover, which instantly made Sophia suspicious. Letitia was not that good an actress. Oh, she might be good enough to fool her brother, but not another woman.

Their parties hadn't been separated a full minute before Letitia said, "Oh, drat! I forgot to ask Millicent if she'd care to come to tea on Friday. Do you mind if I just run after them, Julian?"

Ah, there it was. Millicent was one of the ladies in Mr. Wesley's party. This was obviously some kind of ruse to see him again, perhaps to even steal a few private moments.

Julian nodded. He didn't look too happy to be left alone with Sophia. "Very well, but do not dawdle."

Letitia beamed. "I shall be right back. I promise." Then, flashing a quick wink at Sophia, she trotted off after her Mr. Wesley and his party.

They picked along the row in tense silence. This was ridiculous.

"I did not know at the time that Letitia had put me in your mother's room, Lord Wolfram. If you are uncomfortable with the arrangement just say the word and I shall move myself to another room."

He looked up, but not at her. "And when my sister demands to know why, what shall we tell her? That the idea of having the other one so close drives us to distraction? That despite our mutual dislike and distrust we seem to have this inexplicable attraction for each other? No. I do not think that would be a good idea, my lady. I would rather suffer in silence than admit such a thing out loud."

She glanced at him from beneath the veil of her hat. He stared straight ahead, his expression as bland as if they were discussing the weather.

"You just admitted it to me."

He turned his head toward her. It was the first time he had met her gaze since the morning and in the bright light of day the pale brown of his eyes shone like warm honey.

"You feel the same way. That makes a difference, do you not think?"

Blushing, Sophia looked away. She wasn't certain how to reply, so she didn't. Instead she gave Amanté's neck another stroke.

"She really is a beautiful horse."

"I thought of you when I named her."

Again her heart stuttered against her ribs. "Why?"

He smiled at her—a soft twisting of his lips that was both amused yet a little bitter.

"When I first brought her home she was willful, and wild. Everyone told me she could not be tamed." *Just like you.* He didn't have to say the words for Sophia to hear them.

A strange sensation rose up in her stomach. It was mortification.

"But you tamed her." The words spilled out before she

could stop them. And even though she was humiliated by the innuendo of his words, part of her liked the fact that he had once thought of her as wild, for she was so very domesticated now.

He looked at her with an expression that bordered on smug, but his eyes were dark with promise—of what she wasn't quite certain.

"I was the only one she would let anywhere near her and eventually I—"

"Broke her?" Sophia supplied, a wave of ice washing over her body. Wasn't that what Edmund had done to her? He had taken that wild, stubborn girl and turned her into what he thought she should be, a proper lady.

Julian's head tilted as he gazed at her. "I earned her trust."

"Oh." There was a tingling in her limbs, a dance of pinpricks on her flesh that made her muscles twitch. What was he saying, that he wanted her trust as well? He never wanted it when it was offered, why should he want it now?

She opened her mouth to say something—anything that might ease this tension between them, but the words died in her throat as she spotted a very familiar man talking to a group of gentlemen not thirty feet away.

"Oh, God." Was that pathetic strangled sound really her voice?

Julian glanced at her. He must have seen the horror on her face, because his countenance was instantly one of concern. "Sophia, what is it?"

"It is Charles," she whispered, unable to tear her gaze away from her brother-in-law's profile no matter how badly she wished to do so. "He cannot see us."

"Sophia, you have nothing to fear from him while you are here in London," Julian informed her with startling conviction. "I will not allow him to hurt you."

God help her, she believed him. Worse yet, she *trusted* him—at least where protecting her from Charles was concerned. But what about when she returned to Hertford? Julian would not be able to protect her then. She would have to protect herself, and that meant taking steps to do so now. She would have to see Edmund's solicitors while she was in town, but until then she had to be careful.

Shaking her head, Sophia reined Amanté around so that they were facing the opposite direction. "No, Julian. He cannot see you and I here, alone. We must go. Please."

"All right," Julian replied, his brow creased in a frown. "We shall go collect Letitia and leave."

He didn't ask any questions, and for that Sophia would be eternally grateful. "Thank you."

They rode back toward Lord Penderthal's group in silence. Sophia hoped that Letitia and her Mr. Wesley had exchanged whatever looks and messages they had to exchange, because she wasn't about to risk ruination just so her friend could flirt.

She wouldn't risk that for anything.

"Do you mind if I join you?"

Startled, Julian looked up from the pages of *An Unfortunate Attachment* to find the author standing in the door of his study. A glance at the clock confirmed that the hour was very late indeed and had Sophia been dressed in a robe instead of the same violet gown she had worn to dinner, he might have suspected—hoped—she had seduction on her mind.

"Certainly not," he replied, marking his page and setting the book aside. "Would you care for a drink?"

The door closed behind her with a soft click. "Yes, please. Claret if you have it."

As she approached a chair in front of his desk, Julian rose and went to a small table on the far side of the room. He poured two glasses of claret and handed one to her before sitting down again.

Leaning back in his chair, he watched as she took a deep swallow of the rich, red wine.

"I want to thank you," she said. "I am certain you have your own agenda and reasons for inviting me to London, but for now I appreciate everything you have done for me."

Julian knew she referred to the situation with Aberley and he didn't know whether to be amused or affronted, but since he did have his own reasons for inviting Sophia to London, he decided that it would be hypocritical of him to pretend offense.

"You are welcome." He took a sip of wine.

"Why?" she blurted, eyeing him curiously.

Swallowing, Julian arched both brows. "Why what?"

"Why am I welcome? Why did you help me? Why would you do anything at all for me when you so obviously dislike me?"

Did he dislike her? He certainly distrusted her, but could he honestly harbor this attraction for her if he didn't like at least *some* aspect of her besides her obvious physical charms? He had to admit that over the past few days he had developed an admiration for her frank way of speaking. And her obvious affection for Letitia certainly was a point in her favor.

"While I cannot say I particularly like you," he replied, "I am not wholly certain I dislike you either."

She stared at him. "That makes no sense whatsoever."

Chuckling, Julian had to agree. "I know. It is true nevertheless."

Sophia smiled and Julian was struck by just how truly lovely she was. As a girl she had been exotic and intriguing, but the years had softened her somehow. There was a haunted quality to her eyes and mouth that the poet in Julian found wildly appealing.

He wanted to know what had changed her. There was a restrained quality to her when amongst company. It was as though she was trying very hard to be a certain kind of person, and only with him did she show any hint of who she truly was.

It was just one more intriguing aspect of her that made him want to kiss her, arouse her until she broke free of this shell of hers, but after what she had suffered at the hands of her brother-in-law he was ashamed of himself for even thinking such thoughts.

"Oh!"

The soft cry of distress jerked his attention back to Sophia. She was holding a book in her hands, and staring at it in white-faced dismay.

No need to ask what book it was.

"Why are you reading this?" she demanded, lifting her accusatory gaze to his. "Are you planning on exacting some kind of revenge now that I am under your power?"

Revenge? Under his power? The woman read too many gothic novels.

"Do not be ridiculous," he admonished, not bothering to hide his annoyance. "I have never read it before. I thought it might be a good idea given the circumstances."

Sophia frowned. "I sent you this copy. How could you not have read it before this?"

A niggle of discomfort inched down Julian's spine. He couldn't very well tell her he hadn't given a damn about what she had to say about him or how she might choose to defend herself?

"I . . . I never got around to it."

Her frown deepened into a full-fledged scowl. "You mean you never cared to get around to it! I cannot believe your arrogance! I was forced to listen to all the awful things you said about me to anyone who would listen, but you did not even have the consideration, nay the *bollocks*, to face what I had to say in retaliation?"

Julian's eyes widened at the vehemence in her tone. And where on earth did a gently bred woman learn the term "bollocks"?

"I did not care to hear what you had to say," he began calmly, "because at the time I did not assume any of the blame for what happened."

An angry flush crept up her neck to her cheeks. "Of course you did not. How could you? You only planned to take my innocence and toss me aside!"

"I was only taking what had been freely offered!" he shot back, his own ire rising with startling velocity.

"You ruined me!" she cried, slamming her glass down on the desk and leaping to her feet. "Do you have any idea how many men have thought they could grab me or say horrible things to me because they thought I had given myself to you?"

He refused to feel guilty. He remembered what a flirt

she had been. Surely he hadn't been the first man she had toyed with. "You did give yourself to me. Fortunately we were interrupted before I could take what you offered."

She reacted as though he had slapped her and the wounded light in her eyes pierced his heart like a claw. "I only did what I did because I thought you loved me."

Did she think him a complete simpleton? She hadn't loved him. If she had she wouldn't have married the marquess so quickly.

"Did I ever say the words?" he demanded. He was also on his feet now, the force of his anger too volatile to be contained sitting down. "You sure as hell never said them to me!"

She had the nerve to look affronted. "I did not have to say them. I offered you the only thing that was truly mine to give."

A sneer curved his lips. "Your maidenhead? It could not have been that much of a gift. You gave it to the marquess fast enough."

The color that had heightened her cheeks drained rapidly from her face and at that moment, Julian knew what it was to truly hate himself.

"My trust, you bastard!" she shouted, thrusting her face just inches from his own. "My trust!"

Now it was his turn to recoil as if struck.

But Sophia wasn't done with him just yet. She glared at him with eyes that glittered like black opals.

"I offered myself to you because I thought I could trust you not to hurt me. I thought you loved me, and damn it, Julian! I may never have said the words but I loved you as much as a stupid girl could love a heartless blackguard who used her and tossed her aside like a pair of dirty stockings!"

He managed to catch the book before it collided with his chest. She had obviously thrown it as hard as she could if the stinging in his hands was any indication. He barely had time to react before she ran from the room.

Clutching the book against him, Julian sank down into his chair, a bizarre sense of confusion numbing his mind.

Had she really loved him? No, it couldn't be. He couldn't have been so wrong. He had been there! He knew what had happened. She had married the marquess not even a month later . . .

But what if Sophia hadn't wanted Aberley. What if it had been him—Julian—that Sophia had truly wanted?

What if he had been wrong?

After passing what had been one of the longest nights of his life, Julian found himself back in his study again early the next morning. He had spent a good deal of the night pondering what Sophia had said. Another part had been spent reading *An Unfortunate Attachment* and realizing just how unflattering a picture of him she had painted. It wasn't a completely faithful likeness, but it mirrored more than he was ready to admit.

The portrait she had painted of herself was completely different from the girl he had known, so obviously it was biased in her own favor. She forgot to mention her numerous temper tantrums or how she had to be the center of attention no matter where she was. She made him sound like some worldly rake, something that couldn't have been farther from the truth.

Still, he couldn't deny that he had to take at least half of the blame for what had happened, and he was prepared to do just that. There was little else he could do. Besides, how horrible had her life turned out? From what he had seen and heard, the marquess had been good to her. And her reputation had recovered much more quickly than his had. It was years before any mothers would let their daughters anywhere near him. He probably could have been married by now if not for Sophia.

For that matter he could have been married *to* Sophia. Now there was a startling thought. Knowing how both of them had been back then he couldn't see it being a good match, but now . . .

Now it was madness to even think about it. What man in his right mind wanted a wife he couldn't trust? Or for that matter didn't trust him?

She hadn't told him why she had married Aberley so quickly. Was it to save her reputation, or had he been right about her fishing for a fortune? She hadn't told him why she went from living in splendor to near poverty and she certainly hadn't told him what kind of hold Charles Morelle had over her. These alone were reasons not to hand over his trust so hastily.

A knock at the door pulled him out of his thoughts. "Enter."

His butler, Fielding, stuck his head in the door. "Begging your pardon, my lord, but there is a gentleman here to see you."

"Who is it, Fielding?"

"The Marquess of Aberley, my lord."

Julian's jaw tightened as did his chest. Aberley had some nerve coming to his house after his appalling conduct at Sophia's cottage.

"Send him in."

A few moments later, a smug Charles Morelle entered the room, his hat and gloves under one arm. Julian didn't bother to stand.

"Good morning, Wolfram."

Julian made no pretense of amenity. "What do you want, Aberley?"

The marquess was all confusion and mock civility. "Why, I have come to call upon my dear sister-in-law and inquire after her health and well-being."

Did Aberley truly think him daft enough to believe that?

"Sophia does not want to see you."

"Did she tell you that?" The marquess demanded, some of his pleasant demeanor slipping. "Did she say she does not want to see me?"

Julian nodded, saying nothing.

Somehow, Aberley managed to adopt an expression of wounded innocence. "Look, Wolfram. I do not know what Sophia has told you—"

"She needn't tell me anything," Julian's tone was clipped, brooking no argument. "I saw."

Aberley didn't even have the sense to look sorry. He simply shrugged. "What you saw was a lovers' spat, nothing more." He smiled. "You know how women can be."

Julian's blood turned to ice in his veins. A lovers' spat? "Do you make a habit of accosting your lovers until they are in tears and screaming for help?"

Another shrug. Aberley's attention wasn't even on him now. He was looking about at the papers and books on Julian's desk.

"Sophia was being a tease and got mad when I refused to play along." He glanced up. "She used you to get at me, Wolfram, and she will continue to use you until she has decided she has had enough and wants to come home. To me."

His words struck that part of Julian that was still unsure

of Sophia and her actions. One thing he was not unsure of, however, was the genuine fear he had seen on her face the other day in the park. That was not the look of a woman wanting to torment a lover.

Pushing back his chair, Julian rose to his feet. He moved around to the front of the desk. "For now she does not wish to return home to you, Aberley. And until she does I will respect her wishes. Now, if there is nothing else you wish to discuss with me, I am afraid I must ask you to excuse me. I have an urgent commission to attend to. I trust you can find your way out?"

Without waiting for the marquess's reply, Julian turned on his heel and left the room. If Aberley wasn't gone in two minutes he was going to personally throw the bastard out into the street.

He felt like ten times a coward for walking out on the marquess rather than demanding that he leave, but it was the only way he could think of at the time to escape Aberley's words. He didn't want to believe Sophia capable of pitting the two of them against each other. He might not trust her, but he trusted her more than he trusted Aberley, and he would take her side against the marquess anytime.

He went to the red drawing room and stood at the bank of windows that afforded a good view of the drive. A few minutes later a carriage with the Aberley crest on it passed by. Satisfied, Julian left the drawing room and made for the corridor, where he found Fielding.

"Fielding," he said, coming to stand before the man in a few long strides. "If the Marquess of Aberley calls again I want you to tell him we are not at home, especially if he calls looking for the marchioness. Am I understood? He is not to see her."

If Fielding was surprised by the finality in his tone he

did not show it. "Yes, my lord. Of course. I will pass that on to the rest of the staff."

Nodding in approval, Julian turned to leave. A movement at the top of the stairs caught his eye and he looked up to see Sophia staring at him with an expression he couldn't read. But he thought—hoped—it was trust.

Chapter 6

He danced divinely, as most rakes do.

An Unfortunate Attachment by A Repentant Lady

"I look fat."

Standing in front of the cheval glass in her bedroom, Sophia twisted from side to side, frowning critically at her reflection.

The gown that Madam Villeneuve had worked so hard to have ready for that night was a beautiful wine-colored silk creation with a low neckline and gold underskirt. She should have felt beautiful in it, but instead she felt like an overripe pomegranate.

Letitia laughed and crossed the carpet toward her. Letitia could afford to laugh. She was a vision in a russet satin gown.

"You look nothing of the sort," her friend chastised. "You are stunning!"

Sophia didn't know about stunning, but perhaps she did look better than she originally thought. Jenny, her maid, had piled her hair high up on her head in an elaborate style and applied curling tongs to the tendrils that fell around her face and neck. She had even applied a bit of powder and lip color—not too much. She didn't want to look like a tart.

"Now, fetch your wrap and let us be off. We are late." Letitia released her arms and went back to the bed where her own wrap and reticule lay.

"All right," Sophia said, gathering up her things and expelling a deep breath. "I am ready."

Linking arms, the two of them left the room and went downstairs to the hall, where Julian stood waiting.

The sight of him nearly took Sophia's breath away. He held his hat in one gloved hand, leaving the rich warm waves of his hair naked to her greedy gaze. He was dressed entirely in black and white; black coat and cape and fashionably long trousers with a white shirt and cravat and an ivory waistcoat.

He stared at her as openly as she stared at him, but Sophia could not tell for the life of her whether or not he approved of her appearance.

"Ladies," he said with a bow. "Might I say that you both look lovely tonight."

"Just lovely?" Letitia asked with a laugh. "Oh, Julian! Surely you can do better than that! Just look at Sophia. Is she not the most beautiful creature you have ever seen?"

"Lettie," Sophia chided softly, embarrassed.

"Yes," Julian said and her startled gaze locked with his. "She is."

Slow heat spread over every inch of Sophia's body under the weight of his lupine stare.

"Thank you, my lord. You look very handsome as well."

"Oh, my brother is well aware of how handsome he is, Sophia!" Letitia laughed again. "Are you not, Julian?"

Julian looked at his sister as though he wanted to strangle her and said nothing. He helped her into her wrap instead and then turned to offer his assistance to Sophia.

"Oh no," she protested. "You do not need to help me . . ." but her words died off as he took the shawl from her numb fingers and placed it around her shoulders. He didn't touch her at all and yet there was something incredibly intimate about him draping the wrap around her.

Licking her lips, she glanced up. He was staring at her just as intently as he had a few moments before. "Thank you."

His only reply was a slight smile. Could it be that he was just as sorry for their argument the night before as she was? Was that why he told the butler not to let Charles into the house? Was that why he was being so attentive to her now?

She had told him she had loved him. How was she to behave around him now? A voice in the back of her head—Edmund's voice—told her that a proper lady would go on as though it had never happened, but she feared she wasn't a proper lady, despite all of her late husband's efforts.

"I wonder if I might be so bold as to claim a dance with you tonight, Lady Aberley?"

He was smiling at her, smiling as though she had never yelled at him, as though she had never accused him of lacking, uh, *bollocks*.

"Of course," she replied, her voice hoarse. "Which would you like?"

"The first." His smile faded and suddenly he looked very young and unsure. "And the last."

Sophia wasn't certain why, but the fact that he wanted

her to begin and end the evening with him set her heart to
pounding in a most erratic manner.

"Come on, you two!" Letitia called from the door, before Sophia could speak. "We are already late!"

Letitia's anxiety over getting to the ball had nothing to
do with being late and everything to do with the fact that
Mr. Wesley was going to be in attendance. Sophia could
only hope that her friend kept her wits about her. She
knew how dangerous such gatherings could be. A few
dances, too much champagne and a young lady was liable
to drape herself across a desk in a darkened library and
ask that her escort make a woman out of her.

They arrived at Eden shortly after seven. The club was
the only one of its kind in London. It had a club for gentlemen and a club for ladies within its walls, but it also had
a large dining room and assembly rooms where both sexes
mingled freely. No one was allowed to wager more than
they could afford to pay, and if the management believed a
customer was too deep in his—or her—cups to play re-
sponsibly, then that person was cut off.

One would think all these rules and regulations
would have put the club out of business after its first two
nights, but Eden had been up and running for some
months now and was doing quite well. As it was Thurs-
day the assembly rooms were open and teeming with be-
jeweled members of society. Eden was quickly earning a
reputation—rivaling even Almack's—as *the* place to be
seen by the haute ton.

Sophia could have done without the public introductions. It seemed as though a collective gasp rose up from
the crowd as her name was announced, and an even larger
one echoed when Julian was announced next.

Julian, blast him, appeared unperturbed. With Sophia

on one arm and Letitia on the other, he swept into the room as though he owned it.

Sophia tried to ignore the curious gazes that followed them and instead allowed herself the pleasure of taking in the beauty of the room's decorations. What must have been almost a dozen chandeliers glittered and twinkled high above their heads. Swaths of white and blue gauze were draped along the walls up to the ceiling, creating a tent effect. And everywhere she looked, potted palms and huge arrangements of brightly colored flowers gave the room an exotic appearance and a sweet scent. Letitia broke away from them to go speak to some friends. Sophia had no doubt that Mr. Wesley was one of them. Alone, she and Julian walked toward a small group at the far end of the ballroom.

A red-haired woman in the group turned as they approached. It was Lilith. "Sophia!"

Laughing, the two women embraced. Sophia hadn't seen Lilith Mallory since before Lilith's parents sent her away after she had been ruined by some blackguard. Obviously, she had survived the scandal and done quite well for herself.

Perhaps there was hope for Sophia yet.

Lilith introduced Sophia to her husband, Gabriel Warren, Earl of Angelwood. Sophia tried to keep the surprise from her face as she shook the earl's hand. She had been invited to their wedding, but at the time she hadn't made the connection. Wasn't he the same man who had ruined Lilith years ago? And wasn't he an old friend of Julian's? Had these two made it a habit to play fast with young women's virtue in their youth or was it merely a coincidence?

The other couple was Julian's old friend Balthazar

Wycherley, Earl of Braven, and his countess, Rachel. A
lovely couple. Obviously very much in love. Sophia wondered if they had a scandal as well.

Across the floor she spotted Letitia dancing with
Phillip Singleton, heir to the Earl of Wroth and apparently
one of the young men on Julian's list of potential husbands. He was a friendly young man, handsome, rich and
kind. He would no doubt make anyone an excellent husband, but Sophia wasn't certain if he had quite enough
backbone to handle Letitia when she decided she wanted
her own way.

She wondered how much backbone Mr. Wesley had.
Her thoughts were cut short by Julian claiming his dance.

Hours later, Sophia's feet were beginning to feel the
strain of too much dancing. Her stomach also was feeling
the effects, demanding to be fed with an embarrassingly
loud growl.

"Lady Aberley," came a familiar voice from behind
her. "Would you do me the honor of sitting down to supper with me?"

Sophia wanted to ask Julian why he didn't take one of
his many dance partners instead, but managed to hold her
tongue. The last thing she wanted him to know was that it
bothered her to see him with other women.

The refreshment room at Eden was a large, tastefully
decorated room with buffet tables lining the far wall and
dozens of smaller tables throughout the room for guests to
sit, eat and converse away from the noise and heat of the
ballroom.

"I do not see your brother-in-law here," Julian remarked, placing a slice of tomato on her plate with a pair
of silver tongs.

"No," she replied, selecting a hard-boiled egg for each

of them. "This kind of diversion would not amuse Charles at all."

Julian said nothing as he continued piling food on their plates.

Sophia could no longer keep her silence. "Forgive me, I did not get a chance to thank you earlier for what you said to Fielding regarding the marquess."

He glanced at her but briefly before spearing more cold meats for the two of them. "I did not do it to earn your gratitude."

He didn't? "Then why did you?"

Julian's shoulders sagged in a heavy sigh. "Do you have to question everything?" he demanded, his voice even lower than it had been. "I did it because I wanted to."

Obviously that was as good an answer as she was going to get, and that suited her just fine. She much preferred Julian doing things for her because he wanted to rather than out of a need to have her in his debt.

She plopped a pickle onto his plate. "Well, thank you anyway."

He burst out laughing, causing several people in the room to turn their heads and stare.

They sat with Lilith, Gabriel, Brave and Rachel, a surprisingly comfortable arrangement. Sophia knew Lilith well enough to make conversation, and Rachel was so friendly she made it incredibly easy for Sophia to talk to her.

"You were late as usual tonight, Jules," Brave teased as he sliced into a tomato.

Julian grinned at his friend and Sophia envied their easiness with each other. "You, no doubt, had been here for hours by the time we arrived."

"Half of one." His friend returned the smile. "We get

out so rarely that we like to take advantage of it when we do."

Julian turned to Sophia. "Brave and Rachel are the only people ever to have had a child. The responsibility weighs on them from time to time, as you can imagine."

Sophia didn't know how to react to his joke, but joined in the laughter once the others started.

"Someday you will find out for yourself," Brave informed him with mock severity. "And then we shall all have a good laugh at your expense."

Shaking his head, Julian maintained his good-natured expression. "I am in no hurry to have it happen, my friend. I have already partially raised two. I am in no hurry to repeat the experience."

Was that true? Sophia had never met a man who didn't long for a son to carry on after him. Even Edmund, who would have been an indifferent father at best, had been bitter about his inability to sire an heir.

"I am certain you will feel different when the child is truly your own, Jules," Gabriel asserted.

His gaze narrow, Julian turned to his friend. Sophia watched as understanding lit his eyes.

"Good lord, you are with child," he blurted out.

Happy gasps and congratulations poured forth when a beaming Lilith nodded. Gabriel puffed up just like a peacock.

Everyone expressed their pleasure at the announcement, and Sophia gathered that a baby was something Gabriel and Lilith had been wanting since their marriage. She was happy for them, but not being a mother herself, she couldn't relate to the sheer joy on Lilith's face.

"Envious?" A soft voice asked.

Sophia smiled at Julian's nosiness. "More awkward

than anything else," she replied honestly. "It is not something I can relate to."

He nodded, his gaze straying back to the four chattering people before them. "Did you never want children?"

She met his gaze again. "I knew when I married Aberley that he was unable to father children. I was so young and selfish I did not care."

But that was before her husband died and Julian knew that. "And now?"

She shrugged. "Now that I am a widow of seven and twenty I am becoming accustomed to the idea of never having any."

Julian said what everyone else always said when she told them how she felt about motherhood. "You are still young."

She smiled. "I am unmarried, Julian, and unless I happen to fall desperately in love with someone, have little intention of changing that. Do not," she said holding up her hand when he opened his mouth to speak, "tell me that you think I would make a good mother. It is about as convincing an argument as telling me I would make a good coatrack. There is about as much chance that I will become one as the other."

Julian chuckled at that. "I believe I know exactly how you feel."

"Perhaps we should discuss something other than children," Rachel suggested in her soft yet firm tone. "It can hardly be entertaining for Lady Aberley and Julian."

Sophia's cheeks warmed as all eyes turned toward herself and Julian. In a way, she was touched by Lady Braven's astuteness, but it also made her feel like something of a fifth wheel amongst their happy group. Did Julian feel the same?

"Oh, no," he replied with obviously false enthusiasm. "I find it vastly entertaining. I have already composed half a sonnet about it in my head."

Everyone chuckled and the mood was instantly set to rights. The conversation took a different turn—to telling Sophia amusing antecdotes about Julian as a youngster. She found the change of topic wildly amusing. Julian, however, did not. He excused himself after a few moments to fetch a drink a little stronger than the champagne the club served. Sophia watched him go out of the corner of her eye, admiring the gentle sway of his wide shoulders, the way the thick waves of his hair shone under the chandeliers.

"Sophia."

Jerked out of her thoughts, Sophia glanced up to see who had spoken. It was Letitia. A very flushed, very happy-looking Letitia.

"There you are!" The younger woman's good mood was contagious. "Are you enjoying yourself?"

Letitia nodded. "I need you to do something for me," she whispered.

Frowning slightly at Letitia's insistent tugging on her arm, Sophia rose to her feet and allowed the younger woman to lead her a discreet distance away from Julian's friends.

Letitia fixed her with a determined gaze. "They're soon going to start the last dance of the evening. I need you to keep Julian busy long enough for me to dance with Mr. Wesley. Will you do that?"

"All right." She had promised Julian the last dance anyway, so it wasn't that much of an inconvenience.

Letitia grinned. "Thank you! And when the dancing is over, I want you to tell him that I had to say goodbye to a few friends and that I will meet the two of you in the foyer."

Sophia frowned. "Letitia, what mischief are you up to? Promise me you will not sneak away with Mr. Wesley— not even for a moment."

Letitia's gaze was pleading. "It is just so we might say goodbye. Please, Sophia."

Despite her concern, Sophia capitulated. She really was too much of a pushover. Surely a few stolen minutes couldn't hurt. "Oh, all right. But if you are not in the foyer ten minutes after the last dance ends I will tell your brother exactly what you are up to."

Letitia's bottom lip jutted forward slightly. "If it weren't for the fact that I have no other way to get to the Eversham ball, I wouldn't have to worry about Julian finding out."

Sophia started. This was the first she'd heard of Letitia attending another function that night. "You are not accompanying us back to Wolfram House?"

Shaking her head, Letitia began inching toward the door as the first strains of the waltz started. "No. I have another engagement. But do not worry. The ride from the Evershams' to home is not a long one. You will not have to suffer my brother's company for long."

With that, the svelte woman slipped back out into the ballroom, leaving Sophia staring after her. She had promised Julian the last dance of the evening. They were going to waltz together—touch each other—and then they were going to be alone in a carriage where no one could see them or hear them.

Letitia didn't know what suffering was.

"So did you have a good time, or did my friends manage to make you regret coming to London?"

Smiling, Sophia leaned back against the plush squabs of the carriage and sighed. The coachman had lit the lamp inside the carriage and the flame made her delicate features a study in light and shadow. She was a dark angel, sent to test the strength of his will. That he rhapsodized about her in such a fashion was indicative of just how dangerous she was.

"I had a lovely time, but I am not used to having so many people at once interested in what I have to say." Her smile faded. "You are very lucky to have friends who care about you so much."

He grimaced. "I apologize if they offended you."

"Oh no, they did not offend me in the least."

Julian was glad. Tact was not something either Brave or Gabriel had ever learned to perfect and it seemed that Rachel and Lilith weren't much better. They had only been trying to ferret out Sophia's feelings for him—and his for her.

That suspicion had been reinforced after they finished teasing Julian about incidents from his past. That was when Brave asked Sophia to share some of her own experiences with Julian, and Julian knew that she had been accepted into their little circle.

"They liked you very much," he said. "Everyone remarked upon it."

She met his gaze with a lazy smile. "I know they did. No doubt they think I will make a good countess and give you all those sons you want even though you refuse to admit it."

His eyes widened. "You knew?"

She laughed out loud. "How could I not? All conversation this evening was engineered to determine whether or not I am good enough for you. They believe we are involved."

"Are we?" He couldn't help but ask, even though he wasn't certain he wanted to hear her answer.

"Involved? I do not think so." Her tone was hesitant as she licked her lips.

Julian shifted on the seat, trying for all the world to appear unaffected. One arm lay across the back of the carriage seat, the other was propped against the wall. He rested his head on that hand. There was the same amount of space between them now as there had been before and yet it seemed as though the carriage had shrunk around them, squeezing them even closer together.

He couldn't leave well enough alone. "What exactly do you think we are, then?"

She gazed at him in confusion. "I . . . I do not know."

His lips curved up on one side. "I do not know either."

She seemed surprised by that.

"I believe . . ." She paused. "I believe that whatever we are now, we are well on our way to becoming friends."

"Friends." His soft chuckle echoed through the carriage as he repeated the word. Surely she didn't believe that? He liked her too little and too much for them to be something so insipid. "No, I do not think we are that."

"Then it seems that we are right back where we started," she remarked with patently false lightness.

Julian smiled. "Not quite."

Sophia regarded him much like a rabbit regards a fox. "Oh?"

He sat up and leaned forward, bracing his forearms on his knees. His folded hands were just inches from

Sophia's legs. He could reach out and touch her if he wanted.

Obviously she had the same thought, because her hand was halfway to his face before she caught herself. She jerked her arm back.

His gaze dropped from her face to her hand before climbing back to her face again. He said nothing. He didn't have to. All the answers he needed were in her sweetly flushed cheeks and smoldering eyes.

His neck itched beneath his collar as the heat of the carriage caught up with him. He had to cool things down before he ignited. "I have been reading your book."

She seemed surprised by his change of subject. "I know."

His gaze held hers. "It has made me think about what happened between us. Even though your account of things is not an exactly honest rendition of the affair—"

"It is too honest!" Her mouth tightened in indignation.

Amusement curved his lips. Surely it was perverse to enjoy her pique. "On the pages where you describe the night we first met you have me asking you to dance. I admit it does make Lord Foxton—dreadful name by the way—look like more of a rake, but you know as well as I do that you approached me."

Sophia shrugged, her gaze drifting toward the window. "It was just one little incident. It hardly signifies."

Was it his imagination, or was she blushing?

"And you said that I practically had to hold you prisoner the first time we kissed." Amusement turned to something else—something that made his veins feel as though they were filled with molten lava. He remembered that first kiss with startling—and arousing—clarity.

"It was seven years ago," she replied peevishly. "You cannot expect me to remember everything I wrote."

Grinning, Julian reached out and took her right hand in his left. He hadn't bothered to put on his gloves after leaving the club and he could feel the heat of her fingers through the thin fabric of hers.

"I wager you remember the first time we kissed as clearly as I do."

Sophia swallowed—he could see her throat constrict with the effort—but she did not try to pull her hand away, even as he tugged on the fingers of her glove, pulling it farther and farther down her arm.

"If I portrayed you as more of the pursuer than you actually were, then I apologize." She lifted her chin defensively. "But I was not the one who suggested we sneak off to my father's library. *I* was not the one who left you there to face my father alone with your gown unbuttoned and your skirts hiked up above your garters."

"No," he replied. "You were not." But she had done and said plenty of other things—things that Julian didn't feel like bringing up. There were a million and one things he wanted to do with Sophia at that moment and arguing about a past they couldn't change wasn't one of them.

"You raised your hand earlier," he said, yanking her glove all the way off. "You were not planning to strike me, I hope?"

"No. Not that."

"What then?" He lifted her hand. Palm down, fingers toward him, it trembled ever so slightly as he held it. "What were you going to do?"

His hand dropped leaving her own hovering between them. Would she demand he give her back her glove, or would she give in to temptation and touch him as he instinctively knew she longed to?

"I was going to touch your hair," she confessed, lifting her shaky fingers to his temple.

"You always liked it more than I," he murmured, scarcely daring to breathe as the tips of her fingers brushed his skin.

She leaned closer. "It is beautiful. I never understood why you did not like it."

He went perfectly still, his nostrils flaring with a sharply indrawn breath. He did not try to stop her. He simply held her gaze and waited. She hesitated for only a second.

Julian's eyes closed in sensual pleasure as Sophia's fingers plunged into his hair. He pressed his head against her hand and rubbed like a cat seeking affection. No doubt his hair was a mess, but he didn't care. Her touch felt good— so good his heart ached.

She raked her fingers through the strands, rubbed his scalp with the pads of her fingers. She touched him as though she was in awe of him. How could he not react to that?

His eyes opened in silent inquiry as her hand left his hair. She was staring at him so intently, so hotly that his prick hardened to full erection almost instantly.

"I think this is my favorite, however," she murmured, trailing the tip of her index finger along his upper lip. She used the whole pad for his lower. "I used to think a mouth like this was wasted on a man, but then you kissed me and I knew it was not a waste at all."

He stopped breathing. Could she feel it?

She must have, because her fingers froze in mid-stroke and fell away from his lips. She looked horrified.

"What must you think of me?" The anguished whisper cracked through the heart he thought he had hardened against her.

Julian drew a deep breath. "I think you are the most dangerous woman I have ever known," he replied, his voice low and scratchy in his own ears. "What I want to know is," he continued as her hesitant gaze met his, "what do you think of my mouth now?"

Slowly, Sophia leaned forward, inching closer until he could feel her breath against his face. Her eyelids fluttered closed and then her lips met his . . .

Something shattered within Julian's chest. It felt as though something he had imprisoned within himself had broken free of its shackles and rose up joyously, spreading itself through every nerve and fiber of his being. In all the things he had done over the years, nothing had ever felt so right as kissing Sophia.

And he let *her* kiss him. He didn't raise his hands to hold her or try to take over the kiss by increasing the pressure of his lips against hers. He allowed her complete control. Did she know that by doing so he was also offering her his trust?

Sophia reveled in this incredible feeling. She tasted Julian, probed his lips with her tongue and gasped in delight when he opened his mouth, letting her inside. Still he let her control the kiss, meeting the thrust of her tongue with his, but always allowing her to set the rhythm.

He wanted her. She knew that as certainly as she knew the sun was going to rise in the morning. His body hummed with the tension of restraint. He wanted to take control. He wanted to press himself upon her, touch her and make love to her.

She wasn't ready for that. She couldn't let herself go so

completely. She couldn't risk the scandal and she couldn't risk giving him her heart a second time. He knew that. He was asking her to trust him, and by letting her control this kiss, he was proving she could.

The carriage stumbled to a stop, breaking the kiss before Sophia could do so herself. Her eyes flew open. Julian was watching her.

"We are home." His voice was hoarse with undisguised arousal.

"Yes," was all she could think of to say.

Jerkily, she tore her gaze away from his and began collecting her belongings. He handed her her glove and she quickly shoved her fingers into it as the carriage door opened and a footman lowered the stairs.

They entered the house together, Julian holding his hat and gloves in front of him in such a manner that Sophia knew without a doubt his reason for doing so. Their kiss had aroused him as it had her, only her desire was a low, throbbing ache hidden deep within her, while his was a bit more physically obvious.

It was late. Most of the staff, including Fielding, were already in bed, so there was no one to take their hats and cloaks—fortunate for both of them. Sophia would be mortified if any of the servants figured out what she and Julian had been up to in the carriage.

They walked up the stairs together, side by side, each of them looking straight ahead, saying nothing, and yet the air between them positively rang with vows and confessions better left unsaid.

It was dark in the corridor, only one wall sconce illuminating the section between her room and his. No one would know if she invited him inside. No one would know if they spent the entire night in bed together. No one but her. And him.

"Good night," he said, those wolflike eyes boring into hers.

Smiling shakily, Sophia didn't know whether to kiss him or cry. He was making the decision for her.

"Good night, Julian."

Turning the knob, she slipped into the warmly lit haven of her chamber. He was still watching her as she closed the door.

Chapter 7

"I do not want you to kiss me."
Lord Foxton smiled. "My dear lady, if that is true,
then why are you here with me, alone in the dark?"

An Unfortunate Attachment by A Repentant Lady

Only a dead man could possibly sleep after a kiss like that.

Turning away from Sophia's bedroom door took every ounce of strength Julian possessed, and not just because the urge to claim her body with his own was stronger than the need to breathe.

The second the door closed between them he became aware of just how utterly alone he was. The house seemed more quiet, larger and more cavernous. The light in the corridor seemed dimmer and less inviting because Sophia wasn't there with him. Suddenly it was very clear to him just why he felt like an outsider around his friends, why he coveted their happy marriages.

He was lonely. And it had taken Sophia, a woman who had no right to affect him as she did, to show him just how empty his life was. The desire he felt for her body was nothing compared to how he craved her company.

Wouldn't she have a good laugh at that if she knew? As

he walked down the dark hall to the stairs he wondered if she had any idea of the effect she had on him.

For that matter, did he?

Perhaps he would feel this way about any woman who paid attention to him. Another part insisted that Sophia filled a hole in his life. She had a way of making him feel special that no one else had ever come close to duplicating.

She also had made him feel like a pathetic fool, he reminded himself. He could not just forget that, regardless of how sweet her touch was or how incredibly *right* her mouth had felt against his.

Two lamps burned in the great hall—one on the wall between the stairs and the foyer door and one on a small table toward the back corridor. He took the one on the table and used it to light his way to his study.

He didn't bother to close the door. It was so late no one would bother him, and even if they did the interruption wouldn't be unwelcome. At this point anything that could turn his thoughts away from Sophia would be welcome.

An Unfortunate Attachment sat on his desk, its cover staring at him accusingly. He was almost finished reading it, but the scene where he—Lord Foxton—ruins the heroine was just a few pages ahead and he couldn't quite bring himself to go on.

Nowhere in her writing did she say anything about trying to trap him. Her heroine, Jocelyn, was blindly infatuated with the vain, arrogant and somewhat dandyish Lord Foxton, and was convinced that he returned her feelings.

Was that how Sophia had actually seen him? As arrogant and vain? Lord, back then nothing could have been further from the truth. Perhaps he had been a little arrogant—

most men of his class were—but vain? No. His looks had been the bane of his existence. The only thing he had been the least bit vain about was his ability to write, and looking back, that had been nothing to get puffed up about.

The way Sophia described herself contradicted his own assessment of the kind of person she had been. She described herself as being unsure of herself, wondering if anyone saw her for who she really was. Jocelyn was a social creature, treated like a doll by her parents, but who only wanted someone to love her for who she was.

Julian thought he had done that, but he automatically had thought the worst of her when her father burst in on them. He had thought she wanted only to trap him.

No. That wasn't true. He hadn't thought that until her engagement to Aberley was announced a week later.

The truth was he had believed himself in control of their affair. He had thought they could carry on as they had been and then he could decide when they would marry. After her father caught them in the library, Julian had watched as what little control he had over his life was snatched away. Sophia's father had tried to force him to marry her, just as fate had robbed him of his parents and Miranda and forced him to take over the earldom and all it entailed. He was tired of having his life controlled by other forces. He had dug in his heels and lashed out.

And when Sophia married Aberley he covered up his hurt by telling himself she had only been after a title and a fortune. Perhaps she had been, but that didn't change the fact that he had behaved deplorably. Nor did it change the fact that he had publicly humiliated her by refusing to marry her. No matter what her sins might have been, he had been older and he had been the one with the power. He should have known better.

He was more like Lord Foxton than he cared to admit.

"Julian?" Letitia's soft voice floated from the doorway. "Are you all right?"

Looking up, Julian forced a smile for his sister's benefit. "I am fine. You are home very late. Did you have a good time?"

Letitia looked much younger than her four and twenty years as she glided into the room. He could remember seeing the same expression on Miranda's face often enough as well, but that was before. Before she became pregnant by one of their stable hands and took her own life when the bastard refused to marry her.

He had made many mistakes where Miranda had been concerned. He would not do the same with Letitia. He would see her happily and properly married if it was the last thing he did.

". . . danced with Lord Regley and then Victoria Melbourne fainted when Sir Walter Trundel appeared with Lady Jane Sedgway."

Shaking his head, Julian frowned at his sister, who was now seated across the desk from him. What was she talking about? Oh yes, the party she had attended that evening.

"Was Miss Melbourne ill?"

Letitia rolled her eyes. "No. Really, Julian, do you not pay any attention to gossip?"

"Not if I can help it, no." It was his experience that people who listened to gossip eventually heard something about themselves.

His sister was all too happy to enlighten him. "Victoria Melbourne has been after Sir Walter for months. Everyone knows that she has made a complete cake of herself over the man—not that he ever did anything to encourage her."

"Not that you know of," Julian remarked.

Letitia scowled. "Well, everyone knows only a fool pursues a man who has not made his intentions known."

Julian couldn't stop the words that came out of his mouth. "Your friend Lady Aberley pursued me. Would you judge her so harshly?"

His sister colored in the dim lamplight. "It is hardly the same thing."

Julian shrugged. He couldn't believe he was discussing this with his baby sister! "You have no idea what kinds of promises Sir Walter might have made Miss Melbourne in the heat of passion."

Letitia's eyes widened as her mouth fell open in shock.

After a few moments of silence, Julian cleared his throat. "So, did any of the gentlemen there catch your eye?"

Letitia smiled faintly. "Well, I did dance twice with Mr. Wesley."

His brow creasing, Julian searched his memory for a face to go with the name. "Penderthal's heir?"

Letitia nodded, a hopeful expression on her face.

Julian shook his head. Wesley was a friendly young man due to inherit a fine title, but he wouldn't do. "Better not encourage his intentions, Lettie. His father was a gamester and a notorious libertine. Mr. Wesley might very well prove to be the same."

Letitia paled and Julian was instantly contrite. All this talk of vice had undoubtedly offended her sensibilities. Sometimes he forgot that she was much more delicate than her age would suggest.

"I am glad you had a good time," he said, rising to his feet. "Now why don't we go up to bed, hmm? Tomorrow is going to be a busy day for both of us."

His sister stood and, carrying the lamp, Julian followed her from the room. They didn't speak as they climbed the stairs together. Julian's mind was once again taken over by thoughts of Sophia. He did not concern himself with why Letitia was suddenly so quiet.

Over the course of the next week and a half Julian spent more time with Sophia than he had originally intended. He escorted her and Letitia to various social outings, including a trip to the theater, and on those days when their schedules permitted, he and Sophia would sometimes sit and talk. They avoided talk of the past and any other subjects that might cause either one of them discomfort.

The more he got to know her, the more he came to like her. She was easy to talk to and she seemed sincerely interested in what he had to say. She asked questions, gave her own opinions freely and laughed at his jokes, which pleased him immensely.

In fact, everything about her pleased him. She was frank and honest, and yet she was never malicious—not toward him—but she had no patience for mean or stupid people and she made that abundantly clear.

She was also very good with Letitia. There had been a marked difference in his sister's demeanor since Sophia came to visit. Whether or not this change was wholly Sophia's responsibility he didn't know, but he was glad for it all the same. He had talked to Sophia about his hopes for Letitia's future, and she had given her opinion on that very freely as well.

"If she marries just to please you she might very well

end up miserable," she warned, and Julian promised to take her advice to heart. One of the things he was beginning to learn about her was that she did not give advice lightly, and when she did it was usually sound.

Oh, he knew there were things about herself she withheld from him. He withheld much from her as well. As comfortable as they were becoming with each other, neither was prepared to give their trust completely just yet, but he was beginning to realize that while something of that wild young girl still resided, hidden and repressed inside her, the woman she had become was much, much more intriguing and dangerous than that girl had ever been.

Try as he might he could not forget the kiss they had shared that night in the carriage. It had happened less than a fortnight ago and yet it felt like both a lifetime and a mere moment, it had laid such claim to his thoughts.

It didn't help that she seemed to be there every time he lifted his head. He needed to put a little distance between them, needed to get away from her before he said to hell with it and knocked on her bedroom door.

Unable to bear it any longer, he left the house that afternoon bound for White's.

Heads turned as Julian entered the club. Loud whispers and even louder chuckles followed him as he strode toward the table where his two friends sat. This was curious. What could they possibly have to talk about where he was concerned?

Gabriel and Brave were deep in conversation as he approached—conversation that broke off abruptly when they noticed his arrival. Two guilty countenances gazed up at him.

That his friends were talking about him wasn't surprising. The three of them had no secrets from each other and their lives had always been open topics of conversation. What was strange was the fact that Brave and Gabe looked so decidedly uncomfortable.

"What is going on?" he demanded as he sat down at the table with them.

Gabriel smiled. It looked forced. "Good day, Julian. How are you?"

His gaze drifting suspiciously back and forth between his friends, Julian frowned. "Other than the fact that I seem to be the subject of much conversation today I am much the same as I ever am."

His two friends exchanged glances.

Bracing his arm on the table, Julian leaned forward. He looked first at Brave then at Gabriel. "The two of you know something that I do not, and I want one of you to tell me what it is. *Now.*"

Before either of them could reply, a hand came down heavily upon Julian's shoulder.

"By God, Wolfram, hell hath no fury, eh?"

Scowling, Julian looked up to see Lord Pennington, one of his least favorite people in all of England, grinning at him. From the looks of it the man was already well on his way to becoming thoroughly foxed and it wasn't even four o'clock yet.

"I am afraid I do not know what you mean, Pennington," he replied coolly.

The red-faced man shook his head. "Trust a woman to stroke your staff with one hand and stab you in the back with the other, what?"

A cold sensation washed over Julian. He still had no

idea just what the hell the man was talking about, but he
was getting a pretty good idea *who* he referred to.

"Ah well, those ones to pretend to be above reproach
are just as much whores as the rest of them—worse in
fact. At least a whore will name her price up front." Pennington laughed heartily at his own joke and slapped Julian hard on the back. "Well, if you have had your fill of
her, feel free to send her my way, Wolfram. I always did
have a preference for women with black hair."

Julian watched as Pennington staggered away. Normally he would have demanded satisfaction for someone
talking about a woman that way, but there was a heavy,
sinking feeling in his stomach—a feeling that told him
that it wasn't Pennington that deserved his wrath.

His jaw and fists tightly clenched, he regarded his com-
panions. "Tell me now before I decide to beat it out of one
of you."

Brave and Gabriel looked at each other, worried brown
eyes meeting steely gray.

"Show him," Gabriel said.

Brave hesitated for a moment, his fretful gaze falling
briefly on Julian before he reached beneath his chair and
withdrew a small book. It looked brand new. He offered it
to Julian.

He knew what it was before he even touched it. How,
he did not know, but the sinking feeling in his stomach
worsened as he felt the weight of it in his hand.

He flipped to the title page.

*An Unfortunate Attachment: being the true and
scandalous tale of a young woman seduced.*

By Sophia Morelle, Marchioness of Aberley

Swallowing against the sudden dryness in his throat, Julian turned the page, knowing with a dreadful intuition that there was more.

To Julian. I hope you don't find Lord Foxton to be too unflattering a character. The description is an honest one, if not very kind.

Warmly, Sophia

Bitch.

A little voice in his head urged him not to jump to conclusions. Perhaps Sophia wasn't the one to blame for this, but who else could it possibly be? It was an old scandal. And no one else could possibly know that dedication, not that one precisely, unless they'd either seen it or written it. She had handwritten it in his copy, and his book had been in the same place since he'd received it almost seven years ago.

It had to have been her.

It made no sense. Why would she do this? That night when she had kissed him she seemed so sincere in her desire for him. He thought she was beginning to trust him, and damn it, he had started to trust her.

There was only one explanation. It had all been a game. An elaborate ruse to have her revenge upon him. She believed he had used her seven years ago and she wanted to return the favor by ruining him as she believed he had ruined her.

He should have left her in Hertford, regardless of what Charles Morelle had planned to do to her.

Calmly, he closed the book and rose to his feet. It seemed that every eye in the place was locked firmly on him, waiting for him to react. He wasn't about to give any of them the satisfaction of seeing him lose his temper.

"Excuse me, gentlemen," he said softly, causing Gabriel and Brave to once again exchange worried glances. If they did it again he was going to knock their heads together. "I believe I have some urgent business to attend to."

With the book tucked under his arm, he left the table and strode through the club at a leisurely pace. He kept his head held high as he collected his hat and gloves. Even when he walked outside, aware that he was being watched from the club's bow window, he maintained his illusion of calm. He climbed into his carriage like a man who hadn't a care in the world.

He was saving his rage. Saving it for when he got home. When he finally let it go, Sophia Morelle had better have the good sense to run for cover.

And never come back.

"Tell me again why Julian said you should not encourage Mr. Wesley's attentions."

Raising her cup to her lips, Sophia peered at Letitia over the delicate, gilt rim. They were in the red drawing room, a bright and cheerful room warmed by the midday sun.

Letitia had been in low spirits for more than a week. While it wasn't strange for her mood to swing from one extreme to another, it was odd that she wasn't making a huge drama out of it.

Letitia lifted her gaze from the hearth to Sophia. "He said Mr. Wesley's father was a libertine and a gamester— as though *my* Marcus could ever be either!"

Sophia said nothing. She thought it showed a concern for his sister and her future happiness that was admirable.

A week ago she undoubtedly would have thought it callous and ignorant.

"Letitia, talk to your brother. Once you tell him about your feelings I am certain he will give Mr. Wesley a chance." When her friend remained silent, she added, "Do you want me to speak to him?"

"No!" Her cup clattering against its saucer, Letitia turned imploring eyes to Sophia. "If Julian thinks you and I are in league together it will only make him more resolved. You must promise me that you will not say a word to him about Marcus!"

Sophia stared at her, her cup poised halfway to her mouth. "My dear Letitia, I really think you are over-reacting."

"Promise me you will not say a word, Sophia. Not even if Julian asks." Letitia's eyes were unnaturally big and dark against the pallor of her face. "I need you to do this for me. Please."

"All right. I promise."

It was out of concern for her friend's health and the agitation of her mind that Sophia vowed to keep her silence. Obviously Letitia truly believed that her brother would destroy all her hopes and force her into marriage. Hopefully Julian would never come out and ask her, because she didn't want to have to lie to him, not when the trust between them was so fragile.

It was then, as though summoned by her thoughts, that Julian stormed into the room.

The warm rush of pleasure Sophia felt at the sight of him was immediately cooled by the murderous expression on his face.

"Why did you do it?" he demanded.

Slowly, Sophia set her cup aside and rose to her feet, stunned by this sudden attack. "Do what?"

His eyes darkened. "You know very well."

Letitia stood, her anxious gaze bouncing back and forth between her brother and her friend. "Perhaps I should leave the two of you alone—"

"No," Julian insisted. "I want you to stay. Stay and hear what your friend has done."

Willing herself to remain calm, Sophia stared Julian's anger in the eye. "I would like to hear what I have done as well."

"Do not pretend to be the innocent, Sophia. You know very well I mean this."

He tossed something at her. It landed a short distance away from her and slid the last few feet across the carpet to stop just inches from the toes of her slippers. It was a book.

She picked it up and read the title on the spine. *Oh, dear Lord.* The world seemed to buzz and spin around her. She opened the cover with trembling fingers, and saw the dedication.

She was going to be ill. She was ruined, utterly and completely ruined. How had this happened?

"Where did you get this?" Her voice was little more than a pathetic whisper as she raised her gaze to Julian.

"From Brave and Gabe," he replied. "I talked to a bookseller before I came here. Apparently it was released late yesterday. Even though it is a reprint, the publisher seemed to think it would be an instant success given that the author is the Marchioness of Aberley." His lips thinned. "But you already knew that, did you not?"

Sophia's mind and body didn't seem to be operating at the same speed. Her mind was whirling while her body was slowing down.

"How could I possibly know—?" She stopped. Of course. He blamed her.

The knowledge hurt, but not as much as she thought it would. Of course he blamed her. He didn't know about that damn clause in Edmund's will. He didn't know how hard Charles had worked to drive her to ruin. Were the situation reversed, she would no doubt blame him as well.

She tossed the book back at him. It landed on the floor several feet past him. He didn't bother to retrieve it.

"I know you will not believe me," she said, holding her head high. "But I am not responsible for this."

He laughed—a harsh, wounded sound that nearly broke Sophia's heart. "Oh, I suppose someone else is? Who else could have done it, Sophia? Who else knew about that dedication? Who else knew you wrote the damn thing?"

She had no answer. There was no one else—not that she knew of.

Letitia, who had somehow remained silent throughout the exchange, chose this moment of strained silence to speak.

"Julian, there must be some mistake. Sophia would never—"

If the look Sophia shot her friend hadn't shut her up, the expletive her brother growled certainly did. "Stay out of this, Letitia," he warned.

She scowled at him, too deeply attached to him to fear the darkness of his mood. "You told me to stay and listen."

He turned to her, the muscle in his jaw clenched so hard it ticked. "Listen, yes. If you want to talk you may leave."

Somewhere deep inside, Sophia managed to find her backbone and use it. "Leave her alone, Julian."

A twisted smile curved his lips. "This is *my* house, Lady Aberley," he reminded her, his tone mocking. "I am master here and my demands are the only ones that matter."

He threw the words she had said to him at her cottage back at her with bitter ease.

"You got what you wanted," he continued when she chose to remain silent. "Now you shall give me what I want. You shall leave my house and stay the hell away from my sister."

"No!" Letitia cried. Both Julian and Sophia ignored her.

Sophia dipped her head in a stiff nod. There was no use arguing. He wouldn't listen anyway. "I will depart within the hour."

He looked almost surprised that she didn't protest her innocence or beg for mercy, but what could she possibly say to defend herself?

Letitia rushed to her side, tears in her wide eyes. "Sophia, do not go!"

Summoning a smile, Sophia caught the girl's hand in hers and squeezed. "Come help me pack. That is," she shot a glance at Julian, "if it is all right with your brother?"

Julian nodded, his face as expressive as a slab of granite. "If it serves to get you out of here all the faster."

Pain, sharp and stabbing, pierced Sophia's heart. So this was it. Of all the endings she might have imagined for herself and Julian, repeating history hadn't been one of them. Only this time *she* would at least have the satisfaction of walking out on *him*.

Now, where on earth was she to go?

The offices of Finch, Barrows and Abercrombie were in the area of Gray's Inn, where they had been located for several generations. Being a woman, Sophia had never had any reason to enter the building before, but now, with her future hanging in the balance, she had little choice.

She entered through the narrow door, climbed the narrow stairs, and without the accompaniment of even a maid, entered the office and faced the narrow little clerk behind the great oak desk.

"May I help you?" he asked, his gaze raking over her in a most insolent fashion.

"I am the Marchioness of Aberley," she informed him in her haughtiest tone. "Please tell your employers that I wish to speak with them."

"Y . . . yes, my lady." The clerk jumped to his feet. "I won't be but a minute."

Sophia watched him scurry off with a vague sense of satisfaction. After today she doubted anyone would ever jump to do her bidding again.

Perhaps her situation wasn't so very desperate. Perhaps once Sophia talked to misters Finch, Barrow and Abercrombie—something she should have done long before this—and told them of Charles's machinations, perhaps they would be able to help her. Perhaps there would be a way around Edmund's will. After all, while she did write the book years ago, she wasn't responsible for any scandal it might cause now.

With that thin strand of hope clutched firmly in her breast, she sat down on one of the hard oak chairs in the reception area and waited for the clerk to return.

She had dressed in a modest and sedate gown of slate blue, a gray pelisse and a matching bonnet in the hope that her appearance might somehow convince the solicitors that she was innocent of any wrongdoing. But the clothes had been paid for by Julian and that was damning in itself.

What if Charles had already gotten to them? What if they didn't believe her? Where would she go? She would rather die than go to her parents. The only friends she had in town besides Letitia were Lilith—and Lady Wickford. Letitia could not help her and she very much doubted if either Lilith or Lady W would either, both of them being such close connections of Julian's.

The pale-faced clerk came back for her. "They will see you now, Lady Aberley."

Rising with as much dignity as she could muster, Sophia clutched her reticule to her waist and allowed the young man to guide her down the corridor to an office.

The interior was mostly wood—oak—and decorated in strong earth tones. It was a manly office, made to impress other men and intimidate women such as herself.

But it wasn't the office that intimidated her. It was because of the men sitting in the office staring at her with such damning expressions that Sophia knew all hope was lost.

One of them was Charles. *Damn*.

They all rose. Finch, Barrow and Abercrombie did not smile. Charles did.

"Lady Aberley," one of the solicitors said. "We were expecting you. Please sit down."

Charles held a chair for her, still smiling. It was a smug smile. Sophia wanted to drive her fist into it until either it or her hand began to bleed. Instead, she took the offered seat. To refuse would be unflattering in the eyes of the other men.

It only took a few minutes for the fat man behind the desk and his two only slightly less pudgy associates to tell her that she was finished. The present marquess had already apprized them of the "unfortunate incident" that was undoubtedly her reason for calling on them.

"Yes," Sophia intoned, casting a knowing glance at

Charles. "No doubt he did." No doubt it was Charles who managed to orchestrate the whole thing! But how? He hadn't seen her since her arrival in London.

No, that wasn't true. He had come to call at Julian's. Julian had instructed the staff to refuse him entry again. Could he have somehow seen the book then?

Good Lord, had he told Julian his plan to ruin her and convinced him to help her?

No. That was unlikely. No man would put himself through such public humiliation for the sake of revenge. Especially not a man as proud as Julian.

The fat man was talking again. He was reminding her, even though she needed no reminding, of the clause in her husband's will. The clause that made arrangements to provide for her for the rest of her life *provided she not bring any scandal upon herself or the family.* If she did act in such a way that disgraced both herself and her late husband's family, then she was to be cut off without a penny, forced to leave behind any comforts her widowhood allowed her.

It had been Edmund's one condition upon marrying her. He had wanted a pretty wife—a trophy. For some reason he had wanted *her.* And in agreement for marrying her and saving her family's good name, he had demanded nothing short of her total obedience and supplication.

Her father had promised it.

She rose to her feet before the fat man had finished speaking. "Thank you, Mr. . . . whoever you are, but I am quite aware of my husband's wishes. Good day."

She had known as soon as she laid eyes on them that these men would not help her, so there was no use in even trying to tell them of Charles's deceit. Besides, standing there in her new, albeit simple, clothes, there was no way she could prove that he had denied her every comfort he possibly could in his quest to break her to his will.

The men, even Charles, gaped at her as she strode from the room. Behind her, Sophia heard a chair scrape across the floor, followed by footsteps. Charles was coming for her.

The urge to hurry was overwhelming, but she kept her steps dignified. She would not run from him.

"Sophia."

She stopped in the narrow hall and turned to face him. *Please, God. Do not let him see just how afraid I am.*

He came toward her, all stiff-backed arrogance and smug assurance. "It is your own fault, you know," he told her. "You brought this all upon yourself."

Silently, she stared at him. Her refusal to be baited obviously annoyed him. His expression turned sour. "How glad I am that I picked up that book I saw on Wolfram's desk. You really should have known better than to write something so personal as a dedication, Sophia. A little bit of investigation on my part and it wasn't difficult to prove you were the author of that foolish little book."

"I will keep that in mind for next time," she replied, her tone surprisingly casual.

He frowned. "Next time?"

Sophia nodded. "I shall have to make my living somehow. I thought perhaps I would write a book about my life with your brother. Or perhaps I will just skip that part and tell the world what it was like living with you panting after me like a rutting dog."

Oh, what satisfaction to watch a flush of deep crimson color his face!

"You would not dare."

Her only response was to arch a brow.

Charles lunged. It was all Sophia could do not to shriek in alarm as he pinned her between the wall and the hard, angry weight of his body.

"You do not have to live the rest of your life as a pauper, Sophia," he murmured, his breath hot against her cheek. "You can still come home with me."

Defiantly she raised her gaze. "And live the rest of my life as your whore? I would rather sell myself in Covent Garden than spend one night with you."

He jerked away from her, his face a contorted mask of rage. "Fine," he snarled. "Try to make it on your own. It will not be long before you come crawling back to me, and then you will beg to become my mistress."

A slow, sure smile curved Sophia's lips. "By all means, keep thinking that, Charles, if it gives you pleasure. But I will see you in hell before I beg you for anything."

Stepping away from the wall, she left him standing there, staring after her with a mixture of fury and disbelief. There was a lightheartedness in her step as she walked through the reception area. She smiled at the gaping clerk and exited the office, closing the door firmly behind her.

The afternoon was warm and inviting as she stepped outside, even though the sun was slowly starting to sink over the horizon. She had enough money in her bag to hail a hackney. Where she was going to go, she had no idea.

There were many things she was uncertain of, but as she hailed a hackney, there was one thing Sophia knew for certain. She alone held her life in her hands. Now she knew what it was to be free.

Chapter 8

How I envy men their clubs and their pursuits.
Perhaps if our own lives were not so idle,
we women could forget men
as quickly as they seem to forget us.

An Unfortunate Attachment by A Repentant Lady

"**Y**ou are quite possibly the biggest ass I have ever known."

Julian lifted his unseeing gaze from the papers on the desk before him and focused it on the angry young woman standing in the doorway of his study.

"Yes," he replied drily. "I have abused you your entire life. I deny you even the simplest of life's pleasures. I am a tyrant."

She scowled at him, her expression a dark and startling contrast to the cheery yellow gown she wore.

Julian didn't like yellow. It was such an obnoxious color. It seemed to suit Letitia, however. She looked like a tall, slender daffodil against the gray London afternoon.

"That is not what I meant and you know it."

Yes, he did know it, but he had no intention whatsoever of allowing her to make *him* the villain.

"Where have you been?" he asked with deceptive lightness. Inside, he churned with anger, knowing full

142

well with whom she had spent the last several hours. He wanted to hear her say it, so he could then release the emotion raging inside him.

His sister didn't even have the sense to look apologetic. "I was at Lady Wickford's with Sophia."

Sophia. Just the sound of her name was enough to set his heart pounding with betrayal. For the past three days since he'd discovered her deception he had heard of little but her.

There was the laughter, of course, that seemed to follow him wherever he went. People seemed to think it was wonderfully fun to quote certain unflattering passages of her book at him whilst slapping him on the back with false camaraderie.

And then there were those who thought they were showing their alliance to him by making cutting remarks about her and snidely insulting her character. Julian did not respond to their comments, but inside him a war raged. He wanted to hate her but he couldn't, not completely.

"I thought I told you I did not want you seeing her."

Letitia's expression was one of pure rebelliousness. "You did. And I told you I did not care. She is my friend."

Sighing, Julian rubbed a hand over his face. He was so tired of always fighting Letitia. All he wanted was what was best for her, but she didn't see that, not at all.

"Fine," he said, leaning back in his chair. "Do what you want. Just promise me one thing, when you are poised on the brink of ruin, come to me before you drown yourself."

Anguish flickered briefly across his sister's features. "I thought you had accepted that you were not to blame for Miranda's death."

"I have," he replied, running a hand through his hair. "I blame myself for the life leading up to it."

Closing the door, Letitia crossed the carpet and perched herself on the corner of the desk nearest him. "Julian, after Mama and Papa died you did the best you could for both Miranda and me. No one could ever fault you as a brother, or as a parent."

He glanced up at the softly spoken praise. "No? If I was so good, why did Miranda fall prey to such a man? And why do you seem to think that I am some kind of monster out to ruin your life? All I have ever wanted is to see you happy and safe."

Letitia smiled and nudged his leg with her foot. "I know. But Julian, you have to realize that what you think will make me happy and what I think will make me happy are not always going to be the same thing. You have to trust me to live my own life and make my own decisions, just as Miranda did—as confusing and wrong as her decisions were."

Julian stared at her, his chest tight. "I do not want to fail you, Lettie. You are all I have left."

She held out her hand and he took it, squeezing her slender fingers within his own. "You could never fail me. Infuriate me, perhaps, but never fail. However, there is one person you are in very sad danger of failing."

Julian's mouth twisted into a sardonic smile. "Sophia?"

"No. You."

Her words jolted him. "Me?"

She nodded, her expression one of patient amusement. "I have seen how you look at her, Julian. She makes you happy—happier than I have ever known you to be."

"You are mad!" He pulled his hand free of hers and sat up in his chair.

"No, I am not," Letitia replied, in that same gentle tone

that reminded him so much of their mother. "You miss her and she misses you. You should go to her."

Julian leaped to his feet. Rounding his desk, he ploughed both hands through his hair as he strode toward the nearest window.

"And say what? That it does not matter that she lied, or that she has humiliated me a second time? I am sorry, Lettie, but it does matter."

"Any humiliation you feel stems from your own actions, Julian. Yes, Sophia wanted to marry you and yes she wrote that book, but I have asked questions, and I know that your behavior was not much better."

Julian stared out the window. He did not want to think about his own behavior. He could only imagine what Sophia told her.

Letitia hopped off the desk and walked toward him. "Julian, Sophia did not have her book reprinted."

"Then who did?" There was no one else who knew about that dedication. If not for that he could have believed Sophia's innocence, but it really was asking too much of him given the evidence.

"Her brother-in-law, Aberley. He admitted it to Sophia shortly after she left here that day."

Julian couldn't believe his ears. Aberley? How? More important, why? It seemed rather convenient for Sophia to dump the blame in the marquess's lap. Julian already knew him to be a low sort of man, but what could he possibly stand to gain by ruining his brother's widow?

Letitia continued, "He mentioned the dedication specifically. Sophia told me she wrote those words in your copy of the book alone. Julian, that day Aberley came here, could he have seen the book?"

"Of course not—" he stopped. Aberley had been obvious in his scrutiny of his desk that day. Sophia's book had been there, and he had left Charles alone in his study when he left the room.

Oh Christ. It couldn't have been *that* simple, could it? It seemed too fantastical, the idea that Aberley might have picked up the book, opened it and saw the dedication, but it was possible.

Pathetic as he was, he wanted to believe it. He wanted to clear Sophia of all guilt, but it was impossible. It was too small a thing—too much of a coincidence to think that in the few minutes Aberley was in his library, he had found Sophia's book, memorized the inscription and put two and two together.

It would have been easy enough to do if Aberley had also seen Julian's own notations on several pages. And he wouldn't have had to memorize the inscription; it was short enough that he could have written it down.

"Why would he do such a thing?" he asked his sister. "What could he possibly have to gain by ruining his brother's widow in such a fashion?"

"Because of a clause in the late marquess's will," Letitia explained. "He wanted to ruin Sophia."

Julian didn't bother to hide his surprise. "I think you had better tell me everything you know. Start from the beginning."

The story she told him was an amazing one. She told him that Sophia had confided to her little about her marriage other than the fact that Edmund Morelle expected his wife to be a model of propriety, so much so that he had it written into his will that if Sophia ever brought any kind of scandal or shame upon herself and the family that she would be cut off without a penny. The men who were left to decide her fate were Edmund's solicitors and his brother Charles.

"Surely Charles did not need the money," Julian mused out loud. "Why did he want to ruin Sophia?"

Letitia flushed a dark crimson, answering his question without words. A chill crept over Julian's entire body as realization sank through his damnably thick skull.

"He wanted her at his mercy," he whispered, memories of that day at her cottage flooding back unwanted and ugly. He could see Charles forcing Sophia down on the table, and the tears in her eyes as she tried to fight him off.

The bastard had been trying to deprive her into submitting to him, and when that didn't work he'd reverted to physical force.

And then he had been handed the perfect weapon with which to bring Sophia to her knees. And if the information Letitia repeated was correct, then he, Julian, had been the one to give it to him.

"Why was I not told this earlier?" He couldn't help but think this could have been avoided if Sophia had only confided in him.

Letitia's eyes widened. "I have been trying to tell you for the past three days."

Julian shook his head. "Not you. Why did Sophia not tell me about Aberley's machinations herself?"

Folding her arms over her chest, his sister regarded him with a mixture of annoyance and amusement.

"Despite the fact that it was none of your concern, if she had told you, would you have believed her?"

Probably not, no.

Letitia was right. He was an ass. Possibly the biggest in all of England. The question was, what was he going to do about it?

"Where are you going?" Letitia demanded as he strode past her toward the door.

"I'm going to pay Murray a visit," Julian informed her, pausing on the threshold. "He is not only Sophia's publisher, but mine as well. And if he wants any more of my poems, he'll damn well tell me who ordered the reprint of that blasted book."

John Murray was a shrewd-looking man with thinning hair, a long, hooked nose and eyes that saw more than they should. Normally Julian didn't mind having that intrusive gaze fixed upon him, but today was the exception.

"What makes you think anyone wanted the book reprinted?" Murray asked. "Perhaps I made the decision on my own."

Julian arched a brow. Murray might be a good publisher—God knows he had made Julian a small fortune—but as a liar he was poor at best.

"Did you make up that dedication on your own as well?"

Murray smiled affably. "No, but then I think you already knew that." His eyes narrowed. "You know who wrote the book, my lord. The same person wrote the dedication."

Julian's patience was almost at an end. "That is not what I asked. I want to know who came to you about having the book reprinted. Was it So—Lady Aberley?"

Julian held Murray's gaze as the publisher peered into his soul. Finally, Murray nodded. "Yes. It was Lady Aberley who requested the book be reprinted with her name and dedication attached."

Julian sat stock-still, struggling for breath as a band of ice squeezed his heart and lungs. Part of him had known—

even hoped—that his suspicions about Sophia would prove right but that didn't stop it from hurting. It hurt more than he ever could have thought.

"Of course, I did not deal with her directly this time," Murray went on. Julian raised his head, barely hearing him above the roaring in his ears. "The Marquess of Aberley was our go-between. It was he who took care of the business—rightfully so, given his relationship with the marchioness."

The pressure around Julian's heart ceased so suddenly that his heart gave a mighty thump against his ribs. Murray hadn't dealt with Sophia at all. He had dealt with Aberley.

Thanking Murray for his information, Julian took his leave. As he climbed into his carriage, he ordered his driver to continue on to Gray's Inn and the offices of Finch, Barrows and Abercrombie, the Aberley solicitors. He was familiar with the firm, having done business with them in the past. That previous association—and the hundred pounds Julian had offered—made Mr. Barrows very accommodating. After all, the late Marquess of Aberley's will was hardly a *secret*, now was it?

Barrows told Julian everything—and more—that he wanted to know about Edmund Morelle's will. Sophia hadn't lied to Letitia. There was a clause that demanded Sophia keep her behavior within the bounds of propriety or risk being cut off without a cent—a clause the present marquess had been loathe to act upon, of course.

Julian left the office with a very unpleasant taste in his mouth.

What kind of husband would do such a thing to a wife? If he made such demands as a dead man, what had he subjected Sophia to while he was alive? He had killed

Sophia's confidence, her joy, the reckless abandon that Julian had found so contagious and arousing, and turned her into a dim shadow of herself.

But Julian knew the real Sophia was still in there somewhere. When no one else was around, she had shown herself to him. Sophia trusted him enough to be herself with him.

Look at how he had repaid her. He owed her an apology. He thought perhaps he owed her even more than that.

Rapping on the roof of his carriage for his driver to move on, Julian settled back against the squabs with a hard lump in his throat—it was his pride.

And he was going to have a devil of a time swallowing it.

As she stepped into the foyer of the house in Grosvenor Square, Sophia was struck by the realization that no matter how much some things might change, others would forever remain the same. Her parents' house was one of them.

"Well, bless my soul!" The butler, Jenkins, grinned broadly. "Look who has come to call."

Sophia returned the smile, even as the butterflies in her stomach threatened to eat her alive.

"Good day, Jenkins," she greeted as she removed her gloves. "How is Margaret?"

The balding butler's dark eyes twinkled. "Oh, she's very fine, my lady. Just been blessed with her second child."

Sophia had always liked Jenkins and didn't mind having her mission waylaid by small talk. She didn't relish the idea of facing her parents. But she was not a coward—not completely—and so she left Jenkins after hearing about his grandchildren and made the walk to her mother's parlor on her own. She would spare Jenkins the pretense of announcing her. Her mother had no doubt expected her long before this.

Down the narrow hall she walked, her knees trembling with every step. Portraits of disapproving ancestors stared down at her from their pegs high above her head. Only one featured a smiling countenance—that of the fifth Viscountess Haverington. She had been notoriously scandalous her father said. He had compared Sophia to her before marrying her off to Edmund.

She supposed he could have had made a worse comparison. At least the late viscountess seemed happy.

She rapped softly on the door to the parlor.

"Come in."

Drawing a deep breath, Sophia squared her shoulders and turned the knob. It had been Lady Wickford's idea for her to call upon her parents. Sophia would have rather avoided the humiliation all together, but she had little choice. If her parents didn't offer her their support, she would have to find employment. Lady W had offered her hospitality for as long as Sophia wanted it, but she didn't want to be dependent upon the old woman. She didn't want to be dependent upon her father either.

The door swung open, revealing the familiar blue-and-white interior of the little parlor. A quick glance proved that it too remained relatively unchanged. Perhaps there were a few new porcelain figures on the mantel, a new carpet and one or two new chairs, but the room was pretty much the same as it had always been.

Maria Everston looked up as Sophia closed the door behind her. Aside from the fact that her mother was much darker—given her Spanish heritage—it was like looking into an aged mirror. Startled black eyes stared at her, full lips parted in a silent gasp.

"Sophia."

Clasping her hands before her, Sophia clenched her fingers until her knuckles turned white.

"Hello, Mama."

Her mother was everything Sophia would have become had Edmund not wasted to an early death. The daughter of a Spanish aristocrat, she had been a spirited young girl when Viscount Haverington found her. He married her, brought her back to England and set about turning her into the perfect English viscountess.

Her father had succeeded where Edmund failed. But every once in a while, Sophia used to think she saw a glimpse of that girl whenever her mother let her rigid guard down. This was one of those times.

"*Querida!*"

Sophia hadn't felt her mother's arms around her since Edmund's death, and the warmth and strength of her embrace was much more needed now than it had been then.

Fighting the ache in her throat, Sophia gave her mother a quick squeeze before stepping out of her embrace.

Maria's gaze was assessing, yet without judgment. "I heard you were in town. I had hoped to see you sooner, before all this . . . unpleasantness."

Sophia only nodded. What could she say? That if it hadn't been for this "unpleasantness" she might not have called on them at all?

"I meant to come earlier, Mama. I am sorry."

"You are here now. That is all that matters." Her mother seemed to know that she was sorry for more than not coming to visit sooner. She took one of Sophia's hands in hers and tugged her toward the small blue settee by the far bank of windows.

There would be no tea, no cakes to fill the awkward stretches of silence as Sophia struggled to find the courage to ask her mother for help. Maria detested tea, even after all these years of living in England. She liked coffee, strong and black, but only in the morning.

"I have heard rumors, Sophia," her mother said in that deep, musical voice of hers. Her accent was still as strong as it had been when Sophia was a child. "Is it true that Aberley cut you off?"

Sophia nodded, knotting her fingers together in her lap. "It is."

"And is he also responsible for this—" Maria's fingers moved in the air, as though trying to grab the right word. "—this *novel* I have heard about?"

Meeting her mother's gaze at that moment was one of the most difficult things Sophia had ever done. "He is responsible for this new edition, but I have to claim the blame for its existence."

Maria clucked her tongue as she shook her head. There were strands of gray in her ebony hair and new lines around her eyes and mouth. She looked tired and weary.

"Oh, Sophia," was all she said.

Gathering all her courage, Sophia seized the opportunity to appeal to her mother. "I need your help, Mama."

Her mother's head lifted. Her eyes and mouth were grim, but she nodded in acquiescence. "What do you need?"

Sophia's heart beat heavily in her chest. Thank heaven her mother was going to help her. It was as though a tremendous weight had been lifted off her shoulders.

"I need somewhere to stay. Either here with you and Papa, or perhaps the house in Brighton, until the scandal passes. Perhaps a loan so I can go to the Continent or the Americas and start over. I am not certain."

She wasn't either. She had no idea what the future might hold for her, but at the moment, getting as far away from England as possible was definitely appealing.

Her mother nodded. "Whatever you need, you will have it."

Sophia's euphoria was shattered by a voice from the opposite side of the room. "She most assuredly will *not*."

Mortification, hot and as acute as only a child can feel, swept over her. Slowly, unwillingly, she turned her head to face her father as he entered the room.

He was just as imposing as she remembered, but the years had not been kind to Henry Everston. His hair was thinning across the top of his head, revealing the pink scalp beneath, and he was much thinner than Sophia remembered. He looked tired, as though he had not been sleeping well. It wasn't much of a reach to figure out what kept him up at night—the damning look in his eyes said it all.

"Hello, Papa." It was a hoarse, pathetic whisper, but at least she met his gaze when she said it.

His blue eyes narrowed. "I cannot believe you have the nerve to come here, asking your poor mother for assistance after all the shame you have wrought upon this family."

She hated having him look down his nose at her. Defiantly, even though she knew it would not warm him toward her, Sophia stood and faced him directly.

"You are my parents," she replied, her voice stronger than it had been. "Where else am I to go?"

Lord Haverington's expression was as impassive as a

statue's. "Go to your lover. Or did he not appreciate being made such a public spectacle again either?"

"He is not my lover." Why she bothered to explain, she wasn't certain. Her father would never believe her.

"Have you learned nothing?" Haverington demanded, showing more emotion than Sophia had seen in a long time. "Have you no shame, no regard for anyone other than yourself? It was only the good fortune of your marriage that protected your reputation before. You will not be so fortunate again this time."

Sophia stared at him. "You do not know anything about my marriage, sir. Nor do you have the right to decide whether or not I was fortunate in it. You did not care what kind of match it was, only that you would be relieved of the embarrassment of having such a daughter. All you ever cared about was yourself."

Haverington's nostrils flared as he sucked in a deep breath. "You ungrateful child! You are lucky that *anyone* wanted you, let alone a marquess!"

The fight draining out of her, Sophia shook her head. "No, Papa. *You* are lucky that a marquess wanted me. You made a tidy sum off my marriage, I believe."

The viscount's eyes narrowed again. "How much do you want?"

Sophia's breath caught in her throat. "I beg your pardon?"

"Do not play dumb with me, gel. You mentioned money. I know what you are after. Name your price. I will give you what you want, and then I never want to see you again."

God, she couldn't believe her ears! He thought she wanted to extort money from them? Even more disturbing was the thought of a father paying his daughter to stay away from him. Did he think he could control her so easily? It was almost as tempting as it was insulting. All her life she had gone from the control of one man to another. She would not give her father any more power over her.

"I do not want your money. I came here in search of something you cannot give me."

Her father's expression was one of haughty disbelief. "Which is?"

"Love," Sophia replied. "And support. I see now that I came to the wrong place. You are not capable of giving me either."

Her father sputtered. "I raised you, didn't I? Put a roof over your head, fed you. Saw you well married, didn't I?"

Well married? Is that how he saw it? Just because Edmund had a title and a fortune he was supposed to be a good husband? Dimly, she wondered if that's how Julian viewed his selections for Letitia. God, she hoped not.

"You sold me to a man who saw me as something to display to his friends. He degraded and mocked me at every turn. No, Papa, you most assuredly did *not* see me well married."

She didn't even take the time to enjoy his stupefied stare. Instead, she turned to her mother, kissed her cheek and gave her a quick hug. Maria tried to hold on to her, whispered for her not to go, but Sophia shook her head. She wasn't going to stay another moment in this man's house.

She was almost to the door when his voice called to her. "If you want my money, you had best take it now, because you will not be allowed into this house again."

Turning, Sophia saw her mother try to speak, but her father silenced her with a look.

"I am staying with Lady Wickford, Mama. I would like very much to see you again."

Haverington flushed at her blatant defiance. "I mean it. Do not show your face here again. You are not my daughter."

Sophia smiled coolly. "Thank you, my lord. It makes me very happy to know I no longer have to claim you as my father."

Leaving him gaping after her, Sophia pivoted on her heel and left the room with as much dignity as her trembling knees would allow. For the second time in her life she left her father's house, but this time she had no intention of ever coming back.

"Is there anything Gabriel and I can do?"

Standing in an alcove of Lady Penderthal's crowded ballroom, Sophia shook her head, smiling at Lilith's concern.

"A position at your club would be lovely, but I cannot expect you and Lord Angelwood to get involved—not when he is such good friends with Julian." She was not nearly as casual as she sounded. She could not live without an income. A small one would do—she was used to being thrifty.

But no one would hire her. She had scandal attached to her. No one wanted her for a governess for fear of what she'd teach their daughters. No one wanted her as a lady's maid because she was "too attractive." And she wasn't skilled to do anything else. Her sewing was atrocious, her musical ability nonexistent. If it weren't for her pride, she would be very tempted to go back to her father and beg him to give her the money he had offered two days ago.

But she would no sooner go crawling back to him than she would Julian.

"Have you seen Julian at all?" she asked, giving into her weak-willed curiosity.

"No." Lilith shook her head. "I know Gabriel has been to see him several times, but he has not dared to show his face to me, and perhaps that is for the best. I would be sorely tempted to give him a piece of my mind, and that would only upset Gabe. You?"

"No." She had seen Letitia several times however. "I have not seen him since the day he asked me to leave his house."

Lilith's expression was dark. "I cannot believe he tossed you out without giving you a chance to explain!"

Shrugging, Sophia took a sip of her champagne. Being scandalous was different now that she was a widow. Not everyone had excluded her from their guest lists. In fact, hostesses like Lady Penderthal seemed to think it exciting to have her attend their functions. It gave people something to talk about other than the refreshments.

"He believes I publicly humiliated him." She swirled her glass, watching the bubbles pop as she did so. "I wish I had. Perhaps then we would be even."

"So by flaunting yourself in public, you hope to dig the knife in a little bit farther in retaliation, is that it?"

Was she that transparent? A hot flush crept up her cheeks at the thought of being so easily discovered. Yes, a part of her wanted Julian to know that she wasn't sitting at Lady W's lamenting the loss of him. She wanted him to know that she was being seen at parties and at balls, looking for all the world like she hadn't a care.

In truth, she had too many cares. She couldn't possibly impose upon Lady Wickford much longer, but short of becoming a courtesan, she had little options. Her hope was so lowered that she had seriously given thought to Lord Phillip's offer to make her his mistress. He was attractive and he seemed good-natured enough. He would probably make a very fine protector, but then he would own her, and that was unacceptable.

"Perhaps I am trolling for a husband," Sophia remarked with mock lightness. "That would certain put an end to my problems."

Lilith rolled her gray green eyes. "And give you a whole set of new ones. Seriously, Sophie, what are you going to do?"

"I have no idea." It was the truth and it was terrifying. The bane of being a gently bred female. She was totally hapless without money or a man.

"If only I had been born to the lower classes I might be able to find work somewhere." She flashed a self-deprecating grin.

"You could always start your own business," Lilith suggested. "I could back you."

Sophia was touched by her friend's support. She reached out and gave one of Lilith's gloved hands a firm squeeze. "Thank you. You are such a good friend, but it would not be a worthy investment for you. I cannot do anything."

A highly arched brow rose even farther on Lilith's smooth forehead. "You could write another book."

Choking on a mouthful of champagne, Sophia coughed and sputtered and took the handkerchief Lilith offered to wipe her eyes.

"That is what got me into this mess!" She exclaimed around coughs.

Lilith's shoulders lifted in a delicate shrug. "So it

stands to reason that another could get you out of it, does it not?"

Another sip of champagne smoothed the roughness in Sophia's throat. "I would be no better a writer than I would be a mistress. In fact, I think I would rather be a mistress. At least then I would not be required to think."

Lilith laughed at her caustic tone. "And who would you choose for a protector?"

"Yes," came a deep, unmistakable voice from behind Sophia, sending a shiver of awareness all the way down to the base of her spine. "Who?"

Chapter 9

*"Some young ladies put as much effort into shopping
as they do into finding a husband."*
Lady Eloise smiled. "Is it not the same thing? A new hat.
A new husband. My dear Jocelyn, what is the difference?"
*"You cannot simply toss out a husband
when his brim begins to droop."*
"No. But you can give him to the upstairs maid."

An Unfortunate Attachment by the Marchioness of Aberley

For one split second, Julian considered walking away.
It was foolhardy of him to approach her in such a
public place, but he knew she would not receive him if he
went to Lady Wickford's to see her. Here, she could not
run away without making a scene.

And he truly wanted to know whose mistress she
might agree to be. The idea of another man touching her
was enough to ignite his temper. A part of him had laid
claim to her a long time ago and it wasn't prepared to
give it up.

Her eyes were like smoldering embers beneath the
chandeliers. The light shimmered and flickered in the
ebony depths, making it seem as though the glow came
from within her rather than from ceiling above. Clad in a
rose silk gown with little rosettes on the sleeves and hem,

161

her flesh warm and creamy in the blazing light, she looked as fresh as a morning blossom. A rush of erotic flower analogies flooded Julian's mind—things like flushed petals opening for him, dew on his lips and fingers. They were foolish and far too poetic, even for him, but his prick didn't seem to care. It stirred uncomfortably in his trousers.

Sophia took care of his arousal in short fashion. "I am afraid, Lord Wolfram, that any protector I may or may not choose is no concern of yours."

If words were spears she would have impaled him to the wall with the sharpness of her tone. Even Lilith, someone he thought of as a friend, shot daggers at him with her stormy eyes. It hadn't occurred to him that sides might be taken, but so far, Sophia's side was much more effective— Lilith, Lady W and Letitia. Three women who figured prominently in Julian's life, all of whom had no trouble telling him exactly what kind of idiot they thought he was. Wonderful.

"You are right," he conceded, rather than thumping his chest and insisting that she was his. His gaze jumped to the other woman. "Good evening, Lilith."

Jaw tight, Lilith bobbed a stiff curtsey. "Julian."

"I wonder if you might excuse Lady Aberley and myself for a moment?"

Sophia opened her mouth, but Lilith beat her to it. "I do not think—"

"There you are, my dear!"

Julian smiled as Gabriel strode toward his wife, a bright grin curving his lips. Lilith might have chosen Sophia's side, but Gabe was still on his. If Lilith wouldn't give Julian a chance to speak to Sophia alone then Gabriel would provide a little persuasion.

"Come dance with me before I have to take you home," Gabriel coaxed, taking his wife by the hand.

Lilith was obviously not impressed. The pale expanse of her chest revealed by the neckline of her dark green gown flushed a hot pink. "Gabriel, I told you there is no need for us to leave so early."

"And I told you I do not want you to overextend yourself." Gabriel's gray gaze was so full of love as it rested upon his wife that Julian was almost embarrassed to watch. A sliver of jealousy added to his discomfort. He envied them their happiness and their love. He wanted someone to share tender glances with.

He looked at Sophia. She was glaring at him.

If he was going to make his move it would have to be now. As it was, people were already beginning to watch them.

"We need to talk."

Her nostrils flared ever so slightly as she lifted her chin. "I have nothing to say to you."

His lips curved at one corner. "Ah, but I have plenty to say to you."

"That I do not doubt," she replied, her tone as warm as the Thames in January, "but do not think I have any desire to hear it. Good night, Lord Wolfram."

He watched impotently as she walked away, unable to stop her without handing the gossips more fodder. Damnation, but she had spirit. *This* was his Sophia. She walked away without hearing what he had to say, even though she must surely sumise that he knew the truth about the book by now. She wanted nothing to do with him, and he couldn't help but admire her for it.

But that did not mean he was prepared to let her just

walk away. He had come there tonight in order to apologize and he would do that, if for no other reason than to appease his own guilt. He did not mind the idea of lowering himself, not when it would light her eyes with such surprise.

He turned to excuse himself from Gabriel and Lilith, but they were already gone. A quick survey of the dance floor revealed them weaving in and out amongst the other couples, their movements a more languid version of the waltz being performed around them. Lilith still looked mildly perturbed with her husband and Gabriel seemed to be enjoying it. There was nothing more stimulating for a man than to have a contest of wills with a woman. It was the modern, civilized version of the hunt.

Out of the corner of his eye, Julian caught a glimpse of his own prey leaving the ballroom. Winding his way through the crowd so as not to attract any unwanted attention, he followed her. Sophia could make him a villain if she wanted, but he was not going to make it easy for her. He owed her an apology and she was going to hear it. She was also going to hear his offer of assistance. If she chose not to take it that was her own concern, not his. What happened to her after that was none of his concern.

It would be the concern of whatever gentleman she chose to become her protector.

He'd kill any man who dared touch her.

He stepped out of the ballroom into the corridor. A dozen sconces lit the area, allowing him to see down both sides. A flash of rose disappearing into a room to the left caught his attention. The soft click of a latch followed. It was Sophia, he was certain of it.

Hoping that it wasn't the ladies' retiring room that she had ducked into, Julian moved swiftly down the corridor.

Glancing over his shoulder to make certain there was no one around, he clasped his fingers around the glass knob and turned.

The door opened to reveal not a ladies' withdrawing room but a small library. In the dim lamplight, Julian could see the walls were lined with books and maps. A heavy globe of the world sat in one corner and the air smelled faintly of musty books and pipe tobacco.

Sophia stood with her back to him, staring out one of the windows behind the desk on the far wall. She turned as he closed the door behind him. The one sconce in the room was on the wall beside her and Julian could see her shock as plain as day.

"What are you doing here?" she demanded.

He stepped forward. "I followed you."

Dark eyes narrow, she watched him like a mouse watching a hawk. "I do not want to be anywhere near you."

He deserved her anger but it still stung. He gestured to the door behind him. "Go ahead and leave then."

"I was here first. *You* should be the one to leave." As if realizing how childish she sounded, she shrugged indifferently. "Besides, you are blocking the door."

Julian smiled. "Then it appears you have a bit of a problem, does it not?"

Judging from the tightness of her jaw she obviously didn't share his humor. "My reputation has been damaged enough, Lord Wolfram. I do not need to add being caught alone with you to it."

"I do not wish to add further damage to either of our reputations."

"Then why are you here?"

"I told you, I want to speak with you."

She folded her arms beneath her breasts. If she had known how the gesture accentuated the deep valley of her cleavage she never would have done it. "I believe you said enough the day you threw me out of your house."

He kept his gaze fastened on her face. "That is what I want to talk about."

"I cannot imagine what you could possibly have left to say."

"If you would just kindly shut up for a moment I would tell you."

Oddly enough, she fell silent.

"I want to apologize." He moved further into the room, watching as her eyebrows rose in shock. "I reacted badly when I discovered your dedication in the book. In my mind there was no one but you who could have been responsible. When Letitia told me of the clause in your husband's will and Aberley's . . . interest in you, I realized what I mistake I had made. I am very aware of your current situation and I want you to know that I will offer any assistance within my power."

There. He had said it. It was done.

Sophia stared at him. "Thank you, but I am not your responsibility. Nor do you owe me an apology for your assumption. It was the logical conclusion, one I would have made had I been in your position."

Julian shook his head. He couldn't have heard her correctly. "You do not blame me?"

Her lips twisted into a faint bitter smile. "Not for reacting as you did, no."

Something in her tone made him ask, "But you do blame me for something. What?"

Her arms still folded protectively in front of her, Sophia

leaned one hip against the side of the desk. The fabric of her dress pulled taut, outlining the generous curve.

"I blame you for making me believe things had changed between us, that you actually held me in some kind of regard. I thought that even if you didn't quite trust me you might at least respect me. I was wrong."

Her words cut him to the very quick even as he rebelled against them. "Why do you think I reacted as I did, Sophia? It was because *I* thought things had changed between us. I did—do—respect you. I had no reason to suspect Aberley of such deceit. If the book hadn't contained that dedication I would not have made the conclusions that I did."

She didn't reply. Frustration kindled in Julian's gut. Surely she saw the truth in his words? Surely she could see his side as he saw hers? He had hurt her badly, but could she not see how deeply he had been wounded as well?

Finally she nodded. The gesture was painfully defeated and it tore at Julian's heart.

"I felt so foolish," she whispered. "I thought—"

He pulled her into his arms and kissed her before she could finish. He didn't want to know what she had thought. He didn't want to hear any more about how he had let her down or what expectations she had harbored toward him. His entire life had been filled with expectations and trying to live up to them, and so far he didn't think he had done a very good job. That was why it was so important to him to see Letitia well married, at least then he would have done his duty by her. But he didn't want to hear any more about how he had disappointed Sophia. He couldn't take it.

Her lips parted beneath his. He felt rather than heard

her gasp as he grazed her with his teeth, slipping his tongue into the champagne sweetness of her mouth. Sophia's arms unfolded between them and came up to twine around his neck. The tempting fullness of her body pressed against his, bringing him to full arousal with the promise of all it offered.

Julian splayed his fingers across her back, the silk of her gown warm and light against his palms. One hand slid down her spine, along the gentle dip above her buttocks to cup the generous swell of flesh there. He wanted to feel this part of her naked in his hands, to squeeze and knead the ripe curves as he drove himself inside her.

He wanted all of her. He wanted to press her legs apart and delve into her heat. He wanted her mouth, her hands, her slick cove, all of it wrapped around him. He wanted it hot and urgent and he didn't give a damn about finesse. He didn't want to make love, but he didn't want a mindless coupling either. He wanted something more. Something that scared him. He wanted to make himself a part of Sophia Morelle and he wanted to make her a part of him.

He had her pinned against the desk, one hand cupping her breast, fumbling for the hardness of her nipple through the fabric of her gown, the other rucking her skirts in an attempt to get underneath when the soft click of the door latch reverberated like a shot through his desire-fogged mind.

Sophia heard it too. The soft cradle of her thighs tensed like a vice around his.

"Not again!" Her voice was little more than a breathy anguished whisper against his lips, but Julian heard it as clearly as a scream. He almost chuckled at the irony—in fact he probably would have were it not for the acute frustration throbbing between his legs. He and Sophia were about to be discovered in the most compromising of circumstances for the second time in their lives.

At least now there would be no one demanding he marry her.

Sophia pushed him away as the door opened.

"Oh, I did not—pray excuse me."

Julian closed his eyes in annoyance. Their intruder was Leander Fitzroy, Lord Patterson—one of the young men vying for Letitia's hand.

Sophia rushed from the room with a muffled cry. Patterson had to step further into the room so she could pass. Both men watched her go.

The whole situation had done much to cool Julian's ardor. He didn't even have to clasp his hands in front of his groin as he faced the young viscount.

"I assume I can trust you not to mention this incident to anyone else?"

Patterson regarded him coolly. He was in his late twenties, with a kind face and light brown hair. He also possessed a moral air that Julian had never noticed before now.

"Of course," he replied.

"Good." Nothing more needed to be said and Julian wished to remove himself from the room, from the entire house as quickly as possible.

"Lord Wolfram." Patterson's voice stopped him before he reached the door.

Julian regarded the younger man over his shoulder. "Yes?"

Patterson swallowed. "It is not my place to pass judgment on you—"

"You have that right," Julian growled, suddenly in a very foul temper.

Patterson was undaunted. "But I cannot condone your treatment of Lady Aberley. I have no knowledge of the circumstances surrounding your relationship, but I have heard rumors. And now I have seen for my own eyes how you and the marchioness herself willfully disregard her reputation and social standing."

"What exactly are you saying, Patterson?" Julian demanded with a scowl.

The viscount lifted his chin in an imperious manner. "A true gentleman would marry her, my lord, and cease playing fast and loose with what little good name she has left."

Julian laughed harshly. As if this pup could possibly understand his relationship with Sophia. Patterson probably had no idea what it was like to lose all reason where a woman was concerned.

"You do not know me well enough to tell me what I should do, Patterson."

"No, I do not. But I have seen enough to know that I have no desire to form an alliance with a man who would behave so appallingly toward a lady. I am withdrawing my suit for Lady Letitia."

Julian couldn't believe his ears. "What?"

Straightening his shoulders, Patterson fixed him with a cold gaze. "As charming as your sister is, I cannot help but wonder if perhaps this kind of behavior runs in your family. Might I remind you of the scandal surrounding your other sister—"

"You may not!" Damnation, but the little bastard would be lucky if Julian didn't knock his teeth down his throat!

Obviously Patterson realized how close he was to having bodily harm done because he chose that moment to skirt past Julian to the door.

"I am not the only one questioning the risks of align-
ing with your family, Lord Wolfram. Do not think for a
moment that your actions do not affect your sister. If you
have any regard for her future at all, you will set a better
example yourself."

Julian watched the viscount leave with a mixture of
rage and disbelieving amusement. For the second time in
his life someone was telling him it was his duty to marry
Sophia.

And this time, they were right.

"Staring out the window will not bring him any sooner."

Smiling, Sophia turned. Lady Wickford glided into the
parlor much like a frigate into port—a frigate in a big,
feathered turban, pearls and a gray silk dress.

"What makes you think I am watching for someone?"

Lady W lowered herself into a delicate armchair and
smiled at Sophia. "While I believe I can boast one of the
loveliest drives in all of London, it is not worthy of the
study you have given it this morning."

No, it was not. Leaving the window, Sophia moved
across the bronze and gold Axminster carpet and sat down
in a chair close to her friend's. Thank heaven for Lady
Wickford. The older woman hadn't even blinked an eye
when Sophia arrived on her doorstep asking for a place to
stay. She had no idea what she would have done had Lady
W not taken her in.

It would be so easy to stay here, to remain in the warm
cocoon of Lady Wickford's hospitality, but Sophia was
not a beggar. She would find her own way. She had to.

"Be patient my dear," the older woman instructed, fid-
dling with one of the many pearl ropes around her neck.
"He will come eventually."

Somewhere over the course of the past few days Julian had ceased to have a name. He was simply "he" or "him." She had no idea how Lady W knew it was him she was watching for, nor did she bother to ask. The old woman was right. After seeing—kissing—Julian at the Penderthal ball she had thought of nothing but him and the foolish desire to see him again, even though she knew it would be best for the two of them to stay as far apart as possible.

What if the gentleman who walked in on them told what he had seen? She would be branded the loosest of women. She would have to leave the country if she wanted a new life.

"I do not care if he comes at all," Sophia responded, straightening the cuff of her bottle green morning gown.

"I wager my mother's pearls he will be here by tea time," Lady W announced.

Sophia raised both brows. "All of them?" Lady W's mother had owned *a lot* of pearls.

The older, portly woman laughed heartily. "All of them!"

Smiling, Sophia wondered which end of the wager she'd rather be on, the losing or the winning. If Julian came to her as part of her so desperately wished, what would she do? She'd just had her first taste of freedom, and as frightening as it was, she embraced the idea of being able to live her life exactly as she wanted and not by someone else's rules.

There was a knock at the door. Lady Wickford's housekeeper stepped inside. "Begging your pardon, my ladies, but a letter just arrived for the marchioness."

"Thank you," Sophia said, taking the letter from the small silver tray the woman offered her. Was it from Julian? Somehow she didn't think it was. Julian might be a lot of things—ruinous was the first thing that came to mind—but he wasn't what she would ever consider a coward.

"Would you like me to leave you alone with your letter?" Lady Wickford asked once the housekeeper had left.

Sophia smiled thankfully at her friend as she popped the unfamiliar wax seal on the back of the letter. "Of course not. I have nothing to conceal from you."

Opening the folded parchment, Sophia looked down at the spidery handwriting there. Her heart accelerated at the sight of it, but not from excitement, not from happiness.

It was from Charles. He must have deliberately used a seal other than the Aberley insignia to insure her opening the letter.

My dear Sophia:

I have heard the reports of your behavior at certain social functions you have attended recently. I do believe you are slowly proving my brother correct—you do need a firm hand to guide you. How long do you reckon Lady Wickford will support you if you succeed in making an even bigger spectacle of yourself? Then where will you go? My patience wears thin. Come to me soon and I will make certain you have all the comfort you could ever wish for. Deny me and you deny yourself. Say the word and you can have the life you were meant to have.

Yours, Charles

Sophia trembled with rage. "The arrogance!"
Lady Wickford looked up. "Is it from Wolfram?"

Normally, her friend's wry remark would have coaxed a chuckle from Sophia, but not at this moment.

"It is from Charles. Apparently there is still time for me to come to my senses and become his mistress."

Lady W's round face lost all of its usual good humor. "I sorely wish that man would go to perdition where he belongs and leave you alone."

Shrugging, Sophia tossed the letter into the low fire burning in the hearth. "He will eventually realize that I will never be his." As dismal as her prospects seemed, she would never give in. Never.

"For some men, that realization is a long time coming, my dear." Lady W's voice had the heavy certainty of someone who knew firsthand.

Sophia smiled at her friend. "I can resist the Marquess of Aberley for the rest of my life if necessary."

"What about Wolfram?" the older woman asked with as sly smile. "Can you resist him as well?"

"That is a moot question. One cannot resist what is not there to pose a temptation." But last night! Last night Julian Rexley had been temptation personified.

As if on cue, there was another knock at the door and the housekeeper entered again. "The Earl Wolfram is here, my lady Wickford."

Stunned, Sophia stared at Lady W.

The older woman shot Sophia a triumphant glance. "Send him in, Mrs. Long."

"Did you plan this?" Sophia hissed once they were alone again.

Lady Wickford was all innocence. "My dear, you know me better than that. I may have urged Wolfram to bring you to London, but I would never dream of interfering in such a manner." Her smile grew. "No, the boy is here of his own accord."

Her heart pounding embarrassingly fast, Sophia curled her hands into fists. Her nails bit into her palms as she tried to keep her breathing from becoming too shallow and erratic.

Julian. He was here. He came.

She barely had time to wrap her mind around the realization before he walked into the room. Surrounded by the delicate furnishings of Lady W's parlor he was breathtakingly masculine and undeniably the most beautiful man she had ever laid eyes on.

He was dressed in snug buff breeches that hugged the long, athletic lines of his legs, black boots, a biscuit-colored waistcoat and a coat of dark brown superfine that pulled smoothly across the breadth of his shoulders. In this light his hair was a deep, rich brown with just a hint of auburn and his eyes were a clear, pale sherry.

They bore into her as though trying to read her very soul.

"Wolfram!" Lady Wickford cried, rising to her feet. "What a pleasure to see you!"

He said something about the pleasure being all his as Lady W engulfed him in a warm embrace.

Sophia also stood, despite the fact that her knees threatened to dump her to the floor at any minute.

He had no right to affect her as he did. No right at all. The fluttering in her stomach was nothing compared to the absolute joy in her breast. And neither were brought about by fear. They were because of this strange attachment she felt for him.

Had he spent the night reliving their kiss as she had?

Had he spent the early dawn hours trying to figure out just what this attraction between them meant? It was overpowering and dangerous. It made her forget everything else— such as the fact that Julian Rexley was as deserving of her trust as a snake. That he was a man determined to have the world play by his rules.

Her gaze locked with his, Sophia spied Lady Wickford out of the corner of her eye. The older woman was watching the pair of them with great interest.

"Well," the older woman said after a moment of pregnant silence. "I suppose the two of you have much to discuss. I shall leave you to it."

Sophia watched her friend for as long as she could, until the door closed softly behind her, leaving only Sophia and Julian in the room. Alone.

Slowly, she turned to face him, meeting his suffering gaze with an expression that she hoped was much, much blander than she felt.

"I will get right to the point," he said quickly. "I have come to ask you to marry me."

She could not have been more surprised if he had told her he was dying. Blindly, Sophia's hand reached out for something to support her as the ground shifted beneath her. Unfortunately, Julian was the closest thing to latch onto. Her fingers grabbed the left lapel of his coat and clung to it with every last ounce of strength she possessed.

"Why?" she demanded, trying to calm the pounding of her heart.

He looked at her as though he thought the answer should be obvious. "It would certainly remedy your current situation, would it not?"

Or put her in the middle of an even worse one, depending on the bridegroom. But Julian hadn't suggested marriage in general. He had offered himself as her husband. Why?

She frowned. "Marriage might prove to be a 'remedy' as you put it, but why are *you* asking me?"

He thought for a moment. "Because you will be able to continue living the kind of life you were born into."

No more smokey fires and creaking floors. But she had gotten used to creaking floors. She didn't need opulence and riches anymore. Besides, Julian wasn't asking her out of some misplaced sense of charity. He thought too much of his own freedom to do that. "Not good enough. Give me a reason, Julian. A real one."

He regarded her strangely, and for a split second Sophia was terrified he could see into her soul and know that she didn't want to hear why she should marry him. She wanted to know why he wanted to marry her.

"Is this a good enough reason?" he asked, lowering his head.

Closing her eyes, Sophia sighed as his lips touched hers. Soft and warm, yet firm and unyielding, his mouth claimed her. Her fingers tightened on his lapel, pulling him closer as her other hand slid up the solid wall of his chest and higher, to tangle in the thick waves of his hair.

She opened her mouth to him as his arms closed around her, hauling her flush against him, lifting her up onto her toes. His tongue swept inside her mouth, tasting her as she tasted him. He tasted of heat and salt with the faintest touch of brandy.

His torso was warm and firm against the softness of her breasts, his pelvis pushed against her stomach, the evidence of his arousal becoming more and more apparent as their kiss continued.

Moaning softly, Sophia shivered and pressed closer,

running the ridge of her tongue along his. Not even Edmund, who had known her body more intimately than she, had been able to elicit this kind of fevered response from her. Her body thrummed with sensual awareness. Her flesh craved touch—so much so that her clothes felt restrictive and abrasive against her skin. She burned all over from a volcano of desire that simmered low and deep within her.

Oh yes, this was a very good reason for the two of them to marry.

But would it last? And what price would come attached to it?

Opening the fingers holding his jacket, Sophia placed her palm against his chest and pushed, stepping back as she did so. The kiss was broken, even though Julian did not immediately release her.

"That was lovely," she told him, her voice hoarse with desire. "But even that is not enough for me to marry you. Tell me the truth, Julian. Please."

Tilting his head to one side, his gaze roamed over her entire face, from her tingling lips, up her burning cheeks, to finally stare her straight in the eye.

"Because this does not affect just you and me anymore. Someone else stands to be hurt by my actions and it is time I took responsibility for them."

"Letitia," she said softly, knowing his sister was the only person he would make such a sacrifice for. The knowledge hurt.

"The gentleman who found us last night was one of the young men interested in marrying Letitia. He has withdrawn his suit because of my treatment of you."

Sophia's eyes widened. "Your treatment of me?" If anything she thought it might be his association with her—the fact that she was viewed to have such loose morals.

"You are not the only one with a blackened reputation, Sophia," he told her with a faint smile. "My refusal to marry you was a mark against me as well. Patterson viewed last night's . . . indiscretion as just one more example of how little respect I have for your reputation. In a way he was right."

It was all so hard for Sophia to absorb. "R . . . right?"

He brushed his lips across her forehead, down to her temple. It was so soft, so light a caress, that Sophia's breath halted with it. It was as if he couldn't help himself.

"I have very little control where you are concerned, Sophia." His breath was warm against her cheek. "All I can think about is you and how much I want you."

Heart hammering, thighs trembling, Sophia raised her gaze to his as he lifted his head. She knew exactly what he meant. It might not be much to build a marriage on, but he was right about their actions reflecting upon Letitia. She would rather die than hurt the young woman who had become much like a sister to her. Letitia might like the idea of her suitors ceasing to court her, but what if Mr. Wesley or his family decided the better of such connections? What if Sophia's reputation began to tarnish Letitia's? She would never forgive herself.

"My husband tried to mold me into his idea of the perfect wife." It was humiliating to even admit that much of her marriage to Edmund to him. "I do not want to go through that again. I will not."

One of the hands on her back lifted to come around and cup her cheek. His thumb stroked the expanse of cheek just below her eye. "I want you as you are, not as you could be."

Sophia's stomach clenched. He wanted her? And not just sexually, but as a person? As a wife?

"Neither of us is perfect," he continued, "but we will be going into this marriage with a lot more than some *ton* marriages have. I will be a good husband to you. I promise to respect you and give you the trust you deserve. All I ask is that you offer me the same."

Silence permeated the room as they stared into each other's eyes. "Please, Sophia. You and I will never outrun our past if we do not do this. Please do not make my sister pay for my mistakes."

It was the *please* that was her undoing. That softly spoken plea helped Sophia find her voice. It came from deep within her, from her heart and soul, from the very tips of her toes. It was the voice of that girl who had taken one look at Julian Rexley and knew that she had never wanted anything as much as she wanted him.

"Yes."

Chapter 10

"You do not mean to marry him!"
Jocelyn had never been a young woman given to half-
truths and empty promises. "I most certainly do.
I am his for the asking. If only he would ask."

An Unfortunate Attachment by the Marchioness of Aberley

She was early.

"Lord Wolfram is in the ballroom, Lady Aberley," Fielding informed her as she stepped inside the foyer. "Shall I announce you?"

Sophia smiled. "That will not be necessary, Fielding, thank you." Was Julian alone in the ballroom? Was he making plans for their wedding?

Fielding returned the smile. There was a twinkle in his eyes that puzzled Sophia. It was as though there was some kind of private joke between them, one that Sophia wasn't aware of.

"As you wish, my lady," he replied with a bow. "And might I say that it is lovely to have you at Wolfram House again."

Whether the butler was being honest or simply polite, Sophia didn't know, but she appreciated the sentiment all the same.

Thanking Fielding, she strolled into the great hall,

across the gleaming tiled floor to the hallway that led toward the back of the house, slipping her moist hands out of her gloves as she went.

She still couldn't quite believe that Julian had proposed, or that she had said yes. She had meant to refuse him, but how could she when faced with the prospect of hurting Letitia? And a part of her wanted to marry him. She could admit that, if only to herself.

And now she wondered if she had made the right decision, because it seemed that every decision she made that concerned Julian was the wrong one. That was why she was an hour early for dinner, and why she was dressed in a new gown of dark plum silk that warmed her skin and enhanced her figure. She needed to see Julian. Needed to see for herself if he was having second thoughts.

And she needed to see Letitia. She hadn't seen her friend since Julian proposed two days earlier. She'd received a lovely note but no visit, and that hurt more than she was willing to admit. Did her friend disapprove of Sophia marrying her brother?

One of the pairs of French doors leading into the ballroom was partially open. Slightly breathless voices drifted wordlessly into the corridor. One of them Sophia recognized as Julian's. The other she didn't recognize. A loud grunt followed the sound of something being struck.

Wide-eyed, Sophia slowly pushed the door open even further. She peered inside.

A large, square, roped-off ring sat in the middle of the ballroom floor. It was startlingly out of place amongst the Italian marble tiles and delicate plasterwork.

Light from the sinking sun poured in through the many windows lining the walls, bathing the room and the men in the middle of the ring in a golden-pink hue.

The men were naked from the waist up, their skin aglow with sweat, circling each other with their fists raised.

One of the men was of average height and heavily built, with a thick chest, big arms and wide shoulders. His head was as smooth and bald as a pebble on a beach, but his chest, back and arms were covered in so much hair it almost looked like fur.

Her gaze went to the other man. To Julian. Dear heaven.

While not as thickly built as his opponent—nor as hairy—Julian Rexley was still a sight to behold. His long, muscular arms lashed out with lightning-fast accuracy. Muscles rippled beneath the smooth golden skin of his back as he dodged the meaty fists of his adversary.

Slipping into the room, Sophia inched closer, her gaze fastened on Julian's chest and the reddish brown hair that tapered down the flat plain of his stomach and disappeared beneath the waist of his trousers.

She'd waited seven years to see him with his clothes off, and while he still had his trousers on, Sophia knew the rest of him would be just as dry-mouthed beautiful as the rangy, whipcord perfection bared to her now.

For a moment, all her misgivings about marrying him disappeared, and yet her anxiety seemed to double tenfold. How would that body feel against her own nakedness? What would it be like to feel those muscles bunch and tighten beneath her hands?

But the beauty of Julian's body made Sophia all the more aware of how imperfect her own was. She was short and soft and round and things weren't quite as . . . pert as they had once been. Would Julian find her lacking, or would he like what he saw?

His opponent swung his left arm, the meaty fist flying at Julian with terrifying speed. It seemed certain that it would connect with Julian's face. At the last second Julian dodged the blow, landing one of his own on the shorter man's midriff. Sophia gasped out loud at the near miss.

She should have kept quiet. Her gasp was just loud enough to grab Julian's attention. Foolishly, he turned his head to glance at her, his expression as surprised as hers must have been. That split-second lapse in his attention was his undoing. The other man's fist came up and connected with his jaw. Julian's head flew back as he stumbled into the side of the ring, catching himself on the rope to keep from falling.

Hands over her face, Sophia cried out in horror. Oh, dear God, Julian was hurt and it was all her fault!

She raced toward the ring. Julian's opponent was already helping him to his feet, apologizing profusely. Julian shook him off.

"It is not your fault, Harper," he replied, pressing a hand to the side of his mouth.

"No," Sophia agreed, standing at the foot of the ring directly below them. She gazed up at Julian, hoping he could see how sorry she was. "It is mine. Forgive me, Julian."

"It is not your fault either." His tone was gruff. "'Tis mine for losing my concentration."

Picking up a small towel, Julian dabbed at the corner of his mouth with it. It came away bloody. Sophia cringed at the sight of it.

"That will be all for today, thank you, Harper."

"Same time next week, my lord?"

"No." Julian's gaze locked briefly—hotly—with Sophia's. "I am to be married next week. I will send for you when I am ready."

The burly Harper nodded. After congratulating Julian on his upcoming marriage, he gathered up his belongings and departed, leaving Sophia alone with her half-naked fiancé.

He didn't bother to put on a shirt as he ducked beneath the ropes and stepped down to the floor in front of her. The heat of him rushed at her, carrying the scent of him with it. Sweat, soap and that beguiling spicy sweetness that was Julian invaded her senses, throwing her equilibrium horribly off balance.

"I am sorry," she said, nodding at the blood-spotted towel in his fist.

He held it to his mouth again and looked at it as he pulled it away. There was hardly any blood this time.

"I should not have lost my concentration." He watched her for a moment, his expression so guarded Sophia couldn't even begin to guess at what he was thinking. "You are early."

Should she make something up or should she just be honest and stop this foolish wondering that had plagued her ever since he'd come to see her at Lady W's.

Honesty won out. Not so much because it was a good way to start earning his trust, but because she couldn't stand herself any longer.

"I wanted to give you a chance to change your mind before we announce our betrothal. You can still walk away from this if you wish."

She held her breath as he stared at her, his face and gaze completely expressionless. Was he trying to find the words to tell her he didn't want her after all? In some ways it would be a relief. In others it would be a devastation.

"Is that what you want?" he asked finally, taking a step toward her. "To walk away?"

Sophia raised a hand between them. Whether it was to touch him or ward him off, she wasn't certain.

"I—" She faltered as he took another step toward her, pressing the hairy warmth of his chest to her palm. She could feel his heart beating beneath her hand, feel the heat of his body on her fingers. His own hand came up and covered hers, holding it against him.

"No," she whispered, painfully, honestly. "I do not want to walk away." She didn't want to look away either. Her gaze remained locked on the strong, red-knuckled hand holding hers, on the golden flesh that made her own seem white and bland.

"Do you like what you see?" he asked, his voice a low, rough purr.

I love it.

The words, unwanted and unbidden, sprang to Sophia's tongue so quickly it was all she could do to keep them from spilling out. It was more truth than she was willing to own at this moment.

Raising her gaze to his, she looked deep into those pale, golden brown eyes for the arrogance she expected to accompany such a question. There was none.

Not trusting her mouth not to humiliate her further, Sophia simply nodded. Yes, she liked it very much.

He took another step toward her. "Enough to wake up next to it for the next forty or so years?"

Forever. Again she nodded.

Sophia knew he was going to kiss her before he lowered his head. Raising up on her toes, she dropped her gloves to the floor and pressed her other hand against his chest, feeling the hair there spring against her palm. She lifted her face, sighing as his mouth came down on hers with tender yet firm insistence.

He still held her hand. His other arm slid around her

waist, holding her tightly as though he feared she might pull away. There was little chance of that happening.

It was just a kiss and yet Sophia's head swam with it. She could think of nothing but the warm, moist feel of his lips, of his tongue sliding against hers—of his heart pounding beneath her palm.

Her own heart battered her ribs as she gave herself up to the wonderful sensations washing over her. This was what a kiss should be. Edmund's kisses had been pleasant, even arousing, but not like this. Her husband had never made her feel as though a keg of gunpowder was about to go off inside her. He had never made her feel as though a thousand butterflies were caged inside her chest. No one but Julian had ever made her feel this way.

She moved closer, pressing as much of herself against him as she could. His body was a solid wall of heat that seeped through her clothes, through her skin right to her very bones. Her mouth clung greedily to his, meeting every caress with a wanton demand for more. Her lips tasted of him, the scent of him filled her nostrils and yet it wasn't enough. She wanted his salt on her tongue, wanted to breathe him into her lungs and never exhale. It was as if there were some huge void inside her, as if a piece of her were missing, and Julian was the only one who could make her whole again.

He must have felt her rein over her control slipping, because he broke the kiss then. Hot and hungry, Sophia gazed up at him, her lids as heavy as his.

Still holding her palm to his chest, he raised his other hand to brush his fingers across her cheek. "I have to get ready for dinner," he said hoarsely.

And just like that he released her and moved away.

Sophia watched in stunned silence as he snatched his shirt from the corner of the ring. He paused long enough to pull it over his head before striding toward the door.

"I will meet you in the red drawing room in half an hour," he promised without looking at her and was gone.

How long she stood there, alone and her body throbbing, Sophia didn't know. As soon as her trembling limbs were capable of movement, she bent and retrieved her gloves from the floor where she had dropped them. Slowly, she made her way out of the ballroom and back down the corridor toward the stairs. She still had to see Letitia.

But it wasn't her friend that occupied her thoughts as she climbed the stairs, pulling on her gloves. It was Julian. Why had he left the room as though the hounds of hell were nipping at his heels? He'd said he wanted to marry her. Hadn't he?

No, he hadn't. In fact, he hadn't said much of anything. He'd turned it around and asked her what she wanted to do and then he'd kissed her. Yet, she had offered him the chance to walk away and he hadn't taken it.

Was it possible she had been wrong about his feelings for her? Perhaps his desire for her wasn't equal to what she felt for him. Perhaps that was why he had stopped the kiss. Perhaps he'd been disgusted by her obvious hunger for him, although that hardly seemed likely.

Maybe, a small voice in her head whispered, he didn't want to take you right there in the ballroom.

Maybe she was making more out of this than was necessary. It wouldn't be the first time she'd allowed her imagination to run away with her. She would wait and see how he treated her for the rest of the evening, and if she was still uncertain at the end of it, she would ask him.

After all, hadn't he as good as come out and said he wanted there to be complete honesty between them? He wanted her to trust him, did he not? Well then, she could start by trusting him to be truthful with her when she asked. Even if she was a little scared of what his answer might be.

Pushing Julian as far from her thoughts as she could, Sophia turned down the hall at the top of the stairs and rapped on Letitia's door.

"Come in."

Sophia stepped into the frilly peach-and-white bedroom with a tentative smile. "Hello, Letitia."

"Sophia!" The younger woman jumped up from her dressing table, leaving her maid staring after her, and ran to Sophia with open arms. "Oh, how good it is to see you! I cannot believe that it took you this long to come see me!"

Drawing free of her friend's embrace, Sophia laughed. All her concerns about Letitia's thoughts on her engagement to Julian disappeared. "I was waiting for you to come see me!"

Her eyes bright, Letitia laughed as well. "That will be all, Dulcie," she said, dismissing the maid.

When the young girl was gone, Letitia gripped Sophia by the hand and led her toward the bed with barely suppressed girlish exuberance.

"I want to hear everything. How did Julian propose? Was he a gentleman or did he manage to make a mess out of it?"

"He was a perfect gentleman," Sophia replied, sitting on the bed beside her. Perhaps a perfect gentleman wouldn't have branded her with a kiss that made her toes curl, but who on earth wanted to marry a perfect gentleman?

"I cannot believe you accepted him," Letitia admitted

with a grin. "I expected you to tell him to go straight to the devil!"

Sophia smiled. "I thought about it, but he was so very sincere about wanting to make things right. It was the right decision given my other options."

Wrinkling her nose, Letitia shook her head. "That is not very romantic."

"No, it is not." Sophia chuckled. There were things that she would never tell Letitia, how Julian made her feel was one of them.

"I hope this will not change our relationship?" Sophia couldn't keep the hopeful tone from her voice.

Letitia patted her on the knee. "Of course not! I could not ask for a better sister. Although it might very well drive me to strangle my brother."

Sophia's eyes widened. "What has happened?"

Letitia rolled her big eyes. "Only that his own impending wedding has made him all the more anxious to see me married off as well."

"Oh, dear." Sophia winced. "He is still pushing for one of his own choices?"

Her friend nodded, a wry expression on her face. "Oh, yes! He has it narrowed down to two and he will not stop talking about them whenever we are together. I have told him I have no interest in marrying either man, but he refuses to listen."

Sophia felt truly sorry for Letitia and for Julian as well. He only wanted what was best for his sister, but his love for her made it hard for him to listen to her own wishes.

"Have you tried talking to him about Mr. Wesley?"

Letitia looked away. "Only once since that day he told me to forget him. I mentioned that I had seen Mr. Wesley at a party and he told me again to stay away from him."

Her angry gaze returned to Sophia's. "He cares nothing about my happiness!"

Sophia soothed her friend with a soft shush. "My dear, of course he cares about your happiness! He just believes he knows what will make you happy better than you do." She smiled.

Scowling, Letitia rose to her feet. "If he will not listen to me I will have to *make* him listen. I will—"

"You will what?" Sophia asked, a frisson of dread creeping up her spine.

Letitia shrugged, all the anger seeming to drain out of her. "What can I do?" she demanded, averting her gaze. "Only refuse to marry whoever Julian chooses. That and hope that dear Lord Penderthal dies soon, so that my Mr. Wesley might come into his inheritance."

It was awful of Letitia to wish for someone's death, but Sophia couldn't blame her for it.

"Would you like it if I offered to try talking to your brother?"

"No!" Letitia's expression was earnest. "Promise me you will not tell Julian about Mr. Wesley and me. I do not know how he will react."

"If he knew you were already in love it might help to change his mind."

The younger woman shook her head. "It would only make him more adamant to keep me away from Mr. Wesley. Promise me, Sophia, that you will not say anything until I give you leave."

Against her better judgment Sophia agreed. As much as she wanted to believe Julian would change his mind where his sister's marriage was concerned, she could not truthfully say that he wouldn't turn out to be like her father. As long as Letitia thought it a real possibility, and as long as

Julian continued to act in such a heavy-handed manner, she had no choice but to be cautious. She would hate to see Letitia forced into marriage, just as she would hate to see her hang all her hopes on one young man. What if Mr. Wesley didn't propose?

And she would hate to see Letitia end up resenting Julian as Sophia resented her father.

"Let us have no more melancholy talk," she suggested, also rising. "It will all work out, you will see. Why don't we go down to the drawing room and have a glass of sherry before the other guests arrive?"

Smiling, Letitia replied that would be a lovely idea. As they left the room, the younger woman began to talk about Julian and Sophia's wedding. Would Sophia prefer white roses or red? And surely she didn't *really* want a small reception, did she?

Sophia answered all her questions absently as they walked arm in arm down the stairs. Her mind wasn't focused on the wedding but rather on her future husband and whether or not it was possible to earn his trust.

And still retain Letitia's.

"I have an announcement to make."

Julian waited until all eyes were upon him before continuing. His gaze traveled from Letitia on his left, around the table to Gabriel, Lilith, Brave, Rachel and finally settling on Sophia. He held her gaze as he spoke. Sophia blushed but she didn't look away.

"Sophia and I are getting married."

A collection of gasps rose up from the other couples at the table. Julian couldn't help but chuckle at them. He could only imagine what must be going through Brave and Gabe's heads right now. And Lilith's for that matter.

She had made her disapproval of him very clear that night at Penderthal's.

But what he really wanted to know was what Sophia was thinking. Had she really come there earlier to give him the chance to back out of the marriage? Did she think so little of him and his word that she thought he'd take it back so easily? If so, the kiss they shared in the ballroom should have done much to change her mind.

Christ, that kiss had shaken him so badly, affected him so deeply he had to leave the room lest he fall to his knees and beg her to allow him to make love to her right there in the ring!

It was becoming more and more obvious that concern for Letitia was only one of many reasons for marrying Sophia. His desire for her was quickly shadowing all else. He wanted her in his bed and in his life, and he couldn't imagine ever getting tired of her.

His jaw was sore where Harper had hit it, the inside of his mouth a little raw from scraping against his teeth, but it was all worth it when he remembered the way Sophia had looked at him.

She liked his body. She liked his long arms and the shoulders that he believed relatively narrow when compared to Brave and especially to Gabriel. No woman had ever looked upon him as appreciatively as Sophia. No woman had ever made him feel more like a man or more desirable. And at that moment he wanted her more than he had ever wanted anyone else.

Thank God they would be married in a week, and then she would be back under his roof and in his bed where she belonged. He used to laugh at people who said they would die if they couldn't have someone, but it had killed him to walk away from Sophia that afternoon.

And now here she was, looking more beautiful than any woman had a right to, in a plum-colored dress that flaunted her creamy skin and delectable breasts, and he wasn't allowed to touch her. Only under the table, where his knee pressed against her leg, could he feel her warmth. It wasn't nearly enough, but it would have to do.

". . . toast."

Julian's head snapped around. How long had he been sitting there, staring at Sophia like an idiot?

Brave had his glass raised. Everyone else followed suit. "To Julian and Sophia," he said. "May they have a long and happy life together."

Julian raised his own glass as his friends all murmured their agreement. He drank deeply, hoping the wine would take an edge off his passion for Sophia. It was as though he were a boy again, only instead of being aroused by anything and everything, it was all focused on one woman.

Pushing back her chair, Sophia rose to her feet.

Julian followed. "Where are you going?"

Some women might have taken offense to his possessive tone, but Sophia simply smiled.

"I thought the ladies and I might retire to the drawing room and leave you gentlemen to your port and cigars." She flashed that same smile at Brave and Gabriel. "I am sure your friends have many questions they would like answered. If you would excuse us, gentlemen? Ladies."

Brave and Gabriel also rose as the women prepared to take their leave. Sophia was right. No doubt his friends had many questions they wanted answered.

"Have you gone completely mad?" Brave demanded once the three of them were alone.

Julian arched a brow. "Why do you ask?"

His friend looked at him as though it should be obvious. "Because you are marrying a woman who wrote a book about you—and not a very good one at that!"

Smiling, Julian met Brave's worried brown gaze with an easy one of his own. "You married Rachel to atone for your past."

"This is not the same." Brave leaned back in his chair, his posture relaxing somewhat. "Regardless, I seem to remember you questioning my motives and sanity at the time."

Julian tilted his head in acquiescence. "I also trusted you to know what was in your heart." His gaze flickered to Gabriel. "That goes for both of you. Can you not give me the same?"

Gabriel's gray eyes were earnest as they met Julian's. "Perhaps you might care to tell us what is in your heart then, Jules."

Good question. What was in his heart? There were so many things swimming around in his head where Sophia was concerned, he couldn't sort them all out.

"I cannot tell you," he replied honestly after several seconds of sitting under their scrutiny.

Brave leaned forward in his chair again, his forearms coming to rest on the table's polished surface. "Then why are you marrying her?"

This time Julian didn't need to think. "Because it is what I should have done seven years ago. Because I do not want my actions to reflect poorly upon my sister. Because . . . because I want to." He looked from one man to the other, daring them to question him further.

He could offer up whatever explanation he wanted for his decision to marry Sophia, but the simple fact was that he wanted to marry her. He wanted to know her secrets and share his with her. He wanted to trust her.

Gabriel nodded. "Sounds like a good enough reason to me." He glanced at Brave.

Brave smiled. "To me as well. You know we only want you to be happy, Jules, and if you think Sophia is the woman to make it happen then I wish you every happiness."

Julian stared at them, uncertain if they were being sincere or simply humoring him.

"Well," he said warily, "now that we have that settled, shall we join the ladies? Or would the two of you prefer to question me further?"

"I am for joining the ladies," Gabriel replied, standing. "They are much more pleasing to look upon than you two coxcombs."

Julian took his wine glass with him. "You sound just like Sophia. She thinks I have an abundance of vanity."

"Out of the three of us you *are* the biggest dandy," Brave remarked, also retrieving his glass.

Gabriel walked ahead toward the door. He tossed a good-natured grin over his shoulder. "And you are by far ten times prettier than Brave or I."

Flushing under their teasing, Julian laughed. He had known them both too long to take offense.

"It is not difficult to be better-looking than you two ugly curs," he informed them with a broad smile. "Fortunately you both married handsome women, so I needn't fear for your poor offspring."

This friendly teasing continued as the three men walked from the dining room along the corridor to the red drawing room. They entered the drawing room to find all four women laughing heartily—laughter that died abruptly as they saw that they were no longer alone.

Julian watched the dark flush that flooded Sophia's cheeks with a mixture of emotions. He was desperately curious to know just what they were talking about that made her color so.

He asked her about it later as he escorted her home. They were inside his carriage, and finally alone.

"You are awfully sure of yourself," she hedged. "What makes you so certain we were discussing you?"

He smiled as she struggled to hold his gaze. "You blushed. You do not normally do that—not so deeply. If it was not for my benefit then I demand to know the black-guard's name."

Her expression turned serious under the dim glow of the carriage lamp. "I know ours will not be a marriage in the true sense of the word, Julian, but you may trust me not to cuckold you. I hope that I might do the same."

Julian's smile faded. It never occurred to him to be un-faithful to her. His father had always been true to his mother and he planned to do the same in his marriage.

"As long as you do not deny me, you alone will have my attentions." It didn't come out the way he meant to say it, but he couldn't very well take it back.

She regarded him for a moment. "Then I will make you the same promise. I will be true to you as long as you do not deny me."

He wanted to tell her she'd be true to him or suffer the consequences, but he didn't. He understood what she was saying. She would trust him provided he trusted her.

"I cannot imagine any man ever denying you, Sophia." It sounded so much nicer than demanding she be faithful.

"You did," came the soft reply.

He did? "When?"

Her gaze didn't quite meet his. "Earlier tonight, in the ballroom."

His eyes widened as he stared at her. She was upset because he had stopped himself from ravishing her before dinner?

"Would you have preferred that I make love to you there? On the floor, wrinkling your gown and polluting you with my stench?" Good Lord, had she not smelled him? He'd worked up quite a sweat fighting Harper.

"No." She was silent for a moment. "Did you even want to?"

The sweet vulnerability of the question, combined with that low, faint Spanish lilt was enough to make his groin tighten uncomfortably.

"I want to every time I see you."

Instead of shying away from his honesty, Sophia seemed to be nothing more than astonished. "Really? Do you want to now?"

Was it not obvious? Perhaps not in the dark, but Julian was all too aware of how tight his trousers were becoming. "My God, woman, do not tempt me."

She scooted forward on the seat, closing the distance between them. "But I want to, Julian. I want to tempt you as you tempt me."

He wasn't quite certain how it happened, but one minute she was sitting across from him and the next she was in his lap—and he had put her there. "Do you feel that?" he demanded against her mouth, lifting his hips against her bottom so she could feel the heavy ridge of his arousal through the thin silk of her skirts. "This is what you do to me."

Sophia—his dear, tormenting Sophia—smiled. "Would you like to know what you do to me?"

Julian growled low in his throat. Oh Lord, would he! "What?"

Her lips brushed his as she spoke. "You make me feel hot, Julian. Like there is an itch deep inside me. A hot, *wet* itch."

A shiver of desire raced down Julian's spine. "My God, where did you learn to talk like that?"

It was as though he had tossed a glass of water in her face. She stiffened and pulled back. "Do you not like it?"

Cupping his hand around the back of her head, he hauled her closer. "I love it." He kissed her slowly, teasing her with his tongue as his other hand slid up her ribs to capture her left breast. He found the hard thrust of her nipple and rubbed it with the pad of his thumb.

Sophia's moan echoed in his mouth. She tangled the fingers of one hand in his hair, the others clutched at the lapel of his coat. Her breast pushed against his hand as she squirmed against the straining hardness in his lap.

He had to stop. If he didn't he was going to end up tossing up her skirts right here in the carriage and they were only minutes from Lady Wickford's.

Reluctantly he released her breast and tore his lips away from hers. Her black eyes heavy-lidded and glazed with passion, Sophia gazed at him in bewilderment. "Why did you stop?"

Julian reached up and brushed the tips of his fingers along the smooth warmth of her cheek. "I have waited seven years to make love to you. When it finally happens, it will not be clumsy and hurried in a carriage. It will be in my bed, when I have all the time in the world to do whatever I want to you."

Sophia shifted on his lap, pressing the full curves of her

buttocks down upon his aching erection. "What do you want to do?"

Driven to the point of desperation, Julian was tempted to say to hell with it and show her, but just as the thought crossed his mind the carriage rolled to a stop.

They had arrived at Lady Wickford's.

"It is a surprise," he whispered, pressing a soft kiss against her lips. But he had a feeling that Sophia wasn't going to be half so surprised by him as he was by her.

Chapter 11

*Jocelyn was certain Lord Foxton would propose,
for she knew without a doubt in her heart of hearts
that they were made for each other.*

An Unfortunate Attachment by the Marchioness of Aberley

The day of the wedding arrived bright, sunny and about seven days too late for Julian's liking.

"For God's sake, Jules! Stop that infernal pacing, will you? You are making me queasy."

Laughing, Brave pressed a drink into Julian's cold hand. "Leave him alone, Gabe. It is his wedding day."

"I did not pace on my wedding day," Gabriel boasted proudly.

Julian stopped moving long enough to face his friend. "True, but I believe you had already begun the honeymoon by the time you and Lilith finally decided to say 'I do.'"

"Ah, so you are randy rather than nervous, is that it?" Gabriel chuckled.

Julian shot him an unamused glance. "We shall see who is laughing after your son is born and Lilith is unable to bed you for several weeks." He took a drink of brandy.

All the humor drained from Gabriel's face. "I beg your pardon?"

Brave flashed the darker man a broad grin. "He is right.
It will be some time after the baby is born before Lilith
feels like herself again, Gabe. You had better take advantage of what time you have left."

Julian listened to his friends talk about the pitfalls of fa-
therhood with half an ear. His mind was on the wedding—
and the wedding night. Even though he was only minutes
away from making Sophia his wife, he was still hours
away from being able to make her his. Why had he agreed
to break tradition and have an evening wedding? The private ceremony was at six, with drinks to follow and dinner
at eight. By the time everyone left, he and Sophia would
have just enough time to prepare for the party Gabriel and
Lilith were hosting at Eden in their honor. There would be
no time for the kind of intimacy he craved until after the
party.

"It is ten minutes to the hour," Brave announced, con-
sulting his watch. "Shall we go in?"

Julian's heart slid down into his stomach. It was time.
Drawing a deep breath, he nodded. "Yes. Let us go in."

He straightened the soft, dark blue wool of his coat and
tugged gently on his cuffs. "How do I look?" he asked.

Brave gave him a quick once-over. "Brummell himself
could not fault you."

Gabriel was a bit more critical. "You look like a puffed-
up peacock."

Plastering a false smile on his face, Julian told his
friend where he could stuff that analogy.

They left Julian's study and made the short walk to the
blue drawing room together. The room had been his
mother's favorite, and Letitia had pronounced it the most
suitable room in the house for Julian and Sophia to be
married in. A large portrait of their parents hung above the

mantel. A portrait of Miranda graced the opposite wall. Being married in this room would be almost like having his entire family blessing his marriage.

The guests were already there when they entered. Only a few close friends and acquaintances had been invited to the ceremony. Other than Gabriel, Lilith, Brave and Rachel there were only Letitia, Lady Wickford and Sophia's mother. Her father had refused to come. Julian, for one, did not miss Lord Haverington's presence. He'd never liked the pious old bastard.

The Marquess of Aberley had not been invited, of course. Julian had no doubt that news of their betrothal had reached Aberley—all of London was talking about it. He would have gladly given his right arm to witness the marquess's reaction to the news.

Julian took his place at the front of the room with the minister, clasping his trembling hands in front of him. Letitia shot him a grin from her seat at the pianoforte. She seemed so very pleased by his and Sophia's marriage, and Julian was glad for it. He hadn't told her of Patterson's withdrawal, or why it had happened. She had been so out of sorts lately; he hoped that the wedding might cheer her up.

If only he could see her married herself. He knew that marriage wouldn't stop Letitia from ever having problems, but marriage would afford her more freedom and protection than she had now as an unmarried miss. Once she was safely wed he would stop worrying about her.

Stop worrying that something horrible might take her from him as it had Miranda.

All thoughts of his sister were wiped from Julian's mind as Sophia entered the room on the arm of her mother. Julian was struck by how alike mother and daughter looked. Maria Everston was a darker, older version of her daughter, although years of marriage to the viscount had made her a little harder-looking as well.

Sophia was breathtaking in an ice blue satin gown with matching gloves and a delicate diamond pendant around her neck. Her hair was a braided coronet with tiny white flowers woven in amongst the ebony strands. She smiled at him from behind a demure bouquet of posies. He smiled back. She was actually going to be his.

When she reached his side, he held out his gloved hand. Releasing her mother's arm, she took it. Julian couldn't be certain, but he thought he heard the viscountess mutter something in Spanish under her breath. Julian didn't understand the words, but her tone was one of relief.

They held hands throughout the ceremony, with Julian's parents smiling down upon them from their place above the mantel. When Sophia stumbled over her vows, he squeezed her fingers encouragingly. When they were finally pronounced man and wife, Sophia squeezed his.

After the ceremony, they went to the red drawing room for drinks before filing into the dining room for the wedding dinner. Tradition normally called for a breakfast as marriage ceremonies were usually held earlier in the day, but Sophia declared that they had broken every other tradition on their journey to the altar, so what did one more matter?

Their guests began departing shortly after dinner. Lady Wickford was the first to go, presenting them with a wedding gift of a pair of heavy silver goblets that had belonged to her parents.

"I wanted the two of you to have them," she told them with moist eyes. "For the both of you are as dear to me as any children could have been."

His throat tight, Julian embraced the older woman after Sophia released her. "Thank you," he whispered near her ear.

Brave and Rachel left next, anxious to get home to their son, Alexander, especially since they would be away from him again that evening. Gabriel and Lilith followed shortly after.

By the time Sophia's mother left, it was time to start getting ready for the evening. Just before taking her leave, Maria gave Sophia a stunning ruby necklace that had belonged to the women in her family for generations. The two women spoke softly to each other in Spanish. Julian had no idea what they were saying, but the conversation ended with both of them embracing and on the verge of tears.

"What did she say to you?" he asked as they climbed the stairs toward their bedchambers. Unfortunately, he would go to his and she would go to hers in order to prepare for the evening.

"She told me she was proud of me," Sophia replied, dabbing at her eyes with his handkerchief. She clutched the box containing the jewelry against her breast. "That she wished me joy. And she told me I was the most beautiful bride she had ever seen."

Julian smiled. "I have to agree with her there." Bending down, he murmured against the soft ridge of her ear, "I cannot wait for tonight."

She blushed to the roots of her hair. "Nor can I." They reached the top of the stairs. "But you are the one who said you wanted to take your time and, alas, we haven't much."

"We have some," he corrected, following her into her chamber. "You may leave us," he said to the maid.

The young maid smiled coyly and dipped a curtsey before scurrying from the room. Sophia turned on him with flashing black eyes.

"Why did you do that? Who will help me with my toilette?"

"I will." He shrugged out of his coat and tossed it on her bed.

Hands on her hips, she arched both brows. "Oh, so you are going to help me undress and help me bathe . . ." Her voice drifted off. Obviously she realized that was exactly what he intended.

"Precisely." He rolled up his shirt sleeves. "Turn around."

Placing his hands around her waist, Julian pushed her across the carpet toward said room. A huge copper tub sat in the middle of the floor, steam rising from the water in it.

"I really do not know if this is a good idea," she protested as his fingers set to work on the tiny buttons on the back of her gown.

"Why?" Frigging buttons! Why did they have to be so blasted small?

"I . . . because if you undress me then you will probably want to touch me."

Julian didn't pause in his struggle against the buttons. "I do want to touch you."

She turned to face him, the neckline of her gown sagging. "If you touch me I will not want you to stop."

He smiled at her, at the high color in her cheeks and the defensive angle of her chin. "That is the whole point."

She didn't even crack a smile, but her eyes twinkled. "We have a party to go to, remember?"

Still smiling, Julian untied his cravat, pulling the starched length of fabric from around his neck. "We'll get there. We just might be a little late."

Sophia laughed. She still held her sagging bodice to her chest. "You know as well as I do that there will be no turning back if we start something now."

He knew. Christ, yes, he knew. Hearing her say it was another matter, however. Her matter-of-fact tone—as though their wanting each other was a force of its own—aroused him more than explicit words or touches could have. His prick was as hard as a rock.

"All right," he growled, conceding finally. "You win."

Reaching out, she laid a hand upon his arm. He stood very still, even though he wanted nothing more than to pull her into his arms.

"Thank you." Her gaze was so sweet and so full of trust as it met his that Julian almost believed it was worth the frustration sizzling in his veins.

"Do not thank me," he replied more gruffly than intended. "If it were up to me we would both of us be in that bath right now, and it would not be my back you would be soaping."

She flushed again, but not before a giggle escaped her lips. It was an odd sound coming from her. He'd never thought of her as a giggler. Was it possible that she was nervous about making love with him? What could she possibly have to fear—other than the force of their mutual desire?

Whatever Sophia's reasons for being nervous, Julian knew she wanted him as much as he wanted her. And he respected her enough not to pressure her.

With a quick, chaste kiss, he left her and her gaping gown and retired to his own room. There, a bath waited for him in his own dressing room. He stripped off his wedding clothes, tossing them on a nearby chair to be taken care of later by his valet, and stepped into the warm bath.

He stayed in until the water cooled, waiting for it to cool his blood as well. But it did not work, for all he could think of in his bath was of Sophia in hers.

"I want to take you home now."

Beneath the burning chandeliers of Eden's assembly rooms, in the warm circle of her husband's arms, Sophia shivered as Julian's hot breath fanned her ear.

"All right," she replied softly, unable to meet his gaze. She wanted to please him, but she was frightened. Frightened not only of disappointing him, but of the passion that raged between them. It was like a fire waiting to consume them. Would it consume her entirely? Would she lose something of the self she had fought so hard to find after Edmund's death? She didn't want a man to have any kind of control over her again, and that included Julian.

And she was a little bit scared of him seeing her naked. She knew she wasn't ugly, but her body didn't look like it had seven years ago—she and Julian both had gotten larger over the years. Edmund had watched her weight like a hawk, putting her on a diet if she gained the least amount of weight.

Since his death she had gained almost a full stone.

Sophia did not miss the teasing glances Julian's friends shot him as they said their goodbyes. It was more than a little embarrassing, all these people knowing they were going home just so they could make love.

The carriage ride home seemed to take forever as she struggled to make conversation. Then Julian moved to sit beside her, kissing her until she was breathless, and the trip was over.

Her maid, Jenny, was waiting when she entered her

room. A half dozen candles bathed the room in a soft, mellow light.

She had Jenny unbutton her gown and that was it. She undressed herself after the maid had left, and slipped into the delicate pink peignoir set that Lilith and Rachel had helped her pick out.

The gown itself was little more than a long sheath of gauze with thin straps and a plunging neckline. It clung to her breasts and hips and Sophia was certain it hid very little, if anything. Looking down, she could see the shadowy outlines of her areolae and erect nipples through the transparent fabric. It felt as though she was already naked. Hastily, she pulled on the matching robe.

Her fingers trembling, she sat down at her dressing table and began plucking pins from her hair. It fell heavily around her shoulders, the thick black strands almost poker straight despite having been coiled on top of her head. She brushed it until it crackled, until her breathing was normal and she felt somewhat relaxed. It was then that the door in the far corner of her room opened and Julian appeared.

He stood in the doorway wearing nothing but his shirt and trousers. Even his feet were bare. Sophia's mouth went dry at the sight of him. There was something incredibly sensual about his appearance, even though he was still covered.

He carried a wine bottle in one hand, two glasses in the other. No doubt the wine was for her benefit—a little something to calm her nerves and make her relax.

She rose to her feet as he crossed the carpet. He didn't bother to try to hide his frank appraisal of her attire.

"Very nice," he murmured.

"Lilith picked it out," she replied inanely.

A small smile curved his lips. "I do not doubt that she did. Drink?"

She nodded and he set the glasses on her vanity, pouring a liberal amount into both. He offered her one.

Sophia's fingers trembled as she took it. Raising it to her lips she took two long, deep gulps to soothe her jangled nerves. Smiling, Julian refilled her glass and then set the bottle on the surface of her dressing table.

She watched as Julian took a long swallow of wine. His Adam's apple shifted against the long, smooth column of his throat as he drank. His tongue flicked over his lips in a manner that probably wasn't meant to be seductive, but had the same effect.

He caught her staring and stared back, his gaze filled with tender humor. He moved closer, bending down to brush his lips across hers. He took his time, lazily probing with his tongue.

"Let us move to the bed, shall we?" he suggested, taking her wine from her and setting it on the dressing table beside his own.

Anticipation shivered down Sophia's spine as he backed her toward the bed. "Shall I snuff out the candles?"

"No. Leave them. I want to see you."

The back of her legs hit the trunk at the foot of the bed. Sophia's eyes widened as her stomach fluttered. "Oh."

Julian chuckled, but it wasn't a mean sound. "Do you not want to see me as well?"

She hadn't thought of that. Without the candles she wouldn't be able to admire his nakedness, wouldn't be able to study his body and put her curiosity to rest at last. The idea of offering herself up for such intimate scrutiny was humbling. She so desperately wanted him to approve of her body, to find it as desirable as she found his. It had nothing to do with Edmund and her marriage to him. This was Julian, the first man she had ever loved, and even though it had happened years ago, there was still something special about him.

Obviously he saw the indecision on her face. Either that or he read her mind.

"Are you nervous about me seeing you naked?"

Sophia nodded, a faint blush coloring her cheeks. "A little. Yes."

Tilting his head, Julian moved closer. She could smell him now, a warm, spicy sweetness that sent a tremor through her thighs and made her knees weak.

"We will do this together," he suggested. "First I will take off my shirt and then you can remove something."

Sophia nodded, her tongue dry and her head spinning from the wine.

Julian grasped the hem of his shirt with both hands and pulled. The soft linen slid up over his hips, baring the flat expanse of his stomach, then the hard, hairy width of his chest. Yanking the shirt over his head, he tossed it to the floor and faced her in nothing but his trousers.

Sophia stared at him. In the low, flickering candlelight his body was all smokey shadow and warm highlights. Her eyes drank in every detail—the knobby bones of his shoulders, the hard plains and valleys of his chest and abdomen, the shallow indentation of his navel—even the fine dusting of hair on his forearms. His skin was a natural warm, golden color—not pale and pasty like so many gentlemen of his class. The dusky candlelight only deepened the hue, and Sophia couldn't help but liken him to a bronze statue. But he wasn't bronze; he was flesh and blood and he was hers.

"Touch me."

He didn't have to ask—no, *command*—her twice. Hungrily, she stretched her hands toward him, settling the flat of her palm against the hard curve of his breast. She slid her palms up, over the warm, satiny smoothness of his shoulders, stroking those fascinating knobs of bone and the long stretch of firm muscle that bridged his shoulders and his neck. The pulse at the base of his throat beat against the pad of her thumb, its urgent pounding proof of his excitement.

He watched her silently as she touched him, as her greedy hands devoured him from the waist up. He made no move to touch her in return. She knew it wasn't because he didn't want to. It was because he wanted her to trust him. The realization was as humbling as it was arousing.

"Now it is your turn." Still he did not touch her. Something in his gaze told her what he wanted and compelled her to do it.

Fingers trembling, Sophia unfastened the bow that held her wrapper closed. Her heart beat a staccato rhythm in her chest as she shrugged the flimsy fabric off her shoulders. It slid down her arms, pooling at her feet. She knew how much of herself was revealed to him through the equally thin nightgown, and could only imagine how the candles behind her accentuated it. Shyly, she raised her eyes to Julian's face.

There was only heat and appreciation in his expression. She did not have to invite him to touch her.

"This is lovely," he murmured, his thumbs hooking around the straps of her gown. "But it is hardly fair. I am bare from the waist up and you are still quite covered."

Before Sophia could react, he slipped the straps off her shoulders. Without that support the entire top portion of her gown slithered down around her hips, baring her breasts and torso to his gaze.

Instinctively she lifted her arms to cover her breasts, her body pulsing. He had surprised her, but that wasn't what caused the low thrumming deep down below her waist. His bold action had aroused her.

He caught her wrists. "Do not hide yourself from me."

There was no anger in his voice, but it was a threat all the same. Sophia shivered at the warning, her skin prickling and her nipples tightening in response.

Julian lowered her arms to her sides, his gaze dropping to the flesh he had revealed. She did not want to watch as his hungry gaze assessed her nakedness, but she could not bring herself to look away. Did he think her breasts too heavy? Could he tell that one was slightly bigger than the other?

His fingers skimmed the tops of her shoulders, traced the faint ridge of her collarbones. The heat of his hands was a startling contrast to the anxious chill of her flesh. Her body tightened further, heightening the tingling low in her abdomen that spread downward into her loins and trembling thighs.

His topaz gaze, dark in the soft light, locked with hers as his hands slid slowly along the indent of her waist and drifted across her ribs.

"You are beautiful," he whispered. "Everything about you, your hair, your skin, your breasts—all of it."

She believed him. He wasn't that good of a liar, but even still, she couldn't seem to stop herself from refuting him. "My breasts are too big. They sag."

His attention fell to those heavy globes of flesh. Sophia held her breath. Part of her needed him to find her wanting. Maybe then she would stop feeling as though her entire life had led to this moment.

Smiling almost coyly, Julian cupped her breasts in his long, warm hands, lifting them. "Now they do not," he replied, brushing his thumbs across the hard, sensitive peaks of her nipples.

Sophia gasped, a bolt of sensual need spiking from her breasts to the wanton, wanting part between her legs. Staring down at the golden brown fingers wrapped around her flesh she realized dizzily that he was right. In his hands the only thing her breasts wanted was his touch.

Still stroking the puckered tips, Julian lowered his head to hers and kissed her, the wet velvet of his tongue invading her mouth. Sophia grasped his shoulders in an effort to keep herself upright as his lips and hands slowly turned her bones to jelly.

His teeth nipped, his fingers pinched, each movement ever so lightly, each drawing another gasp from deep within her. His lips left hers, brushing a tantalizing, shivering trail along her jaw and throat down to her chest. And when he lifted one of her breasts to his mouth, Sophia's gasps became moans.

Clinging to the hard curves of his biceps, Sophia arched her back, giving him full access to her body. The sight of his mouth on her breast was shockingly arousing. She could not look away, even when the suckling pressure of his mouth threatened to draw her lids closed in a lazy sigh of pleasure.

Every flick of his tongue drew her deeper and deeper under his spell. He knew just how much pressure to apply to keep the sensation that of pleasure and not pain. And

when Sophia thought she had taken all she could, he trans-
ferred his attentions to her other breast.

Crying out, she released his shoulders, even though her
knees threatened to buckle beneath her, and tangled her
fingers in the thick, silky mass of his hair, pulling him
closer as the sharp edge of his teeth closed delicately
around her nipple. The throbbing below her waist was
acute, almost painful in its intensity. She burned inside
and most of that heat was centered between her thighs.

Julian lifted his head from her breasts, her fingers still
caught in his hair. His hooded eyes were bright with sexual promise, his sensual mouth dark and moist.

"Shall I remove my trousers now?" he asked, his voice
little more than a rasp.

Emboldened by the wine and her desire for him, Sophia
reached for the tented fabric before her. "Allow me."

He said nothing. He just stood there, an expression of
hungry expectation on his face as her fingers unfastened
the falls of his trousers, and slid the soft, black fabric over
his hips.

Kneeling before him, she removed his clothing and
tossed it aside. He stood gloriously and unashamedly
naked in front of her. As beautiful as she dreamed he'd be.

Her fingers started with his feet. They were long and
slender just like the rest of him, the sharp bones of his an-
kles hard beneath her palms. She moved up to the firm,
hairy curve of his calves, past his knees to the hard muscular length of his thighs and narrow hips. And then,
wickedly, she slid her hands around to cup the high, tight
curves of his buttocks and squeezed.

"Do I meet your approval?"

Sophia's gaze drifted to the one part of his anatomy she
had yet to inspect. It jutted out from a thick crop of brown

curls at the base of his abdomen, and seemed to grow even bigger under the awed weight of her stare.

"Yes," she whispered, running her fingers along the satiny length. Julian gasped as she closed her fist around the hot, hard flesh. Pumping gently, she brazenly raised her face to look at him. "Would it please you if I kissed it?"

A strangled sound seemed to tear itself from his throat. "Yes," he rasped. "That would please me very much."

Closing her eyes, Sophia moistened her lips and wrapped her mouth around Julian's rock-hard erection. He groaned above her. Sophia hadn't enjoyed pleasuring Edmund in this way, but she thrilled with every groan and sigh that Julian made. His fingers clutched at the back of her head, pulling her closer, pushing more of himself between her lips, and she readily took him in, running her eager tongue all over his slick stiffness.

Suddenly, he tugged on her hair, pulling back on her head and easing himself out of her mouth.

She lifted an anxious gaze to his. "What? Did I do something wrong?"

Julian chuckled hoarsely as he helped her to her feet. "Hell, no. You did everything right."

She stared at him dumbly. "Then why did you stop me?"

Bright, predatory eyes bore into hers with such intensity that for a moment Sophia thought he was going to toss her on the bed and thrust himself inside her at that very second.

"Because the first time I come with you, it is not going to be in your mouth," he growled. "Now I believe it is your turn."

With one flick of his hand, he sent her nightgown

plummeting to the floor in a soft heap around her feet. Sweeping her up into his arms, he carried her around to the side of the bed, laying her on the counterpane as though she were some kind of exotic treasure.

"You are the most beautiful woman I have ever seen," he murmured, looming above her. "I have thought so since the first time I saw you."

Sophia stared at him, a hard lump in her throat. "Really?"

The gaze that met hers was painfully tender. "My God, Sophia. How could you doubt it?"

She couldn't think of an answer.

His fingers brushed the inside of her thigh and she stiffened, but only for a split second, because after that, she felt him part the hot, swollen lips of her sex and her bones turned to molten lava.

"Your body knows how much I want it," he told her, slowly sliding a finger deep within her. Sophia gasped, both at his words and at his heavenly invasion of her most private spot.

"Your body knows how desirous it is," he continued, his finger moving in and out, making her writhe in frustration and pleasure beneath him. "And this—" Sophia cried out as his thumb rubbed the hard, sweet spot further up the wet furrow of her sex. "—This knows how beautiful you are to me, because every time I touch it, the most exquisite expression of pleasure washes over your face. 'All the soft hills and hidden valleys of her vista formed a sweeter garden than Eden ever dreamed.' "

Sophia wanted to ask him what that was from, but words deserted her as Julian delved deeper into her smoldering flesh. She didn't care that she was spread naked before him. She didn't care that she was making the most unladylike sounds and she didn't care if he noticed that she was moving her hips in time with his manipulations. All she cared about was the pleasure he gave her.

"Oh! Julian, I . . ." She was close. So close. The pressure within her body was wound almost as tight as it could go.

"Do you want to come, Sophia?" he demanded, ruthlessly stroking her with his thumb.

"Yes!" And she was going to. Just a few more strokes and—

Julian withdrew his hand from between her legs. Frustrated and throbbing, Sophia opened her eyes and stared at him. He was smiling. A playful, sensuous smile that made her either want to hit him or molest him. She wasn't certain which.

"Then come take me." He climbed up onto the bed beside her, stretching himself out along the bedspread. His erection stood tall and thick from his groin, the tip glistening with arousal.

What? Had she heard him correctly? Her, take *him*?

"I do not know how," she whispered, her cheeks flaming as her body screamed silently for release.

Taking her hand, he drew her closer. "Yes you do. Climb on top of me. Put me inside you."

Hesitantly, Sophia did as he bid. She had never made love this way before, but she knew that men and women fit together only so many ways. This was just another position. A position that put her in control instead of Julian.

A flood of heat rushed between her legs at the realization that he was giving her power over him. He *wanted* her to have this power.

Reaching down between their bodies, Sophia grasped the heavy length of him and guided the blunt head to the opening of her body. He pushed, gasping as her body stretched to accommodate him. Instinct demanded that she take him all—*now*, but pleasure commanded that she savor each and every hard inch as she took Julian deeper and deeper inside her.

Slowly, even though her body hummed with impatience, she lowered herself down onto Julian's hips, spreading her thighs wide along his flanks, until her pubis pressed against the firm ridge of his pelvis. She kept her gaze fastened on his face as she took him into her body. His eyes fluttered closed, the dark fringe of his lashes soft against his cheeks. His lips parted, a soft gasp escaping them as she opened herself to him.

He was completely inside her. A shuddering sigh rippled through her body. They were one. The man she had tried so hard to forget and despise for so many years was part of her. Her body claimed a part of his.

She was still for a moment, letting her body adjust to having him inside her, and then she began to move. Bracing her hands on his ribs for support, she used the muscles of her thighs to push herself up and down on the delicious intruder that slid effortlessly in and out of her. With every thrust she felt her climax building, felt Julian tense beneath her. Neither one of them was going to last very long. They had the rest of their lives to take their time.

She quickened the pace, thrusting faster and faster, panting with exertion as she pushed herself closer and closer to release. The ache between her legs was so good—she wanted it to last forever and yet she couldn't wait for it to arrive at its inevitable conclusion.

Beneath her, Julian's breath came in labored gasps. His hips arched up against hers, pushing himself as deep within her as he could. He grasped her waist in his hands, holding her firmly to him, trying to set the rhythm of their mating.

"Oh, God, Sophia," he groaned, his hands moving up to cup her breasts. "Do not stop."

Gasping as he squeezed her nipples between his thumbs and forefingers, Sophia felt her tenuous grip on her control snap. Leaning forward, she braced most of her weight against his hands and his ribs, riding him furiously as the dam within her burst, releasing a torrent of pleasure like nothing she had ever felt before. It washed over her in waves of mindless ecstasy, driving her onward, even as she heard Julian cry out in his own release. He bucked beneath her, grinding his pelvis against hers and sending aftershocks of acute pleasure rippling through her.

Her body still firing sparks of sensation, Sophia collapsed onto Julian's chest, her hair tumbling them both into darkness. A few seconds later, his hands smoothed the mass back from her face and she was able to see him again.

He was smiling. "Are you all right?"

He had to ask? Good Lord! If she were any better she would need medical attention.

"More than all right," she replied. "You?"

He nodded.

Silence followed. Lowering herself to his side, Sophia was very much aware that he was watching her. When she again met his gaze, she was humbled by the tenderness she saw there. She had pleased him, and he hadn't had to tell her how to do it, as Edmund always seemed to. He hadn't instructed her on how to touch him or how to kiss, and he had set her body aflame with the simplest of caresses. How did he do it? Better yet, how did she?

She was going to fall in love with him. She knew it with such clarity that it was as if her heart were caught in a vice. Loving Julian would be wonderful, provided he loved her in return. If he didn't, her life would be even more miserable with him than it had been without.

"Was it worth waiting seven years for?" she inquired, wanting to put an end to her thoughts.

Chuckling, Julian wrapped his arms around her. "Yes. Only I hope you do not plan to make me wait another seven before we do it again."

Sophia laughed and kissed him. "My dear Lord Wolfram, I expect you to be ready in seven *minutes*."

He stared at her in mock horror. "I do not think that is possible."

But six and a half minutes later, a very happy Sophia and a very surprised Julian discovered that it was.

Chapter 12

*The hardest thing for a man to comprehend
is the woman who does not fall at his feet.*

An Unfortunate Attachment by the Marchioness of Aberley

"Tell me about your marriage to Aberley."

Sophia glanced at him over one soapy, wet shoulder. "What do you want to know?"

It was late in the evening and they were in Julian's dressing room, soaking in the large copper tub near the fire. Sophia sat nestled in the *V* of his legs as Julian reclined against the head of the tub, lazily washing the warm flesh of her back. The firelight danced over her wet skin, turning it various shades of golden perfection.

They had been married two days and he was still in awe of her.

Julian squeezed the cloth over her back, rinsing away the suds. "Why did you marry him?"

Her answer was a slight, noncommittal shrug. "Because I had too."

Julian stilled, his hand poised over her back. Water trickled down his arm. "You had too?"

"My parents were still trying to recover from the scan-

dal. No one else would have me—" Julian winced. That
was his fault. "—so when Aberley said he wanted me, my
father was all too happy to oblige. He made it very clear
that if I did not marry Aberley I would be tossed out with
the morning's slop."

Her tone was so matter of fact, so devoid of bitterness,
that Julian didn't know what to make of it. He rinsed the
rest of the soap off her back. "Aberley was beyond proper.
Why would he offer for a young woman who was—" he
couldn't finish.

"Supposedly spoiled goods?" his wife supplied lightly.
There was a trace of bitterness in her voice now, but instinct told Julian it wasn't directed at him.

"He wanted to make an example out of me. He wanted to
mold me into a proper lady and then show me off to all of
society as his creation so he could brag about 'taming' me.
And he desired me." She turned her face away. "Aberley
was not quite the proper gentleman behind closed doors."

Julian's fingers tightened on the washcloth. "He did not
hurt you?"

Sophia shook her head. "No, but he broke me all the
same. He turned me into someone I did not recognize."

He drew her backward so that her shoulder blades
rested against his chest and slipped his arms around her.
"You can be whomever you want now."

Her hands closed over his. "Thank you."

"I am sorry." How hard it was to say the words!

Tilting her head so she could look up at him, Sophia
smiled kindly. "It was a long time ago and we are different
people than we were back then."

God, what had he done to deserve her understanding?
"If I had done the right thing you never would have had to
marry Aberley."

Sophia shrugged, seemingly unaware of his regret. "At least my time with him was brief."

At that moment Julian sincerely hoped that Edmund Morelle was burning in hell.

"Was he that awful?" He didn't want to know. Truly he didn't, but a part of him wanted desperately to hear that Aberley was worse than *him.*

She seemed to think about it for a moment. "No, I do not think so. He was never cruel, just . . . persuasive."

He should have known better than to ask. "Did you ever resent him for not being able to give you children?"

Sophia seemed surprised by the question. "I knew when I married him there would not be any. Besides, I was still a child myself in many ways. I had no desire to bear any."

Julian nodded. He was still thinking about what she had said about Aberley's reasons for marrying her. Aberley's little experiment to show off to the *ton.* Look how the Marquess of Aberley turned the little hoyden into a proper lady.

She pulled away, turning her body to face him more fully. "Why the sudden interest in my marriage? Were you perhaps also wondering how you compared to Edmund as a husband?"

Was he that transparent? "Perhaps."

She faced him, water sloshing over the sides of the tub as she moved between his bent knees. In the firelight her eyes were so black there was no distinction between iris and pupil. She slid her arms around his neck, pressing the warm, wet heaviness of her breasts against his chest.

"Forget about Edmund, Julian. He is in the past and you and I have enough problems without bringing him into it."

Slipping his arms around her waist, Julian pulled her closer so that her entire front lay flush against his. "I will do everything in my power to give you the future you deserve."

She didn't say anything. She just stared at him with those unreadable ebony eyes of hers, and for a moment Julian wondered if maybe he had said too much.

"How is it?" she asked, after what seemed like an eternity. "That you always seem to know exactly what to say to make me feel like the most incredible woman in all of England?"

Julian's heart swelled with an emotion he didn't dare try to name. "Because you are." In the world, in fact, but now wasn't the time to admit that, because then he'd have to examine it and he didn't want to. "You are like myth, nature and fantasy rolled into one—a sweeter garden than Eden ever dreamed."

"You said that on our wedding night," she reminded him, conjuring images of all the pleasureful things they had done that night. "What is that from?"

Dare he tell her? What if she laughed? What if she suspected how deep his feelings for her ran? He scarcely knew their depths himself.

"It is from a poem I am writing." He didn't have to say about whom.

Sophia didn't speak. She kissed him instead, and as her lips pressed against his, Julian's understood everything she didn't say.

The kiss seemed to last forever. Every last detail burned itself into Julian's mind with heart-wrenching clarity; the soft, supple rhythm of their lips, the gentle poke of Sophia's nipples against his chest, the delicate brush of her sex against the thickening length of his stirring erection.

"Take me to bed," she whispered against his mouth.

Julian did as he was bid. Rising to his feet in the tub, he drew the warm, wet curves of her body hard against his. He stepped out onto the rug, sweeping Sophia out of the bath with a splash and up into his arms. They dripped a trail of suds from the dressing room to his chamber.

He laid her on the bed, their slippery limbs entwining as he slid between her parted thighs. He kissed her—her mouth, her breasts, her belly, the hot, salty furrow between her legs. She writhed beneath him, every whisper fanning the flames of his desire.

"Tell me what you want," he demanded, as he hovered above her. He wanted to please her, wanted to give her everything that was in his power to give.

"You." Drowsy dark eyes shone up at him. "I just want you."

He gave himself to her. Filling her slowly, he groaned as he slid deeper and deeper into of her sultry tightness. Time stood still as her strong, round legs clamped around his hips. The muscles of his arms trembled with tension as he struggled to make this moment last.

It ended much sooner than he would have liked. Sophia's cries of release sent Julian spiraling unstoppably toward his own.

He fell forward on his arms, body shuddering as the spasms rocked him. Never before had lovemaking affected him so strongly. It felt as though his soul had exploded.

As his senses returned and the spots dancing before his eyes cleared away, Julian reluctantly withdrew himself from Sophia's softness and rolled onto his side next to her.

Silence descended as they lay there, staring into each other's eyes, smiling. Whoever would have thought that they could ever have this level of comfort between them? Never in a million years could he have guessed that it would feel so right to have Sophia in his life. It felt as though a door long shut had been opened, letting fresh air and sunlight into an otherwise dank and darkened room.

Julian's smile faded. Sophia was that fresh air and sunshine. His heart was that dank and darkened room.

"I promise I will never turn my back on you again."

Her expression softened. "Let us hope you never have reason to test that vow."

"As long as we do not keep secrets from each other I can see no reason for it to be tested."

Something flickered in the darkness of her eyes, something that jerked his heart against his ribs and made him want to ask what it was she was hiding, but that wasn't what trusting someone was all about, and he was determined to trust Sophia.

"Come," he commanded, sitting up. "We will get washed, put on our robes and sneak downstairs for a glass of wine in the library. If you are good I shall read to you."

"And if I am naughty?" Smiling seductively, Sophia also sat up and allowed him to help her to her feet.

Julian returned the smile. Lord, but she made him feel young and carefree!

"If you are naughty then you shall have to read to me."

An exaggerated pout pursed her lips. "That does not sound very enticing."

Walking behind her, Julian placed both hands on her full hips and leaned down to whisper in her ear, "Yes, but you do not know what I plan to do to you while you are reading."

She shivered beneath his hands and he chuckled.

The water in the tub was beginning to cool and so they washed quickly, drying off with soft, warm towels before slipping into their robes and slippers.

Like two mischievous children, they crept quietly through the dark corridor and down the stairs. Once they were in the library, Julian locked the door and stoked the fire dying in the hearth. Within minutes he had a nice blaze going, bathing the room in flickering light and snug warmth.

Kicking off his slippers, Julian padded barefoot across the plush carpet to the liquor cabinet and retrieved two wineglasses. He filled each with a generous measure of rich, red wine.

"So, what book would you like?" he asked as he turned toward her, a glass in either hand. As soon as his gaze fell upon her, he froze in stunned and aroused amusement.

His wife—his very, very *naughty* wife—reclined on the chaise, her pale skin even paler against the dark blue velvet. She had taken her hair down and the thick, black curtain fell straight and heavy around her shoulders.

She was also stark naked.

"I shall read whatever you like, my lord."

Grinning, Julian closed the distance between them. "Oh, shall you?" He offered her a glass.

"Oh, yes." A seductive smile curved her lips. "I only ask one thing."

"And what is that?"

The smile grew. "Pick something *long*. I want you to keep me reading for a while."

Early the following afternoon, joined by Lilith in a shiny wine-colored carriage with the Angelwood crest on the door, Sophia realized that she had yet to give her husband a wedding gift. She wanted to give him something that might measure up to all he had given her, but how could she possibly match a poem?

"First we shop for us," Lilith informed her with a grin as the carriage rocked into motion. "Then we shall find something suitable for Julian."

They made small talk as the carriage bore them through the city toward Bond Street. Lilith's maid Luisa was with them, and while the maid spoke little English, her understanding of it was apparently much, much more advanced. It would not do to discuss private matters in front of her.

When they entered a fashionable dress shop some time later, Lilith wasted no time in putting as much distance between them and the maid as possible.

"So," she began, linking her arm through Sophia's. "Is that husband ever going to take you away for a proper honeymoon?"

Sophia smiled as they walked down an aisle laden with bolts of material on either side. "At the end of the season, after he is certain of Letitia's situation." Her smile faded a bit.

Julian was becoming increasingly anxious to see his sister wed, and Letitia was becoming increasingly secretive and withdrawn. Sophia was scared that her friend was going to do something foolish, but her vow prevented her from saying anything to Julian. She didn't like keeping secrets from him, especially after what he'd said yesterday about the two of them being honest with each other. Her concern that Letitia might be right about him forcing her to marry—Lord, she hated thinking he might prove to be like her father!—warred with her promise to Julian. She hoped Mr. Wesley proved himself worth all this secrecy.

"Excellent." Lilith's voice cut through her thoughts.

"And how are things between the two of you? Good?"

The suggestive, hopeful rise to her friend's voice brought a blush to Sophia's cheeks. "Very good."

The stunning redhead squeezed her arm. "Wonderful! Oh, Sophie, I am so very happy for you."

"I am happy too." And she was. These past few days as Julian's wife were the happiest of her life.

"I knew it would all work out." Lilith smiled smugly. "I told Gabriel and Brave it would all work out."

Her brow creasing, Sophia stopped to admire a bolt of garnet velvet. She really couldn't blame Julian's friends for their concern. The three of them were all very solicitous of one another, like family—or rather, like family *ought* to be. Sophia could not remember the last time someone had treated her in such a manner. Only Julian when he told his staff not to allow Charles in the house.

"You should have a ball gown made out of that."

Lilith's voice pulled Sophia from her thoughts. She glanced at the deep red velvet beneath her hand. It was a gorgeous color. Julian would like it.

"I think I will." What a wonderful feeling to see a bolt of fabric and know that she could have it. Not since Edmund's death had she been able to enjoy such extravagance.

Lilith grinned. "I have to shop while I can. Pretty soon nothing will fit me."

The joy on the other woman's face made it obvious that she wasn't complaining.

"Then, by all means, shop. It has been so long since I've had new gowns, I certainly have no problem indulging you."

They spent the next two hours in the shop, picking out fabric and designs for gowns, pelisses and lingerie.

"Is there anywhere else you would like to go?" Lilith asked as they exited the shop. "The milliner's perhaps? Or the glove maker's?"

Oh, a new hat would be divine. Sophia couldn't believe how much she was enjoying buying a new wardrobe. Certainly Julian had paid for her to have some new clothes upon her arrival in London—Letitia had insisted—but she hadn't felt right spending his money. Now, knowing that he liked to see her in pretty things, and wanting to look pretty for him, she had a hard time controlling the urge to spend a fortune on clothing.

She wanted to please him, but not like she had once wanted to please Edmund. She had wanted Edmund's approval and acceptance. All she wanted from Julian was his smile and . . . his heart.

"Let us save that for another day," she suggested. "I would like to find a gift for Julian now, if you do not mind. Do you know of any gentlemen's shops?"

"There is one just down the street. Let us walk there." Turning to her maid, Lilith said something in rapid Italian. When she had finished, the maid scurried off to do her bidding.

"The carriage will follow us down," Lilith explained, opening her parasol. "Shall we?"

Sophia opened her parasol as well, the dainty green umbrella shielding her face from the warm afternoon sun. Despite her pale complexion, her mother's blood ran strong in her veins and the slightest exposure to the sun often resulted in her skin turning a deep gold. From a very young age she had it drilled into her head not to allow the sun to touch her, and to this day she tried to make certain it did not.

The shop Lilith picked was remarkable. There were

snuff boxes and cravat pins, rings, watches and hundreds of other little vanity and personal items for the discerning gentleman, but none of it grabbed her attention. There were any number of things that Julian might enjoy, but nothing that struck her as special.

In the end she chose a ruby cravat pin and a shiny silver pocket watch, which she planned to have engraved. They would do until she found something more personal.

"Hello, Sophia."

Sophia froze over the tray of watches, the one she had chosen for Julian still clutched in her palm. Lifting her chin in blatant defiance, she turned to face her former brother-in-law.

"Charles." If the temperature were any lower, her words would have had ice on them.

The Marquess of Aberley smiled, but it didn't reach his eyes. They were as cold and pale as they ever were. They drifted over Sophia from head to toe, lingering on her breasts in a most insolent manner before finally lifting to her face again.

His tone was even more insulting than his gaze. "What brings the *Countess* Wolfram to a gentlemen's shop?"

Schooling her features into a cool mask, Sophia replied, "I would think that obvious. I am buying a gift for my *husband*, the earl."

Charles's handsome features tightened. He didn't mind reminding her of her lowered social status—something that hardly mattered to her—but he didn't like to be reminded that she had chosen marriage to Julian over being his mistress.

"Ah, yes." That insultingly charming tone was back in his voice. "And where is Wolfram? Do not tell me he trusts you out of his sight."

Sophia turned to the curious clerk who stood just a few feet away watching them. "Could you wrap these for me, please? I would like to take them."

Once the clerk had relieved her of her purchases, she turned her attention back to Charles. "One of the many things I adore about my husband, Charles, is that he does not treat me as a possession. Something I doubt you would understand."

A dark flush crept up Charles's chiseled cheeks. "I am surprised it took you this long to spread your legs for him."

"Careful, Charles," Sophia warned, grateful that no one seemed to have heard his insult. "You do not want to cause a scene, do you? You would not want to do anything to humiliate or bring scandal down upon yourself, would you?"

The marquéss's gaze was glacial. "You are nothing but a common whore. My brother knew it, I know it and someday your precious Wolfram will know it."

Sophia's blood ran cold even as her skin flushed with anger. "If I am a whore, Charles, it was your brother who made me one the day he bought my innocence from my parents. His whore I might have been. Julian's I might be as well, but one thing is for certain, Charles, I will never be yours."

Darkness flickered over his face, contorted his features into a sinister mask. And suddenly, Sophia understood everything.

"I was the one thing of your brother's that you wanted and did not get when he died. I am the one thing of Edmund's you were not able to have." She shook her head. "That is pathetic, Charles. Truly pathetic."

He didn't say anything. He just stood there, his barrel

chest heaving, his face dark with rage, and Sophia knew without question that if they were alone he would have hit her by now.

"As much as I sometimes despised your brother," she said, twisting the knife a little deeper despite the warnings of her brain. "I never pitied him as I do you, Charles."

His nostrils flaring, Charles whipped his hand into the air, but he didn't hit her—not just because he suddenly remembered himself, but because suddenly Lilith was there, looking for all the world as though she'd like to plant Charles a facer herself.

"Lilith," Sophia said, never taking her gaze from the marquess. "It is time for us to go."

As if on cue, the clerk returned with her packages. Anxious to leave the shop, Sophia asked him to start an account for her and slipped the small bundles into her reticule.

Charles grabbed her as she turned to leave, his fingers biting painfully into the bones of her wrist. Sophia gasped. She couldn't help it. It hurt so badly it brought tears to her eyes.

"You will pay for this," he whispered harshly against her ear, smiling so as not to alarm the other customers. "Do you hear me? I will make you sorry you ever crossed me."

Sophia met his gaze evenly, praying that he couldn't see how much he scared her. She smiled as well; it was perhaps a tad more sincere than Charles's. "You cannot do anything to me, Charles, and you know it. Now let go of me before I start screaming and really give these people something to talk about."

When he did not release her immediately, she added, "I have never cared much for my own reputation, Charles. I certainly would not hesitate to damage yours as well."

He hesitated a fraction of a second before releasing her. "We are not finished."

Sophia smiled coldly. "My dear Lord Aberley, you and I never even started."

With that parting shot, Sophia turned to Lilith, and gladly taking the arm her friend offered, left the shop with as much hauteur as her trembling limbs would allow.

Chapter 13

There are some truths, my dear Jocelyn,
that are better left untold.

An Unfortunate Attachment by the Marchioness of Aberley

Julian left word that he was not to be disturbed that afternoon as he entered his study, so when his sister came sashaying in twenty minutes later, he was somewhat perturbed—until he saw the look on her face.

"What is it, pet?"

Letitia closed the door. "I need to talk to you—if you are not too busy."

He put aside the correspondence from his Yorkshire steward and leaned back in his chair. "I am never too busy for you. You know that."

Smoothing the skirts of her pale green gown, Letitia sank into one of the armchairs, folding her hands primly in her lap.

"What is it you want to talk about?"

She was silent for a moment, as though collecting her thoughts. Finally, she raised her head.

"I do not wish to marry any of the gentlemen you have suggested."

He would have been more surprised if his difficult sibling had announced she *did* want to marry. "How would you know? You have not made any effort to become acquainted with any of them."

Her expression was mulish. "I do not wish to become acquainted with any of them."

No, of course she didn't. Heaven forfend she might actually *like* one of the young men he had chosen.

"Lettie, you promised me when I agreed to bring Sophia here that you would at least give the young men a chance."

"I have," his sister replied peevishly. "They are boring."

Julian sighed. "You haven't spent more than an hour or two in the company of any of them."

Jaw set, Letitia shrugged. "Long enough to know I would expire of boredom before the honeymoon was over."

Julian raised his brows at that, wondering just how much Letitia knew about what happened between men and women. He had tried to explain it to her once, years ago, but when it came to discussing such issues with either of his sisters he never felt as though he had done a proper job of it.

Or perhaps in Miranda's case he had done too good a job.

"You would rather marry someone exciting and unpredictable, is that it?" From the look on her face he knew that was exactly what she wanted. Something akin to panic rose up from deep within him. "I will not allow you to be taken in as Miranda was."

His sister's eyes flashed with indignation. "I am *not* Miranda."

Julian's eyes widened at her vehemence. "I know that,

but you are still a naive young woman. You would be surprised how agreeable some young men will make themselves to get their hands on a dowry the size of yours."

She scowled. "You make it sound as though it would be impossible for a gentleman to love me for myself."

"Of course not," he chided. "Any young man would be lucky to have you fall in love with him. Just take care that you fall in love with someone suitable."

She was downright haughty now. "And which one of us decides who is and is not suitable?"

She already knew the answer to that. He knew it too. "I do."

"That is not fair!" she cried, jumping up from her chair and slapping her palms down on the top of the desk. "It is my life, my future. It is my choice!"

"No," he informed her in a quiet tone. "As your guardian, it is mine."

Letitia's mouth opened but nothing came out. Despite the remorse burning in the pit of his stomach, Julian held her gaze, giving away nothing of the turmoil inside him. He wanted to see her happy, but he knew how easy it was for young men to prey on romantic, spirited, naive women like Letitia. He had done it himself once upon a time.

Tears welled in her eyes, wringing his heart even further. "You said you would not force me to marry a man I did not love."

"I would not force you to marry even if I could, which we both know I cannot."

She straightened, some of the self-assurance slipping back into her demeanor. "Good. Then we are agreed."

"Not quite," he replied as she turned to leave.

Halfway across the carpet she froze and faced him. "What do you mean?"

Steepling his fingers, Julian regarded her coolly over the tips. His sister expected him to give in to her demands too often. It had been one thing when she was a child, but it was an entirely different matter now that she was grown.

"I will not force you to marry, but I have every intention of making certain you keep your promise to me and start spending time with the young men I have selected."

"You cannot," she informed him with more bravado than she had a right to. "There is nothing you can do to make me."

His remorse was quickly giving way to anger. Where had he gone wrong? Were all young women this difficult, or had he made a colossal mess out of his sister's upbringing?

"How about no more credit at the dressmaker's?"

Her face fell a bit, but she still gazed at him like a queen upon a serf. "I have enough gowns to do me the entire season as it is."

"True," he allowed. "But what good will they do you when you have nowhere to go?"

That got a reaction out of her. She looked utterly shocked. "You would forbid me to go out?"

Julian lowered his hands. "Every invitation that arrives at this house is delivered to me. I allow you to open them because you are my sister, but if you will not do as I ask, then I will ensure that you do not see any of them and give the hostess your regrets for any I choose to accept."

Her face was devoid of color. "I cannot believe you would do that to me."

Julian refused to be swayed. "Yet you would go back on your promise to me. Now, are you going to act your age and give some of these gentlemen a chance to court you, or are you going to make things difficult?"

Letitia glared at him, her slender form practically shaking with rage. "I will keep my promise."

Julian felt little victory. "Good. Lord Rutherford sent flowers this morning and a note." He plucked the still-sealed missive off his desk and held it out to her. "Perhaps you would like to start with him."

His sister came close enough to snatch the paper out of his hand. "I have never despised you as much as I do at this moment."

He winced. Did she think he was made of stone? "I know, but someday I hope to see you so happily situated that all of your anger will have been worth it."

She didn't seem to like that response at all. In fact, she snorted in disgust at it and whirled around to stomp out of the room.

Her exit would have been much more dramatic had she not almost knocked over Sophia on her way out.

His wife turned to him with a puzzled expression. "Whatever is the matter with her?"

Rising to his feet, Julian rounded the desk to meet her near the sofa. "My sister makes it a point to hate me at least one day a week. Today is the day."

She smiled at his humor, but her gaze was earnest. "Is everything all right between the two of you?"

With a sigh, he steered her toward the sofa and gestured for her to sit. He seated himself beside her.

"It will be. Letitia was trying to renege on her promise to spend time with the gentlemen I've chosen as potential husbands for her."

Sophia's brow knitted. "Julian, you do not plan to force her, do you?"

"To marry? No." At her nod he didn't bother to mention that he would do whatever necessary to get Letitia to at least *meet* some of the young men. "But I want her to marry well."

His wife's frown deepened. "What of love? Surely you want her to marry for that as well?"

Taking one of her hands in his, Julian raised it to his lips. "It is possible to enter a marriage without love and still be content, is it not?"

He chuckled as she colored softly. "It is different for us. We are both practical, logical people. Letitia is a romantic."

"You were once a romantic," he reminded her. "I believe that I am one still, in my heart."

She flushed darker. "You know what I mean."

"No, I am afraid I do not." Perhaps he did understand on some level, but he didn't want to spend the rest of their lives together as nothing more than friends making love. He wanted Sophia to love him. He wanted to love her.

Good Lord. When had this come about?

When she didn't respond, her consternation evident, Julian asked, "Do you think you might come to love me one day, Sophia?"

She went as still as a deer who knows the hunter is nearby. "I do not know."

It was better than *no*. "What if I said I had every intention of making you love me?" *And loving you in return.*

Her entire body jerked. Her emotional withdrawal was as obvious as the pounding of the pulse in her throat. He held tight to her hand, preventing her from withdrawing physically as well.

This was not the reaction he had hoped for, but it didn't surprise him, either. Perhaps he shouldn't have been so blunt about his intentions, but he had been raised by parents who loved each other, and since marrying Sophia he had decided that nothing less would do for his own marriage. It was all right if Sophia didn't love him now. She would one day. He would make certain of it.

"I am not sure I know how to love."

He pulled a face. "Nonsense."

Her gaze was shadowed as it met his. "Nor do I think I am the kind of woman with whom gentlemen fall in love."

Her voice, so low and hesitant, pierced his heart with its stark vulnerability. "Why do you say that?"

She looked down at her feet. Following her gaze, Julian saw that she was curling her toes inside her dainty green slippers.

"Because no one has ever told me they loved me. Not my parents—although now I believe that my mother does—not Edmund, certainly not Charles." She looked up, accusation and pain in her eyes. "Not you."

Like a well-timed blow, her remark hit him square in the chest, knocking the breath from his lungs.

"That was then," he murmured, finding it hard to speak. "I want more than that now."

She watched him, her gaze searching his face as though looking for some sign of falsehood.

"So do I."

Julian hadn't even been aware of holding his breath until it all came rushing out. He didn't know what to say, didn't know if anything needed to be said.

They sat in silence for what seemed like an eternity. It was as though there were still so many things they both wanted to say and neither knew how to say them.

"I have something for you," she said finally, holding out her other hand. There was a small wrapped box in it.

She had bought him a gift. When was the last time any-one had bought him a gift?

"Thank you." He took it from her. "What is the occasion?"

Sophia shrugged. "No reason. I just thought you might like it."

Feeling somewhat like a child, he released his hold on her hand and tore off the ribbon securing the wrapping. The paper fell free, revealing a polished rosewood box. He lifted the lid. Inside was a gold and ruby cravat pin and a pocket watch.

No one had ever bought him jewelry before. They seemed such personal items—fitting gifts for a wife to give a husband.

"They are lovely." He kissed her. "Thank you."

"You have done so much for me I wanted to give you something in return."

His good mood lessened. "I do not want you to give me gifts because you feel indebted to me, Sophia."

Her hands came up to cup his face, preventing him from pulling away. "I know." Her eyes sparkled with humor. "You really should not be so quick to jump to conclusions, Julian. I bought you presents because I wanted to buy you presents. That is all."

She let go of his face and he nodded. He was such an idiot at times. "Forgive me."

Sophia smiled.

"I have to tell you something," she said after a moment's silence. "Something that happened while I was out with Lilith."

There was a hesitancy in her voice, almost as though she was afraid of his reaction to what she was about to tell him. It both worried and pleased him. Worried him because she was so obviously distressed. Pleased him because she trusted him enough to share it.

"What is it?" He kept his tone carefully neutral.

She held his gaze regardless of her obvious discomfort. "I ran into Charles."

Just the sound of the marquess's name was enough to kindle his anger. He didn't give a damn if the man was a marquess, if he so much as breathed on Sophia, Julian would demand satisfaction for it.

"What did he say to you?"

He listened, rage bubbling inside him as Sophia recounted the details of her run-in with her former brother-in-law. Julian suspected she left some details out to keep him from getting too angry. She needn't have bothered. He didn't think he could possibly want to kill Aberley any more than he already did.

"Promise me you will not confront him." Her tone was anxious.

"You ask too much. I cannot make such a promise."

"Julian." She caught him by the arm as he started to stand and pulled him back down beside her. "I do not want to give the gossips more to titter about. Neither should you, if you truly wish to see Letitia receive a suitable offer of marriage."

She was right, of course. Julian was learning that she often *was*, damn her. The scandal surrounding their marriage wasn't huge, but it still had yet to die down. People still whispered about them at parties, still made thinly veiled comments about *An Unfortunate Attachment* to them both. Most of society treated it as a joke at worst, a charming tale of reunited lovers at best. But if word got around that Julian went looking for a fight with the Marquess of Aberley, and that it was over Sophia . . .

"All right," he grumbled. "I won't confront him, but if he comes to me I will make him sorry for it."

A coy smile curved her lips. "My protector."

Picking up on her change of mood, the subtle shift in her body language, Julian grinned. "Do you like it?" He leaned closer, turning his body so that he pinned her against the sofa.

She moved to accommodate him. "Very much."

He cupped her breast in his hand. "Does it excite you?"

Sophia nodded, gasping as his thumb brushed the hardened peak of her breast through the material of her gown. Her body reacted so wonderfully to his touch.

"Is the door locked?" she asked, winding her arms around his neck.

He drew back. She barely touched him, and already he was half erect. "No, but it could be. What did you have in mind?"

Smiling softly, she flicked her tongue across his lips. "I think I have thought of a way for you to thank me for your gift."

Julian chuckled as he stood. Quickly, he crossed the carpet and turned the key in the door. Then he returned to his beautiful wife, who was already starting to struggle out of her clothes.

Oh yes. He was a very *thankful* man indeed.

Sophia opened her eyes as the clock in the downstairs hall struck three. Beside her, Julian snored softly, his features bathed in silvery moonlight. Sophia smiled. For a man who claimed not to snore he was certainly very good at it.

But Julian's snoring was not the reason for her restlessness. Their earlier conversation was.

What was all this nonsense about wanting her to love him and wanting to love her in return? He didn't mean it, did he? Love was the last thing she would ever expect him to want from her.

When he told her he wanted her love, it was all she could do to keep her mouth shut.

She had already fallen—or at least stumbled.

How or when it had happened she had no idea. There hadn't been enough time, but she knew with frightening clarity that it was true. She couldn't—wouldn't—tell him until she was certain of his feelings for her. She was not about to give him that kind of power over her. Oh, she knew their marriage shouldn't be about power, but it didn't matter how much they had both changed. The fact remained that she had told Julian she loved him once before and the feeling hadn't been returned. The next time she told him she would be certain of his feelings first.

After her run-in with Charles earlier, all she had wanted to do was run home to the safety of Julian's arms. When she asked him not to confront Charles, it wasn't because of Letitia's reputation as she claimed, but rather because she couldn't bear the thought of anything happening to Julian because of her. She had purposefully left out or altered many of the things Charles had said to her as well. Julian would have been even angrier had she told him the truth.

That was three times in one evening that she had lied to him. How could she ever expect to earn his trust when she did not even try?

Perhaps it wasn't so completely wrong to lie to someone to protect them, or to be honest, protect oneself. It was petty of her, she knew, but she couldn't help it.

But these pointless thoughts were not the only reason she could not sleep. Other questions plagued her, such as whether or not she should betray Letitia's trust and tell her brother about her attachment to Marcus Wesley. Letitia would never forgive her if she did. Julian might not forgive her if she didn't. Which would be worse?

She was not married to Letitia. She wasn't *stumbling* into love with Letitia, but neither was she prepared to expose her friend in such a manner. She would have to talk to Letitia and tell her what a difficult position she had put her in and beg her to confide in her brother.

In the meantime she could not lie here worrying about things any longer. Silently, she crept out of bed and slipped into the plum velvet robe she had dropped to the floor at Julian's request earlier that evening. A glass of wine would calm her mind.

Julian didn't stir as she left the room. Drawing the door shut behind her, she tiptoed down the corridor to the stairs and picked her way down in the dark.

She didn't see the person at the foot of the stairs until it was too late. A sharp gasp issued forth from the stranger's throat as Sophia stifled a scream.

"Sophia?"

It was Letitia. Even if Sophia hadn't been able to tell by the voice, now that her eyes adjusted to the dim light in the hall, she could make out her sister-in-law's shadowy form.

And that she was wearing evening clothes.

"Have you been out?" Surely she hadn't been. Hadn't she pled a headache shortly after dinner and retired to her room? She had told Julian she was going to bed and would see them both in the morning.

The guilt-ridden silence that followed her inquiry was answer enough.

Catching the younger woman by the arm, Sophia
steered her away from the stairs, where someone else
might stumble upon, or worse, overhear them. She guided
Letitia out into the great hall, so she could better see her
face.

"Where have you been?" she demanded, struggling to
keep her voice low.

Letitia's expression was sullen. "Why, so you can tell
Julian?"

Sophia scowled at the taller woman. "It would serve
you right if I did. Honestly, Letitia, this is hardly the behavior of a full-grown lady."

Letitia sucked in her cheeks. "I do not think you are the
appropriate person to lecture me on propriety, Sophia."

The remark should have stung, especially since it was
delivered with such venom, but it only made Sophia angrier.

"On the contrary. I am the perfect person to lecture
you, for I know the consequences of behaving impulsively
and stupidly. Do you want to end up as I did?"

Letitia's expression was still sulky. "You do not seem
to mind being married to my brother."

Heat pulsed in Sophia's blood. "Of course I do not, but
I was once married to a man whom I allowed to treat me
badly because I was so terrified he'd leave me if I did not.
All because I had behaved inappropriately. Is that what
you want?"

Letitia's mouth dropped open, and for a moment her
petulant facade disappeared, only to return again seconds
later. "That will never happen to me. Marcus would never
treat me in such a way. He is going to marry me."

Sophia arched a brow. "Has he proposed?"

Letitia frowned. "Not officially, no. But we have talked about it."

"About marriage?"

Her chin came up defiantly. "About our future."

"You had better make certain, do you not think? A young man might talk as though he will marry you, but he may say whatever necessary to get what he wants. And you will give it to him, because you believe he is going to give you what you want."

Letitia snorted. She had to know Sophia was talking from firsthand experience. "I have a hard time imagining my perfect brother behaving in such a way."

Smiling coolly, Sophia moved in for the kill. "Then try to imagine how a lesser man—a man with less to lose— would behave."

All the haughtiness drained from Letitia's face, leaving only anger and resentment. "Marcus is not a lesser man."

"Then why has he not been to see your brother? Why does he never call on you?"

Thin arms folded across Letitia's chest. "Because he knows Julian is against him and he is waiting to hear about a business venture that might make him more financially suitable in Julian's eyes."

Sophia sincerely hoped that was the truth and that Mr. Wesley wasn't acting a part to her friend.

"In the meantime you sneak out to see him, risking your very reputation in the process."

If Letitia lifted that pointy chin of hers any higher Sophia wouldn't be able to see anything of her face but her nostrils.

"Being with him is worth any risk."

Sophia tried to ignore the warning bells clanging in her head.

"Letitia, promise me you will not do anything foolish—at least not before Mr. Wesley makes his intentions known."

Letitia stared at her, and even though it was too dark to see the expression in her eyes, Sophia knew it wasn't favorable.

"There was a time when you would not have asked me such a question," her sister-in-law countered. "You used to trust me."

Sophia offered the only reply she could, "Love makes a person do things they would not normally do."

"Is that why you are so concerned? Or is it because you are becoming like my brother?"

Sophia was all astonishment. "Like your brother?"

Letitia shifted her weight to one leg, thrusting her hip out in a most belligerent manner. "Yes. You are even beginning to sound like him, treating me as though I were a child, unable to tell when someone is lying to me."

Perhaps this wouldn't be a good time to inform Letitia that if she felt like a child it was because she was acting like one. "I did not say that. I just want you to be careful."

"You mean you do not want me to be happy."

Oh, this was ridiculous! "You are right, Letitia. That is exactly it. I want you to be miserable. Perhaps I should go wake your brother and tell him why you are so reluctant to spend time with any of the suitors he has chosen. Why did I not think of it sooner?"

A hand caught her arm as she turned to go. "No, Sophia, please!"

It was Sophia's turn to be belligerent now. She faced

Letitia with a challenging gaze. "Give me one good reason why I should not."

Letitia seemed to think about it, undoubtedly searching for a good enough reason in that mystifying mind of hers. "I will never speak to you again if you do."

Sophia was unmoved. "Right now that sounds more like a favor than a threat, Letitia."

The young woman's face fell. For a moment Sophia feared she might actually burst into tears. That would not be good, but it didn't stop her from continuing, "You accuse me of being untrustworthy, yet you have yet to give me good reason to trust you. You keep secrets, skulk about like some kind of criminal and now you try to threaten me. That does not make you much of a friend, Letitia. It does not make you someone I can trust."

Letitia's chin trembled and Sophia braced herself, waiting for the deluge to start.

But it didn't. "You are right," the younger woman replied in a shaky voice. "I haven't been much of a friend to you lately. In fact, I haven't been your friend at all. I have been petty and jealous."

"Jealous?" This was something new.

With a great deal of obvious hesitancy, Letitia met her gaze. "Yes. I see how happy you and Julian are and it makes me angry. I want you to go back to disliking him so I can feel that you are on my side again, and I am jealous because I want a husband to laugh with."

As angry as she had been, Sophia was touched by her friend's candor. She couldn't help but be sympathetic.

"And you will have one someday. I promise." She couldn't resist adding, "Just take care you do not get yourself into trouble, being in such a hurry."

Letitia nodded. "I will. Forgive me, Sophia, please."

Smiling, Sophia ran her hand down the other woman's arm. "It is already forgiven, but I want you to promise me that there will be no more sneaking out at night. No more behavior that might expose you to scandal."

Again Letitia nodded. "I promise."

The vow was given rather quickly, perhaps a little too lightly, but Sophia was satisfied with it for now. "Good. Now why don't you get off to bed? It is late."

Letitia hugged her and said good night. Sophia stood at the bottom of the stairs and watched as the young woman climbed them into the darkness beyond. A few moments later she heard the soft click of a door opening and closing again.

Dealing with Letitia had left Sophia more exhausted than any amount of wine and reading could have. She wanted nothing more than to climb back into bed beside Julian and press her cold toes against his warm legs.

She did just that, shucking off her robe before she slipped under the covers. He woke up as she placed her feet in the soft crook of his knees.

"Bloody hell, those are cold!" he cried hoarsely, rolling toward her. "Where the devil have you been?"

"Downstairs," she replied. "I thought a glass of wine might help me sleep."

Hauling her against him, even though he growled about how cold she was, Julian put his nose near her mouth and sniffed. "I do not smell wine."

"I did not have any. I ran into Letitia and ended up talking to her instead." At least that was the truth.

Obviously he didn't find it strange that Letitia was also up at this late hour. He merely nodded, his cheek sliding against her pillow. He was so lovely when he was sleepy.

"I trust she is feeling better?"

Stroking the soft fullness of his hair, Sophia kissed his forehead. "I believe so, yes."

"Good. It upsets me to cause her such distress."

Wrapping her arms around him, Sophia closed her eyes and didn't reply. He would be so much more upset if he only knew the truth.

The truth she had promised not to tell him.

Chapter 14

There are few things that are quite as painful
as unrequited love.

An Unfortunate Attachment by the Marchioness of Aberley

Julian saw the fist a split second before it came crashing into his jaw.

"Bloody hell, Jules. I thought you were looking. Are you all right?"

Shaking his head to clear the stars dancing before his eyes, Julian stretched his jaw open and then closed it again. At least it still worked, even if it did hurt like the blazes.

He was in one corner of Gentleman Jackson's pugilism club. All around him, aristocratic gentlemen with varying levels of skill made a show of trying to pound each other into some kind of barbaric pecking order. He was one of them.

A few feet away, he could hear Gabriel chuckling. "Have a care with that pretty face of his, Brave."

Julian scowled at his friend before turning his attention back to his sparring opponent. "I am fine. It is my own fault—I should have been paying attention."

254

But he hadn't been. His mind had been busy thinking of Sophia and how preoccupied she had been over the past few days. She seemed to have something pressing upon her thoughts, something she didn't seem to want to share with him. He didn't think she was unhappy in their marriage, but she was certainly preoccupied with something.

He asked Sophia what was troubling her—several times in fact. She had smiled and replied that it was nothing, that she was simply woolgathering.

Perhaps it was the confrontation with Aberley that had her so morose. He knew full well she had left out details of the meeting when she told him of it—he could hear it in her voice. Why did she not tell him the truth? Was she embarrassed, or was she truly worried that he would challenge the marquess? She should know that just the fact that Aberley had dared approach her was reason enough in Julian's mind to beat the man senseless.

"I wager I know what has you so addlepated." Gabriel flashed him a rakish grin as he helped Brave out of the mufflers—thick, padded gloves—covering his hands. As a rule the gloves were used for practice matches while bare knuckles were still the weapon of preference in the ring.

"And what might that be?" Julian didn't step up to have his gloves removed. He was still brimming with restless energy. He still wanted to hurt somebody. Gabriel was beginning to look like the perfect candidate.

"You are a newlywed," the darker man replied, holding Brave's now-empty gloves. "Your mind is on your wife— where it should be."

"You are very astute." Julian lifted his chin toward the gloves in the other man's hands. "Put those on and come fight me, Gabe. You do not mind hitting me half so much as Brave does."

Gabriel's nose wrinkled as he looked down at the used mufflers. "They are damp."

"So?"

His friend glanced up, distaste still plain on his face. "They smell."

Laughing, Julian gave up. "Never mind then, you big coward. I shall just have to find someone else to spar with."

"I would be pleased to spar with you, Wolfram."

Julian froze, the laughter dying in his throat. He knew before he turned around—knew from the expressions on Gabe's and Brave's faces—who his challenger was.

"How very kind of you, Aberley," he replied with frosty civility, "but I must decline."

Aberley flashed a grin at the two men flanking him. "You are not afraid of me, are you, Wolfram?"

It was the most childish thing the marquess could have asked. It was also the most effective. No man could walk away from an affront to his courage, especially not one who had spent much of his school years proving his slender stature didn't mean he couldn't hold his own.

But he had promised Sophia . . .

No. He had promised Sophia he wouldn't *confront* Aberley. He remembered distinctly telling her that he could not make her any such promise if Aberley came to him. And in this arena, where men fought each other every day, any violence between them would not raise half the scandal as some kind of duel might.

"No," he heard himself reply. "I am not afraid at all. Get yourself a pair of mufflers, Aberley. I will fight you."

His smile perhaps a little less smug than it had been,

the marquess nodded. He still looked more pleased with himself than he had a right too. Julian knew from simply looking at him that Aberley planned to beat him, and not just beat him but publicly humiliate him.

"Do you know what you are doing?" Gabriel demanded, coming up behind him as the marquess and his cronies went in search of gloves.

Glancing over his shoulder, Julian nodded. "Yes, I do."

"I have seen Aberley fight before," Brave joined in. "He is very good."

Julian didn't take his gaze off the marquess's retreating back. "So am I."

Apparently unsatisfied by his answers, his friends came forward, confronting him face on now, rather than from behind.

"Surely you are not going to fight the man just because he challenged you?" Gabriel demanded. He frowned. "Why did he challenge you anyway?"

"I presume it has something to do with Sophia," Julian replied, deliberately vague.

Julian had never seen fit to tell his friends about Aberley's physical assault on Sophia. Sophia wouldn't want them to know. He told them about how he kept her in lowered circumstances, and of course they knew he was responsible for the reappearance of Sophia's book, but they had no idea that Aberley hated him for stopping him from forcing himself upon Sophia. Hated him for marrying her.

What Aberley didn't know was that Julian hated *him* even more.

His friends dropped back again, no doubt to discuss him behind his back. Julian didn't care. He knew that Brave and Gabriel were merely concerned for him and his safety. They needn't be. Even if Aberley bested him, Ju-

lian was still going to hurt the marquess—very badly, with
any luck.

Aberley returned a few moments later. Stripped down
to his shirtsleeves, he looked even bigger than he had before. The sleeves were rolled up to reveal beefy forearms,
and the gloves he wore only made his huge hands even
more gigantic. Julian made a mental note to keep moving
as much as possible. No mistake, if Aberley hit him, it was
going to hurt. A lot.

Shrugging his shoulders to loosen the knotted muscles
there and in his neck, Julian waited for Aberley to come
to him.

"'Tis a good thing you and Braven are here, Angelwood." Aberley grinned. "Wolfram will have to be carried
out of here when I am done with him."

Julian fixed his opponent with a level stare. "Are you
going to stand around grunting all day, Aberley, or are we
going to fight?"

All traces of mockery faded from the marquess's face
as his features twisted into a bitter mask of contempt. "I
am ready if you are, Wolfram."

Julian only nodded. Slowly, he raised his fists, adopting
a defensive stance. As he predicted, Aberley made the first
move, coming at him with such speed and ferocity that
Julian dodged the blow at the last possible second. As he
came back up he struck out at the other man's thick midsection, catching him in the ribs with a hard jab. Aberley
grunted and reacted instantly, catching Julian in the jaw
with such force Julian thought his neck might break as it
snapped backwards. He had been right. It did hurt when
Aberley hit him. A lot.

Shaking off the colored lights dancing before his eyes,
Julian managed to recover just as the marquess charged

again. This time he managed to land a hard punch to Aberley's temple. He couldn't help but smile as the larger man stumbled backward, obviously dazed.

How long they danced like this Julian didn't know. His jaw ached, there was blood inside his mouth and his gut felt as though someone had driven a battering ram into it, but he would not stop. He couldn't.

Aberley looked much better off, even though Julian knew he had managed to land enough well-placed blows to make the marquess suffer. It wasn't enough.

Oddly enough, it was Aberley himself who tipped the scales. Obviously he had decided that physically battering Julian wasn't enough. He wanted to taunt him as well.

"Do you really think she's worth taking this kind of abuse for, Wolfram?"

Julian made no reply. He held Aberley's glittering gaze as he circled him slowly.

"I sincerely hope you have not made the mistake of believing she cares about you, my boy. Money is the only thing she cares about."

His expression did not change. "If money was all she wanted, Aberley, why did she not choose you?"

The barb was more effective than a right hook. Aberley's eyes lost some of their malicious sparkle. "I did not make the mistake of offering her marriage."

"No. You did not offer her much at all." Julian smiled. "Only yourself."

That was all it took. Gone was any composure or appearance of civility as the marquess snarled in reply. He charged at Julian like a rampaging bull.

Julian was ready.

It all happened in a matter of split seconds, and yet Julian saw everything as clearly as though time had slowed to a crawl. He lashed out, his gloved fist catching Aberley in the chin, sending the fairer man's head whipping backward over his shoulder.

The heavier man staggered backward, but rather than waiting for him to recover, Julian followed after him, hitting him in the stomach this time. And when Aberley doubled over from the force of the wind being knocked out of him, Julian hit him in the face again. Every blow knocked Aberley backward and with every blow, Julian advanced forward.

It hadn't taken long for other patrons to notice the brawl taking place in the lower corner of the room. It was hard to miss, especially since the Earl of Wolfram was driving the Marquess of Aberley across the floor with a series of blows that made even Jackson himself wince.

But then the marquess rallied. His big fist struck Julian again in the jaw, sending a spray of blood from Julian's mouth into the air. Thankfully, his jaw was unbroken, but the inside of his cheek was cut from being smashed against his teeth.

"Is she really worth this, Wolfram?" Aberley demanded as Julian dodged another swing. "Do you think she truly cares what happens to you? She is probably laughing at you right now; congratulating herself for pulling the wool over your eyes and making you believe she's worth having."

Julian punched Aberley high on one cheekbone. "You certainly went through a lot of trouble to have her yourself."

Aberley's expression was half smile, half wince. "It was no trouble at all. How does that feel, Wolfram? To know that your wife has had another man's cock inside her?"

For a moment, Julian stopped. He dampened the rage boiling inside him with a force of will he never knew he had.

"How do you feel knowing it was your brother's and not yours?" he countered, landing another blow to his opponent's face. "How do you feel knowing that I am the one who shares a bed with her now?" Another jab. Aberley's head snapped back.

The anger flowed heavily now and Julian let the fever pour over him. He let it guide his arms, felt its strength behind every blow.

"How do you feel knowing it will never"—he punched the marquess in the mouth—"ever"—a left jab to the stomach—"be you?" He finished with a lightning-fast jab to Aberley's nose. It crumpled beneath his glove, sending Aberley to his knees with a cry of pain.

Julian would not have stopped were it not for Gabriel and Brave. He would have kept on battering Aberley's handsome face until not even the man's mother would recognize it if his friends hadn't grabbed his arms and pulled him backward.

"Enough," Gabriel muttered harshly near his ear. "You have won. Now let us put an end to it before it becomes more a scandal than it already is."

A scandal. Damnation. He had promised Sophia he wouldn't cause a scandal.

"Whoa!" Brave said with loud, forced joviality, clapping Julian on the back as he did so. "Got a little carried away there, did you not, Wolfram?"

It was then that Julian managed to lift his hate-filled

gaze from Aberley's bent form and noticed the crowd of spectators. The gazes ranged from curious to disapproving. He noticed that no one rushed to the marquess's aid, however.

He forced what he hoped looked like an apologetic smile, for he was no more sorry for breaking Aberley's nose than he was for waking up that morning.

"I do not know what came over me." Pulling his arm free of Brave's grip, he extended a glove to the marquess. "My apologies, Aberley."

Blood running from his nostrils, Aberley glared at him as he slapped Julian's hand away.

"Go to hell, Wolfram."

Julian laughed then. Turning a sheepish expression to the spectators, he shrugged.

"Rightfully so, the marquess is not in humor to accept my apology." Some of the men laughed as well. Someone from the back yelled that Aberley should be a better sport.

If anything, the lightened atmosphere of the club made Aberley even more hateful. His two cronies were at his side again. One tried to help him to his feet, but he pushed them away, rising on his own.

He held a handkerchief against his nose. "We're not finished, Wolfram."

Holding his gaze, Julian smiled. "Yes, we are—or next time I will break more than your nose."

And then, just to add to Aberley's rage, Julian addressed the crowd. "Lord Aberley has forgiven me for getting so carried away. All is settled between us." This last statement was directed at the marquess alone.

"What the devil happened back there?" Gabriel demanded some time later when they were in his carriage and on their way home. "You went after Aberley like a madman."

Julian dabbed at a spot of blood on his lip with his handkerchief before replying, "What I am about to tell you goes no further than this carriage."

His friends nodded in agreement.

"Aberley tried to force himself upon Sophia. That is why I brought her to London in the first place."

"No wonder you went after the bastard the way you did," Gabriel remarked. "I wonder that you did not kill him."

"I wanted to," Julian replied.

It wasn't Aberley Brave was concerned with. "What are you going to tell Sophia?"

Oh, Lord, Sophia! He hadn't even thought about facing her. Even if he had managed to convince the men at the salon that his pummeling of Aberley had been an accident, there was no way he could convince Sophia of the same. She was going to know he had broken his promise to her.

"I have no idea," he replied honestly. "But I had better think of something fast."

When Julian entered the gold drawing room that afternoon, Sophia stared at his beautiful face with something akin to horror.

She had been waiting for him to return home from his afternoon with Brave and Gabriel so they could discuss Letitia. She might have promised her friend that she wouldn't tell Julian about her engagement to Mr. Wesley, but that didn't mean she couldn't drop a few well-placed hints in his direction. She wanted him to tell her that all that mattered to him was his sister's happiness. She wanted him to be different from her father.

Setting aside the invitation she had been reading, she rose to her feet and went to him, her mouth dropping open at the sight of his bruised features. "What have you done to yourself?"

Julian smiled weakly and winced. "I did not do it. Someone else did."

He refused to lean on her, but allowed her to take his arm and lead him toward the long gold brocade sofa.

"I cannot believe either Gabriel or Brave would inflict such injury upon you." But what did she know of men and their barbaric sports? They sometimes seemed to *enjoy* hurting one another.

"That is because they were not at fault either," he replied. "Well, perhaps Brave is a very little. He did plant me a good facer earlier." He sank onto the sofa, grimacing as he did so.

Sophia sat down beside him, a niggling sense of unease worming its way up her spine. She could tell from her husband's obvious discomfort that whoever it was who had beaten him had *meant* to harm him.

"Who were you fighting, Julian?"

He seemed reluctant to meet her gaze. "Aberley."

A chill settled over her flesh. Hadn't she asked him just the other night not to confront Charles? He had promised her that he would not.

He had also told her that he wouldn't walk away if Charles came after him.

"Did he challenge you?"

Julian nodded. "He did."

Sophia drew a short breath. "And you could not walk away."

His gaze locked with hers. "I could not."

"Why not?" She wanted him to make her understand how his pride, or even she herself, could possibly be worth taking such a beating for.

"He insulted you."

"I do not care what he says about me, Julian."

"I do."

"And do you think allowing him to hit you changes any of that? You cannot change what he thinks. You cannot change what he says. All your bruises and cuts are for naught, save perhaps for giving people reason to talk behind your back."

He watched her with a most peculiar expression—part indignation, part incredulity.

"You think I lost."

Sophia blinked at the wounded amusement in his tone. Of course she thought he had lost! What other outcome could there be? He looked awful and Charles outweighed him by a good four stone at least.

"It does not matter who won or who lost," she replied in a careful tone. "I am certain you both have cuts and bruises enough between you."

He was decidedly affronted as he rose to his feet, grimacing and pressing a hand to his midsection as he did so.

"I will have you know that I did *not* lose." He scowled at her as he spoke. "I might look a little worse for wear, but Aberley walked out of there with his nose snapped like a twig."

Sophia stared at him, her stomach churning in a most uncomfortable manner. Just how hard did a person have to be struck in order to have their nose "snapped like a twig"? Quite hard, she imagined.

"Oh, God, Julian," she whispered. "What have you done?"

He must have heard the distress in her voice, because he sat down beside her again.

"Oh, for heaven's sake!" she snapped. "Can you not just stay still? You are making *me* sore with all this up and down foolishness!"

His lips twitched as he arched a brow at her. "Forgive me. I shall try to keep my discomfort to myself."

Sophia frowned at his droll tone. "You deserve to be uncomfortable! How am I supposed to feel knowing you broke a man's nose?"

He was frowning now as well. "You seemed perfectly content to think me the loser of the match. You did not seem to mind the idea of him hurting me. Why now so pale?"

She stared at him. "Because I expect such violence from Charles. I expect better from you."

Perhaps it wasn't the most tactful way to word her concerns, but it was certainly the most direct and the most honest. The idea of Julian being capable of such brutality, such violence—and that he could be proud of it!—appalled her. And yet . . .

Yet at the same time, she had to admit, what appalled her even more was the pleasure that had blossomed in the pit of her stomach when he told her he had won. As a woman, she wasn't allowed the luxury of being as physically strong as a man. She might be able to hurt Charles with words, but she could never do what Julian had done—and publicly, no less!

Julian's face was ashen beneath the red and purple

patches where Charles had struck him. "You would prefer that I allowed him to get away with harassing you in shops? That I pretend he has not insulted you to the lowest level?"

Sophia understood the anger in his voice. He was frustrated, hurt and indignant. There was a certain helplessness to being told you couldn't fight back—or not having any weapons with which to fight. As a man, it would be even harder for him to walk away from a confrontation. He probably did not know what it was like to be told what to do, bullied or preyed upon because he was weak. How could he? He was Julian. He was nothing if not strong.

"Do you honestly think that what happened between the two of you today will stop him from saying what he pleases to me whenever I see him?" From the glare in his eyes she could tell that was exactly what he thought. "You publicly humiliated him and he will never forgive either of us for it."

He rose to his feet yet again. This time she winced as well. "What I did today was show him that I will not tolerate his insulting you or myself."

"Walking away would have had the same result."

He shot her a look that blatantly told her she didn't know what she was talking about. "It would have made me look like a coward."

Ah, masculine pride. It drove men to do the most outlandish things, suffer the most excruciating pain and oftentimes lose those they love just because they couldn't bring themselves to do something that might make them look weak in the eyes of another man.

"So what you are saying then, is that you did not fight Charles because of any injury to me, but because you feared what others might say about you."

Julian's face darkened. "What if I had not fought him, Sophia? How would you feel the next time we were out at a ball and someone called me a coward in front of you? Would you be proud to be the wife of a man all of society sniggered at?"

"I would be proud to be your wife no matter what people say about you, Julian. I know what kind of man you are. I do not need others to tell me."

For a moment, he just stood there, staring at her, an unreadable expression on his face.

"You are mine. I will fight for you."

The possessive edge to his voice dotted Sophia's arms with gooseflesh. He said it like he owned her, and yet she couldn't help but feel that it meant much more than that.

"You do not have to fight for me," she informed him. "We are husband and wife, you have already won me. So why do this to yourself?"

He looked for all the world as though he would rather face Charles again than answer her question.

He raked a hand through his already messy hair and turned away from her. "I spent much of my life doing what I was told I *had* to do. I will not allow anyone to control me again."

"And that includes me." It was a statement, not a question.

He turned, an expression on his face that was both determined yet regretful. "Yes."

It didn't really hurt to hear him say it. She didn't want to control him. She couldn't respect a man who would allow her to walk all over him. What woman could?

"I will not allow you to control me either." Holding her breath, she waited for his reaction. Edmund would have laughed, because he would have known, just as she did, that she was in no position to make such demands.

Not so, Julian. "I do not want to."

Her sigh of relief was almost audible.

"But I do intend to possess you, Sophia. Body, heart and soul. Make no mistake about that."

A wave of heat rippled across her flesh, blossoming into flame in the deepest, darkest recesses of her body. Had it been any other man saying such things to her, Sophia would have been terrified. Angry. Defensive. But not with Julian. She wanted to be his.

"Would you offer the same in return, Julian?" she asked softly. "Do you offer me your body, heart and soul?"

He was unflinching. "You only have to want them."

Something that tasted very much like fear rose up in Sophia's throat. This didn't seem possible. It was too much.

It wasn't enough.

Hands folded in front of her, she rose to her feet, moving toward him with carefully measured steps. "What of your trust? Do I have that too?"

Golden brown eyes flickered over her face. "With my life."

If he had struck her as he had struck Charles she wouldn't have been less shocked.

He took a step toward her. She couldn't tear her gaze away from his poor battered face. Even bruised and swollen he was the most beautiful thing she had ever laid eyes on.

"Do I have your trust, Sophia? Would you put your life in my hands?"

Hadn't she done that several times already?

She moved her hands behind her back. "You promised me you would not fight Charles. I believed you." It certainly wasn't a yes, but it wasn't quite a no, either.

He took another step. They were touching now. His torso pressed softly against her breasts. She could push him away if she wanted. One shove and he would give her room to breathe without inhaling his scent. Room to feel without feeling him all around her, making her want to say things safer left unsaid.

"You lied to me, Sophia." He traced the tip of one finger along the side of her cheek.

"I most certainly did not," she replied with as much hauteur as she could muster.

He was insistent. "You did." His finger slid down to brush the sensitive flesh just above the neckline of her gown. "You told me you did not think you were capable of love."

He was toying with her. She could see it in his eyes. To what purpose, she did not know, but she knew that she did not like this side of him. It made her uncertain, anxious—itchy deep inside.

"Julian, this is ridiculous—"

"You love me."

The softly spoken pronouncement rang in Sophia's ears. Her head swam like a fish through reeds. Her skin flushed hot and cold at the same time.

How could he know? She did love him. She loved him but she couldn't tell him—not until she knew how he felt about her. She just couldn't.

"You are very sure of yourself," she croaked, hoping she sounded more lighthearted than she felt.

"I wish I were," he replied, seeming to gaze deep inside

her. "Perhaps then I would be able to ascertain just how I managed to win your heart so that I might continue winning it, but I think you are the better equipped to answer than I."

She backed away from him. "I do not know what you are talking about." Could he hear the panic in her voice? "It is impossible. People do not fall in love so quickly, especially not when those people are you and I, Julian."

He followed her. "I could argue you that point, but I suspect it is just a clever ruse on your part to avoid telling me you love me again."

Stopping, she held her ground. She would not run from him. "I've yet to say it once, let alone again."

Shaking his head, his lips curved ever so slightly, smugly. "You did not have to say it. Only a woman in love could be so angry that her man broke such a trifling promise to her. Only a woman in love would stand in front of a man and deny her love without actually denying it."

She would argue his logic if she had words to do so.

And if he wasn't right.

"Say you love me, Sophia," he whispered, reaching for her. "Tell me."

Shaking her head, she eluded his embrace. "I cannot." She didn't know why, but she just couldn't. She would not say it only to have silence meet her in return. Or worse, say it and have him kiss her as though he loved her without actually saying the words. That's what he had done the first time and she had believed he returned her feelings. She could not afford to be so foolish now, not when she feared her feelings for him seven years ago had been nothing more than an infatuation compared to how she felt about him now.

He reached for her again, his brow creased with concern. "Sophia—"

"I need to be alone," she hedged, scurrying toward the door. "Please, just let me go."

And he did.

Chapter 15

Trust is something more easily given
than it is earned.

An Unfortunate Attachment by the Marchioness of Aberley

"**A**m I doing this right?"

Julian's only reply was a soft grunt. He didn't dare do anything else—not when Sophia held a razor to his throat.

It had seemed like the perfect way to show her he trusted her, but now, with his head tilted back and her hand heavier than it should be, Julian wondered if perhaps he might have found a better way.

"Not quite so hard," he murmured, hoping this wouldn't be the last shave of his life. "That's it. Stroke upward."

They were in his bedroom, each still in their dressing gowns. Julian sat near the hearth listening to the heavy pat of rain against the windows, the hissing of the fire when an occasional drop managed to slip down the chimney, and the scratching of the razor as Sophia removed a full day's worth of whiskers from his face.

"I cannot imagine having to do this every day," she re-

273

marked, rinsing the blade in the basin of hot water at her elbow.

"Sometimes I am lazy and allow my valet to do it." He tilted his head so she could scrape the razor down his cheek. Her hand was lighter as it skimmed over the bruises Aberley had left behind.

Another stroke. She was definitely getting better at this. "It seems an awful inconvenience."

He shrugged as she rinsed the blade again. "I would rather shave every day than bleed five days out of the month."

Her hand stilled. The flush that flooded Sophia's face was so bright Julian was tempted to shield his eyes from the glow. He waited until she lowered the blade again to speak. "What? Did you think me ignorant of such things?"

Sophia shrugged, her cheeks still red.

He shook his head. "I declare, Sophia, you are a mystery to me. You think nothing of speaking your mind to me but when I bring up a natural function of your body you turn all *missish* on me. Why is that?"

"I do not know," she replied, flicking the razor along his upper lip and chin. "I suppose it is because Edmund was very frank about wanting to use my body, but only when it was clean, and usually in the dark."

Wiping the remaining lather from his face with a towel, Julian watched her curiously as she cleaned the razor one final time.

"Clean," he said. "That is an odd way to put it."

She turned toward him, her color still quite high. "That is how he phrased it."

Lovely man, the former marquess. Julian sincerely hoped he was burning in hell at that moment.

Tossing the towel aside, Julian rose from the chair. "Well, he was wrong. When are you next due?"

If possible, she flushed even darker. "Not for some time. I . . . I do not have a normal cycle—at least not normal compared to other women I have known."

He waited for her to elaborate. When she didn't, he asked, "What is it?"

Sophia set the razor aside and clasped her hands in front of her. "It only comes once every other month."

She made it sound so terrible. Julian smiled. "I think most women would agree that you are fortunate."

Her gaze narrowed suspiciously. "The doctor said it would make it very difficult for me to conceive a child."

Tilting his head, Julian shrugged one shoulder. "I am not in any hurry to become a father."

"Edmund used to say that it was a good thing that he could not sire children, otherwise I would have nothing but my looks to recommend me as a wife." There was just the slightest tremble to her chin as she spoke.

"Edmund is dead," he bit out, his jaw tight. "Blessedly so, the bloody bastard."

Moving around to the back of the chair, Julian laid his hands on Sophia's shoulders. "Sophia." He waited until she lifted her gaze to his to continue, "I have already raised two sisters and I did not do a very good job at that. If God decides to give us a child, then we will have a child. If we do not, then we do not."

"You are not a normal man," she whispered, something very much like awe in her voice.

Julian laughed. "Perhaps not. But even seven years ago I knew that I wanted you for how you made me feel, not for the heir you might produce."

He knew even before her eyes widened that he had revealed too much, damn it.

"If you wanted me then, why did you not marry me?"

He should have known he could not conceal the truth from her forever. He should have known that one day he would have to tell her that he had truly cared for her—that he had been a coward.

Releasing her, he turned away. He didn't want to see the look on her face when he told her the truth.

"I thought I could do whatever I wanted, live my life the way I wanted, without there being any consequences," he replied. "I had thought to propose to you, and then when your father found us so conveniently, and you did not seem surprised to see him at all, I thought you were trying to trick me."

There was silence behind him. Unable to bear it any longer, he turned. Sophia watched him with a guarded expression.

He plunged on. "I had spent my entire life doing what other people told me was right. And when your father told me I had to marry you . . . well, that was the last straw. I told myself you had tried to trap me, and when you married Aberley, it was very easy to hide my hurt by congratulating myself on escaping the clutches of a fortune hunter. I convinced myself you did not care for me. I know now that I was wrong. And I am sorry."

And there it was. Told in such a condensed manner, it made considerably less sense than it had seven years ago. He waited for her reaction to his confession. He could have prevented her marriage to Edmund Morelle. He could have spared her all that she had suffered with the bastard, and the only reason he hadn't was because of his own childishness.

"Thank you."

Those two little words, so quietly and meaningfully spoken were *not* what he had expected.

"I have a confession to make as well."

Something in her voice made his gaze narrow as it snapped to hers. She looked every bit as uncertain as he had felt just a few moments ago.

"I did try to trap you."

Julian's jaw dropped at the same time as his stomach. "What?"

Her fingers knotting together before her, Sophia took a hesitant step toward him. "I wanted my father to find us— perhaps not in that particular state of undress, but I hoped that his discovering us would induce you to propose. It was underhanded of me, I know, and I am sorry for it— more so because it did not work out as I had planned. I wanted to marry you, and not for your fortune or your title as you came to believe."

Julian couldn't believe it. It should give him some sense of vindication, some sense of satisfaction that he had been right. It should make him angry that she had purposefully tried to trap him, but it didn't. Instead, it confused him. Why would she go to such lengths just to have him?

It hurt as well. There was a dull ache in his chest, very near his heart, because even though he knew they both had a lot of growing up to do at the time, Sophia could have been his wife these last seven years if they had only been a bit more honest and trusting with each other.

"Why?" he demanded when he at last found his voice. "What did I ever do to make you want me?"

She smiled a tad regretfully. "You made me feel lovable."

Her words deepened the ache in his chest. "You made me feel like a man."

"In my eyes you were a man. The man I adored."

They stood there a moment, just staring at each other. The tightness in Julian's chest was acute now. It was hard to breathe, so great were his regrets, so overwhelming were his feelings. Why had it taken them so long to come to this? Why did it feel as though his very soul depended on having her forgiveness, on having her give herself to him, and allowing him to show her just how much he was beginning to love her?

One second he was staring into the endless depths of Sophia's eyes and the next she was in his arms, her mouth warm, wet and open beneath his.

His arms locked around her waist, Julian lifted her and carried her to the bed, taking care not to break their kiss. Bracing one arm and one knee on the mattress, he gently lowered her onto the coverlet.

Raising his head, he watched her face as he fumbled with the closures on her dressing gown with his left hand. He pushed the robe open, baring her body to his eyes.

She was so damned beautiful to look at. Sophia would be the first to point out all the flaws with her body, but Julian could not see them. If she called her breasts big and heavy, he called them full and ripe. If she said her belly was too big, he said it was soft and gently rounded. While it was true that he had known women who were possibly more aesthetically perfect, he had never seen a body more beautiful than Sophia's.

Rising up above her, he removed his own dressing gown, tossing it on the floor without so much as a glance as to where it landed. A wave of pleasure washed over him as he watched her gaze travel the length of his nude body. In her eyes he saw the same hunger and wonder that he felt when he looked at her.

He kissed her neck, the warm hollow of her throat where her pulse fluttered like a butterfly's wings. He tasted her there, where she smelled faintly of lavender soap and clean skin, and lower—down her chest to the baby-fine skin between her breasts.

He cupped the weight of her breasts in his hands, lightly dragging his thumbs across the puckering peaks. A shudder raced through him as Sophia gasped in pleasure. Her nipples were so sensitive, so incredibly receptive to his slightest touch. The pink buds beneath his fingers stood high and erect, their color deepening under his attentions. Julian lowered his mouth to one, sucking it between his lips and tasting it with the flat of his tongue.

God he loved the feel of her in his mouth. Loved her taste, the texture, the way she cried out when he nipped lightly with his teeth. He suckled her flesh until her fingers tangled in his hair, then he turned his attentions to the other breast. When he had her writhing beneath him, he knew it was time to move on. Downward he traveled, planting kisses along the soft flesh of her ribcage, dipping into her navel with his tongue, nuzzling her belly and rubbing his freshly shaven jaw over the pale curve there.

Kneeling between her legs, his hands braced on either side of the generous flare of her hips, Julian eased toward the thatch of ebony curls at the juncture of Sophia's thighs with heart-pounding anticipation.

How long would this fascination with her body last?

How many years would pass before he ceased to worship every inch of her? He had thought that once he bedded her a few times his interest would wane, but it hadn't. If anything, it had grown stronger. He didn't just want her; he craved her. And not just her body—it was her. Sophia.

He pressed his lips against the curls, feeling the dampness there.

"Do you want me to taste you?" he asked softly, gazing up the breathtaking length of her.

Her black eyes were heavy-lidded and bright with passion. "Yes."

A low groan broke free of Julian's throat as he lowered his head to the humid valley before him. All that mattered now was pleasing her. He wanted to hear her pants of pleasure, wanted to feel her shudder around him as her climax rocked her. He wanted to know he was the only man to ever make her feel such joy.

The only man who ever *could* make her feel such joy.

He worked her into a frenzy with his tongue, concentrating on the firm, hooded nub that would eventually lead to her climax. He stopped just before her cries of pleasure reached that exquisite peak. Normally he would relish sending her crashing into the abyss of pleasure this way, but he had something else in mind.

She stared up at him, eyes glazed with sensation and confusion.

"Roll over," he told her, his voice low and rough in his own ears.

Her expression was uncertain, but he knew that at this point her body would do almost anything he asked, with the hope of him finishing what he had started.

Sophia rolled onto her stomach, revealing the long,

delicate indent of her back and full round curve of her buttocks to his appreciative gaze. Julian ran his hands down the smooth ivory of her spine, cupped the blushing cheeks of her bottom.

Nudging her legs apart with his knee, he moved between her thighs. "Lift your hips for me."

She lifted her head, watching him over her shoulder. "I beg your pardon?"

He reached down, sliding his hands beneath her pelvis. Gently, he pulled upwards, guiding her hips toward his. She was hesitant, but she didn't try to stop him. In fact, she braced herself on her forearms for support.

"What are you doing?" She inquired with a gasp as he probed the opening of her body with his aching erection.

He slid the head inside her. His eyelids closed on a sigh of ecstasy. "Have you ever made love this way before, Sophia?"

"N—no." There was uncertainty and desire in her voice as he penetrated her even farther.

"Do you like it?"

"I—" Whatever she was going to say was cut off by a low keening moan as he buried himself inside her.

"You will," he promised. "All you have to do is trust me."

Holding her tightly, Julian began to move. The angle of her hips made every stroke more acute than the last. The sweet grip of her body around his and the soft coos of encouragement slipping breathlessly from between her lips heightened the urgency in his blood.

He reached beneath her with one hand, his fingers parting the silky curls between her thighs and finding the tiny mound his tongue had savored moments earlier. He stroked it, eliciting a sharp gasp from the woman beneath him.

The rhythm of his body matched that of his busy fingers. Thrusting in as his fingers stroked up, Sophia rocked her hips against him, spreading her thighs wide and arching her back.

"Do you trust me, Sophia?" He asked, increasing the tempo of his thrusts as his fingers quickened their pace.

He could feel her body tensing, could feel the tremble of her arms and thighs as she pushed herself toward climax. She was getting close. So very close.

"Yes." She gasped as he thrust hard, plunging deep within her. "Yes, Julian. I trust you."

Bending over her, Julian was without mercy as he stroked her with his body and his fingers.

"Do you love me?"

His only answer was the cry that tore free of Sophia's throat as her body tensed and shuddered around him. Her release triggered his own and he just barely managed to grab hold of one of the posts to keep from falling when his knees buckled beneath him. Everything else ceased to exist except for this mind-numbing moment.

Some time later, as they lay together, he turned his head to look upon her. Her expression was one of utter contentment; her breathing was that of a person in the deepest of slumbers.

Sighing, Julian drew the coverlet over them. It wasn't long before he was drifting off himself, and as sleep claimed him, he realized that even though she hadn't said a word, Sophia had given him a pretty satisfying answer to his question.

*   *   *

When Sophia awoke for the second time that morning, it was to find herself alone on Julian's bed, the coverlet pulled down over her back and her dressing gown bunched beneath her.

Lifting up on her forearms, she looked groggily around the richly masculine bedchamber. Her husband was nowhere to be seen.

Insufferable swine, she thought with a smile. How dare he not sleep away the day with her. He was probably off somewhere with Brave and Gabriel, challenging anyone who dare impugn her honor. Foolish, wonderful man.

She had almost told him she loved him. Only the fact that the pleasure his body gave hers robbed her of any ability to speak had saved her.

Why was it so important that he hear her say it? He had yet to make any such declaration of his own. He could hardly expect her to make herself so vulnerable to him—not a second time, no matter how much she might be tempted to.

Edmund used to ask her to tell him she loved him, and she had said the words because they pleased him, not because she meant them. Julian was different. He wanted her to mean them and that scared her more than Edmund's demands ever could. Love wasn't something one could take back once it was given, and just once, Sophia would like to be certain that when she pledged her heart to a man he would give her his in return.

Perhaps next time she was in control of their lovemaking she should ask Julian if he loved her and see how he responded. Perhaps he would tell her the words she wanted to hear. No, if she ever gathered enough courage to ask him, she would do it when his mind was on something other than sexual release. She did not want him to say he loved her just because his body loved how hers made him feel.

Tossing back the coverlet, she gathered up her dressing gown and rose from the bed. She crossed the carpet to the wash stand and cleaned away the residue of their love-making from between her thighs.

Once she finished washing, Sophia shrugged into her dressing gown and rang for her maid. Half an hour later, dressed in a fashionable morning gown of bottle green muslin, her hair swept up into a simple knot on the back of her head, Sophia entered the breakfast room. It was going on eleven. Julian was gone, but Letitia—who kept more socially acceptable hours—was just sitting down to breakfast.

Sophia had seen little of her sister-in-law since that night she had caught her sneaking into the house. She was pleased to see that the younger woman looked much like her old self this morning. Dressed in a simple peach-colored gown, Letitia looked like a sprite sitting at the round oak table.

She smiled as Sophia entered the room—a good sign that everything was fine between them. "You are up late this morning."

Sophia couldn't help the heat that crept into her cheeks. "I was up earlier but found I needed a nap. May I join you?"

"Of course." Letitia gestured to the sideboard behind her. It was laden with silver covered dishes. "Cook always prepares far too much for me."

Taking a plate from the low cupboard in the buffet, Sophia piled it high with buttered eggs, ham, sausage and toast. She was ravenous. Nothing like being ravished in the morning to give a woman an appetite.

Letitia arched a thin brow when she saw the amount of food on her plate. "Your nap made you hungry, I see."

Sophia's expression was one of mock hauteur. "I am a restless sleeper. I always wake up hungry."

"Hmm. I have always wondered why so many women gain weight after they marry," Letitia remarked with a grin. "I am beginning to understand now. All those . . . *naps*."

Sophia couldn't help but laugh, even as she flushed clear up to her hairline.

"I would be impertinent and ask you for details, as any inquisitive friend would," the younger woman continued, "but since it would involve discovering things about my brother that I have absolutely no desire to know about the tyrant, I will abstain."

Despite the jovial tone of her friend's voice, Sophia's smile faded. "Have you spoken to him?"

Letitia shook her head as she spread marmalade on her toast with the back of her spoon. "Not since we fought, no."

"How long is this silence going to last?"

Letitia took a bite of toast, making Sophia wait for an answer until she had chewed and swallowed.

"Not very long, I expect." A slow smile curved the young woman's lips. "Marcus is coming to speak to Julian either today or tomorrow."

Unable to contain her squeal of delight, Sophia muffled it with her hand. "Oh, Lettie! How wonderful!"

Grinning foolishly, Letitia nodded. "I could scarcely believe it when Marcus told me. He is convinced that his invesments will soon pay off and that he will be able to prove to Julian that he can provide a good life for us until he inherits the earldom."

It certainly sounded as though they had everything planned out, and Sophia wasn't about to start asking questions that might burst her friend's bubble. She was happy for Letitia, blissfully so. She only hoped that Julian would share in the joy rather than squashing it by being the overly protective elder brother.

Julian still saw his sister as a child. He expected her to believe that he knew what was best for her, and he truly believed it himself. It was fairly ironic coming from a man who had refused to marry her the first time because he felt it was expected of him.

Putting thoughts of Julian and what could happen from her mind, Sophia concentrated on her sister-in-law's happiness. As they ate their breakfasts they talked of fashion and society, and filled each other in on all the collective gossip they had both heard.

Lord and Lady Carnover were expecting their second child, Letitia told her. Apparently the earl was hoping for a girl this time. And some young woman rejected by her lover had attempted to drown herself in the Serpentine as the poet Shelley's wife had done more than two years earlier, but changed her mind when she discovered how cold the water was.

"I have never understood taking one's own life by drowning," Letitia remarked, a slight edge to her voice. "It does not seem a very nice way to die."

Sophia gazed at her friend in dismay. She was not good in such situations. She never knew what to say. If it were anyone else, she would dismiss it, but Letitia's sister had committed suicide in such a manner and obviously the wound her death had left behind had yet to fully heal.

"Perhaps we might blame it on Shakespeare," she

replied, with a degree of forced lightness. "Ophelia made it seem quite tragic and romantic in Hamlet."

Much to her surprise Letitia smiled. It was a sad smile, but a smile all the same. "Miranda would have liked being compared to Ophelia, I think. Everything was tragic and romantic as far as she was concerned."

Was there any other way of thinking as far as the Rexleys were concerned?

Thankfully, a knock at the door interrupted the melancholy drift to their conversation. Mrs. Yorke bustled into the room, a pleasant smile on her round face.

"Begging your pardon, my lady," she said, addressing Sophia, "but this is just arrived."

She handed Sophia a sealed missive, which Sophia accepted with thanks. The plump housekeeper smiled even broader and bobbed a quick curtsey before exiting again.

"Who is it from?" Letitia asked, slicing off a bite of ham.

Turning the letter over in her hand, Sophia shrugged as she studied the handwriting on the front. "I have no idea."

"Well, open it!"

Chuckling at her sister-in-law's impatient tone, Sophia broke the seal and opened the letter. There was a bank draft inside.

"Oh dear." Lifting the draft, she stared at it, her eyes widening.

"Well?" Letitia demanded.

Sophia glanced down at the letter, her eyes quickly reading the few lines written there.

"It is from Mr. Murray, the man who published *An Unfortunate Attachment*. He says this draft is mine—monies earned from sales of the book. He writes that since revealing myself as the author demand for the book has been overwhelming. He wonders if I might consider . . . writing another."

Sophia turned her astonished gaze to Letitia. "That book was awful, and he wants another!"

Squealing, Letitia punched her hands into the air. "Take that, Lord Aberley!"

Sophia couldn't help but join her laughter. Oh, wouldn't Charles have a fit if he knew his attempt to ruin her had resulted not only in her marriage to Julian, but to some degree of success for her as well.

Tossing her napkin on the table, Sophia tucked the bank draft back into the letter and rose to her feet.

"Come, Letitia. You and I are going shopping courtesy of the Marquess of Aberley."

Letitia was out of her chair in an instant. "You know I never turn down the opportunity to go shopping."

"I will even buy you a treat," Sophia said with a smile.

"What about me?" came a familiar voice from the doorway. "Will you buy me a treat as well?"

Flushing with warmth, Sophia turned to face her husband as he walked toward her. "Do you think you deserve one?"

The sparkle in his golden eyes thrilled her right down to her toes. "Do you?"

There was no mistaking the meaning in that low, gravelly tone. He was referring to earlier that morning—and the pleasure he had given her.

She flashed a teasing grin at him. "I shall think about it."

"Would you like to come with us, Julian?" Letitia asked, surprising not only her brother, but Sophia as well.

That Julian was touched by her offer was plain to see in

his expression. Sophia's gaze went from sister to brother. This was what it meant to be family—to love someone so much that even anger and personal injury couldn't sever it. This was unconditional love.

Lord, how she envied it.

"No, thank you, Lettie," he replied, emotion thickening his tone. "I have business to attend to. I just received a note from a certain young gentleman requesting an audience with me later this afternoon. He says he has something of great importance to discuss with me."

Sophia's breath caught in her throat as he smiled. Such a sweet, hopeful smile, the likes of which she had never seen on his face before. Could it be that he had changed his mind about Mr. Wesley?

Letitia's smile was almost as painful to look at as her brother's, it had so much expectation in it.

They prepared to leave, Letitia exiting the room first. Sophia took advantage of this time alone to plant a quick kiss on Julian's cheek. "You will go easy on this young man, will you not?" she asked. "And hear him out before making your decision?"

His expression was one of amusement. "Of course I will. I am not a complete ogre, you know. Besides, I am already persuaded to give my permission."

Sophia threw her arms around him. "Oh, Julian, that is wonderful! Letitia will be so very happy. *I* am so very happy."

"Do I deserve that treat now?" he asked, smiling.

Sophia reluctantly stepped out of his embrace. "Oh, my dear Lord Wolfram, I believe you deserve more than just one." She lowered her voice seductively. "And if you are good, I just might buy you something as well."

And with that, she hurried from the room, anxious to assure Letitia that her dreams were about to come true, and thinking that the next time she was alone with Julian, she might just have to tell him how much she loved him.

Chapter 16

*Everyone makes mistakes. Some are simply
easier to conceal than others.*

An *Unfortunate Attachment* by the Marchioness of Aberley

"**I** look forward to having you as a brother-in-law,
Lord Wolfram."

Julian smiled at the younger man as they shook hands.
Even more pleasing than the fact that such a fine, worthy
gentleman wanted to marry his sister was the knowledge
that Letitia wanted him as well. He knew she would come
around eventually.

"I look forward to it as well, Rutherford," he replied
sincerely, as Fielding opened the door for him. "As soon
as I have had a chance to confer with Letitia I will call on
you to discuss the particulars."

Grinning like an idiot, Rutherford bowed his sandy
head and took his leave. Julian watched him go with
amusement. The young earl practically skipped down the
steps to his waiting carriage.

There was a slight spring to Julian's own step as he
walked back to his study. He didn't have to worry about

Letitia's future anymore. He was finally free to concentrate on his own. With Sophia.

He had just sat down to resume work on the poem he was writing for her—a task that was taking him longer than usual, he labored over it so—when Fielding knocked on the door.

"There is a young gentleman here to see you, my lord."

"Who is it, Fielding?"

"He said his name is Wesley."

Marcus Wesley, Penderthal's heir? What could he possibly want? Julian hardly knew the man.

But Letitia did. She had mentioned him several times since the start of the season. Unease crept up Julian's spine as he remembered his sister's smile that morning when he told her a young man was coming to see him.

Damnation. He hoped to hell that smile hadn't been because she thought he meant Wesley.

It couldn't have been. She knew how he felt about Wesley. He seemed like a good sort of man, but he had no title yet, little money and came from a deplorable background.

"Send him in, Fielding." Perhaps there was another reason for the young man's visit. Julian sincerely hoped there was. Just because he didn't think Wesley suitable didn't mean he wanted to have to tell *him* that.

"Yes, my lord." The butler bowed out of the doorway.

A few moments later, Marcus Wesley appeared.

Wesley was a smart-looking young man with dark hair and bright eyes. He was handsome, charming and always at ease. He reminded Julian very much of a young Gabriel. That resemblance and his open nature made it hard to disapprove him, but the fact that he was so unsuitable for Letitia made it almost too easy.

"Good afternoon, Lord Wolfram," the younger man

spoke, his voice low and smooth. "I hope I am not inter-rupting anything of import?"

"Not at all. Come in." The poem for Sophia was cer-tainly important, but hardly enough reason to send Wesley away.

Julian leaned back in his chair. He wasn't going to pro-long the man's discomfort by making small talk. It would be cruel.

"What can I do for you, Wesley?"

Wesley smiled at him, all youthful exuberance. There was perhaps a mere five or six years separating him from Julian, and yet Julian felt as though the gulf were more like six and twenty.

"I want permission to ask for your sister's hand."

The man was blunt, Julian would give him that. No pretty phrasing, no bowing to the guardian, just a straight-out demand.

Julian would give him the same candor. "I cannot do that."

Young Mr. Wesley did not look entirely shocked, as though he had expected the reply.

"Might I ask why not?" he asked. Some of the bright-ness had left his eyes.

A little stab of guilt pierced Julian's conscience. Ignor-ing the sensation, Julian rested his elbow on the arm of his chair and set his chin on his thumb and finger. "Do you drink, Mr. Wesley?"

The younger man frowned. "On occasion, yes."

"Like your father?"

Wesley's jaw tightened. "No. Not like that. Nor do I gamble or whore around as he did either—just in case you thought to ask."

Julian believed him. "What about your income?"

Wesley's gaze dropped for a split second. "I have several investments that are expected to pay off in the near future. And as you know, I am to inherit my uncle's title upon his death."

Julian shrugged one shoulder. "Your uncle is in his fifties. He could live for a number of years yet."

The younger man's gaze narrowed. "I would never wish for his death just to secure my own happiness, Lord Wolfram. I wish him a long and happy life."

Julian did not doubt Wesley's honesty. But even as he wished the young man had better prospects, he could not willingly give his sister to a man with no land, no title and little fortune.

"I am afraid I cannot oblige you, Wesley. I have already given permission to someone else."

All the color drained from the young man's face. Julian almost thought he could hear Wesley's heart as it shattered. "Someone else? Does Letitia know this?"

He could lie. That would put an end to Wesley's pursuit of his sister, perhaps even lessen the young man's pain somewhat, but he couldn't do that.

"No. I do not believe that she does. I suspect she was rather hoping it would be you."

Wesley stared at him, his eyes unnaturally dark and large in his pale face. The guilt stabbed harder this time. "And if she refuses this other man?"

"I still would not give my permission."

The muscle in Wesley's jaw ticked. Anger blazed in his eyes. "Because of my father?"

Straightening, Julian shook his head. He wasn't very proud of himself at that moment. "Because of your financial situation."

Something in his voice must have given his suspicions away, because a sardonic smile curved the younger man's lips as he regarded him.

"You think I am after her fortune."

Julian did not respond. He simply lifted a brow and challenged Wesley to deny it.

Color bloomed on Wesley's cheekbones. "Only the fact that you are Letitia's brother keeps me from wishing you straight to hell, Lord Wolfram."

"I love Letitia," Wesley continued hotly. "An emotion which, with all due respect, I suspect you are not familiar with, my lord."

That rankled, but Julian contained his temper. "It is because I love my sister that I am so concerned about her future, Mr. Wesley. Love is all very well and good, but what can you give her? How much will you love her when the bills from the dressmaker or the jeweler start to pile up and you have no way to pay them?"

Young Wesley's face was as immobile as granite. "We will just have to economize."

Julian surged to his feet, bracing his palms on the surface of his desk as his gaze bore into the younger man's.

"Letitia does not know *how* to economize! She has never had to. How can you demand that of her now? She will come to resent you for asking it of her, just as you will resent her spending. How long will love last when you are constantly arguing over expenditures?"

Wesley was stiff with indignant anger. "You seem to have a rather low of opinion of both myself and Letitia, Lord Wolfram, if you believe we would let something like frivolity come between us."

Sighing, Julian raked a hand through his hair. "Frivolity

is a quirk, Wesley. Letitia's spending is a way of life. She has never been denied anything—ever. I must assume some responsibility for that, I know, but it is something she has spent the last four and twenty years expecting. Would you honestly expect her to give it up just for you? What are you prepared to give up for her?"

Wesley didn't budge. "Everything I have is Letitia's."

Julian's lips curved in a sympathetic smile. "Everything you have wouldn't keep my sister in gowns for a year. I am sorry, Wesley, but my answer is still no."

Face dark with frustration and anger, Marcus Wesley glared at him. "You are no more sorry than you are aware of your sister's wants and needs, Lord Wolfram, but I suspect those are things you will have to discover on your own."

Julian frowned at the cryptic tone in the other man's statement. He would have demanded to know what he meant if Letitia hadn't chosen that moment to come barging in.

"Marcus!" she cried happily as she entered the room. Her joy quickly faded as her gaze went from her lover to her brother.

Wesley didn't try to hide his feelings as he turned to face her. The love in his expression was almost enough to make Julian change his mind. Almost.

"He said no, didn't he?" Letitia asked in a little voice.

Wesley went to her. It was as though the two of them had forgotten that Julian was even there, like the two of them were alone in the world. Julian knew that feeling. He often felt it when he was with Sophia.

Julian watched as his sister laid a hand on her lover's arm and spoke softly to him. Wesley's expression was pained, but he nodded and covered her hand with one of his own before leaving the room.

As the door closed behind him, Letitia turned to face

Julian. She looked as though he had just shoved a sword through her chest.

"How could you?" she demanded. "How could you elevate my hopes as you did this morning only to crush them like this? Do you hate me that much?"

"I do not hate you," Julian replied harsher than he intended. "Has it ever occurred to you that I do these things because I love you?"

Letitia was incredulous. "Love me? How can you stand there and say you care for me when you have just refused to let me marry the man I love?"

Inhaling a deep breath, Julian mentally counted to ten as he exhaled. "How would you live, Lettie? Mr. Wesley's income allows him to live comfortably on his own, but it is nowhere near enough to keep both of you."

She scowled at him. "It would be if we economized," she informed him, her tone mimicking that of Mr. Wesley's. "Marcus has done the math. He says we will be fine as long as we are careful."

And if "Marcus" said it, it must be so. Julian sighed. "*Careful* means one trip to the dressmaker a year, rather than four or more, Lettie. It means not being able to buy a new hat just because it's pretty. It means no baubles, no trinkets unless they are accounted for."

Her chin came up defiantly. "I do not care."

Julian's control on his temper snapped. "For God's sake, listen to what you are saying! You are lying to yourselves, Lettie. He cannot afford to marry you. Even with your dowry, the lifestyle you are accustomed to will not last more than a few years. It could be many more before he inherits the title. What then?"

"We will make do!" she shouted back, stomping her foot on the carpet.

Julian rubbed a hand over his face as he bit back a stinging retort. He was losing control of the situation. He had to regain control.

"I do not believe it will be that simple for you, pet."

Letitia laughed bitterly. "Your faith in me is astounding."

Julian went to her. He set his hands on her shoulders, but she shrugged them off. "This is not about faith. This is about wanting to see you happy. Wesley is a fine man, but he cannot afford to marry you."

Fixing him with a look that could freeze Hades itself, his sister replied, "If our father were alive he would care more about my happiness than money."

With that charge ringing in the air between them, Letitia turned on her heel and opened the door. Julian caught a glimpse of Mr. Wesley standing there waiting before Letitia slammed the heavy oak shut behind her.

His shoulders sagging, Julian went back to his desk and dropped into his chair with a heavy heart. If their father were alive it would be him making this decision, not Julian.

What was he doing wrong? Was there something he just wasn't seeing? Because while he could understand Letitia's anger, he just didn't understand why she couldn't see things clearly. Was she so in love with Wesley that her judgment was completely altered? She had to know as well as he that right now, Wesley was a bad match. She just wanted him so badly that she refused to see the truth.

Normally he would be proud of her for being so determined, but she was only deluding herself.

Who was he to make that decision? A voice in the back of his head demanded. Perhaps Letitia and Wesley could make things work. Perhaps his sister could learn to economize for the sake of love.

No. Despite what the poets—and that included Julian himself—often said, it was impossible to live by love alone. The lack of money and Letitia's inherent extravagance would lead to problems for the two lovers, despite the depth of their regard for each other. The realization did little to ease his guilt.

What if he hadn't been allowed to marry Sophia? What if someone had prevented him the chance to win her love? She made him so whole, so happy.

What if Wesley was the only man who could ever make Letitia happy? Did he have the right to deny her that? But what if Wesley made her miserable instead? How was he to determine the difference? It had taken Sophia and himself seven years to come together. In seven years Letitia would be one and thirty. She couldn't afford to wait that long.

Leaning his head back against the soft padding of the chair, he closed his eyes and wished for Sophia to appear. She would tell him whether or not he was in the wrong.

He could always count on Sophia to be honest.

After arriving home from shopping with Letitia, Sophia went up to her bedroom to sort through her purchases. She would much rather join Letitia in Julian's study to share in her friend's happiness, but she thought brother and sister would appreciate the privacy.

And so she waited a good twenty minutes before going downstairs to her husband's study. She found him at the window, staring out at the back garden, a tumbler of amber liquid in his hand.

"See anything interesting?" she asked lightly, crossing the carpet toward him.

He turned and smiled at her. There was an odd sadness to it. "Not until you appeared." He held out his hand to her.

Blushing in pleasure at his flattery, Sophia took it. His fingers were warm and strong around hers as he drew her to his side.

"Are Letitia and Marcus Wesley still out there?"

Sophia raised her brows and smiled. It wouldn't be right of her to pretend complete surprise, but she didn't want to reveal how much she knew either. "Marcus Wesley, hmm? No. I would imagine they would want to celebrate in private."

"Celebrate?" Julian scowled as he took a sip of his drink. "Commiserate, more like it."

She couldn't hide her confusion. "But this morning, when you said a young man was coming to see you, you acted like it was going to be a pleasant visit."

Julian set his empty glass on a small table near the window. "It was—with young Lord Rutherford. I had no idea Wesley was going to call as well."

Sophia gazed at him with a hollow feeling in the pit of her stomach. The watery sunlight streaming through the window fell across Julian's face, accentuating the tension around his mouth, the tiny lines around his eyes. He suddenly looked much older and much more tired than a man his age should.

She led him to the dark green brocade sofa in the center of the room. He put his head in her lap as he laid down.

Sophia smiled as she began combing her fingers through his hair, massaging his scalp as she did so. "What happened?" she asked when the furrow between his brows was completely gone.

"I made a mess of things, Fe," he replied without opening his eyes. "As seems to be my habit as of late."

She rubbed his forehead with her thumb. "Tell me everything."

He told her how Letitia's exuberance that morning had pleased him, how he believed she knew it was Rutherford he spoke of. After all, she had agreed to spend more time with the young lord and she seemed to enjoy his company. What else was Julian to think?

Yes, Sophia agreed silently. What else was he to think when neither his sister nor his wife had told him the truth?

He had been so pleased when Rutherford left, thinking he had secured his sister's future happiness, only to find out he hadn't. And now he was torn between what he knew Letitia wanted and what he thought was best for her.

Sophia wasn't certain what to say. If she had betrayed Letitia's trust and told Julian the truth they might have been able to avoid this. If Julian knew how much his sister loved Marcus, then he might have tried to find a way to allow a marriage to take place. Certainly he wouldn't have accepted Rutherford's suit had he known his sister's heart was engaged elsewhere.

"Did Letitia never even try to tell you about Mr. Wesley?" she asked instead. Letitia had often insisted that she had tried to talk to Julian about her lover, but Sophia wondered just how honest her sister-in-law had been.

"She mentioned him once or twice. I knew she had a partiality toward him, but I told her how unsuitable he was and that was the end of it. Had I known that she loved him . . ."

"Would it have made a difference if you had known?" Sophia asked when he trailed off. She wasn't certain she wanted to hear his answer.

Julian shrugged, his shoulder blades rolling against her thighs. "Probably not, but at least I might have handled the situation more appropriately. As it is, I would not be surprised if Letitia did not speak to me again for a week."

His words both soothed and worried Sophia. He assuaged her guilt by saying the truth wouldn't have changed things, but his dismissal of Letitia's anger worried her immensely. What if Letitia didn't stop at simply not speaking to her brother?

"You do not think she will do something foolish, do you?" she asked, unable to keep her fears solely to herself.

Letitia was an emotional girl, given to mood swings and flights of melodrama. Sophia wouldn't be surprised if this latest episode played directly to the younger woman's theatrical nature and drove her to do something worthy of a farce on the Drury Lane stage.

"You mean other than locking herself in her room, sobbing and threatening not to eat until I relent?" her husband remarked, his tone rife with mock gravity. "I doubt it. Letitia likes being able to use my credit about town too much to risk losing it."

Sophia feared he was quite wrong. Letitia was more spoiled than Julian ever had been—the fault for which had to rest mostly on Julian's own shoulders. It wouldn't occur to her that Julian would ever turn his back on her completely. Letitia would believe that Julian would pay her bills and take care of her even if she did marry Wesley, and she would be right. Julian would never disown her, no matter what she did.

And that included running away with her lover.

She moved to stand. "Perhaps I should go check on her."

Julian's weight on her legs stopped her from rising.

Opening his eyes, he gazed at her with an expression that made her heart crack against her ribs. It was an expression of loving amusement. It was the loving bit that broke her heart.

"You do not have to do that, Sophia. It is what Letitia will want—someone to sympathize while she rants about her evil brother."

What could she do? She couldn't very well tell him that she thought he was wrong, could she? That she expected to go up to Letitia's room and either find her gone or preparing to leave?

"This has obviously been going on for some time, Julian," she said, her voice carefully measured. "Letitia came to me because she believed you were going to force her to marry. She risked your wrath then. What do you think she will do now that she thinks you have actually chosen a husband for her?"

Stupid, maddening man, he didn't even look concerned! "She knows I would never force her to wed against her will."

Her patience fraying badly, Sophia jumped to her feet. Julian's head bounced back against the sofa cushions.

"I think you are underestimating your sister," she informed him. "And I think I am going to go check on her."

Julian sat up, a confident smile on his face despite his tired eyes. "Go check on her, then, but I reserve the right to gloat when she decides to use you as an audience for her 'My Brother is a Despot' speech."

Sophia wished she could share in his humor. Really, he was so incredibly thick when it came to Letitia.

"I hope you have reason to gloat, Julian. I truly do."

She left him sitting there on the sofa, shaking his head as she hurried from the room.

Hiking her skirt up around her calves, Sophia ran down the corridor and up the stairs. By the time she reached the top she was out of breath, but it did not stop her from running the rest of the way to Letitia's room.

She knocked on the door. "Letitia?"

There was no answer. No sound of crying from inside either. Her heart pounding, Sophia turned the knob and opened the door. As it swung open, she peeked inside.

Letitia's room looked as it always did. The ivory bedspread was neatly smoothed over the mattress of the large four poster bed. A pile of peach-and-white pillows was artfully arranged near the top.

Sophia stepped inside, her gaze searching the rest of the room for any sign that something wasn't right. The vanity drawers were closed, and although the top of it looked a little bare, Sophia couldn't tell if anything was missing or not.

The wardrobe door was open ever so slightly, just enough that Sophia wanted to go open it and look inside. Why she was so compelled, especially when everything else looked normal, she didn't know, but she went and looked all the same.

The wardrobe was filled with some of Letitia's newest gowns, *some* being the operative word. Many of Letitia's gowns were gone. Sophia knew this because she had seen this wardrobe filled with gowns just a few days earlier, and now empty hangers dangled where those gowns had once hung.

Below the gowns, almost an entire row of footwear was gone as well.

Heart thumping, Sophia turned from the wardrobe, leaving the door hanging open as she whipped across the room to Letitia's dressing table. There were empty spots where several items had once stood, and when Sophia opened her sister-in-law's jewelry box, her worst fears were confirmed.

All of Letitia's jewelry was gone.

Back downstairs she flew, as fast as her feet could carry her. She almost fell halfway down, but managed to regain her footing just in time. She ran into Fielding at the bottom.

"Ah, Lady Wolfram," he said, his tone as warm as his smile. "Would you be on your way to his lordship's study?"

"Yes, I am," Sophia replied gasping for breath. "But I—"

"Then would you be so good as to give him this note from Lady Letitia?"

Sophia froze as the aging butler held a folded, unsealed sheet of paper to her. She took it with numb fingers. Letitia had left a note for Julian. Notes were never a good sign.

"It was very good of Mr. Wesley to offer to take her to Lady Wickford's like he did," Fielding went on. "I so dislike seeing young ladies travel unaccompanied, even if it is just around the corner."

Sophia could only stare at him. Poor, misguided, gullible Fielding. Letitia was going a lot farther than just around the corner, and since the person taking her wasn't in Julian's employ, there would be no way of knowing exactly where she went. One thing was for certain: Her destination was *not* Lady Wickford's.

"Thank you, Fielding," she heard herself say. "I will take this to Lord Wolfram at once."

As soon as the butler bowed and left, Sophia spun on her heel and ran to the study, Letitia's note crumpling in her sweating palm.

Julian looked up as she burst into the room, his expression of expectant amusement giving away to something much more raw and worried when his gaze fell upon her.

"She is gone," she said, offering him the note as she stumbled toward him. "Letitia has run away with Mr. Wesley."

Chapter 17

Saying one is sorry is very much like seeing a ghost.
It does not mean a thing if the person
one is telling does not believe.

An Unfortunate Attachment by the Marchioness of Aberley

Dumbfounded, Julian opened the note Sophia gave him.

Gone. Letitia couldn't be gone. Even *she* wouldn't do something so stupid as to run off with Marcus Wesley. Would she?

The words on the paper confirmed his fears. He could scarcely breathe as he read.

Julian, by the time you get this I should be long gone. I wish I could tell you that I am sorry it had to come to this, but I cannot say it. I am not sorry to be marrying the man I love.

No, of course she wasn't.

Do not try to follow us, you will not be able to.

That's what she thought. Julian wasn't about to sit back and let Letitia make the worst mistake of her life. He

307

would go after her. He'd start this instant if she hadn't written more that might give him some clue as to where they were bound. Gretna Green, no doubt—to be married by a blacksmith in Scotland.

> *Tell Sophia I am sorry. I tried to act as she wanted, but that did not work, and now I must do things my way. I hope you will both forgive me.*

Lowering the note, Julian raised his gaze to his wife, who stood not three feet away, watching him with an anxious expression, twisting her hands in front of her.

"You knew." It came out such a softly spoken accusation, even though inside it felt like the loudest of roars.

She didn't try to deny it. "I knew she loved him, yes," she replied, equally as quiet. "I urged her to tell you the truth."

Julian's lungs felt like a bellows, expanding his ribs with air so that his chest felt as though it might explode with the force of his emotion.

"You are my wife." He might be able to contain his anger, but he couldn't contain the hurt. "*You* should have told me."

Her face was terribly pale now. Her hands, no longer twisting, were tightly knotted at her waist. "I gave my word to Letitia that I would not."

His chest was so tight now his ribs felt as though they were breaking. Or perhaps it was just his heart.

"You made a vow to me in front of God," he choked out. Had that meant nothing? She lied to him, even after everything they'd said and been through together. What else had she lied about? Had she lied about wanting him?

She had the grace to look shamed. "I made my promise to Letitia before we married."

She had known all along. Sophia had come to London

with his sister's secret already in her possession. She had promised to trust him, knowing full well that she wouldn't.

It hurt. It hurt more than anything he could remember. The death of Miranda, even the death of his parents, had left him feeling hollow and empty inside. What he wouldn't give to have that feeling again. Anything would be preferable to the pain in his chest, the hot sting of betrayal deep in his gut.

He had been played for a fool and he had walked into it with a smile on his stupid face. He had only wanted what was best for Letitia and now he had lost her because of Sophia's duplicity.

No. He had to be fair. If he had indeed lost Letitia, it would be because of his own folly. He had stupidly underestimated his sister, and his wife. He should have seen the signs. If he hadn't been so caught up in trying to provide a good future for Letitia, he might have seen that she already had a future in mind.

"Julian," Sophia's voice drew him out of his thoughts. She looked at him with an entreating expression, one pale, slender hand reaching out to him. Julian stared at it. He knew what it was, but he wasn't quite certain what she expected him to do with it. He certainly didn't want to touch it. If he touched it, he would be touching her, and if he touched her he'd forgive her just so some of this pain would stop.

"I am sorry."

He laughed. He sounded like he was choking. "It is a little late for that, do you not think?"

"If it was not too late to forgive each other for seven years of bitterness, it is not too late to forgive me for a lapse in judgment."

"A lapse in judgment?" Incredulity colored his tone

and brought his brows snapping together. "I have lost my sister because of your 'lapse in judgment.' "

The pleading left her features and he was glad for it. It was too difficult to stay angry at her when she looked so sorry.

. "No. You lost your sister because of you."

If words were blades she would have exposed bone.

"And," she continued, her tone less harsh than it had been, "because of her. There were problems between the two of you long before I reentered your life."

She was right, of course, but that didn't take away any of the pain. This wasn't really about him and Letitia, and Julian knew it. They both knew it.

He looked at her—really looked at her. What he saw was more than just the most beautiful woman he had ever seen. She was strong and opinionated and she had endured years with a man who hadn't seen her true worth. Julian himself hadn't seen her true worth or he wouldn't have walked away all those years ago. He had betrayed her far worse than she could have ever betrayed him. Perhaps keeping the truth about Letitia from him had been a little bit of revenge on her part.

And why not? He had ruined her and turned his back on her. The few times he saw her in public after that he had given her the cut direct and smiled while others blatantly whispered as she walked by, even though he honestly hadn't felt much like smiling.

And she had acted like she didn't care. No matter how long he stared at her, she never once looked back. She treated him like something meaningless, when what he had wanted was some sign that she had cared.

Then she sent him that damn book and he believed she thought him a fool. Now that he had read the book, he knew how deeply he had cut her. How could he have been so foolish as to think he could atone for it so easily? Did he truly believe marrying her and offering her the heart he hadn't bothered to give her seven years ago would make up for everything else?

Yes. Yes, he had, because he *wanted* it to make up for everything else.

If she only knew how complete her revenge now was. Perhaps if he gave her that she would just leave him alone.

He locked gazes with her, and for a moment he thought he saw regret in the ebony depths of her eyes.

"I love you," he whispered, confessing what he only now knew was true. Only it was far too late. He knew that as well.

Sophia stared at Julian, her jaw slackening as her dazed mind made sense of his words.

He loved her? It was too shocking to dare believe, not when she thought she had ruined any chance of ever hearing him say those words. Before she could tell him she loved him as well, he spoke again.

"Or rather, I loved who I wanted you to be. That was a mistake and I am sorry for it."

It felt as though someone had reached into her chest and yanked out her heart. There was nothing he could have done to hurt her any deeper.

"I never lied to you about anything, Julian," she informed him. "I might have kept Letitia's involvement with Mr. Wesley from you, but I never lied about anything between us. Never."

He looked as though he wanted to believe her, and that hurt even more than his telling her he loved her. "Your revenge is complete, Sophia. You do not have to pretend anymore."

Revenge? Pretend? He thought she had kept Letitia's secret to revenge herself upon him?

"There was no revenge, Julian. I made a promise to your sister, that is all. I tried to make you see what was going on, but you wouldn't listen. You didn't see."

"No," he murmured, his honey brown gaze boring into hers. "I did not see because it never occurred to me to look—not in you."

Oh, but he knew just what to say to cut her. He knew just how to look to make her feel like the worst sort of woman, and she despised him for it, because, unlike Edmund and his manipulations Julian only wanted her to see how badly she had hurt him.

"I love you," she blurted. It was stupid and inane, and the only thing she could think of to say.

Julian's face darkened. "No, you do not," he countered. "You have to trust someone to love them. You do not trust me."

His accusation sparked a fire inside Sophia. "You believe I was trying to avenge myself on you. Clearly you do not trust me either, Julian. Perhaps you did not love me as you thought."

His mouth—that beautiful mouth—twisted bitterly. "Oh, I loved you. Your betrayal would not hurt quite so much if I had not loved you."

Betrayal! She clung to the word. It kept the cruelty of his words from slicing too deep.

"I did not betray you."

"You deliberately kept the truth from me." She could hear the restraint in his voice. She wanted to push him, make him lose that volatile temper of his. She needed to know she could drive him to the extremes of his emotions, because if she could make him mad enough to yell, then perhaps there was still hope for them.

"Yes," she replied calmly. He was shocked by her admission, she could see it in his eyes. "I kept the truth from you, because you would not have accepted it even if I told you. How many times did I tell you that I was worried Letitia might do something foolish? Every time I brought it up, you dismissed it because you arrogantly assumed you knew better than I, or even Letitia did."

A muscle ticked in his jaw, but he said nothing.

Sophia kept going, her own anger building. "You are so used to everyone doing what you want them to do that it never even occurred to you that Letitia might want some control over her own life. You were doing to her what you told me you once felt everyone had done to you. Except that she didn't run away from a marriage, Julian. She is running into one. You cannot keep her a little girl anymore. She is a grown woman and she's chosen the only way she knows to prove that to you."

Did he even hear her, let alone understand? His expression revealed nothing. Only the color in his cheeks was any indication that she might have struck a nerve.

"Yes," he said stiffly. "Thank you for clarifying things for me. Now if you will excuse me, I need to find my sister."

Sophia's shoulders sagged. He had heard what she said, and like everything else he dismissed it because it wasn't what he wanted to hear.

She tried to stop him as he brushed by her. "We have to talk."

He didn't even look at her. "I am afraid that right now I have more important things to do than listen to you tell me how wrong I am—how wrong I have always been, apparently. I need to stop a huge mistake from being made."

"It is not your mistake to stop!" she cried at his back. "It may not be a mistake at all!"

No, Letitia's marriage might not be a mistake, but Sophia knew that letting him walk out that door without settling things between them would be.

"Julian." How she hated the pleading in her voice. "Do not leave me like this."

At the door, Julian turned finally to face her. He looked at her as though she were a casual acquaintance, not the woman whose heart he held in his hand, and certainly not as though he cared.

"My darling Fe, I do not believe you are mine to leave."

Julian's words echoed in Sophia's head long after he left her there alone in his study. They taunted her while she stood there, silently staring at the door, hoping he would return so they could talk. They whispered to her twenty minutes later, when, convinced that he wasn't coming back, she decided she had to do something. And they haunted her now, a full hour later as she sat in Lady Wickford's parlor, washing down the cake stuck in her throat with a cup of tea that smelled divine but tasted like dishwater on her tongue.

"So the gel's finally gone and done it, has she?" Lady Wickford clucked her tongue with a resigned shake of her graying head. "I suppose I shouldn't be surprised. Every Rexley I've ever known had more will than good sense."

Sophia forced a smile. "I have no doubt that you are right. I thought perhaps Letitia might have given you some hint as to where they might have gone."

"Only one place they could have gone, as far as I can see," the older woman remarked, stirring a generous amount of sugar into her cup. "Letitia's always been captivated by Gretna Green. Chit seemed to think it romantic to be married by a blacksmith next to a dirty forge."

"Then you believe Mr. Wesley does indeed intend to marry her?" Sophia took another cake even though her stomach rolled at the thought of eating it. Maybe if she ate enough cakes she could fill the emptiness inside her.

Lady W seemed surprised by her question. "Oh, I see. Worried that he might prove to be a cad, eh? Well, I can't say as that I blame you, given your own history, but I do not think you need worry about Mr. Wesley. I have known his family for years. He's never been anything but a good lad."

Sophia regarded the sturdy woman thoughtfully. Was it her own experience with ruination that made her worry about Letitia, or was it that no one else wanted to think of the consequences if Mr. Wesley turned out to be less than they all hoped?

"Still," Lady W added, almost as an afterthought. "It will cause a scandal once word gets out that she's run off with him. I hope they marry and return quickly before the stories have much of a chance to tarnish her reputation."

"Yes," Sophia agreed softly. She knew firsthand what it was like to be the object of jeers and whispers. She would hate for that to happen to Letitia, even if the young woman did invite them upon herself by eloping as she had.

"I wager Wolfram was none too pleased by the news?"

Taking a bit of cake, Sophia forced herself to chew and swallow before replying. It was a difficult task, considering the very sound of his name sent her heart into her throat.

"That is putting it mildly."

The old woman's gaze was as sharp and shrewd as a hawk's. "And how did he react when he learned your part in it?"

Tea sloshed over the side of Sophia's cup. How had Lady Wickford known she had been involved? She had never spoken of Letitia's secret before now.

The old gal laughed at Sophia's shocked expression. "My dear girl, no one could have such a sorry, guilty countenance as yours without reason for it."

For a brief second, Sophia entertained the notion of throwing herself into Lady W's arms and confessing everything. She wanted to feel someone's arms around her, have someone pat her on the head and tell her everything was going to be all right, but she had never had anyone do that for her before, and she wasn't about to start asking for it now.

"He was understandably upset," she replied finally, carefully.

Lady Wickford smiled. It was far more sympathetic and knowing than Sophia was comfortable with. "So why are you here with me, stuffing yourself full of enough cake to choke an elephant, when you should be at home trying to make your husband understand why you acted as you did?"

Setting her cup and saucer on the tray on the table before her, Sophia hesitated a moment before answering. She was unused to discussing her problems and wasn't so certain she would know where to stop if she started now.

"He did not want to understand," she said simply. "He left."

Again she felt the pierce of Lady W's pale gaze. "So for the second time in your relationship, Julian Rexley walked out on you and you let him do it."

Thank God she had set her cup aside, otherwise she would have surely dropped it.

"I did not *let* him. I had little choice in the matter."

Lady W arched a thin, pale gray brow, furrowing the creases of her forehead. "Oh? Your feet were stuck to the floor and you could not follow him?"

Sophia scowled. "What good would following him have done?"

The older woman drained the last of her tea. "It is hard for someone to leave when you refuse to let them go. So why did you let him? It was not because you are not strong. I know how you fought that bounder Aberley. You did not let him have his way with you, so why do you allow those close to you to do whatever they want?"

"I do not know," Sophia replied hotly.

"I think you find it easier to live down to the expectations of those you care about rather than trying to live up to them," the older woman informed her haughtily. "I believe you are so convinced that you are going to disappoint someone that you do not bother to try not to."

"That is ridiculous!" Sophia didn't care who Lady Wickford was, or how good of a friend she had been in the past, she would not sit there and listen to someone else tell her what kind of person she was!

She opened her mouth to tell the old woman exactly that, but was cut off.

"Or is it that no one has ever lived up to your expectations that makes you let them fail *you*?"

Anything Sophia might have thought to say died in her throat. Was that true? Had she become so accustomed to having people disappoint her that she didn't expect anything better? It certainly eased the pain when it happened.

She never truly expected things to work between Julian

and herself, no matter how much she might have wished for them too. She saw that now. Perhaps that was why she had kept Letitia's secret. Not because of loyalty to her friend, but so she would have something to blame it on when Julian finally turned his back on her. Again.

"I think it is time for you to go home now," Lady Wickford said. There was no rancor, no disappointment in her voice, nothing but patience and warmth. "I think you need some time by yourself to think things over, and decide what you really want out of your life and your marriage. You will feel much better once you realize what you must do."

Sophia nodded dumbly and rose to her feet at the same time as Lady Wickford. Her friend took her by the arm and personally escorted her out into the foyer, where the butler went to get her pelisse and bonnet.

Lady Wickford gave her a fierce hug and kissed the air by her cheek. "Let me know how it all works out," she murmured before practically pushing her out the door.

Outside, Sophia stood on the step for what felt like an eternity, just listening to the birds chirping and feeling the sun on her face. Her life had just been drastically changed, although she couldn't quite put her finger on just what Lady Wickford had said to change it.

Julian had said he didn't believe she was his to leave, and she understood that now. She had blocked a part of herself off from him and he knew it. She had been afraid of disappointing him, and she had been afraid of being disappointed by him again as well. Her fear had been so great that she hadn't allowed herself to trust him completely, nor had she given him reason to trust her.

Back at Wolfram House, Fielding informed her that Julian was still out. Sophia's heart sank a bit, but she buoyed it back up by deciding to wait for Julian in his study until he returned. Perhaps she would send a note around to Lilith asking for her assistance. The day they had run into Charles at the gentlemen's shop, Lilith had told her that she knew of a man who could very discreetly look into Charles's private affairs if Sophia so desired it. Perhaps this man could also discover if Gretna Green was indeed where Letitia and Mr. Wesley had gone.

It was something that Julian had probably already thought of, given his relationship with Gabriel, but it was worth a shot.

Sitting at Julian's desk, Sophia wrote the note and had a footman deliver it. Then she waited. She had Mrs. Yorke bring her a tray rather than dine alone at that huge dining room table. She was still waiting when Fielding came in and asked if there was anything else she required before the servants went to bed. She told him no.

Even as she drifted off in a chair by the fire, Sophia waited for Julian to return to her.

He never came.

Julian left Lord Penderthal's later that afternoon no closer to discovering where Letitia and Marcus Wesley had gone than he had been when he first learned of the elopement.

Penderthal was as surprised by the situation as Julian had been. His nephew had sent him a note saying that he had been called out of town on business and would return in a few days. It hadn't crossed the old earl's mind that his heir might be lying to him.

At least Julian had the old man's word that he would contact him if he heard anything.

He went to Wesley's club next and asked a few discreet questions. No one seemed to know anything. Then he went to Sir William Lewis's house to question his daughter. Miss Lewis had assisted Letitia before, and he thought there might be a chance that the girl was aiding her again, but if she was, nothing could entice her to loosen her tongue this time. She did, however, promise to keep Letitia's elopement to herself. Julian knew it could not be long before word leaked out.

By the time he had done all this, it was early evening. His next and final stop before returning home was Gabriel's. He knew Lilith had connections of a dubious nature because of her days as a gaming club owner. It was his last hope of finding Letitia before she managed to put too much distance between herself and London. They were traveling by coach, which would slow them a fair bit, and they would have to stop at night, but even with these obstacles, they would soon be far enough away that Julian would not be able to catch them in time to stop a wedding.

He tried very hard not to think about Sophia while he was gone. He was hurt and angry, and he wanted her to do something about it, even though he had no idea what she could do.

She had lied to him. And then she had the nerve to say she loved him. Was he supposed to believe it? Just like that? He had been trying to get her to tell him she loved him for days and she refused. It seemed a little too convenient for her to tell him when he was mad at her.

Even so, it had been damn sweet to hear, regardless of whether or not it was true. And part of him hoped it wasn't true, because that would just be too much in the face of her betrayal.

It *was* a betrayal too. It was more than just keeping

something from him, although he couldn't quite articulate how. That was how deep his disappointment ran.

The Angelwood mansion rang with laughter as he crossed the marble floor of the great hall toward one of the house's many drawing rooms. Gabriel and Lilith, Brave and Rachel sat in the center of the room, drinking and laughing as though they hadn't a care in the world.

Lucky them.

"Jules!" Gabriel cried, looking up as he entered the room. "We were wondering if you were going to come."

Julian stared at him. "Come?" he repeated dumbly. He had been expected?

Gabriel came to him and clapped him on the shoulder. "Lilith sent the invitation round a few hours ago. We knew it was short notice, but we figured you would not mind. Where is Sophia?"

"She is at home," he replied as Gabriel glanced over his shoulder at the door. "Or at least, I think she is. We—that is, I—did not receive any invitation. I have not been home all afternoon."

Gabriel's smile faded as his gaze locked with Julian's. He must have seen then that something was not right.

"What is the matter?" he asked.

Julian glanced at the others, who were still laughing and chatting, unaware that his life was falling apart before them.

"I need your help. Letitia is gone."

He didn't think he had spoken all that loudly, but the conversation died abruptly all the same. Brave, Rachel and Lilith all turned to him with almost identical expressions of surprise and horror.

"Gone?" Rachel asked. "Where has she gone?"

Seating himself in the nearest chair, Julian explained

everything. He even told them about Letitia's note and Sophia's involvement in the whole thing. He left nothing out, except for how utterly destroyed he felt inside.

When he had finished, everyone seemed too stunned to speak—except for Lilith.

"So that is why Sophia sent me that note."

Just the sound of her name on another's lips was enough to send Julian's heart slamming against his ribs.

"What note?" And when had she sent it?

A small frown puckered the otherwise smooth skin of Lilith's brow. "I received a note from Sophia earlier this afternoon asking if I knew of anyone who might be so skilled as to find someone who did not wish to be found. I was going to call on her tomorrow to discuss it. Had I known it was so urgent I would not have waited." Her gaze was keen as it met Julian's. "I assume you have come here personally with a similar request?"

Julian nodded. "Yes. I need to find out whether or not Letitia and Wesley have indeed set out for Gretna Green. It seems the logical choice, but Wesley is not stupid. He might have another destination in mind that would be harder to discover."

Lilith rose to her feet in a rustle of russet satin skirts. "I will send for Mr. Francis directly. If anyone can find them, it is he."

Thanking her, Julian watched as she pulled a cord on the wall and went to a small desk in the corner of the room. There, she hastily scribbled a note, which she gave to Robinson, Gabriel's stocky butler.

"Do not worry, Julian," she said in a voice far more soothing than her usual crisp tones. "Mr. Francis is the best there is. He will not dally in responding to my summons."

And Lilith was right. Hardly a half hour later—most of

which Julian spent trying to project some semblance of his normal self—Robinson announced Mr. Francis's arrival.

Francis was a large, sturdy man of average height. He possessed the thickest head of silvery hair Julian had ever seen. He also possessed, Lilith told him, the uncanny ability to uncover information.

Julian wasted no time in explaining the situation. He gave Mr. Francis descriptions of both Letitia and Marcus Wesley, what clothing they had been wearing, what Wesley's carriage looked like—everything he could think of that might be of use.

"Everyone leaves a trail, Lord Wolfram," Mr. Francis informed him confidently. "Your sister and Mr. Wesley will be no exception."

Julian thanked him for giving the matter top priority and also for his promise of discretion. No one needed to tell him what would happen to Letitia's reputation if word of this leaked out. No one would want to marry her then.

One thing was for certain, he wouldn't marry her off to the first bastard who offered, not like Sophia's father had done to her.

Sophia. What was he going to do about Sophia?

Nothing for now. He was so damned tired, he didn't want to think anymore.

He stayed and had dinner with his friends. He ate very little and drank much, much more. By the time he took his leave, late that evening, he was so deep into his cups he was seeing double.

The servants were all abed when he finally arrived home. He staggered down the corridor to his study. Why he was going there this late at night he didn't know, except that he had the strangest desire to see if Sophia was there, waiting for him.

She was. He found her in a chair in front of a dying fire, a blanket pulled up around her shoulders, her mouth slightly parted in slumber. He could wake her, but then he would have to talk to her, and even if he knew what to say, he wouldn't be able to say it so that it made sense, not in his present state.

So he left her there by the fire, and made the slow, weaving climb through the dark, upstairs to his own chamber, where his big, empty bed sat waiting.

Julian's last thought before sleep claimed him was of Sophia, asleep in the chair in his study. She had waited for him, just like he had hoped she would. The realization should have made him happy.

It didn't.

Chapter 18

*The chase is so much more appealing when one
is certain their quarry wishes to be caught.*

An Unfortunate Attachment by the Marchioness of Aberley

He felt like hell.

The clear golden light of a spring morning poured through Julian's bedroom windows. He had been so drunk the night before he had forgotten to close the drapes, and now he would pay for it.

Rolling onto his back, he forced his eyes to remain open, despite the stabbing pain in his head. He deserved whatever discomfort the morning had in store for him. He had known this would happen as he guzzled glass after glass of Gabriel's brandy the night before. He had wanted the drunken stupor and this splitting ache in his head and roiling in his stomach—it kept him from thinking about Sophia. It kept him from thinking at all.

But even now, the pain in his head seemed dull compared to the pain inside. He would give anything to change things; anything except Sophia.

He loved her. That was the real thorn in all of this. Seven years ago, when he could have had her love, he had turned his back on it. Now that he wanted it with all his heart, it turned its back on him.

Groaning, he sat up. The pain behind his eyes was almost unbearable. His stomach protested as he weakly rose to his feet. He hadn't even removed his boots the night before. He toed them off now. His feet were sweating inside his stockings. Ugh.

He smelled. He felt dirty. He needed a bath and a shave and a good strong cup of coffee.

Twenty minutes later he was soaking in a tub of hot, lemon-scented water. The sharp, clean smell seemed to help clear his senses. Just being clean made him feel infinitely better.

He reclined in the tub, freshly shaven and drinking a cup of coffee that was so strong he could have polished his boots with it. Yes, this was better. He could face the day now. He could face anything. Even his wife.

He wanted to forgive her. His heart and his head told him it would be a simple thing to do. His pride wasn't so convinced.

Some time later Julian emerged from his chamber, feeling much better for being clean and dressed in fresh clothes. He wore a dark green coat that his valet swore put color in his cheeks and diminished the circles under his eyes. Julian didn't care what the hell it did just as long as it made him look better.

Sophia wasn't in the breakfast room when he sat down and forced himself to eat some breakfast.

"Lady Wolfram has not come down yet, my lord," Fielding informed him as he filled Julian's cup with hot coffee. "Shall I have one of the maids check on her?"

Julian shook his head. "Let her rest." He didn't want her to see him like this.

After eating, he went to his study. Despite all he had to do, he did nothing but stand and stare at the chair she'd slept in.

This was ridiculous. He had to stop mooning over her like some love-struck youth. Rest assured she wasn't pining over him.

He had just sat down at his desk when a sharp rap on the door made him wince. His headache had eased considerably, but it still felt as though Gentleman Jackson himself were pounding on his brain.

"There is a Mr. Francis here to see you, my lord," Fielding informed him.

Julian's heart leapt with hope. Had Francis news for him then?

"Send him in, please, Fielding."

A few moments later Francis entered the study looking for all the world like a prosperous merchant rather than a man who made his living prying into the affairs of others. Julian didn't care how the man presented himself—he could walk around in ladies' undergarments for all Julian cared, so long as he uncovered just where the hell Letitia had gone.

"Mr. Francis," Julian said, standing. He offered his hand. "I hope you have news for me."

"Lord Wolfram." The heavier man took the offered handshake. "I do."

Gesturing to a chair in front of the desk, Julian reseated himself and waited for Mr. Francis to get to the point.

He did not have to wait long.

"Your sister and her companion seem to indeed be bound for Gretna Green, Lord Wolfram."

Julian was hardly surprised by the information, but

what did surprise him was that Francis had discovered it so quickly. Letitia and Wesley wouldn't be anywhere near Scotland yet.

As if hearing his unspoken question, Mr. Francis elaborated, "I tracked them to an inn north of Bedford late last night. One of their horses threw a shoe and they were forced to stop. Apparently they are traveling as brother and sister—with separate rooms."

Julian found that little piece of information vastly relieving.

"They had not left the inn as of six o'clock this morning," the investigator also informed him. "On horseback you might be able to catch up with them by late evening, early tomorrow morning."

Julian had every intention of doing just that. As soon as Mr. Francis left, he penned a note to Gabriel and a note to Brave, asking them to come immediately. He gave them to a footman to deliver and ran upstairs to pack a small bag to take on his journey. A clean shirt and undergarments would be all he would need.

Before the end of the day he would have stopped his sister from making the biggest mistake of her life. He could only hope she would forgive him for it.

"What can we do to help?"

It was the first thing out of Brave's mouth when Julian told him and Gabriel that Mr. Francis had found Letitia and Wesley. It would be Gabriel who would want to know the particulars—Brave just wanted to know what to do. Perhaps that was because he had once held himself responsible for Miranda's death.

"The two of you need to make certain no one realizes

how odd my sudden departure from town is," he told
them, putting papers away in his desk and locking the
drawers.

"We can do that," Gabriel answered. "It shouldn't be
too difficult. You are traveling north. We will simply
say you had urgent estate business to attend to in Yorkshire."

Yorkshire. Julian froze. What if Letitia and Wesley
weren't headed for Gretna Green as Mr. Francis suspected? Letitia's intelligence might be questionable at
times, but the girl wasn't stupid, and she was sneakier
than she should be. She would have to know that Julian
would chase after them. She knew him too well to suspect
otherwise. She would also know that Gretna Green would
be his first assumption.

But what if they weren't going to Scotland?

It all made sense now. Letitia had left the house with
Wesley not even twenty minutes after leaving Julian yesterday morning. How had she managed to pack so
quickly? For that matter, how had they made the decision to elope, written a note, retrieved Letitia's belongings and Wesley's own before setting off? Such things
could not be rushed, and Fielding said both of them
seemed so calm when they left—not in the least bit hurried.

They'd had it planned. That was the only explanation.
All Letitia had to do was run up to her room, stuff a few
essentials into her already packed valise, retrieve the note
she had written—probably the night before just to be
safe—and go back downstairs to where Wesley waited.
His own belongings were already stored in his waiting
carriage.

No doubt a special license among them.

"Damnation," Julian muttered.

Gabriel's gaze narrowed. "What is it?"

Julian's gaze went from him to Brave. "They are not going to Gretna."

Understanding dawned in Brave's dark eyes. "You think they are going to Heatherington."

Julian nodded. Heatherington Park was his Yorkshire estate. The place where Miranda had committed suicide. Letitia hadn't been there in years. Normally it would be the last place Julian would think to look for her. She knew it as well as he did.

He walked across the room to the bookcase and hid the key to his desk underneath a volume of Rochester. No one but he ever read it.

"I would also ask that the two of you take care of Sophia while I am gone."

Gabriel and Brave's expressions softened and a shard of uncertainty pricked Julian's heart. He didn't want their pity, and he certainly didn't need to be second-guessing his own actions right now.

"Have you spoken to her?" Brave asked.

Julian shook his head. "No. I will do that when I get back."

Gabriel folded his arms across the breadth of his chest. "You should do it before you go."

"I do not have time," he replied gruffly. "I have to go after Letitia. She is all I have left."

Gabriel corrected him. "You have Sophia."

It was a well-aimed dig—one that struck Julian right between the ribs, somewhere in the vicinity of his heart.

"Yes," he scoffed. "A wife who does not trust me. It is not much of a marriage, is it?"

Brave shrugged. "Mine wasn't either at first. Both of you know I had my own reasons for marrying Rachel. But you love Sophia. You always have."

Julian didn't bother to argue his feelings. "What good does that do me when she keeps secrets from me?"

"Oh, I don't know," Gabriel replied lightly, a smug smile on his face. "Lilith and I kept our share of secrets from each other at first and we loved each other. I think we turned out all right."

His gaze darting from one friend to the other, Julian despised them both at that moment, but he was not about to admit defeat.

"I have to do this. Will you look after my wife while I am gone, or not?"

Gabriel and Brave exchanged glances. Julian didn't comprehend the meaning behind them. It was obviously some secret code that only happily married men could decipher.

Bastards.

"I do not have time to debate this with either of you," he announced crossly, snatching his valise from the sofa where it sat. "I have to leave now if I want to catch up with them before they reach Heatherington."

He was at the door, his hand on the knob, when Gabriel's voice came from behind him.

"Yes. We shall look after Sophia while you are gone."

It was an effort to keep his shoulders from actually sagging in relief. Glancing over his shoulder, Julian cast a brief smile at his friends. "Thank you."

He checked his watch as he strode down the corridor. It was late. He would have to make good time if he wanted to catch up with them. Fortunately he knew of a few short-cuts to Yorkshire that might give him an advantage, provided that Wesley or his driver didn't know them as well. "Julian."

His feet stuck to the floor as though they had been glued there. Against his better judgment, he turned his head to face her. It was a mistake.

Sophia stood on the stairs dressed in a gown of pale blue muslin. The color normally would have looked quite fine on her, but this morning it only accentuated the pallor of her face and the bluish circles beneath her stark, wide eyes. She looked tired. She looked sad.

Julian didn't speak. He couldn't. He simply stared at her for what seemed an eternity. Finally, he turned away, but not before he saw the rejection in her eyes. She thought he was leaving in order to punish her. What she didn't understand—what she could have no possible way of knowing—was that it wasn't her he was trying to punish.

He was punishing himself.

He didn't say goodbye.

Never mind that, he never even said *hello*.

From where she stood in the hall, Sophia could see out into the foyer, and through the windows that flanked the front door. Through the spotless panes, she watched as Julian hoisted himself up onto the back of his horse. He spoke to someone standing beneath him—Fielding probably—and then glanced up.

Their eyes met through the glass for the briefest of moments—long enough to hurt—and then he was gone, the gelding's hooves kicking up stones as it galloped down the gravel drive, its rider bent over its neck.

Within seconds he was out of sight, and Sophia was left alone, the emptiness of the house echoing around her.

Where was he going? When would he return? Had he discovered where Letitia and Mr. Wesley had gone? Gretna Green was the obvious answer, but perhaps Julian knew differently. Or perhaps he didn't know anything at all.

If it weren't from the missive she received from Lilith late yesterday evening, she wouldn't have even known that Julian had anyone trying to find his sister—although she probably would have assumed it. Julian was not the kind of man to allow anyone to run away from him. Nor was he the type of man to run himself, except where she was concerned.

Lilith's note had been brief, explaining that Julian had come to see them, also asking for her help. She had given him the name of a man who might be able to help. She asked how Sophia was faring and offered her assistance and friendship, however either might be needed. Sophia was touched.

She was also angry as hell.

Julian must know that she had asked Lilith for help as well, yet he said nothing. He must know she was feeling awful for everything, yet he remained silent. She hated silence. She had endured years of it while married to Edmund. He could go for days without speaking to her, ignoring her until she came to him, having worked herself into a state wondering what she might have done to displease him. Most times she wouldn't have done anything at all. He just liked making her think she had because then she was suitably grateful when he decided to bless her with his attention again.

Well, she wasn't that stupid girl anymore, and Julian, for all his faults, was a better man than Edmund ever thought of being. Her husband was upset with her, she could understand that, but if he thought she was going to let him avoid her, he had a rude awakening coming.

Holding her head high, even though there was no one to see her brave front, she walked across the hall to the parlor where she and Julian usually took their breakfast.

A piece of toast, lightly buttered, was all her stomach felt like eating, and she nibbled on it as she left the parlor, her cup of tea in the other hand. If Julian left behind any trace of where he was going, or what he had discovered about Letitia, it would be in his study. If she didn't find anything, she would have to resort to questioning the servants, even though she would rather not have them gossiping about the state of her marriage to their master.

It was possible that Julian had been on his way after Letitia when she saw him. Had he any luggage with him when he left? She couldn't remember. She hadn't noticed. Her gaze hadn't gotten past his face and the betrayed expression in his gaze when it met hers.

The door to his study was open. That was odd. Normally Julian made certain it was closed at all times, unless he actually allowed the staff in there to clean it. The room was his little haven, his sanctuary. He wouldn't like her pawing around in it.

One more thing to add to her list of sins, she thought wryly. She'd apologize for that too, if he ever spoke to her again.

Gabriel and Brave were standing in the middle of the study having what appeared to be a very serious conversation, given the gravity of their expressions and the hushed severity of their voices.

"Gentlemen," she said loudly from the doorway. "Why am I not surprised to see you?"

They jumped like boys caught at mischief, and turned to face her with almost identical aspects of chagrin.

"Sophia." It was Gabriel who found his voice first. "Good morning." He bowed. Brave followed suit.

"I challenge you to name one thing good about it," she said, softening the remark with a smile as she crossed the carpet toward them.

"The sun is shining," Brave replied when Gabriel turned to him for help.

She would give them that. "Where was my husband going when I saw him just a little while ago?"

Brave glanced first at Gabriel then at Sophia. "I'm not certain we should—"

"Yorkshire," Gabriel blurted. "He's gone to Heatherington Park."

The scowl on Brave's face was almost laughable. "Gabe!"

The dark-haired man shrugged. "Julian would interfere if it was one of our marriages and you know it."

Sophia didn't give a damn who interfered in whose marriage. "Why did he go to Yorkshire?" Good lord, he wasn't angry enough to leave her, was he? Normally it was the woman who was banished to the country, not the husband.

"That is where he thinks Letitia and Wesley have gone," Gabriel replied.

Sophia frowned. But in her note Letitia said that she and Marcus were eloping. "Not Gretna Green?"

Gabriel shook his head. "Julian thinks Gretna Green is what they want us to believe. He believes they plan to be married by special license in Yorkshire."

Sophia's brows were still knitted, even as relief washed over her. At least Letitia hadn't taken complete leave of her senses. If this was true then she must have known Wesley's intentions before running off.

"Where would Mr. Wesley get the money for a special license?" Licenses were expensive—too expensive for a man of Marcus Wesley's income.

"It would be easy enough for him to get the funds. He could borrow, or if he did not want anyone to know, he could always fence something, a piece of art, silverware, jewelry."

Jewelry. Sophia's head snapped up. "Letitia's jewelry case was empty when I checked her apartments yesterday. I thought she had taken it all with her, but perhaps they 'fenced' some of it, as you put it, to pay for the license."

"It would not surprise me," Brave replied, obviously deciding he'd stayed out of the conversation long enough. "Wesley might not have a lot of his own cash, but as Penderthal's heir, he would have plenty of friends who would know where to go to discreetly pawn items."

Pacing the carpet, Sophia rubbed her hand along the back of her neck. Her shoulders were so tight she could have run a bow along them and played a jig.

Damn Letitia. She had duped them all—Sophia especially. Here she had believed the younger woman when she told—no, *promised*—her that she wouldn't do anything stupid. It had merely been a bid to buy them time to get the license and make their plans.

And Sophia hadn't seen it coming. She should have. Letitia was more like her than Sophia cared to admit. Of all people, she should have recognized the signs. Letitia had taken to keeping to herself more often. She had become guarded and secretive, and she had talked about the situation with far more calm than she usually possessed. Sophia probably would have noticed had she not been so caught up in her own life. Julian claimed more of her thoughts than was healthy.

And now he was gone—running after a sister who didn't want to be caught, trying to keep her a little girl when it was so obvious that Letitia needed to grow up. And she had just let him go.

Perhaps Lady Wickford was right. Perhaps she set the standard for herself low as well, so it wouldn't be a surprise when those whom she expected to love her turned their backs in aversion. Had she always done this? She couldn't remember.

Well, it was time it stopped.

"I am going after him," she announced, daring either man to try to stop her. "If Julian thinks he can just avoid me by running away again he is sorely mistaken. He cannot just turn his back and forget about me. I am his wife, and I will dog him until the day he dies if I have to."

Point made, she fell silent. Both men stared at her as though they believed her to be completely out of her wits, but Sophia didn't care. She was in charge. Julian might be her husband, and by law her master, but this marriage was half hers, and she would be damned if she'd let it go just because his pride had been hurt.

At least, she hoped it was just his pride that had been hurt, because Sophia knew what it was like to have one's heart broken and she didn't like the idea of having done that to Julian. Never mind that he had been the one to do it to her. The whole point of her epiphany was to ensure that their past didn't repeat itself, which it was very much in danger of doing if she allowed Julian to walk away.

"There is something you should see before you go chasing after him," Gabriel informed her, the shock gone from his expression. Brave remained silent as Gabriel strode across the room to the bookcase. He pulled a key out from underneath a book and used it to open a drawer in Julian's desk.

"He keeps all his poems in here," Gabriel explained, rifling through papers in the drawer. "The ones he's working on, at any rate. Ah. Here, read this one."

He had given the papers the briefest of readings. Sophia wasn't certain how he had determined that *this* poem was better for her to read than any others, and she wasn't certain she wanted to look at one of Julian's unfinished works. He really wouldn't appreciate it.

She took the parchment and lowered her gaze to it. What she saw made her chest tight with emotion and her eyes fill with tears.

For Sophia, it read. Even if it hadn't stated so bluntly that it was for her, she would have known after a verse or two, when she read that line about the garden of Eden that Julian often quoted to her. Sophia was almost ashamed to read it. It was so personal, like peering into Julian's heart.

But what she saw made her so happy she could just burst. He loved her. He had said it and this poem was proof of it. That wasn't something lost over one little lie. Was it? Not if she could help it.

"All right." Sniffling, she wiped her eyes with the back of one hand. "Which one of you is going to take me to Yorkshire?"

Brave and Gabriel exchanged glances and something

seemed to pass between them even though all Sophia saw was Brave's nod.

Gabriel met her gaze, determination and resignation in his pale eyes.

"I'll take you."

Chapter 19

It does not matter how long or how fast you run, my dearest. One's past always catches up.

An Unfortunate Attachment by the Marchioness of Aberley

There was something oddly poetic about chasing Letitia to Heatherington. The irony was not lost on Julian as he tore across the countryside on the back of yet another horse. Miranda had made a horrible mistake at Heatherington. He would not allow Letitia to make one as well.

He had spent the entire day and the better part of the blessedly moonlit night on the road, pushing each mount he rode to its limit before stopping for a fresh one. Other than that, he stopped only when nature made it necessary for him to do so.

The sun had risen a few hours ago and the coolness of the morning was slowly giving in to its heat. Thank God the weather had remained fine for his journey. Rain would have slowed him down to the point of futility. He wasn't far from Heatherington now.

He had no idea of knowing how many hours Letitia and Wesley had on him, and they had almost a full day of

340

travel before that. They might very well be at Heatherington already, depending on how fast their carriage made the
journey.

What if he was wrong? What if Yorkshire wasn't their
destination? What if they actually were bound for Gretna?
This foray into Yorkshire might very well cost him any
chance of stopping their marriage.

Would that truly be all that *un*pleasant? He couldn't believe he even entertained the thought. Certainly Letitia
would be married to a man who at this time was beneath
her and could not afford to keep her, but she would have
her dowry, and Julian wouldn't let her starve. It might do
his sister good to not get everything she wanted as soon as
she asked.

And if Letitia *was* indeed married, he could just turn
around and go back to London—back to Sophia.

The memory of the look on her face when he left her
remained with him all the way from London. He shouldn't
have left her, not with things between them as they were.
Chasing after Letitia was only part of it. The real reason
he left was because he was a coward. He was terrified her
declaration of love had been another lie.

And he couldn't face her, because that same part of him
that wanted to believe she loved him didn't feel worthy of
her love—not after all the blunders he had made where
she was involved. She was wrong when she accused him
of not trusting her. He had—or at least he had wanted to—
but the truth of her betrayal had cut him deeply. What else
was he to think but that she had been out for revenge? It
was what he would have done.

He couldn't think of this now. It was too painful, and he
had more pressing matters demanding his attention.

Was there anything more pressing than saving his marriage? Why couldn't he just leave Letitia to the mess she had made? He knew the answer to that as surely as he knew his own face.

He could not bear to lose Letitia, and that was exactly what it felt like. He was losing the only family he had left.

Gabriel had told him he had Sophia, but it wasn't the same. Letitia was all he had left of his parents, of Miranda. She was a living, breathing memory of happy times, of love and warmth and security. Letitia had depended on him for more than a decade. He had been everything for her. He had a responsibility to her to protect her.

Who would look at him like he could move the sun and the moon if she was gone? Who would make him feel as though he could do anything with their blind faith? There would be an empty place in his life without her—a place he didn't know how to fill. For years he had worried about his sisters, and then just Letitia by herself. Her life became the focus of his. He didn't know how to let go of that.

For years he had thought he wanted control of his own life. As a youth he had rebelled against those who tried to tell him what to do. He had turned his back on Sophia because of it. And now, faced with the possibility of having the responsibility of only his own life, Julian felt as though his world was falling apart.

He didn't like change. Change for him usually meant loss. He had lost his parents and Miranda to death. He had lost Gabe and Brave to their new lives, and now he was losing Letitia.

But he had gained Sophia. He only hoped he hadn't lost her in the interim.

His mount carried him swiftly over a hill. The sun struck him, brilliant and blinding and square in the face.

And there, set in that low, fertile lap of nature, surrounded by lush, green foliage, was Heatherington Park.

An Elizabethan mansion with gothic influences, the house was something right out of Mrs. Radcliffe's novels. Perhaps that was why Miranda chose to end her life there. Her death had ruined the house for Julian. He had spent much of his youth there with his family and Gabe and Brave. It had been a happy place. Now it seemed just a sad, old house. A sad, old house that he still paid to staff and care for.

Mrs. Berry, the housekeeper, confirmed his suspicion that this was Letitia's destination.

"Lord Wolfram!" she cried as he crossed the threshold into the foyer. "We weren't expecting *you!*"

There wasn't much of a staff at Heatherington, just Mrs. Berry and a few others—enough to care for the house and what few rooms were in use. It seemed foolish to have a full staff in a house he rarely used.

He smiled warmly at the plump older woman. "I hope my arrival is not a disappointment, Mrs. Berry."

She took his coat and gloves, clucking her tongue at his teasing. "Of course not, my lord. It is just that in her note, Lady Letitia did not mention that you would be joining her."

Julian kept his tone casual. "It is a surprise. Is my sister here?"

Mrs. Berry folded his coat over one short arm and smiled up at him. She had to lean her head all the way back to do so. She only stood as high as his chest.

"Not yet, but we expect them by luncheon. Would you care for breakfast, my lord?"

As if on cue, Julian's stomach growled an affirmative.

He hadn't eaten a decent meal since breakfast the day before.

The housekeeper chuckled. "I will take that as a yes! You go on in to the dining room, my lord. I'll have some of that awful coffee for you in a wee minute."

Smiling despite himself, Julian did as she instructed. How could he have forgotten how dear Mrs. Berry was? He remembered her fussing over him and the girls, sneaking them tarts and other treats whenever Renfrew, the butler, wasn't around.

Old Renfrew was dead now. The house hadn't had a butler in years. There hadn't been a need with it being closed up as it was. Mrs. Berry was perfectly capable of running things as they were.

Julian walked through the marbled hall, past the staircase that was as wide as two men placed end to end, down the corridor to the dining room. Everything was exactly as it had always been. The furniture gleamed, the house was bright with light and the air smelled sweetly of beeswax and the outdoors. Mrs. Berry had cleaned and aired the house for Letitia and Wesley, just as she aired and cleaned it whenever she knew Julian was coming.

How difficult was it for the servants to live there? Every day seeing the pond where Miranda had drowned herself, every day caring for a house the family had, for all intents and purposes, forgotten?

The long mahogany table glowed in the morning light as Julian entered the dining room. He sat down at the head of it and waited, his gaze drifting around the room to the paintings that lined the walls. There was one of a foxhunt on the wall directly across from him that made him smile. His mother hated that painting, but his father had loved it, and so he hung it where it would be at her back so she wouldn't have to look at it, but he could.

There had been a lot of laughter in this house. There were a lot of tears of well.

Mrs. Berry brought his coffee—an entire pot of it—a little while later, and shortly after that she brought him breakfast as well. There was a small plate piled high with freshly baked bread slathered with butter, a pot of strawberry jam, and a large plate positively heaped with eggs, sausage, ham and kippers.

And of course he ate it all, even though he swore he wouldn't be able to. He left the dining room and went to the blue drawing room. He sat on a blue high-backed chair, his feet propped on the windowsill, and watched the lane that led from the road to the house for his sister.

The carriage arrived about two hours later. Julian was waiting in the hall when Letitia and Marcus Wesley came flouncing through the door, laughing as though they hadn't a care in the world.

"Good morning," he said.

Letitia screeched and dropped her reticule. It landed on the marble tiles with a loud *clank*. She must have had a lot of coin in it. Julian couldn't help but wonder where she got it.

The lovers stared at him as though he were a ghost—an awful, moaning, pustuled ghost.

Now that he had caught them, Julian didn't know what to say. *Boo* just didn't seem appropriate, but neither did ranting and raving. He was tired and drawn and he just wanted to sit down and see if the three of them couldn't be honest with each other for a change.

"What are you doing here?" Letitia demanded, her

cheeks blooming with color where just a few seconds ago there had been none. "You cannot stop us, Julian. I do not care what you do—"

"Oh, Lettie, do be quiet!" he snapped.

She opened her mouth to reply, but Wesley stopped her with a hand on her shoulder. He smiled soothingly at her, then turned his gaze to Julian.

"Perhaps we could go somewhere a bit less . . . public, Wolfram?"

Yes. Privacy would be good. He didn't need the servants hearing him and Letitia rip into each other like fighting children, and he didn't need them overhearing the particulars of Letitia's elopement.

"Follow me," he said and he kept glancing over his shoulder to make certain that they did.

Inside the blue drawing room once more, Julian turned to face his sister.

"I imagine you are surprised to find me here." He managed a small smile. "Imagine my surprise when I discovered you were gone."

Letitia's chin came up in a gesture he was beginning to hate. "What did you expect me to do? Meekly accept your dictate and marry a man I do not love?"

"Yes," he replied honestly. "I believe that is exactly what I expected. When you put it that way I see why you did not find it so appealing."

Letitia gaped at him.

"I also expected your honesty. I do not want you to marry a man you cannot love, Lettie." His gaze left hers and settled on Wesley. "Nor am I about to allow you to marry someone unsuitable just because you think you *do* love him."

Wesley didn't even flinch. Julian's estimation of the younger man rose a notch.

"That is not your decision to make, Julian," Letitia informed him quietly.

He didn't raise his voice. "I'm afraid that, by law, it is."

"Why?" she cried, her sudden outburst of passion hitting him like a blow to the chest. "Why are you doing this? I love Marcus. He loves me. I do not care if he is not rich. Why do you?"

"You are my responsibility."

"I am your sister!" Pressing her clasped hands to her breast, she gazed imploringly at him. "This is my life. *Mine*. Why will you not allow me to have control of it?"

Julian scowled. "You think I want to control you?"

She looked as though the answer was obvious. "Ever since Mama and Papa died you have not allowed me to make any decisions on my own unless it was what color of gown to buy. It is as though you have never wanted me to grow up, as if you hoped to keep me a child forever."

Her words struck a chord deep within him. He thought he was protecting her from the world, keeping her safe, since he had failed with Miranda. He realized, with the sickening feeling that came with seeing one's own actions clearly, that he hadn't just been protecting Letitia. He had been protecting himself, keeping her close so he couldn't lose what family he had left.

He had been Letitia's age when Sophia's father tried to force him to marry her. He had reacted by refusing and by turning his back on Sophia and what was right. He didn't want Letitia to turn her back on him. And she would.

"I do not want to see you get hurt," he rasped, jerking his gaze back to hers.

"With all due respect, Lord Wolfram," Wesley said, coming up to stand by Letitia's side. "I plan to love and care for your sister for the rest of her life, not hurt her."

Letitia and Wesley smiled at each other. It was a lovers' smile. They loved each other, it was painfully obvious. How could Julian deny his sister the joy of loving and being loved? He couldn't, not when he envied her so terribly for it.

It was time for another confession. "I do not want to lose you."

Letitia's eyes widened, filling with tears at the admission. "You will always be my brother, Julian. I will always need you, but I need Marcus too."

It felt as though someone were sitting on Julian's chest, it was so tight. She was right. When had his brat of a little sister grown up? She was her own woman and if he didn't allow her to live her own life and make her own mistakes she would never forgive him and then he really would lose her.

Sophia had been right.

"Will you at least allow me to give you away?" his voice was so thick he almost didn't recognize it.

Gasping, Letitia broke away from Wesley and launched herself into Julian's arms. He held her tightly, pressing a hard kiss to her temple. Her arms twined around his neck, lifting herself up on her toes so that she could brush her lips against his cheek. He squeezed his arms tighter around her as though he could make her see how much he loved her by the force of his embrace. And then he did what he had to do.

He let her go.

Good lord, just how far away *was* Yorkshire anyway?

It was late morning now. They had traveled all day and all night. Even though Letitia and Mr. Wesley would no doubt be a bit more relaxed in their speed, given the fact that they didn't expect to be caught, Gabriel didn't want to waste time. They didn't stop longer than the necessary time to purchase food and answer nature's call—not that Sophia would have agreed to stop for anything else. She wanted to find Julian, and would have gone on horseback if she'd had to!

"How much longer?" she asked, stretching her cramped legs out before her.

Gabriel glanced out the window. "Another hour or two." He smiled. "Is being cooped up with me beginning to fray your nerves?"

Sophia smiled. "Lord, yes. I never want to travel from one end of the country to the other with you ever again."

He laughed and Sophia joined him. She liked Gabriel. He teased her and made her comfortable. Brave was more serious and he had a way of looking at her that made her feel as though he were trying to see inside her soul. It made her uneasy. Quiet people always made her feel very self-conscious. She preferred loud, boisterous people—people who talked more than she did, so she didn't feel compelled to reveal things about herself.

And then there was Julian, who actually made her *want* to reveal things about herself. He knew more about her marriage to Edmund than anyone else, except herself. There were some things she would never tell him—he didn't need to know all the sordid details. They didn't matter anymore.

"Do you think he managed to catch up with them?" Sophia asked. As much as she wanted to see Julian, she hoped that Letitia had succeeded in eloping with Marcus Wesley. Then Julian would have to acknowledge her as an adult and allow her to live her own life.

Gabriel shrugged. "If Yorkshire was truly their destination, then I think yes, he probably caught them. But if they really were headed for Gretna Green I think they will be man and wife before he finds them."

Man and wife. Another smile tugged at Sophia's lips. Letitia would never be satisfied just to be a wife. She would not lose her identity as Sophia had when she married Edmund.

Poor Mr. Wesley. Did he know what he was doing?

For that matter, did she? She was chasing Julian across the country. He would not be impressed when she arrived at Heatherington Park demanding that he face her.

All the soft hills and hidden valleys of her vista formed a sweeter garden than Eden ever dreamed.

Other lines swam around in her mind, but it was that one that stood out because he had obviously written it before their marriage, which meant he had been falling in love with her even then.

"How many other poems has he written about me?"

Gabriel started at her question. Perhaps she should have asked in a nicer tone.

"I could not begin to suppose," he replied with a shrug of his wide shoulders, made even wider by the capes of his great coat. Lord, he was big. How could Lilith stand it?

When he didn't offer any more information, Sophia frowned. "Well, when did he start?"

She should be ashamed of her own insistence, but Gabriel already knew so much about her relationship with Julian, what did it matter if he knew how much it meant to her to find out how long Julian had been writing about her? It wasn't as though she asked out of a sense of vanity, although every woman liked to hear such things.

She wanted—needed—to know because . . . because she *needed* to hear it. Needed to know that when she stopped and thought of him during all those years apart that he had thought of her too.

"The poem that launched his career was written about you."

Sophia's brows went up in shock. She remembered reading that poem—she had read almost everything he ever published. Never once had she stopped to think that he might have written it about her, although now she realized she should have. It was about a man haunted by the memory of a woman he had loved and been betrayed by. If she recalled correctly the poem was not a flattering one. The man in it did not want to remember his lover at all.

I followed blindly her siren song—into darkness, into temptation— and never again found my way free.

Was that true?

"Sophia?" It was Gabriel's voice, hauling her back to the present, to the jostling carriage that seemed to be crawling like a turtle over the countryside.

She looked up at him.

"Surely you must have known?"

"If I had known, Gabriel," she replied, a hard lump in her throat, "you and I would not be in this carriage right now. This situation would be very different, I assure you."

Yes, different. She would have driven herself mad by now, looking for mentions of herself in his work.

There were so many things they needed to talk about when she caught up with him, but the first thing she was going to do was tell him she loved him and make him believe it.

"Are you all right?"

Sophia smiled at the concern in Gabriel's voice. "I am fine. Thank you."

There was silence for a moment.

"He loves you, you know."

The tightness in Sophia's throat increased. Hot wetness pricked the backs of her eyes as she jerked her gaze toward the window. "I know."

"Julian is my friend. I do not like to see him hurting."

When Sophia's gaze came back to meet his, it was devoid of tears. "He is the man I love. I do not like seeing him hurting either. I dislike even more knowing I am the cause of it."

Their gazes held for what felt like an eternity. Obviously Gabriel saw what he wanted in hers because he smiled kindly before turning his attention to the scenery passing outside.

They passed the rest of the journey in relative silence. Occasionally Gabriel would offer some tidbit of information about Yorkshire and the time he spent there as a boy with Julian and Brave, or Sophia would ask a question about either, but mostly she kept to herself and wondered whether or not Julian would be happy to see her.

"We are here," Gabriel said finally as the carriage turned down a long, wooded drive. "We should be at the house by the quarter hour."

Her heart thumping brutally against her ribs, Sophia sat up and plastered her face to the carriage window. There was nothing to see but trees, but every tree they passed brought her closer to Julian.

It seemed to take forever, but eventually the house

came into view. It was bigger than she expected, its rosy gold stone far more inviting than she would have expected given the tragedy that had taken place there.

She didn't want to imagine the foolish, dramatic girl who must have felt like Ophelia as she sank beneath the surface to her death. And she didn't want to imagine the anguish in Julian's heart. She knew him well enough to know he would have put on a brave and stoic face for all those present, but alone he would have wept like a child.

Or a parent.

"Julian's parents and sister are buried just beyond that copse of trees," Gabriel informed her, pointing out the window to a spot far beyond the house, on the opposite side from the pond, where a path cut through the forest.

"There's a small chapel there," he continued as the carriage rolled up in front of the house. "The family used to have services, but the last time it was used was for Miranda's funeral."

"You were here for it?"

Gabriel turned his sorrowful gray eyes to hers. "I helped carry her casket. I carried Julian's mother's as well."

Sophia didn't have to ask to know that Brave had been there as well, helping to bury Miranda, the girl he had thought he loved.

"Thank you for being there for him."

Gabriel's eyes widened at her words, but before he could reply, the carriage door opened and a footman lowered the steps.

"Are you coming inside?" Sophia asked, as her stiff legs awkwardly carried her to the ground.

"I think I will walk around a bit first," Gabriel replied, stretching. He smiled. "He needs to see you more than he needs to see me."

Sophia watched the large, dark-haired man as he set off in the direction of the forest. She knew exactly where he was going.

Draping her shawl around her shoulders, Sophia took her bonnet in both hands and climbed the steps to the house. A robust woman with pale eyes and gray curls peeking out from beneath her cap opened the door.

"Good morning. May I help you?"

An uncertain smile curved Sophia's lips. Would Julian let her inside? "I am Lady Wolfram," she replied. "Is my husband here?"

The woman's plump jaw dropped and Sophia thought she saw something very much like tears in the old gel's eyes.

"Oh, my dear lady!" she gasped. "Come in, come in! I'm Mrs. Berry, the housekeeper. I cannot tell you how happy I am to meet you!"

Sophia found herself enveloped in a fierce embrace as she stepped inside. Stunned, she could do nothing but stand there and wait for the woman to release her. She had never been hugged by a housekeeper before.

"His lordship's in the blue drawing room," Mrs. Berry remarked, wiping her eyes with the backs of her strong little hands as she released Sophia and took her belongings. "Second door on your right down the corridor there."

Sophia gazed around at her surroundings as she cautiously walked in the direction Mrs. Berry had pointed her in. The great hall was soft white-and-gray marble with dark heavy wood that looked to be mahogany. It could have been oppressive were it not for the floor-to-ceiling windows along the front of the house.

The house smelled of beeswax and fresh air and just the faintest hint of something warm and spicy—something baking in the kitchen perhaps. Sophia wasn't sure why, but to her Heatherington smelled like a house longing to be a home again.

Down the corridor she walked, her heart hammering faster and faster against her ribs until she thought it might break right out of her body. She stopped in front of the second door, took a deep breath, and raised a trembling fist to knock.

Julian's voice answered, muffled by the heavy door. "Enter."

Gripping the door handle, Sophia pressed her thumb down on the lip. The latch clicked open and she pushed. The door swung open, revealing a large, bright room with comfortable furniture and a high ceiling, but what captured her attention was the man standing by one of the far windows, his back to her.

Julian turned, the sun dancing red and gold in his hair. The smile on his face faded into an expression of astonishment at the sight of her.

"Sophia." His voice was hoarse. "What are you doing here?"

Summoning all her strength, Sophia smiled. "Hello, Julian. You did not truly believe I would let you walk out on me again, did you?"

Chapter 20

*True happiness always reveals itself to those
who have suffered enough to recognize it.*

An Unfortunate Attachment by the Marchioness of Aberley

Julian couldn't believe she was actually real.

"You followed me." *Very clever, Wolfram. Now
count to ten.*

Sophia nodded, her dark eyes bright with determination as she sauntered closer. As she walked, her hips
swayed beneath her skirts, a natural display of her sensuality. Julian didn't know if he should be angry at her for
coming or haul her into his arms and kiss her until he took
complete leave of his senses.

He had missed her. It felt as though years had passed
since he last held her, laughed with her. He despised her
for making him feel so needy and weak, for making him
want to beg for her forgiveness rather than offer her his,
and yet just the sight of her filled him with such joy it
would take him the rest of his life to find the words to describe it.

She stopped just scant inches away from him. Her
black gaze compelled him, mesmerized him. He couldn't

have looked away if he wanted to. He didn't want to.

"You have an annoying habit of walking away from me, Julian," she murmured, her breath tickling his chin.

"I did not walk away—"

"No. You ran."

Indignation flared. "After Letitia, not away from you."

A thin, black brow rose high on her forehead. "Oh?"

He mimicked her expression, unable to suppress a smile as he did so. "Oh."

She didn't touch him. Didn't move any closer and yet he could feel her body just as certainly as though it were pressed against his.

"You did not even say goodbye. That sounds like running away to me. It must be something in your blood. You and Letitia both have a penchant for it."

He would have laughed at her assessment were it not for the spark of hurt in her eyes. He and his sister had reached an understanding and repaired the rift between them. Now it was time to do the same with his wife, if he could.

"Perhaps you are right," he replied, lifting his hand to her cheek. "But I was coming back to you, Sophia."

Her lashes fluttered at his touch. The knowledge that just the merest caress could affect her so thrilled him to the depth of his soul.

Her gaze warmed. "I could not wait that long."

A gentle smile curved Julian's lips. "Missed me that much, did you?"

"Yes."

That simple admission broke what was left of his already battered heart. His hand slid down, curving around the warm, slender column of her throat.

"I am sorry." He had thought apologizing would be

more difficult, but it was surprisingly easy to tell her he was sorry.

Her expression was completely open. "I was the one who lied, not you."

His smile faltered. "What good would telling me have done? You said yourself I would not have listened."

Her expression was one of gentle curiosity, but he could feel her concern, her hurt and her affection for him just as certainly as he felt his own. "What changed your mind?"

"You," he replied honestly. "And Letitia. I had an entire night alone to put things in perspective."

It was her turn to smile. "What did you discover?"

"That you were right. That I was trying to control Letitia's life. I had to let her go to keep from losing her forever."

"Are you all right?"

That simple question, and all the unspoken meaning behind it was his undoing. He pulled her closer. "Better than I would be if I lost you."

"You will never lose me." Her voice was low and throaty. "I'll chase you to the ends of the earth if I have to."

Julian smiled at her. There was something both frightening and comforting in her words, knowing she meant them. There were no absolutes in this life, and Julian knew all too well how cruel fate could be. Sophia could be snatched from him in a heartbeat, just as his parents were. The frightened boy inside him never wanted to have to face that kind of loss again. But he knew what a gift he had been given when life threw them together again. Sophia filled the emptiness inside him and he would rather risk losing her one day than never take the chance at all.

Death was the only thing that would ever separate

them, and even then it would only be temporary.

"I am not going anywhere," he informed her, his fingers massaging the back of her neck.

She was so close he could actually see the almost imperceptible change of color between her iris and pupil.

"Neither of us are perfect." There was the slightest tremor to her chin as she spoke. "There will be things we keep from each other, intentional or not. Sometimes we will hurt each other, regardless of how hard we try not to."

She didn't need to say these things. He knew already. It didn't matter. "Sophia—"

"But I will always forgive you, Julian." Her fingers curled tightly around the lapels of his coat. "Can you forgive me?"

"Always." And he meant it.

Her eyes were downcast. "I have not had very good timing telling you how I feel about you . . ."

"You do not have to tell me. You are here. That's all the declaration I need."

He lowered his head again to kiss her, but she stopped him with a gentle push against his chest.

"No. The first time was just before my father found us. The second time was after you found out I lied to you. I want to tell you now, when there is no chance of you doubting it."

He wouldn't doubt it. It had been his own stupidity that made him doubt it before and he was going to make every effort to never be stupid again.

"So say it," he urged, wanting to hear the words so he could show her how he felt about her.

"I love you—"

Anything else she might have said was lost as he pulled her to him, capturing her lips with his. He kissed her with all the emotion he felt inside, every word he couldn't find to express himself springing from his lips to hers on one inarticulate groan that said it all.

She parted her lips for his tongue without any coaxing. She tasted faintly of cloves and the inherent sweetness that was her. He slid his tongue along hers, over her teeth, flicking it against her lips as though he could slake this hunger inside himself just by tasting her.

It wasn't enough. He needed to devour her.

She pushed him backward and he let her, but he refused to relinquish his claim on her mouth. It wasn't until the hard edge of a sofa bumped against the backs of his legs that he realized her intent, but then it was too late. She had already knocked him off balance.

He fell back onto the sofa, taking her tumbling into his lap as he went.

Sophia straddled him, her skirts settling around them like a fluffy blue cloud. Her knees flanked his hips and he could feel her heat through the clothing that separated him. He had wanted her before he kissed her. Now he was hard as a rock and aching for the relief only she could give. He wanted to take her upstairs, to his room—the room no other woman had ever seen—and make love to her the way she deserved to be made love to. He didn't care how long it took, or how much frustration he would have to endure, he wouldn't rest until she was limp with satisfaction.

Her eyes were hot and black like coals. The hands that had clutched so tightly at his coat slid down his chest, across his stomach and lower, down between their bodies to the falls of his trousers.

"I want you," she whispered, her fingers deftly freeing the hard, eager length of him.

Julian jumped as her fingers curled around his sensitive

flesh. His breath caught harshly in his throat as she stroked him.

"Do you like that?" Her breath was hot against his ear.

"You know damn well I do," he growled.

Chuckling softly, Sophia continued to pump him with her hand as she tugged at her skirts with the other. Within seconds, Julian could feel the hardness of his body nudging the moist warmth of hers.

He closed his eyes as she took the head of him inside her.

He clutched at the matching sofa cushions as she took him even deeper.

He bit his lip when she took him deeper still.

And when she settled her weight on his lap, the entire length of him buried inside her, Julian lost what little control he had left. Arching his hips, he pushed against her sweet softness, wrapped his arms around her waist and prayed for this moment to last forever.

Beneath her skirts, his fingers dug into the soft flesh of her buttocks. He tried to control her movements, tried to set the rhythm of her hips. The muscles in his arms strained with the effort, but somehow she fought him and won. He could feel her thighs tremble from the exertion. She was in complete control.

Julian had never begged for release in his life. Male vanity had made him demand the same kind of supplication from lovers in the past, but never had anyone taken him to the brink of such exquisite torture that he would do anything they asked just to experience the pleasure they offered.

"Sophia . . . please."

She stilled, poised so that the head of his sex pushed against the wet, beckoning entrance of her incredible, lush body. Her face was flush with desire. "Tell me you love me."

The little minx! Julian would have laughed if she hadn't chosen that moment to take more of him inside her slick heat.

"I love you," he admitted, gasping as she slid down even farther. "I have always loved you and I always will."

His words must have driven her to the brink because the next thing Julian knew, Sophia was grinding her body down on his like a wild woman. Seizing her by the hips, he arched his body off the sofa, digging his heels into the carpet until his legs shook with the pressure.

He could feel the tension coiling in her body as they moved together. His own body reveled in it, tightening in response.

Her release struck first, arching her spine as she shuddered all around him. Her head thrown back, she cried out—the most satisfied sound Julian had ever heard. It was so incredible that it triggered his own orgasm immediately, stealing his breath, his sight, even his mind as an explosion of pleasure rocked him. The world ceased to exist.

Eternity passed.

Reason returned some time later, when Sophia lifted her head from his shoulder, she didn't try to pull away—not that he would have allowed it.

She smiled lazily at him. "That was pleasant."

He couldn't help but laugh. She looked like a cat that had just cleaned out an entire pot of cream. *Pleasant* was an understatement and she knew it.

"Yes," he replied with mock blandness. "It was, wasn't it?"

Her smile faded. "I love you."

Holding her tightly he kissed her—hard and fast. "I love you too."

They sat in silence for a few moments, basking. It seemed so strange to Julian that they had fought over Letitia, had spent so many hours apart and not speaking, and now they were in each other's arms, happily sated after making love. It had been so easy to set things right between them.

"You never did tell me what happened with Letitia," she said.

Julian grinned. "You never gave me a chance."

She shifted on his lap, sending a jolt of sensation through his groin. "Tell me now."

"She and Marcus Wesley are getting married here at the end of the week."

He wished he could capture the wondrous expression that lit up her face. "Oh, that's wonderful!" she frowned. "But why are they waiting so long?"

Heat suffused his cheeks under the weight of her stare. "I thought that was how long it would take for you to arrive."

She looked like she didn't know whether to laugh or to cry. "I am here now."

Julian rubbed his cheek against her hair. "Letitia will be pleased not to have to wait. Now all we have to decide is where to have the ceremony."

Lifting her head, Sophia gazed up at him in surprise. "I know the perfect place."

Letitia and Marcus were married in the family chapel two days later.

It was the perfect place for a quiet wedding. Letitia had been ecstatic when Julian told her he was having the chapel cleaned just for her and Marcus. It hadn't taken much coaxing on Sophia's part to convince him the chapel would be perfect. It would be a happy occasion to erase the bad memories of too many funerals, and with the family plot so close, it would almost be like having Julian's parents and Miranda in attendance.

It was a glorious spring morning, complete with a gentle breeze and birds singing in the trees. The little stone chapel looked like something right out of a fairy tale, nestled in the shade of towering oak trees, and Letitia looked just like a princess.

Julian wore a strange expression as he gazed upon his sister. "That is probably the last gown I will ever pay for her to wear."

Sophia would have laughed if he hadn't looked so crestfallen. Julian was holding up tolerably well, but she could see just how hard this was for him. He was setting Letitia free to make her own mistakes and solve her own problems. To say he didn't like it would be an understatement, but he knew it had to be done.

The ceremony was small—only the four of them and the vicar, as Gabriel had returned to London the day before—afterward they went back outside, where they said goodbye to the vicar, who was unable to join them at the house for breakfast due to another appointment. Letitia, as radiant as any bride ever was, whispered something to her husband and then took her brother by the arm.

"Come with me," she said, and steered him toward the garden of headstones and monuments surrounded by a small stone wall.

They stood before three newer-looking markers, their backs to Sophia and Marcus. Sophia couldn't help but wonder what they were saying.

Feeling like an interloper, she tore her gaze away from her husband's back and turned to Marcus, who was watching Letitia with so much love in his gaze that Sophia didn't know which made her more uncomfortable—watching the private scene at the graves, or this.

He was a lovely man, Letitia's husband. Handsome and strong, yet kind and gentle. He would be good to Letitia, very good. But he would not allow her to run roughshod over him. It was a good match.

And Sophia knew for a fact the two of them would never have to worry about money. Julian would never allow his sister to suffer, and she could only hope that Mr. Wesley's pride wouldn't allow it either.

Letitia rejoined them a few moments later, but Julian remained at the graves. A few moments later, Letitia and Marcus left to return to the house. Reluctant to intrude upon Julian's privacy, Sophia waited for him to finish whatever it was he was doing. Her heart in her throat, she watched as he straightened the flowers—Letitia's bouquet—on one of the graves.

When he finally joined her, his eyes were red and his lashes wet, but he smiled when she looked at him in open concern.

"Thank you," he said, slipping his arm around her shoulders as they began walking back to the house.

"For what?" She hadn't done a thing that she knew of.

"Everything."

She waited for him to elaborate. He didn't.

"You're welcome."

Letitia and Marcus left for London again late that afternoon. Everyone agreed that it would be better for them to return quickly as man and wife to staunch any gossip.

Plus, they would be able to spend their wedding night alone—without the bride's overprotective elder brother in the house.

After the newlyweds left, Sophia went upstairs to nap and then bathe. She half expected Julian to join her, but he didn't. When she came downstairs, hours later, she asked Mrs. Berry if she had seen her husband.

"He was in the library for a while, my lady," the house-keeper replied, "going through his father's books, but he went outside about half an hour ago. I am not sure where he went."

But Sophia was. Over the last few days she had witnessed Julian facing his past in many ways. This house, which he had begun to associate with many tragedies in his life, was suddenly a place of happiness again. He and Sophia had reconciled there. Letitia had been married in it. It did not seem so painful for him to be there anymore, but there was one place he hadn't visited yet—not with her—and Sophia knew that's where he was now.

She didn't bother with a bonnet or gloves, but wrapped a light shawl around her shoulders and went out to look for him. Even though the sun was setting low in the west, the day was still uncommonly warm. She really didn't need the shawl, but she took it anyway.

Grass rustled against her slippers and gown as she walked around the side of the house, down the low sloping lawn toward the pond that nestled like a sparkling gem on a bed of green velvet. As she rounded the copse of trees that hid most of the water from view, the sunset seemed to set the water on fire, and the sky danced with flames.

She did not find him standing on the shore as she expected. All she found there was a pile of clothes. Julian was in the water, his long arms glistening in the sinking sun as they cut through the water with powerful strokes.

Sophia's heart skipped a beat at the sight of him. When Julian decided to face his demons, he certainly didn't do it halfway. She'd wager he hadn't swam in that pond since Miranda's death and now there he was, alone in it.

There was no reason for him to be alone anymore. Glancing over her shoulder to ensure they were indeed out of view of the house, Sophia struggled with the buttons on the back of her gown. She pulled the garment over her head and laid it on top of Julian's clothes so it wouldn't get stained. Then she stripped off everything else until she stood on the grassy shore in nothing but her hairpins and the skin God gave her.

The water was cool as she stepped in, but not as cold as she feared. It wouldn't have mattered even if it was frozen. Julian was in it and she was going to join him.

"I wondered when you might find me," he said with a smile once she was directly in front of him, the water lapping around her shoulders.

Suddenly Sophia wondered if she might have made a mistake. "I am sorry. Did you want to be alone?"

His smile grew. There was something boyish about it. He looked . . . happy. "I do not think I will ever be alone so long as you are around."

"I am your wife, not your nursemaid," she replied a little more defensively than she intended. "You can be alone all you want."

He came closer, so close that their chests were almost touching. "No matter where I am you will be in my heart. You are my always."

Any other man, and Sophia would have rolled her

eyes—but she knew Julian meant it. He wouldn't say it if he didn't. Her own heart thrilled to hear it, and echoed in reply.

He tilted his head to one side. "Tell me why you love me." He sounded like a little boy asking why the sky was blue.

It just is.

"I do not know if I can attribute it to one thing. I only know in my heart that you are everything I want and need. You are what my life has been missing."

It sounded very lame and senseless to Sophia. Julian made his declaration sound so poetic, so simple and real. Hers sounded idiotic.

Julian didn't seem to agree. In fact, he seemed rather pleased by her words.

"Swim with me," he said. "Make this pond a happy place again like you have done with the rest of the estate."

Sophia watched him as he slipped beneath the surface, propelling himself effortlessly through the water. He thought *she* had brought joy back to Heatherington? Perhaps she had helped, but he and Letitia . . .

Oh bother. If he wanted to give her the credit then she would just shut up and take it. It was time she stopped doubting herself and her own worth. Julian loved her. She could do anything she set her mind to.

Laughing as though a huge weight had been lifted from her shoulders, Sophia swam after him, launching herself onto his back when she finally caught him. They swam until the last vestiges of daylight were almost lost before climbing up onto the low wooden dock to dry off.

Warm in the circle of Julian's arms, despite the cooling air, Sophia smiled in contentment.

"I wish we could stay here forever." She sighed, resting

her shoulder against his chest. She was sitting in the hollow of his legs as he sat cross-legged on the dock, the springy hair of his left thigh tickling the backs of her calves.

He kissed her shoulder, sliding a hand down to cup her breast. "We can if you want."

Sophia's breath caught as his thumb brushed the tightened flesh of her nipple. "We cannot, and you know it."

His teeth nipped gently at her neck. She shivered. "Why not?"

Turning in his arms, she squirmed on his lap until she sat with her legs wrapped around his waist and her breasts pressed against the warm wall of his chest. The evidence of his growing arousal nudged against the curls between her thighs.

Would he always want her like this? Would she always be so ready to receive him? God, she hoped so.

"You have an adoring public," she teased, flicking her tongue along the velvety edge of his earlobe. "Your publisher will expect more poems from you."

Hands going back to her breasts, Julian muttered just what he thought his publisher could do with his poems.

A familiar throbbing began low in Sophia's abdomen as his long nimble fingers worked their magic.

Dear heaven, but she loved him.

"Promise me you will never leave me again," she demanded when he tried to slide inside her.

He lifted his hips. "I promise."

Sophia shifted, and he growled in frustration. "Promise me you will finish the poem you have been writing for me."

His eyes widened. She hadn't told him she had read the poem. "They have all been for you."

She shifted again, narrowly avoiding his insistent erection once more. "You know what one I mean. I want you to finish it."

"That poem is a work in progress," he informed her with a mixture of levity and seriousness. "Every time I discover something new about you I write it down. I expect to be working on it for the next forty or fifty years at least."

He knew exactly what to say to make her chest ache.

He also knew just how to distract her so he could slide the entire length of him inside her with one deft stroke.

Gasping, Sophia wrapped her arms around his neck. Her body barely had time to adust to his exquisite intrusion before he began to move.

"But you plan to finish it one day?"

He gripped her hips. "Yes."

"Oh! I . . . you promise?"

Chuckling, he caught the back of her head in his hand and brought her mouth down to his.

"You will just have to trust me," he whispered against her lips.

And she did.

Epilogue

*We are all authors of our own story.
How it ends is up to each of us.*

Untitled Work in Progress by Sophia Rexley, Countess Wolfram

Fourteen months later

It was the perfect day for a party.

The summer sun was warm, the breeze pleasant and gentle. Alexander Wycherley, the future Earl of Braven, sat on his father's lap, his face dotted with cake crumbs and smeared with icing, some of which had found its way into his fine blond hair as well as onto his father's trousers. The present earl didn't seem to mind.

Countess Braven watched her husband and son with a gentle smile. She had the serene glow of a woman still early enough in a pregnancy that she could sit comfortably in the shade, unbothered by the heat, her hand resting protectively on the gentle swell of her stomach.

Beside her, the Countess Angelwood passed her sleeping daughter to the child's father. She had her mother's red hair and stormy eyes and her father's temperament—

371

something which her father was often heard to profess extreme gratitude for.

"You had her all to yourself for nine months," Lord Angelwood said as he took little Imogen into his arms. "Now it is my turn."

Lady Angelwood rolled her eyes. "You can carry the next one, then."

Mr. and Mrs. Marcus Wesley came up beside Lord Angelwood to admire the child in his arms. They hadn't been blessed with a child of their own yet—not for lack of trying, Mr. Wesley joked, much to his wife's embarrassment.

Mrs. Wesley wore a simple gown of yellow muslin, stylish but hardly the cutting edge of style. She didn't seem to mind. There was a quiet, content maturity to her that hadn't been there prior to her marriage. She was completely in love with her husband and it was obvious that he felt the same way about her. They lived comfortably thanks to her dowry and his business investments, several of which he was expecting a large return on shortly.

The Earl of Wolfram watched them all with an overwhelming sense of joy and fulfillment. They were his friends, his family. It felt right to have them all together here on the terrace at Heatherington. The only thing missing was his wife.

As if on cue, she appeared at his side, linking her arm through his with a bright smile. He smiled back, knowing full well all the love he felt for her was revealed in his gaze. He didn't care who saw it. He was not ashamed to love her as much as he did.

That morning Sophia had told him she suspected she might be with child. Julian had experienced a peculiar pinching in his chest at her announcement. For the first time he thought he might be ready to be a father. Whatever happened, whether they had a child or not, he was thankful for what he had.

And what he had was family and friends who loved him. To think at one time it had just been him, Brave and Gabe—the three of them against the world.

Julian grinned at the two of them—at Brave, who had sworn to never love again and found a love too strong to resist in Rachel, and at Gabe, who had been given a second chance at happiness with Lilith, his first and only love.

And then there was Julian himself. If asked, he would have to say he was the most fortunate of them all. After all, he had been given everything he needed, everything he had ever wanted, when fate brought Sophia back into his life.

"I love you," he murmured for her ears alone.

She smiled up at him, filling his heart with so much joy it hurt. "I love you too."

He kissed her then, heedless of their audience, laughing when Brave and Gabe began to tease him.

They were lucky men indeed.